Heir of the Haloed Sun

ENDORSEMENTS

"Emeriz is the romantasy I needed on my shelf! Lane gives us a perfect blend of magic, adventure, and romance in this tale packed with lovable characters and rich world-building. I was immediately drawn into the land of Emeriz and frequently found myself relating to its heroine, Temperance. The swoony romance and playful banter between the male and female protagonists is enough to make the heart of any romantasy fan flutter. Lane pulls the reader right into her writing with skillfully crafted dialogue and picturesque descriptions. I enjoyed every moment of this story and can't wait to continue the series!"
—Ashley Bustamante, author of the *Color Theory* trilogy

"Lane is an enchantress, weaving a story brimming with mystery and magic, love and adventure. I devoured this sweet romance between a young king and the girl that literally crossed worlds to stumble into his life. *Heir of the Haloed Sun* is a must read for believers of fairy tales and anyone that wishes to fall heart-first into the land of Emeriz."
—Sara K. Anderson, author of *Fractured: The Mind Hunters* duology

Heir of the Haloed Sun

H.C. LANE

Cozy Unicorn Publishing
A MoonQuill Imprint

ISBN (e-book): 979-8-88993-053-2
ISBN (paperback): 979-8-88993-054-9
ISBN (hardcover): 979-8-88993-055-6

Cover and Chapter Header Design by Emilie Haney
Illustrations by Swortoi, Jane S.
Interior Design by Tangcu LLC

Published 2025 by Cozy Unicorn Publishing
Arlington, VA
www.moonquill.com

TABLE OF CONTENTS

CHAPTER 1

TEMPERANCE

The undeniable scent of sweat and steel permeated the large room of the Phoenix Convention Center. Friends and family of the competitors carried on in indistinguishable conversations, anxiously awaiting their moment to cheer for those who remained in the competition.

The emcee made his way to the center of the red-and-yellow mat and announced, "Ladies and gentlemen, we have reached the semifinal of the Teen Full Contact Steel Longsword Tournament!"

The audience burst into applause and shouts that reverberated across the room like thunder.

Only four of us remained in the competition. All I had to do was get the most points within the allotted ninety seconds, and I'd be in the final bracket.

Be with me today, Grammie.

I needed to win to honor her memory. Besides, losing on my seventeenth birthday would be pathetic.

Once the emcee settled the crowd down, he said, "Starting us off, we have Temperance Maher from Mordhau Historical Combat."

I stood up too quickly, and my head swam as I waved to the applauding crowd, but my feet remained planted. It had been months since I'd last entered the ring, and though it wasn't my first bout of the day, each one felt paralyzing. My severe lack of sleep from a recurring nightmare didn't help either. Even in that moment, haunting images played on an infinite loop in my mind.

The locked door.

The spiraling staircase.

The oppressive force coming up behind me…

"Wake up, Tempy!" My brother, James, shoved my sparring helmet into my hands. "What is with you today?"

He wore jeans and a Mordhau Historical Combat shirt that matched the one beneath my sparring suit. The crimson skull emblazoned on the black cotton tee was creased from wearing his protective armor suit. Helmet hair sprouted from his head in a disheveled mess. Even with his blond curls looking like short cockatoo feathers, he somehow still looked cool.

James was nineteen, so he'd already completed and won in his category, Advanced Longsword. The fact that he hadn't stopped competing after Grandma passed both surprised and impressed me.

His nudge on my shoulder snapped me back into the present and got my feet moving again. What was wrong with me? It wasn't even my first time in the ring that day.

"You got this, Tempy!" my dad shouted from the audience. As I looked up to find him, I saw the tripod he had set up with a video camera. While he took photos with a camera around his neck, Mom raised her phone, most likely streaming the competition straight to Grandpa.

"Tempest! Tempest! Tempest!" my friends, Brett and Nora, chanted.

My smile felt forced. I suspected my eyes were rimmed with dark circles, my lips twitching at the corners. I flexed my stiff fingers to release the anxiety that had built up in my body.

My friends continued to call out my nickname, which I'd gained after punching some kid at recess for bullying James back in elementary school. That was also around the time the nightmare had plagued me for weeks until it stopped as suddenly as it had begun.

I shook my head and cleared all thoughts from my mind as I reached the center ring on the mat.

There were three others left in the competition, including Sophia Barley. With hopes of crossing swords with anyone *but* her, I prayed to the universe for the odds to be in my favor.

"Temperance's opponent will be... Sophia Barley from Haloed Violet Community Center Combat," called out the emcee.

I tensed my shoulders to keep them from drooping down in disappointment.

She waved to her screaming fans and walked over to me with her helmet beneath her arm.

With a smile plastered on her face, she said under her breath, "Remember our deal. You win, I lend you photocopies of my family's literature on longsword techniques. If I win"—her eyes flitted to James standing near my bench—"you set me up with your brother."

She knew I'd been aching to study her family's techniques. Most people in the Historical European Martial Arts community were friendly, willing to share knowledge, and were honorable in both victory and loss. With so little information on Historical Combat, and so much of it unclear, we had to be. Even with the vast knowledge we could find on the internet, a lot was open to interpretation due to a lack of proper translation or missing text. Having any additional knowledge that no one else had could give anyone a one-up in competition.

Unlike most people, Sophia was overly competitive and stingy with her knowledge—a difficult combination. Her family had the wealth, status, and lineage that passed down the art of longsword from generation to generation. This prestigious heritage explained why she attended and studied at Haloed Violet, which was essentially an exclusive country club, rather than a community center.

I didn't really care who my brother dated, but knowing Sophia's temperament, she'd walk all over him. I had hoped that we wouldn't have to fight each other in the semifinals and that she'd be defeated before the final round. If I lost now, I'd have to answer to James.

I extended my hand to shake hers. "Looking forward to those photocopies."

As we shook hands, she whispered, "In your dreams."

Irritation grated my mind, and I clenched my jaw as flickering images of the nightmare intruded my thoughts.

The locked door.

The spiraling staircase.

The oppressive force coming up behind me.

I shoved the images down and tucked them away—this was no time for distractions. As the two of us took our positions on the mat, the timer lit up with ninety seconds on the clock. We slipped on our helmets and held our dull steel longswords in the first position as we awaited the signal to begin. I let out a long, slow breath, centering my thoughts in the moment between stillness and action.

The emcee held his hand between us for a moment before shouting, "Begin!"

His hand raised as he stepped back. Sophia and I danced around each other, anticipating who would make the first move. After ten seconds, she tapped her steel blade against mine, feigning a thrust and attempting to provoke me into an attack.

I didn't fall for it.

Revealing her impatience, Sophia thrust toward my head. I

attempted to block it, but being out of practice slowed me down. Her blade struck my helmet, but her strike had left her torso open. I took advantage of this opening and crashed my sword into her left side.

The audience was a mix of cheers and tension.

Why did I bother striking her? She landed the blow first, so the point went to her.

I retaliated with a downward cut, landing the thrust on her hands, but she countered with an after-blow to my arm.

No points.

Frustration flared in my chest, my composure slipping. Anxiously, I tapped her blade, readying myself for my next move. I was determined not to miss. Sophia held her sword higher, anticipating a high blow. I feigned up, but then slashed downward, scoring a blow to her knee.

The crowd cheered.

"Yeah! Get her, Tempest!" Brett shouted from the crowd.

A bit of my confidence returned, and I bounced on the balls of my feet trying to work out the nerves as I reveled in my point.

Tied match.

Blood thrummed through my veins, adrenaline hyping me up and urging my muscles to continue. I had the same feeling in my previous bouts that day. For the first time in months, I felt alive.

I could do this.

I'd missed this.

Why had I waited for so long?

I shook my head, burying down the answer. Too painful.

Our swords danced again, tapping back and forth against each other. One of the lights glinted off Sophia's blade, and a violet light flashed in my eyes.

The locked door.

The spiraling staircase.

The oppressive force coming up behind me.

The door from my nightmares suddenly manifested into my reality and opened to reveal a violent, stormy sea. It lasted mere seconds, and the illusion vanished, throwing me off balance.

Sophia landed a blow to my head, following with a swift cut to my bicep. The hallucination had completely broken my concentration, leaving me open and sloppy. None of my defensive moves proved effective.

It was two to one in Sophia's favor when a loud horn sounded throughout the room.

Time had run out.

The crowd erupted into cheers for Sophia, forcing my heart to plummet into my stomach.

I lost.

We had always ended close in score, but she'd never actually beaten me. White noise blocked out the sounds of the audience, and I became all too aware of my failure.

Couldn't I have just one thing? One normal, *happy* thing?

I mentally kicked myself for getting distracted, then again for thinking I was ever ready for this. What did I expect after months of no practice? The only reason I'd competed in the first place was because Grandma had encouraged it before she passed. Back then she hoped she'd be able to attend.

We all had.

Sophia's satisfied grin practically glowed as she removed her helmet. She swept an arm across her brow, smearing sweat and black strands of hair that had matted against her forehead. "Deal's a deal, and I expect my payment in full," she said smugly as she held out her hand.

I pulled off my own helmet, and stray strands of reddish-brown bangs fell into my eye line. I pushed them behind my ear and took her hand. The AC blew into my face, cooling my warm cheeks.

"Shouldn't you be greeting your adoring fans?" I asked.

"Not until I take this entire tournament."

"I'll leave you to it then."

I was about to head back toward my bench when she said, "You know, I'm willing to set you up with my brother, Ethan." She pointed to the stands opposite my friends and family.

The alleged brother sat next to his dad. Though I'd met him on a few occasions, this was my first time seeing him at a match. Ethan had Sophia's dark-brown skin and tight, black curls, but his were cut short. His right ankle rested on his left knee, and he was nose deep in a hefty book, which seemed a bit odd to me. Not that I didn't appreciate a guy with bookworm tendencies, but this environment wasn't exactly suitable for quiet study.

Ethan was cute, but being so bored at a longsword tournament that he needed a book to distract him told me he had no interest in something that I absolutely loved.

"Sweet of you to offer, but I'm good," I said.

"Your loss," Sophia replied. "He's a nineteen-year-old genius. You'd definitely pass your SATs with him as your boyfriend."

I stole another glance at Ethan, and our eyes met. He immediately pulled up his hood, hiding himself.

I knew I looked like a mess, but I couldn't have looked *that* scary.

His dad yanked the hood back, forcing him to sit up straight. Ethan slammed the book shut and deliberately pulled his hood back up before beelining out the nearest set of double doors.

"Not again," Sophia grumbled in exasperation. "I'll text you to arrange a set up with James. I gotta go."

She bounded after her brother.

I respected her for that. Anyone who put family first impressed me, and I'd probably do the same if it were James.

We'd always been close due to the social anxiety that James had struggled with when we were kids. It had been so bad that he'd missed too many days of school in sixth grade and was held back. After that, he spent most of his time with Nora, Brett, and me. Even now, there were times I'd sit with him during an anxiety attack or help him with grounding techniques. James had come so far since then and had learned how to manage it for the most part.

Crap… He's gonna let me hear it now that I've lost, especially when I tell him what Sophia just won.

I headed to the bench, and before James could get a word out, I handed him the sword and helmet then rushed toward the lockers to change. The last thing I wanted to hear was a lecture on what I should have done.

Besides, I had no way to explain what had distracted me during the fight without sounding crazy.

I'd changed into my favorite pair of jeans and top: a purple shirt with a rounded neckline and sleeves that reached my elbows.

I gripped my duffle bag tighter as I exited the ballroom. My parents and James followed me out, trying to keep up with my quick pace.

"Tempy, stop!" James said, grabbing my arm. "What happened in there? It was like you were somewhere else."

"I don't expect you to understand," I said.

"Oh, stop it," James replied. "I may have been held back a grade, but that doesn't mean I'm stupid." He took a few quick steps in front of me and blocked my path. "You had her, and then you choked."

"Stop it, you two," Mom said. "We can save the match breakdown until after her birthday party tonight."

"Your mom's right," Dad said. He draped an arm around me and squeezed my shoulder. "You'll get 'em next time."

Using his free hand, he adjusted the black-and-red baseball cap with the Diamondbacks logo covering up his dark hair. His matching mustache always gave off a Tim McGraw vibe.

"Thanks, Dad." I shot him a half-smile, but it didn't fool him.

"Can't take seeing you like this," he said. "How about I give you one of your presents now?" Dad pulled from his pocket a small black box tied with a purple satin ribbon.

"Yes, please." I perked up a little and a more genuine smile graced my lips.

"Sweetheart, are you sure now is the right time to give her that?" Mom asked with concern, but oddly, I could sense an undertone of warning too. "Why don't we wait until we get to your dad's house tomorrow?"

We hadn't seen Grandpa since the funeral, so our parents were taking us on a trip to San Diego to visit. Grandpa had plenty of friends, but as Dad always reminded us, *There's no greater love or support than family.*

"I think now is the perfect time," Dad said. "It will be fine." He raised an eyebrow and gave her his *trust me* look.

My shoulders drooped. "Come on, Mom, please!" I said. "I could really use a pick me up."

Mom brushed a few flyaway strands from my face, a wary and defeated grin brightening her pale-blue eyes. She was never one to let her children be lost in sadness if she could help it.

She shrugged, short blonde waves of hair brushing her shoulders. "Fine," she said.

I wrapped her in an enthusiastic hug, then turned back to Dad.

He handed me the box while Mom and James huddled in a little closer with happy yet solemn smiles on their faces. Their weird energy unsettled me a little, but I ignored it, overwhelmed with excitement to open the gift.

I lifted the lid. Resting on a little white, satin pillow was a necklace. Carefully slipping it out of its cushioned box, I examined it closer. A round amethyst was mounted in a gold teardrop pendant with no backing. Four clamps, resembling the petals of a tulip, held the purple gem in place. It looked like it belonged to another time.

"Dad... isn't this?" My heart clenched, stalling my words.

"Your grandma's," he said, finishing the sentence I couldn't bear to say aloud. "She originally wanted to wait until your eighteenth birthday, but... well... one of her last wishes was to give this to you now."

My thumb gently caressed the amethyst as a memory surfaced. During one of our trips when I was six, James and I had been playing pirates, and we'd borrowed her jewelry box to use as treasure. While we were counting our loot, this particular necklace captivated me. Grandma noticed and thereafter told me tales of a magical world called Emeriz. After that, she wore it every day.

My eyes darted between my dad and the gift in disbelief.

He guessed my train of thought and said, "Yes, Tempy, she entrusted this with you. No one else."

The dam burst as I stared at the priceless object in my hands. "I miss her," I sobbed.

Mom reached over to wipe the tears from my cheeks as Dad took the necklace from my hands and slipped it over my head. The pendant hung just below my chest, and my fingers found their way around it, as if touching the gem would somehow make her feel closer.

Tears welled in his eyes. "Me too, sweet pea… Me too. It suits you, just as it did her."

"The resemblance is uncanny sometimes," Mom said.

Everyone had said I could pass as grandma's doppelganger. It was a bit surreal looking at photographs of my grandparents when they were younger. We shared the same periwinkle eyes, fair skin, hair color, frame… nearly everything.

According to my grandpa, even our souls were kindred spirits. As her granddaughter—not to mention her namesake—it made sense that I took after her in some ways.

Dad pointed from the pendant to my face. "Never lose this." A heavy emphasis sat on his words

Although the necklace hadn't changed in those few seconds, it weighed heavier around my neck.

Regardless of my apprehension, I nodded and assured him, "I won't. Thank you."

We shared a family hug—something our family was no stranger to lately. We'd relied on each other's support a lot over the past few months.

"Happy birthday, Temperance," my father said when we pulled away.

A small smile crossed my face. He only called me by my full name on special occasions. Everyone called me Tempy to avoid confusion with my grandma.

Grandma had been struggling with her health when I was born. Because they weren't sure she was going to pull through, I was gifted with the same name. She was actually in the hospital as a patient while my mom was in labor. They told me that as soon as Dad walked into

Grandma's hospital room and placed me in her arms, she started to improve.

Now it didn't matter what people called me anymore.

Dad patted my shoulder and said, "Well, we'd better get going if you want to have time for sushi before your party tonight."

I adjusted the strap of my bag and followed them to the parking garage where we met up with Brett and Nora.

"I thought you two would have left already," I said and hugged them both.

"Yeah, well, this guy was insistent that we wait," Nora said.

"Why?"

Brett hesitantly scanned the faces of my family and asked, "You got a minute?"

He didn't wait for me to respond before he headed toward his truck a few spaces away. Leave it to Brett to expect you to simply follow him. I almost didn't, just to show him I wouldn't be bossed around—but my curiosity got the better of me. With a "Just a sec" to my parents and a groan from James to "Hurry it up 'cause I'm legit starving," I pushed past my annoyance, forcing myself to walk over to Brett.

"What's up?" I asked when I reached him.

"Sorry about the match," Brett said in a hushed tone.

"Yeah."

"Would a present cheer you up? You know I give the best gifts." He wiggled his eyebrows.

I laughed. "Are you sure you can top last year's?"

"I can't, so I'll just do the same thing and take you to Co-Ed again," he said like the decision was already made.

I knew he was trying to be nice, but it rubbed me the wrong way.

"How original," I teased. "Thanks, but I won't be here, remember?

Tomorrow we'll be on the road to Grandpa's and won't be back until after the dance."

"Oh, I forgot about that," Brett said as his face fell slightly. But in the next instant, he smiled. "You'll just take me to Morp."

That caught me off guard.

"*If* I want to take you," I said in jest.

As Brett headed toward his truck, he said, "You will."

My parents' van horn blared through the garage. When I looked over, I wasn't surprised to see James leaning over Dad, laying on the horn.

"I'm hungry, Tempy!" James shouted out the window. "Let's go!"

Mom scolded him but then gave me a look instructing me to make this conversation quick.

In a move I wasn't expecting, when I turned back around, Brett leaned down to peck me on the cheek. He whispered, "You did great for your first time back in the ring. Happy birthday." He hopped in his truck without another word.

Nora rushed past me, getting into his passenger seat, but not before she shot me a *girl, we need to talk ASAP* look.

My mouth hung open, and I stood there in shock while they drove off. He'd never done that before.

James pounded on the horn again, snapping me out of my daze. I rushed to the van and accidentally put a little too much force into sliding the door closed.

"Honey, are you and Brett dating now?" Mom asked.

I knew that look in her eyes: the wedding march was playing in her head. His mom was her friend, and they'd love nothing more than to set us up at an altar.

"No, Mom," James said, "Brett flirts with every girl."

Not wanting my mom's daydreaming to continue, I agreed. "Yeah, he was just wishing me happy birthday."

Mom raised her eyebrows, and an overly eager smile graced her mouth. "Right…"

"Mom, I swear," I groaned.

Embarrassed, my face flared with heat. Unable to process my feelings, I wrapped my arms around my duffle and pulled it against my chest. I shot James a questioning glance, but he glared in the direction Brett had gone.

"Well, then… ahem. Off we go," Dad awkwardly proclaimed.

James' expression became carnivorous. "Food!"

While Dad pulled out of the parking lot, James whipped out his phone.

My phone buzzed with an incoming text.

> **Do you have to date my best friend? I don't want to spend the last semester of my Senior year watching you two suck face and make goo-goo eyes.**

I rolled my eyes and sent one back.

> **Not your business.**

He tsked and formed another text.

> **Yeah it is. If you date and break up, he's not gonna hang around anymore. It'll make everything in the group awkward. I won't lose a friend due to your hormones.**

James shoved his phone into his jacket pocket to make a point that he was done with the discussion.

I didn't have a retort anyway. His complaint about messing with our group dynamic was valid. On top of that, there were few people in our group that James considered true friends—Brett being *numero uno*. After everything he'd been through, messing that up would be cruel. I looked out the window and played with my grandmother's necklace as I watched the Phoenix skyscrapers pass by.

CHAPTER 2

TEMPERANCE

The allure of celebrating my birthday with a bonfire in the Arizona desert faded quickly, mostly because the guy in charge of bringing the chairs and blankets didn't show. Instead, I had to freeze my butt off in the dirt on what should have been a happy occasion—something to cheer me up and distract me from my abysmal loss at the tournament. I wrapped my black jacket closer to my body and crossed my arms in an attempt to shield myself from the cool February breeze.

At least the fire helped. Large wood pallets—filched from the back of our neighborhood grocery store—had been haphazardly stacked earlier in the evening and set alight. At one point in the evening, we had to hide the lighter fluid from the boys, who had the ridiculous idea of creating a raging inferno that would have melted the cheeks off our faces. However, now that it was nearing 10 p.m., the fire was dwindling. The glowing embers popped, and a piece of blackened wood shifted, tossing me into the throes of a memory.

Over a blazing campfire on the beach, Grandma had once told eight-year-old me fairy tales about a world called Emeriz. Stories of mermaids, fairies, fallen kingdoms, and heroes had captivated my imagination. Grandma would recall them as though they were distant memories while stroking the amethyst necklace she wore. I remembered how the gem caught the light of the fire, drawing me into its violet depths as it always did. Grandpa sat beside her, intently watching the storm clouds forming in the distance.

As my mind slowly slipped back into the present, my fingers found their way around the pendant, and I could almost feel Grandma right there with me. This night wasn't too different from the campout of my memories—campfire, cold night air, and vast inky-blue sky with millions of stars. Though, for some reason, in my memory with my grandparents, I could have sworn that those stars were differing shades of white, blue, violet, and amber. I pushed it off as my own imagination trying to piece together an old memory.

Grandma's words from that night sounded clearly in my mind. *"We need to feel the magic of the ocean before us, the forest behind us, the sky above us, and the earth below us in order to dispel your nightmare."*

"Old people ramblings," I mumbled under my breath. I smiled. That was my initial response to her advice back then—and yet, she'd been right. The recurring nightmare had stopped after that night.

I ran my fingers through my hair and tried to stifle the grief threatening to break through. It was my birthday, so I should have been in the moment, enjoying this time with my friends. They'd done what they could to make this a fun night for me. We had hot dogs, chips, Dr Pepper, and s'mores galore. I did my best to enjoy it.

The fire had died down enough that Brett, James, and the other guys decided it would be a good idea to take turns jumping over it.

Morons.

The other girls watched and cheered them on, which didn't help to discourage the lovable idiots. I was happy to see the others having a good time, but I also didn't want my birthday to be remembered as that time we took a trip to the ER. I was about to intervene when

Nora stepped in front of James just before his turn, arms spread wide and amber eyes aflame in the firelight.

"You guys are being idiots," she said.

James leaned in so his eyes were level with hers. "We prefer the term *adventurous*."

Nora rolled her eyes and crossed her arms, not budging a single inch. The guys collectively sighed.

I stood up and dragged one of the few wooden pallets that remained in our wood pile and tossed it on, feeding the fire a little more.

"Now you can't," I told them as I shrugged.

"Party pooper," James mumbled.

"If someone gets hurt, what are you gonna do?" I asked. "Do you have magical healing powers I don't know about?"

James let out a sort of half-laugh, half-snort, dismissing my comment as he fussed with the leather band on his wrist. It had been a gift from Grandpa. He shoved his hands into his jacket pockets, a clear sign he was holding something back.

"That's what I thought," I said.

"Come on, we all know the real reason Tempy and Nora want us to stop," said Brett as he shot me a playful, challenging grin. "We're brimming with testosterone. They couldn't handle it."

"Yeah, since jumping over a nearly dead fire takes *so* much skill," I teased.

"You're just jealous because you don't have the guts to do it," Brett said.

"I have the guts, but I also have a brain, Scarecrow."

Brett shrugged. "I guess we will never know."

I knew he was baiting me. Brett and I were what one could consider competitive soulmates—no romance involved. It all started with a cookie-eating contest when we were seven. I always drew a line, though. There were some things I simply wouldn't do. He assumed jumping over an open flame without any necessary motivation was a line I would not cross. And normally, he'd have been right.

Unfortunately, I was not in the most stable mindset this evening. All my pent-up frustration and grief filled my heart, weighing it down as it beat against my chest like a hammer.

I took a few steps back and stared at the fire. It had picked up in height from the tinder I'd fed it, flicking tongues of orange and yellow against the darkness.

"Tempy," Nora said hesitantly, "what are you doing?"

My feet propelled me forward in a rush, and I leapt over the flames. The heat was immense; waves of flames curled around my ankles and calves before I landed safely on the other side with my feet skidding in the dirt. I felt invigorated and free from the thoughts that had been plaguing me. The girls cheered, and a couple of the guys high-fived me. I looked behind me to see Nora crossing her arms with a look of disapproval, though I could tell underneath it all she was impressed.

"She got more air than any of you guys," Sophia said as she tossed her ebony curls over her shoulder.

"Yeah," said Brett, who grinned and rubbed his palms together. "I can't wait to beat it."

"You wish," Sophia quipped.

Brett lifted an eyebrow and asked, "Why are you even here?"

"As a matter of fact, Temperance invited me," she replied and glanced at James with a sly grin.

"Whatever," Brett said and backed up to get a running start.

"Na-ah, my jump was the last one," I said in a commanding voice while pointing at each of the guys. "Anyone who tries it again will feel my wrath."

"Yep, she's the birthday girl," Nora said. "So what she says goes."

There were a few mumbled groans, but then Brett grabbed James' shoulder and said, "Hey, I dare you to eat a s'more laced with Cheetos."

"Done," James said, and the other guys followed him over to the food.

Gross, but at least they weren't doing dangerous stunts anymore.

Everyone fell back into individual conversations, jokes, and games while I hung back a little. I wanted a break from acting like everything was all right when inside I was a jumbled-up mess, but Nora stayed to keep me company.

"How's your birthday treating you so far?" she asked.

I sighed. "Let's see, I lost the tournament, my dream resurfaced, and my grandma's gone. It could be better."

"Oh," she said with an understanding smile. "You want to talk about it?"

"No."

"Alrighty then. Let's move on to happier topics. Brett asked you out."

"As *friends*," I quickly retorted.

"Whatever, he likes you!" Nora said and then bumped my side with her hip. "Honestly, he always has."

"Can we not talk about this with everyone just over there?" I said quietly.

"Come on, Tempy. Wake up," she whispered. "He. Likes. You."

I scowled.

She tapped her index finger to her chin and looked up

inquisitively. "*Who* did he ask to Co-Ed for the second year in a row, dashing the dreams of at least five girls?" she asked. "Let me think..."

I playfully shoved her in the shoulder. "Shut up."

"Mmmm... nope!" She bore a wicked grin.

Though she had a point, my brows still furrowed and said, "You're crazy."

Grabbing the chain of my necklace with my hands, I flicked my wrists, sending the pendant spinning around. Then, it occurred to me that Dad would have killed me if he saw me treating Grandma's necklace like that, so I stopped playing with it.

"Seriously, though," Nora said with relentless zeal, "how would you feel if he confessed to you?" She gave me her investigative look that always made me spill anything to her.

I gazed up toward the sky. I'd fantasized about it before, and if I was honest with myself, it wasn't totally unappealing. I always came to the same conclusion, though: Brett and I were like puzzle pieces that almost fit, but we were from different boxes.

"I honestly don't know, Nora," I groaned. "He's one of my best friends, and we have fun together... He knows everything about me. But I always feel boxed in around him."

Nora nodded. "Brett *does* like to do most of the talking and decision making."

"If you don't agree with him, you're wrong. It's like arguing with a wall," I said as I spun the pendant again. I poked her in the arm. "Can we please change the subject now?"

"Okay, fine. What happened in the dream?"

With Grandma gone, it was comforting that I still had Nora to talk to.

"I touched the door but couldn't open it," I said. Frustrated, I slid the pendant up and down the chain.

"That sucks." Nora's brows pulled together before her face lit up again. "Look on the bright side, at least you aren't constantly suffering from déjà vu, like me."

She tucked loose strands of her long mermaid waves back behind her ear. Her brunette hair looked nearly black under the light of the moon.

"I'd prefer that over a confusing recurring dream."

She glanced down at my hands. "Should you really be doing that?"

My hands froze over the pendant, and I mentally kicked myself yet again. It seemed I had no self-control when my mind was a mess. Nora reached over and moved my hands, her eyes sparkling as she looked over the necklace.

"I wish my family had heirlooms like this," she said with a soft tone. "Or that Dad had kept something of Mom's for me."

I was about to wrap her in a hug when she got that look on her face when she was experiencing her daily dose of déjà vu.

"What is it?" I asked.

She shook her head and stepped back. "I just have a strong feeling that you need to be careful with this," she replied.

"So, your déjà vu has turned into psychic visions now?" I teased.

"Shush! Look, I can't explain it." Nora laughed after she said it, but the smile didn't touch her eyes. She let go of the necklace and rubbed her head. One of her migraines was coming on. "Hey, I'm gonna grab some meds from my bag."

"M'kay."

Nora trekked along the path toward the cars and disappeared into the darkness. A sudden unease about her going alone came over me, so I followed her. The campsite was no longer in sight when her shadowed form came into view. What I saw brought a familiar image to mind: a stormy ocean, a flash of lightning, and the silhouette of Grandpa with his arms outstretched toward it all on that beach. It was only a millisecond, but it was clear as day. But that never happened... Did it?

I grasped the pendant around my neck as if it could anchor me to the present. The moment the gold touched my skin, a long-forgotten face appeared in my vision. A nine-year-old boy with blue eyes, soaking wet and shivering lips, wearing an old-fashioned white shirt with a standing collar and laces, blue pants, and black boots.

Did he wash up from a Renaissance Fair?

The thought was strange, an echo of the past. It was my thought, but... it was attached to the vivid memory.

A sharp pain suddenly shot through my head and white flashed, overwhelming me and pulling me to the ground. It slowly faded away, leaving me utterly confused.

What is happening to me?

"Tempy, are you okay?" Nora asked, suddenly at my side. I'd been so dazed I hadn't even heard her approach.

I shook my head.

"I'll go get James. Maybe we should take you home," she said and rushed back to the camp.

Once she'd disappeared from view, I leaned against a rock, trying to gain my bearings. I blinked a couple times and looked down. A dim, violet light shined from the hand enclosed around my pendant. I opened my palm to find the amethyst in my grandma's necklace glowing. My heart skipped a beat.

What on Earth?

I caressed the front of the necklace and turned it over. Small script appeared, engraved into the gold.

"The Haloed Sun rises," I whispered, reading the text.

The words sent a familiar zing humming through my body. One I'd felt every time I'd snuck a peek at the necklace in the past—a strange connection that I couldn't quite understand. Flipping the necklace back over, I ran my thumb over the two tulip-like prongs on its sides, accidentally pushing them up. Worry clutched at my chest. Had I broken it?

But then the top and bottom prongs shifted too, and the gem oscillated, hovering in the small space with nothing to tether it. Was it meant to do this? How *could* it do this?

I spun it experimentally, and my pulse quickened. The faster it spun, the stronger a familiar feeling coursed through my body, and the more entranced I became. The words engraved on the back echoed in my head.

The Haloed Sun rises.

Another memory formed of my grandma comforting me the night of my eighth birthday when the nightmares began, telling me one of her stories of Emeriz and a prophecy. She'd told this one so many times that I had it memorized. I uttered the words aloud as I watched the gem spin.

> *"In the dawning of the red wolf's reign*
> *The Haloed Sun shall rise,*
> *And the true power shall return.*
> *The forces of the staff shall be linked with the moon,*
> *As it draws its sword over the realm.*
> *And they shall be tossed upon the tides of fate,*
> *As two faces of a single being*
> *Tame the lion of the unseen storm.*
> *And the Descended united*
> *Shall reclaim the fiery chain about the wolf's neck."*

The stone slowly came to a stop. When the tulip-like prongs slid back into place, my fingers went translucent. I was fading away, like the moon at sunrise.

I heard James call out to me. "Wait, Tempy! No!"

A gust of wind blew across my face, carrying the scent of salt and a spray of mist. As I came out of my daze, I lifted my gaze from the stone.

The Arizona desert and mountains were gone. Instead, I sat on a beach facing a vast ocean. Overwhelmed with a familiar force that left me breathless, it called Grandma's words back to the surface of my mind; *"We need to feel the magic of the ocean before us, the forest behind us, the sky above us, and the earth below us."*

A sudden wave of nausea hit me like a freight train, and everything went black.

CHAPTER 3

FREDERICK

Misty daylight flickered into the old, tattered war tent as the entrance fluttered against the wind. The bright white linen had faded to a dingy gray, a shadow of the glory it had once held.

Captain Wulfric raised his thick orange brows, assessing me. The grizzled warrior's cheeks were ruddy from sunlight, and his mustache blended into his thick beard sprouting from his face like flame from a hearth fire. The captain sat behind an ancient mahogany desk, a purple cape draped over one shoulder.

Wulfric was captain of Lord Zavain's faction of the Eslanian rebels, and he took up space in the room like a great boulder. Despite being weathered by decades of battle, he stood firm, unmovable. The disbelief was clear in his pale gray eyes, and I understood it well. I'd handed out a request he hadn't expected.

"King Frederick, you want information on the Descended?"

No one had laid eyes on any of the four Descended since the rise of Minerva. Well, at least none that they were aware of. Unbeknownst to Captain Wulfric, he was looking directly at one.

"Yes," I said.

Wulfric sat down and leaned against the back of his chair, away from the map he'd been studying, and snorted. "Specifically, the Descended of the Haloed Sun, blood-daughter to the Superior

Goddess, and the true heir to our fallen kingdom?"

Reactions like this were why I'd kept my search to myself all these years. But, if I had any hope of finding the other Descended, especially their heir, I needed the help of the Eslanian Factions.

"Again, yes," Calix, my Left Advisor, chimed in from his position at the far end of the war tent. Green eyes that turned the head of many a lass narrowed slightly. He sounded agitated at Wulfric's attitude. His arms folded over his brown leather jerkin.

"Your child king expects me to believe in a fairy tale?" the captain asked Calix with a chuckle.

Eighteen may have been young, but I was no child.

"It's not a fairy tale," I said sharply.

"All the Descended are dead," Wulfric said with a swirl of bitterness. "What proof do you have otherwise?"

I had his proof. One display of my abilities, one word of who had sheltered me and my uncle on the night my parents were murdered, would be enough to rally them. However, I couldn't divulge those secrets to anyone just yet.

"I give you my word," I told Wulfric. My gaze unwavering and my stance firm, I enacted my power—enough to add the weight of truth to my words but dimmed enough that my eyes wouldn't glow.

It didn't work.

It hardly ever did even when I used my abilities at full capacity. Without the Haloed Sun, my gifts would always be dampened.

"Trust the word of a boy under High Queen Minerva's thumb?" Wulfric tsked.

I gritted my teeth. "Minerva tortured and murdered my family before my very eyes. Half of Linall burned that night." I hit the edge of the table with my fist, rattling the map weights shaped in the symbol of the Superior Goddess. "She's cut my armies in half by banning the women of my kingdom from serving. And then she cut what was left in half, just for good measure."

Calix cleared his throat, signaling me to scale back my anger. The captain looked me up and down, seeming to enjoy that he'd struck a nerve.

"And yet, your treasury is full of her gold," Wulfric said.

I sat down in the chair behind me, trying to regain some of my regal composure.

"She does whatever she can to hold onto her power," I replied. "Some of which ends up in the lining of your pockets, I might add. Her bribes are financing her own destruction."

Wulfric scrunched up his nose at the mention of my financial support for his armies. With narrowed eyes, he stared me down, as if trying to decipher my thoughts. When he finally spoke, his demeanor had become a little more open, but still skeptical.

"Even if we knew an heir was alive and where she was, why would we—or any of the eleven factions—tell you?"

Under the guise of a natural tic, my finger grazed the sodalite stone in my ring as I once again delicately enacted my abilities. I needed him to see the truth of my intentions.

"I pose no threat to any of the factions by receiving this information," I said. "Nothing would please me more than to see Eslane united and restored, and a proper High Monarch in Minerva's place."

"You?" asked Wulfric, disbelief returning. "Or the mythical heir you speak of?"

"Whichever the people decide. As it was in the old days," I assured. "Instead of jesting at the idea, maybe actually consider it. What is the one thing that can unite the factions of Eslane and give you the strength to defeat the High Queen?"

Wulfric took a long pause, carefully considering my words. "Fine. Believe what you will about your Descended, young king. I will hold back my humor from it. In fact, if you succeed in finding our heir, I assure you that not only this faction, but all eleven, will come together under her one rule."

We were finally getting somewhere, but my momentary relief was washed away by the captain's next words.

"As for the intel you seek, we have none." He took a swig from his waterskin. "And before you ask, no, I will not devote men and resources to your pointless hunt. If there is an heir alive, clearly they have no intention of being found. And if they are dead, the Superior Goddess has certainly deserted us."

"You lack faith for someone who still carries the Goddess' symbol," I said as I motioned to the paperweights and the white-and-violet banners that hung on either side of him bearing the insignia of the Goddess: a violet circle within a golden tear, backed with the sun.

"The Haloed Sun hasn't dawned in forty-five years. That doesn't inspire much faith," Wulfric retorted and then toppled one of the weights on its side. "As for the symbols, you should know the cost of changing a banner or crest. We'd need to replace everything. There's also the convenience of inspiring hope to our people. It keeps them fighting, even if we ourselves no longer believe."

"But it did return. Nine years ago. There were high priests throughout the lands that confirmed it."

"That supposed day was clouded over and didn't clear until the sun had set. Very few claim to have *witnessed* the sight, and the priests will do whatever they can to keep their donation pots and temples full."

"Does it tell you nothing that Minerva executed those who claimed to have seen it and anyone who called her a blasphemer for claiming *herself* a Descended?" I clenched my hands into fists, doing my best to restrain my anger and disbelief at his ignorance, though it still leaked through my tone.

"It tells me she's a demon spawn that needs to be burned for her thirst for power and admiration," Wulfric replied as his oversized brows knit together in frustration. "It tells me that those who helped her rise to power all those years ago should be burned alongside her!" Wulfric's eyes were inflamed with guilt and loss.

So that's when he lost his faith.

My voice took on a more sympathetic tone as I said, "Minerva had everyone fooled when she took down King Domhnall after he ripped Eslane into pieces the first time."

"And the factions backed her, believing she was the true heir to the Goddess, believing she was whom the prophecy spoke of... But it was all lies! Lies conjured by the blasphemous, sinister snake of a Grand High Priest Maxwell." He grabbed one of the weights and knocked over another to take its place. "All we did was remove one tyrannical ruler and replace him with another."

"My grandfather wasn't innocent either. He led our Linallian armies to fight with her."

Wulfric scoffed.

I ignored him. "My parents gave their lives to correct that failure. I carry on that burden."

If he only knew how much.

They loved each other, but my parents hadn't met by chance. It'd been arranged in secret so that one day there would be another Descended in a seat of power—blood tied to the Four First Gifted and a true legitimate heir to a throne.

I stood and placed my hands over the edge of the desk between us. "I will find the Descended, fulfill the prophecy, and restore harmony throughout the kingdoms of Emeriz with a new High Monarch to command them."

"I admire your convictions and faith in the Goddess and her Descended... I once shared them, but I'm older now," Wulfric said, placing the weights back in their corners, standing up. "We've only barely found peace in the factions—ruling ourselves individually after we finally stopped warring with each other. Enough that every now and then, we deign to work together in our missions against Minerva. Our faction's dedication is to Lord Zavain and his rule. We protect our people and fight Minerva on our terms. Not on the cruel whims of a prophecy and a Goddess who won't strike the woman down herself."

I opened my mouth to argue, but he held up a hand to silence me.

"I mean no disrespect, Your Majesty. If we come across information on any of the Descended, we will contact you. In the meantime"—Wulfric lifted the bag of coins I'd given him when I'd entered the camp—"thank you for your donation to the cause. We will see Lord Taren on the night of the hidden moon for your next shipment of goods."

Weapons, food, and more money.

Wulfric bowed respectfully while I lifted my hood and tugged the navy cowl over my nose and mouth. Dressed in my basic leather armor and hunting gear to blend in, no one had recognized me so far. Luckily, I'd never shown my face officially as King Frederick outside the walls of Linall for this exact purpose. The last thing I needed was to draw attention to myself while searching for the Descended. The flaps of the entrance brushed against Calix and me as we exited the tent.

"You need to watch your temper, My King," Calix scolded under his breath. He scrubbed a hand over his well-trimmed beard.

"Don't call me that while we're masking our identities… I think it might help with the whole *secret* aspect of it," I said, sarcasm heavy in my tone. I shrugged and schlepped through the muddied earth beneath our boots.

The sky was overcast with gray clouds, a hint of rain in the air. It had poured the night before, and by the scent lingering in the wind, it would not be the last we would see of the storm. We walked through a makeshift market with wooden stalls that could be easily collapsed in the event they needed to escape quickly. They were slightly slanted or warped in places, indicating that these quick getaways had happened on multiple occasions.

Would Minerva ever let them settle anywhere in peace?

A group of people encircled a nearby campfire, awaiting their turn to receive rations. The man running the meat stall called out a name, and a little girl ran across our path. In her effort to avoid bumping into us, she slipped in a puddle of mud. I managed to grab her arm to steady her, and she looked up at me. Flecks of brown dirt dotted her face, but still she smiled and thanked me. Sincerity twinkled in her blue irises, bringing a flash of memory—a nameless girl who cracked open a door, streaming light into the darkest night of my life.

I released the girl like I'd been burned. "Go on now. Watch your step." I turned toward the tree line where we'd tied up our horses and supplies.

"We should head back to Kanthe to await word from Fjall and Kelurs," Calix suggested.

I shook my head. "Not yet. I want to circle the surrounding area for a day or two."

"What makes you think they'd come back, let alone reside in the same area where you first spotted them? It's been years, sir."

"This is all I have. No other information to go on other than my personal knowledge and instinct."

"We've made this same trip at this time every year for nine years. Nothing has ever come of it."

"And?"

"I don't want you to get any more obsessed, locked into thinking that finding the other Descended is the only way." Calix stopped walking and pulled my arm so I'd face him. "What if they're dead?"

"They had a granddaughter." I sighed. "She'd still be alive. I didn't realize the meaning of her presence until I was older, but she could be our only chance."

"And she could also be—"

"Calix, please. I can't let this go... Not yet."

Calix cocked his head and narrowed his eyes. "Ahem, sir?"

"Let's just focus on the search for now. Then I will discuss if we should move on from this." I wasn't ready to give up. Every instinct in my bones told me I was on the right track. And tracking was one of my special abilities.

"That's not what I was going to speak of, My King." Calix's eyes darted to the side and then back at me.

Irked that he'd used a formal address with me again, I scoffed. "What, then?"

He pointed behind me. "Where's your horse?"

I turned and cursed. My brand-new mare was missing.

A horn sounded, followed by the sounds of wood slapping against wood. Looking back at the encampment, I saw everyone desperately packing up. One of the scouts must have returned with word that the High Queen's men were nearby.

I clenched my hands, determined that one day, the Eslanian Factions would never have to run again. No one would.

CHAPTER 4

TEMPERANCE

The edge of my vision glowed a familiar hue of violet. It was happening again.

Fear pulsed through me as I took that first step up the tall, winding staircase, the emotion so overpowering that it had stopped me dead in my tracks nearly every time I tried to ascend. I buried the fear once again, more determined to reach the top than ever.

I'll make it in time.

With one heavy step followed by another, I gripped the cool stone banister and pulled myself up the staircase. Halfway up, a misty darkness reached out from a glassless window, clouding my mind and paralyzing me with terror. The oppressive force clutched onto me no matter how hard I tried to shake it, weighing me to the ground and stripping me of my will to keep moving.

A bright light flashed, freeing me and giving me the strength to scramble up the rest of the steps until I reached the door at the top. As I ran my hand across the smooth wood of the door, excitement filled my body from head to toe. I'd finally find out what secrets lay beyond it. I turned the handle, but it wouldn't budge.

All that effort and it's locked!

I knelt to inspect the doorknob. Its intricately engraved face resembled those old-fashioned ones that only opened with a skeleton key. Tracing a finger over the keyhole revealed that it was a completely different shape than I'd expected—but I felt certain I'd seen it before.

The violet hue began to fade, a sign that my dream was coming to an end.

No, not yet!

Something prickled against my cheek as though it was being caressed by a small set of twigs. My eyes fluttered open to see a white dove perched on my chest, its beak tapping my skin. I instinctively batted the creature away, and it flew off into the distance toward the sunlit ocean.

Ocean? Daylight?

I froze.

"Where am I? Is this some sort of prank?" I asked aloud, suspicious that somehow my friends had decided to knock me out and take me on a surprise road trip. Not that they'd ever done that, but they had joked about it once or twice. When no one responded, panic set in. "Guys, this isn't funny!"

My eyes darted around, looking for someone—*anyone*—but I was alone.

Closing my eyes, I took a deep breath and told myself not to panic. There had to be a logical explanation. Maybe I was hallucinating. Or, the more plausible scenario, this was a dream. When I woke up, I'd be at home in bed or with my friends.

The salty air tickled my nose, and the cool breeze lightly whipped my hair across my face. Nothing had changed. My heart fell as I opened my eyes and inspected my surroundings. Scooping up a handful of sand, I watched it gently trickle between my fingers like an hourglass.

There was no denying it... This place was real.

To my left, a rocky wall jutted into the ocean and disappeared into the icy waters. It was shallow though—enough that a ship couldn't come in without scraping up the bottom.

Or a boat...

I froze and my pulse stuttered.

A vibrating sensation overwhelmed my mind. When I closed my eyes to shake the feeling away, a memory consumed my vision like I had on virtual reality goggles. In this memory, I was eight years old, camping with my grandparents.

The beach was enclosed in darkness with only the moon, stars, and campfire to bring light. We were camping *beyond* old school without any modern devices, contraptions, or furnishings. We had a simple A-frame tent made of sticks, rope, and white linen fabric. Any dishes we used were made of wood or tin.

Wrapped up in a blanket burrito, I shielded myself from the frosty breeze blowing off the crashing waves of the ocean. Every gust of wind felt like death by a million microscopic icicles. I could've gone inside the tent and kept a little warmer, but there was one good thing about the cold: it kept me awake. My own screaming had already yanked me from the bad dream once that night, and I wasn't eager to have it happen again.

Grandma was in the middle of telling the tale about two sisters and their magical pendants when we were distracted by a violent crash.

Moonlight reflected off the surface of the ocean, revealing two figures swimming up out of the arching black waves surrounded by the debris of a small boat. Grandpa rushed over to the shoreline, his silhouette stark and black against the lightning crackling across the night sky. He stretched his arms out wide, shouting something at them, words stifled by the wind.

Immediately, a dead calm stole the breath from the gales, and the waves settled into nothing. To my sleep deprived eyes, it appeared as if he'd commanded the winds himself.

But of course, that was crazy.

Grandma ran into the tent before emerging with several blankets and a lantern.

"Wait here, Tempy," she told me.

Like I was gonna miss *this*.

I dashed over as fast as my feet could take me, blankets flapping behind me like wings. Even with her head start, I reached the three of them first.

Deep in whispered conversation, Grandpa's hand gripped the shoulder of a tall, burly man. He was bald, with large ears and a long, braided beard held closed with a silver clasp. A boy about my age stood next to him, his hand gripping the man's apron strings.

When Grandma caught up, she said, "Sweetheart, I told you to wait at the—" Her eyes shifted to the man. "Henvick?"

"What's a Henvick?" I asked, out of breath.

Either not hearing me or ignoring my question, Grandma handed Grandpa the lantern and frantically wrapped the stranger in a blanket before hugging him.

When they separated, Henvick addressed them both. "I can't believe my eyes. To see you and Neal here... I just can't believe it! I thought you'd..." He eyed me, seeming to choose his words carefully. "I thought you'd left."

As they continued their reunion, I looked at the boy. Dressed similarly to Henvick, he wore a white, oversized shirt with laces, blue pants, and boots to match. He was that boy!

Did they wash up from a Renaissance fair? thought eight-year-old me.

His outfit was completely soaked through, and he was shivering aggressively. The light from the lantern illuminated his face, and I could see that his quivering lips matched the set of blue eyes above them. I quickly removed one of the two blankets around me and draped it across his shoulders.

His eyes went wide, and he bobbed his head in a quick bow. "T-Thank y-you," he said.

"No problem," I said. "I'm dry; you're soaked."

Grandpa walked over and placed his hand on my head. "Henvick, this is our granddaughter."

Henvick's jaw dropped as he looked at me in awe. "Your granddaughter? So she's the—"

"Why don't we get you over to the fire," Grandpa said, grasping Grandma's hand to lead everyone back to our camp.

Sunlight bled through my surroundings and the memory evaporated with it. I blinked, and I was seventeen again, standing alone on the beach.

What's happening to me?

I glanced behind me to see the fallen tree trunk we'd camped next to, confirming all my feelings that this is exactly where we had camped. As I stood to investigate, I noticed another odd change.

My clothes had been replaced by a purple dress that stopped just above my knees. Along the scooped neckline, floral embroidery reached across from shoulder to shoulder. The sleeves came in fitted around my elbows, belling out at my wrists. Instead of my jacket, I was cinched into a black corset, but I could still breathe easily. A sturdy pair of black leggings hugged my thighs and disappeared beneath a set of matching, well-fitted boots. My grandma's pendant, however, was left unchanged.

Clearly, this *wasn't* a prank from my friends. The last thing I remembered was my necklace glowing unnaturally. If it had brought me here, could it get me home?

Pushing the prongs, I attempted to recreate what had happened before, but to no avail. I clasped the pendant tightly in my fist—the worst thing I could do now was risk breaking it.

"So, I'm stuck here?" I shouted at the sky, dropping onto the sand in defeat. Tears welled in my eyes as I pulled my knees into my chest. The magnitude of how alone I felt crashed into me like the cold waves on the rocks.

A high-pitched voice buzzed near my ear. "It's true... I can see the glow, ever so faintly."

"Who said that?" I demanded as I whipped my head up and choked on a gasp, my eyes widening. Sand kicked into the air as I backed away from it. A giant *bug* was talking to me.

"Oh, don't be frightened," it said. "You belong here!"

I kept shifting back in the sand until I bumped against a log.

"Oh, fiddlesticks. I didn't mean to scare you!" it said as it scurried closer to me.

I could now see two lithe red wings sitting on the back of a girl the mere height of a grapefruit. Rich auburn hair draped around her shoulders down to her feet, framing her flowing red, yellow, and orange dress.

It wasn't a bug at all, but a fairy.

As I struggled between my instinctual urge to swat at it and my curious state of wonderment, our attention was brought to the distant calls of men. Someone barked orders, directing a search party.

"Oh dear!" she squeaked. "Maxwell and his hunters are after me, and I can't have them find you!"

"It appears the blessing of the Goddess is upon us, gentleman," a hauntingly smooth voice said from behind me. "We have found our prey. Our queen will be pleased."

He was a man somewhere in his fifties, wearing attire that clashed with the beach scene—long flowing robes in black and red, with intricate embroidery throughout. His black hair was slicked back, and he sported a mustache and beard to match. If he'd styled the mustache anymore upward, I feared he'd kidnap me and tie me to a train track like a silent movie villain.

The stranger's eyes bore into me in a sort of transfixed shock. "Temperance?"

How does he know my name?

"Run!" the fairy whispered, positioning herself between me and the group of men. "You're too important."

She glowed orange and then crimson before unleashing a bright ball of fire. When it hit the ground in front of the hunting party, a ring of flames surrounded them. But they wouldn't be occupied with the inferno for long. As the men shifted to avoid getting burned, the flames were already fading away.

Weaponless and clearly in danger, I rose to my feet and bolted in the opposite direction. For how long or how far, I couldn't say, but when exhaustion set in, I ducked behind a large boulder.

My body trembled, unused to being driven to that extreme. I placed my hands on my knees and glanced around the rock to check if I'd been followed. Luckily, it seemed no one was on my tail. Relieved, I leaned against the boulder and nearly buckled to the sand.

Guilt from leaving her to fight alone crept into my thoughts. In grandma's stories, fairies were as sweet as candy, but some liked to cause trouble. That one was clearly into some sort of mischief, and I didn't need any more on my plate. But still, she had helped me.

Wait, Grandma's stories! Fairies, the necklace magically bringing me here, and my new wardrobe? If this is truly real, it could only mean one thing.

"Emeriz," I whispered. "I'm in Emeriz."

The truth sank into my soul like quicksand.

Grandma's fairy tales were real, and she'd brought me to this world before. How did they hide it? And why?

All I remembered from that night years ago was getting into their van then waking up in the tent a short time later. I'd apparently slept during the trip home too. Then, I'd woken up in their guestroom with no memory of even getting in the car.

My emotions warred inside me, parrying back and forth so quickly that none could secure the upper hand. I was excited to be walking in the same world as the heroes I grew up hearing about but was infuriated that they'd hidden it from me.

What was I supposed to do? I couldn't sit around waiting for that old guy who knew my name to hunt me down, but I couldn't go home either.

Panic settled in. I rubbed at my chest, trying to calm myself and untangle the knot of pressure building. I wouldn't solve anything by freaking out.

My gaze bounced in every direction, searching for anything that might help my situation. All my senses were on full alert and doubly impactful. I used that to clear my mind. The ocean air smelled like stale seaweed and wet sand. The breeze blew strands of hair across my cheeks sending goosebumps down my neck and spine.

My muscles relaxed and my breathing evened out as I listened to the waves crashing against the sand and a piece of driftwood beating against a nearby rock. It reminded me again of the boy and his uncle. If I found them, maybe they could help. My grandparents knew them, after all.

A flock of multi-colored birds flew overhead, their colorful feathers blending together in beautiful vibrancy. They were Teachdaire birds, heralds of the Goddess.

How I remembered the name of the type of bird or their purpose, I couldn't say. It was instinctually buried deep within memories of Grandma's fairy tales. Three stark-white doves soared alongside them, standing out amongst the others' blue, purple, and yellow feathers.

Doves represent something in the stories too. What was it again?

The birds sang out, and their harmonious chirping pulled a feeling of peace to the surface of my emotions. They disappeared over the treetops, and their song faded into the distance.

The forest tugged on my soul, urging me to enter its tangled embrace. Besides, I had to keep moving, and standing still never got anyone anywhere.

I shivered at the dark shadows in the trees. All my Girl Scout training and survival instincts warned me not to venture there quite yet, maybe not even at all.

Deciding to stick to the beach, I summoned my courage and continued in the opposite direction from my new *acquaintances*, and it wasn't long before I reached another wall of rocks. With no way around the structure, I climbed over it. Getting to the top was easy enough, but I slipped going down the other side, scraping the palm of my hand in the process. After scrambling to my feet, I rushed to the waterline to clean dirt out of the wound, which turned out to be a mistake. The salty water stung, causing me to flinch in pain.

"Ow! Ow! Ow! Duh, you idiot! It's a friggin' ocean!"

I squeezed my palm and wished the pain would stop. An overwhelming calm washed over me, and the stinging sensation faded away. I examined my hand to find that the cuts and scrapes had disappeared.

"What on Earth?" But this wasn't Earth, and the magical healing of the cut was a stark reminder of that. Blood drained from my face.

I didn't fully get the chance to process the miracle because my wrist was yanked down. A mess of dark hair, fair skin, and seaweed filled my vision, and I stifled another scream. A strange girl stared up at me with wild amber eyes peeking out from beneath the tangle of hair and ocean debris that clung to her face.

She was gasping for breath. "F-Finally... H-Help," she said weakly.

I immediately dragged her out of the water and onto the sand. Something pale, shimmering, and slimy lay in place of where her legs should have been.

She was a full-on mermaid—fin and all.

CHAPTER 5

TEMPERANCE

"You're a... a..." I couldn't string a full sentence together.

The mermaid coughed and gripped my arm. "T-Tempy, breathe," she said.

"How does everyone here know my name?" I asked, finally able to form a coherent thought.

The mermaid removed the seaweed from her face and flipped the wet strands of hair behind her.

My eyes went wide as I recognized her face. "Nora?" I said incredulously as I threw my arms around her, thrilled to no longer be alone. "How are you here? Wait... How are you a mermaid?"

She pulled away. "I'm not Nora. Well... I'm also not *not* Nora."

"What?" My relief popped like the bubbles of sea foam surrounding her tail.

"I can explain," Not Nora said, her voice starting to wheeze. "But I need your h-help first."

"Okay."

"I need you... to change me," she breathed.

"Change you? Like, into a human?" I asked, befuddled.

She nodded, still struggling to breathe. Being out of the water was obviously taking a toll on her.

"How?"

She abruptly tugged at the pendant around my neck. "Use... this."

My necklace? How could it possibly help? I tugged it from her grasp and inspected it. The words engraved on the back shifted before my eyes.

Side by side.

One of the rhymes from my grandma's stories came to mind, but I couldn't bring myself to admit it might actually be a spell. And yet, speaking the words that had appeared on the necklace transported me to Emeriz, and I'd healed myself.

I had magic.

It was possible that I could fulfill her wish.

I awkwardly held my hands over her, unsure of what gestures to make. I recited the rhyme slowly and with purpose.

"The tides of fate have turned again,
So I ask the help of a loyal friend.
But first things first, our worlds must collide,
And stand together, side by side."

My muscles relaxed, and I felt a little dizzy. Something shifted in me and a strange pressure took over. No longer in control of my actions, I backed away from the mermaid with my hands stretched out. As I did, she rose from the sand until she was vertical. Then a blast of violet light erupted between us, and she screamed. A sharp pain shot through my stomach, and then everything went dark.

When I came to, she was kneeling over me with her arms crossed and her hands around her shoulders. My vision was still blurry as she helped me sit up.

"Good, you're alive," she breathed. "For a minute, I thought we were both goners! I never expected to feel that overwhelming pressure." Her voice was overly energetic. "Normally, I can only transform on half-moons, but it feels more natural then. I wonder if this permanently made me human. I hope not. I like having the choice. That's not the biggest problem right now though, since the Haloed S—"

I held up my hand. "Please... just slow down a second."

My head throbbed, and I rubbed my eyes to relieve the blurriness. After a minute or two, my vision was set right. I looked over at her and then immediately turned my attention elsewhere.

"Um, Nora... you're naked."

"Again, I'm not Nora. She lives on Earth. Call me Ora. That's what I go by, and it might make things less confusing."

"What? And what?"

Ora waved her hand in front of her, only to clap it back down to cover herself. "I'll explain everything after you help me find some clothes."

"Right... I'll just mosey on over to my traveling wardrobe and grab you something," I said sarcastically. "What am I supposed to do? Conjure some up out of thin air?"

"Exactly," she said matter-of-factly. "You have creation magic."

I checked the pendant, hoping to find another helpful engraving, but there wasn't one.

"Yeah, never done this before, so..."

Ora sighed in frustration. "Wow, your grandmother really didn't teach you anything?"

"No, she didn't. Just some stories and rhymes. No Magic 101 classes for me."

"I suppose it would have been difficult with you living so far away from her. You've mentioned to Nora how much you missed her when they moved." Ora appeared reminiscent for a moment before returning her attention to me. My confusion must have been apparent in my expression because she said, "I'll explain after we get me dressed."

"Okay... but I don't know any spells for something like this. Should we just wrap you up in some seaweed for now?"

Ora shook her head and snickered. "Spells are helpful and can make wielding power easier on our minds and bodies, but a Descended doesn't always need one, especially you since one of your particular gifts is creation magic."

I filed away her comment about the Descended for later inquiry. I needed her to focus on instructing me in the creation magic I supposedly had.

Ora shivered. "When you don't have phrases of power to do so, you need to enact the power on your own. Close your eyes and relax."

Bittersweet anticipation and hesitation thrummed through my veins. For the third time that day, I was going to use *magic*. When I'd cast that first spell on her, a surge of powerful energy had burned inside my chest. It felt like pushing in that last piece of a puzzle, completing my soul. A sliver of myself was lost—one that was both foreign and surreal—and it scared me. Nevertheless, the temptation to use it overwhelmed me, and with Ora encouraging me to explore it, I couldn't resist.

Besides, the girl needed clothes.

I closed my eyes.

"Take a deep breath," Ora said as she placed her cold hand over my chest. "Then focus only here until you feel... *different*."

As I did, warmth spread through my core. Every breath stoked it like a furnace until an image of an ultraviolet flame appeared in my mind. The heat crept up my shoulders and neck until it softly burned behind my eyes, forcing them open.

A smile lit up Ora's expression. "Wow... Okay, now imagine what you want to accomplish, and allow your instincts to guide you."

We stood and stepped back from one another. She remained silent as my hands reached out by their own will. I envisioned what I wanted to create but still focused on the intensity building in my chest. I allowed myself to surrender to it, and a wind rotated around her. It was working. Freaking out a little, I lost my focus, and the power began to slip from my grasp.

"Just relax," she said.

After another deep breath, I shifted my attention back to the task at hand. The seaweed at her feet reached up, transforming into a featherweight fabric weaving its way across her body. I smiled as what I had envisioned took shape before my eyes. A minute later, my hands slowly dropped to my sides, and the winds ceased. Once again, my vision blurred as the world spun, a dull ache blooming at the base of my skull.

"You did it!" Ora pounced and wrapped me in a tight hug. She stepped back and spun in a circle, lovingly touching her new clothes. "This dress is beautiful!"

The fabric draped over her chest and shoulders, held up by two thin straps. It came in tight but delicately at the waist, then lightly flared out at the hem just above her knees, with skirts whispering in the wind. The color was a gorgeous array of blues and greens, starting light at the top and fading into darkness—perfect for a mermaid-turned-human, and reminiscent of Nora's ice-skating dresses.

Not too shabby for my first time. For a moment, I considered the idea of going into fashion back home, assuming I could find a way to return.

Still grinning from ear to ear, Ora caressed the pendant that hung around her neck. "It matches my necklace perfectly too!"

In the center of the silver medallion was a small, blue water opal surrounded with an intricate filigree design. An iridescent finish shimmered underneath.

"That's stunning!" Reaching out to examine it closer, I asked, "May I?"

She nodded enthusiastically while I shook away a sudden feeling of déjà vu. Mere hours ago, *Nora* had asked me the same question.

They were identical... Could they have been long lost twins?

"I'm Descended of the Tides," Ora explained. "Opals can help amplify my abilities and keep me centered the same way your amethyst does. It also holds the secret as to how I know who you are." She grabbed her necklace back. "Are you prepared for this?"

There she went using that *Descended* word again.

"Yes," I said, though I wasn't completely sure I was.

"Here we go!" Her irises illuminated with a quicksilver hue with multi-colored facets like diamonds. The glowing shade spread down through her arms and over her forehead in a wispy pattern. She pulled the filigree of the medallion up like a locket, revealing an opal perched on an iridescent finish. Running her finger over the gem caused it to liquefy and transform into a reflective surface. There were no winds like the ones that'd come when I used my powers, but the tides picked up, lifting the waves to dangerous heights. Her voice echoed while she spoke.

> *Mirrored in our own images and reflected in our eyes,*
> *I attempt to break their sacred ties.*
> *We connect in the only way our hearts will allow,*
> *Even when it severs the immortal vow.*
> *And then someday the time may come,*
> *That we come together as one."*

The waves immediately ceased, and my eyes widened. The surface of the medallion was like watching a livestream of Earth. Brett was in the frame, staring straight at us. From the looks of it, he was on Nora's front porch.

"Hey, Nora!" he said.

"What's up?" I heard Nora's voice reply.

I glanced at Ora. "You can see my world through Nora?"

Ora nodded and smiled. I turned my focus back to the scene unfolding before my eyes.

We missed something Brett had said as Nora responded with, "Fighting another migraine. I've been babysitting all morning."

"Ouch, and after a late night too. Do you need meds?" he asked.

"I'll grab some in a minute," she said.

I was beginning to suspect that it had nothing to do with her siblings or late nights and everything to do with a certain person using a particular spell.

"That's good." Brett smiled and glanced around for a minute without saying anything.

"Did you need something?" Nora asked, sounding a bit uncomfortable.

"I need your opinion on something. Well, *someone*," he said and then sighed.

"What do you want to know about Tempy?" Nora asked, cutting straight to the point.

Anxiety reared her ugly head again inside of me. This felt so invasive, like I was spying... which I kinda was.

He looked at her in surprise, but she must have had her *I-know-all* face on, because he moved right into his dilemma.

"I asked Tempy to Co-Ed, and she couldn't because of her trip. Then I kind of threw a major hint in the air that we'd go to Morp together." He eyed Nora, as if to make sure she was following his train of thought, then continued. "I thought it was a done deal, but I texted her to confirm, and she hasn't responded."

"Are you asking me to try to understand the inner workings of my best friend's mind?"

"That is your job, isn't it? Please?" There he went with his no-fail puppy dog smile to charm her.

"Fine, but first I need to know, why does it matter?" she asked, a tint of wickedness shading her playful tone.

"Uh-oh," I breathed, knowing exactly where she was going.

"Um, what?" he asked, sincerely confused.

"Why is going to Morp with her so important?" She leaned forward and asked, "Is the balance of your friendship tipping?"

"Ora, we can stop now," I said abruptly, stepping away to avoid hearing his response.

The glowing designs faded from Ora's skin and her eyes returned to normal. The opal formed back into a ball and lost its reflective surface. After closing the filigree, she turned to me with hands on her hips and disapproval written all over her face.

"It was just about to get interesting," she scolded.

I shrugged. "Not my business."

"It's about you!"

"But it's not *to* me, and... I don't know. Maybe I don't want to know," I said. "I've got more important things to worry about right now, like why you look like my best friend, and why I can't get home. Not whether or not Brett and I like each other."

Also, why had that fairy saved me from that strange man? And how had they both known me? I needed to get moving just in case those men made another appearance, but I needed answers too.

"How are you able to look into Nora's mind?" I asked. "Are you twins or something?"

"Or *something...*" she said cryptically as she bit her lip.

"Are you trying to be enigmatic?" I waved my hand in a circle to prompt her into expounding.

Ora gave a shaky grin and then said, "We are two halves of the same soul—one person, split into two."

My blood went ice cold and a shuddered breath escaped from my lips.

Nora was... half a person?

What she said felt so wrong, but then again, there she was, a carbon copy of my dearest friend. When I didn't respond, she wrung her hands and launched into speech once more.

"What I just did, it's called *scrying*," she said. "It's an ability unique to the bloodline I'm descended from. Usually scrying into other worlds can only be done through a reflective surface, like a mirror." She caressed the face of her medallion. "Nora, being my other half, offers a unique connection to Earth. I see more clearly through her and feel less strain on my mind."

And all the while, Nora compensated for it with her migraines.

"Can we communicate with her?" I asked, a trickle of hope alighting my chest.

She shook her head. "As long as Nora and I stay separated, I'll never be able to reach my full potential and win complete control of my abilities. I'm at a fourth of what my powers should be."

"A fourth?"

"Being without the Haloed Sun dampens all magic in Emeriz. Until it shines with its violet halo again, we're limited." Shading her eyes, Ora glanced toward the sun. "I thought your return might restore it."

A vague inkling of a memory jingled in the back of my mind. Grandma had mentioned the sun before in her stories.

"How are you here while Nora's on Earth?" I asked.

"That's a long story. Bear in mind, this is just what I've been told." Ora took a deep breath. "My father is from Earth and my mother was from here. The day my parents met, my father was walking along a road on Earth and stepped into a puddle my mother had been scrying through.

"It enveloped him... opening our world and swallowing him down into the icy depths of the ocean. The Descended of the Tides can use portal magic through scrying, but it should've been impossible without the Haloed Sun. Mother used to tell me that only the Superior Goddess herself could allow such a thing. '*Fate*,' she always said.

"Since we're mermaids—and our kingdom, Merald, resides beneath the ocean—my father found himself drowning beside my mother. She saved him, and as these stories tend to go, they fell in love. He decided to stay in Emeriz." Ora gave a nonchalant shrug. "Mermaids have the ability of transforming into humans on half-moons and can stay that way for as long as they wish. If they want to go back to Merald, they'd have to wait for the next one to change back. With the danger High Queen Minerva poses, we usually only do so in times of necessity or trade. Minerva still finds ways to interfere with us, but it's not as bad as land kingdoms."

I remembered stories about the High Queen, but they always seemed vague and incomplete, almost like Grandma hadn't known all the details. What I did understand is that being near Minerva in any way was never good. The fact that she was real and still actively reigning was terrifying.

"So, your parents," I prompted.

"My mom decided to live on land with my dad, and all was well for a short time. Not long after they had me, danger struck.

"When I was around two, Mother was meditating on the direction of the tides when they warned her of a disturbance. Even in human form, she was still connected to the tides, feeling their push and pull. She rushed to where my father and I had been playing on the beach waiting for her return.

"Thank the Goddess for portal magic—she got there in time. One of Maxwell's soldiers had overtaken my father and was in the process of drowning him, while another attempted to kidnap me. Mother summoned her Descended Relic, the Serenity Bow, and shot my father's attacker, killing him instantly. She aimed her arrow at the man holding me captive, and my father ripped me from my captor's arms before my mother took his life too."

The fairy had called that man Maxwell. It could have just been a coincidence, but something told me that it wasn't.

"We still don't know how they found out about me," Ora continued. "My parents became extremely paranoid and worried for my safety, so they sought help.

"Somehow, they contacted your grandmother on Earth, who suggested splitting me into two people, and thus, splitting my aura—dimming it and making it near impossible for someone to find me by magical means. Your grandparents returned to Emeriz long enough to perform the ritual. My parents were still worried, though, so they decided to break their marital bonds and raise Nora and me in different worlds."

That seemed wrong, even with good intentions.

"Why not take you to Earth as one person and as one whole family?" I asked.

"My mother felt that her duty as a Descended was to stay here in case she was called to action." Ora looked a bit sheepish. "Mother didn't exactly approve of your grandparents running away, but who was she to question the Descended of the Haloed Sun? She also thought that this way, I could be trained properly in my abilities. Still, between the lack of the Haloed Sun, not being a whole person, and Mother being... gone, I couldn't get far in my training. The Serenity Bow has been missing since we lost her too. There are things I should be able to do but can't."

Nora's dad always made it seem like her mom had passed away but was vague about the details. I'd had hope when she'd mentioned her earlier that she could actually be alive, but Nora would have to continue living without her. It was like the beginning of the *Parent Trap* gone wrong.

Rubbing at my head and face, I tried to process her story. "Wow..." I said, bewildered. "Has every adult in my life lied to me?"

Ora twisted one of her beach-waved strands of hair around her fingers anxiously. "Everyone has secrets. Adults more so than anyone else."

I nodded my agreement and then asked, "What would happen if Nora ever came here?"

Ora shrugged. "The theory is that we would be brought together as one whole person."

Nora had lived without half of herself her entire life. Wouldn't doing this change her? Would I even know who she was anymore? Would it be painful for her? Had she already been suffering being apart from Ora? Would she want this?

My best friend was involved in all of this, and the longing to go home gripped my heart even tighter. I needed to see Nora and let her speak sensibly like she always did. This other half of her, though convincing and sincere, still sounded far-fetched.

"What are you thinking, Tempy?"

"Honestly, as incredible as this all is, I need to go home and discuss all of this with my family. I need to figure out why they gave me the necklace and why they aren't here." I dropped to my knees and sat back on my feet.

"Why don't you just use the necklace to take you home?" she asked, as if I were crazy to not even consider it.

"I've tried," I said, anxiety gripping my chest again. "The prongs are locked in place, and no words are appearing on the back like they did before!"

"Words on the back?" she asked, bemused.

I explained what had happened the first time they appeared and then again when I transformed her.

"That's unusual," she said, brows raised. "A Descended's power stones don't *train* their users in any way. That's unique to you, I guess."

I groaned and dropped my head into my hands.

"We'll figure it out! I promise," Ora assured me as she placed a hand on my shoulder. "When I felt your presence in the tides, I raced here to help you."

I looked up at her, puzzled. "How?" I asked. "It's not like I have a training manual for any of this."

Her face scrunched up in thought before she frantically shook me. "I know! We go to Linall! Their castle has the most expansive library in the world. According to my grandfather, the king knows just about everything about the Descended. He might be able to help."

Hope colored over my stress in a warm embrace. "Do you know how to get there?"

"I've swam around their southern border, but I'm not sure how to get there by land. It's somewhere east of here." Her shoulders dropped, but she maintained her confidence. "I'm sure we can figure it out. There are some scattered villages around where we can seek directions or a map if we get lost."

I still couldn't be sure those men wouldn't come looking for me, and staying on an open beach would ensure they'd find me eventually. I stared at the unknown forest. There was no telling what creatures we would come across. But my need for information, along with my curiosity for adventure, outweighed the fear that attempted to hold me in place.

"Let's go," I said with a smile, semi-confident about my decision. A mixture of nerves and excitement bubbled within. I was about to explore a magical world that was actually part of my lost heritage.

Ora clapped her hands and hugged me excitedly—an energy Nora didn't typically exude. She stood, but teetered backward, waving her arms around to find her center of gravity.

"You good?" I asked, holding my hands up in case I needed to catch her.

She nodded then helped me to my feet and brushed off any excess sand on my skirt.

"Follow me," Ora commanded and headed toward the forest. She stumbled a bit, her legs shaking like a foal taking its first steps.

I stayed put and eyed her hesitantly, unsure if she could handle this.

Ora glanced back and waved me forward. "This isn't my first time walking on land, but my experiences are few and far between. I should be normal by the time we reach the tree line."

There wasn't much of a choice, so I gave her a trusting smile and took my first steps toward answers. "All right then, let's go."

CHAPTER 6

TEMPERANCE

A light mist blanketed the air above us, glittering in the sunlight. It poured in through any small gap in the lush trees. Rich vines climbed up nearly each one, extending up to the highest branches before draping down when they had nowhere else to go. A twisted outer layer encased a number of them, seemingly shielding the massive trunk beneath. As we walked, I ran my hand against the base of one of the towering, gnarled trunks to observe the luminous, turquoise glow peering through its shell.

The bark faintly pulsated beneath my fingertips, and my heart synchronized with it, creating a connection that resonated within my chest, like an ancient life breathing from within.

"Tempy, pick up the pace," Ora urged. "I knew nature would call to you, but stay focused."

"What?" I said as I jogged to catch up to her.

"You're connected to nature the way I feel connected to water," she explained.

My eyes wandered from shrub to tree, branch to rock, bringing a strange realization to my attention. Not a single animal could be seen or heard. It was common on Earth for animals to remain scarce when humans were around, but Grandma always gave the impression that

Emeriz would be buzzing with magical and fantastical life—fairies, mini dragons, shadow wolves, nymphs, and many others.

"Speaking of creatures, why does it feel so... deserted?" I asked.

"High King Domhnall and his barbaric hunts," Ora said sadly. "He hated all things magical and encouraged their destruction."

What kind of crazed psychopath could harm innocent creatures with no provocation or motivation other than pure hatred?

Anger bloomed inside my chest, darkening my mood. It didn't surprise me when I recalled what my grandparents had told me about him. He had launched a coup, viciously murdering the Eslanian royal family. Fortunately, the younger princess survived and had a family of her own: two daughters with magical pendants and abilities like healing, divination, creation, and traveling through worlds.

Something clicked inside me. A magical pendant, traveling worlds... and Ora had called me "Descended."

"Ora, why am I connected to nature and why do I have powers?" I asked. "Because, from what I'm piecing together, it seems that I'm..."

She watched me intently with her arms crossed.

I'd been so overwhelmed and distracted by everything that happened to me in the past hour that the weight of the truth hadn't hit me until that moment.

"Ho-ly crap," I breathed. "If I'm a female descendant from that particular line, that would mean the prophecy is about... me?"

How had I been so dense? All the signs were there.

"Descended of the Haloed Sun," Ora said. "Which also means you're royalty. A deadly combination." She rushed over to me and excitedly grabbed my hands. "Descendant to the Superior Goddess herself. At least that's what I believe. Some still think your bloodline was simply gifted magical abilities like the other three."

"The Four First Gifted?" I asked weakly, remembering the old tale.

"Yep!" Ora beamed.

"No," I said incredulously.

"Yes! How else would you explain your abilities?" she asked in Nora's jesting *well, duh* tone.

It sounded alien to me.

"Nope, not me. It can't be." I tugged my hands from hers and rubbed my temples in an attempt to relieve the building tension.

Her face fell, but then she said, "Yes. You can help fix it all. Overthrow Minerva, bring back the creatures and create new ones, unite and restore Eslane..."

If it was all true, and my grandma's fairy tales were actual events, that meant High Queen Minerva murdered and stole my Great Aunt Ivy's pendant, defeated Domhnall, and took the throne. Which would also mean that Minerva pursued Grandma to claim her half of the pendant to solidify her rule as high queen.

My fingers caressed the necklace. Thank goodness that fairy drew Maxwell's men away from me. If Minerva got ahold of me, I'd never get home. Unless the only way out was to defeat her.

It seemed as though every path I could choose crumbled to dust, leaving only a narrow beam leading to one I'd be forced to follow.

Panic took hold, building pressure in my chest. "Is this negotiable?" I asked, my voice breaking. "Or is this one of those *I-don't-have-a-choice-in-my-own-future* things? Because, I refuse to have someone else determine my life."

"No one is taking away your future," Ora reassured. She then scolded herself, kicking at the dark soil. "I shouldn't have told you this so soon. Sometimes my excitement overflows and information just slips out."

I crossed my arms and stared at her, waiting for her explanation.

"I don't intend to keep you trapped here, but whether you like it or not, as Descended, the prophecy is about us. You hold the same magic that Minerva is currently in possession of."

"Magic I know nothing about."

Ora breathed in deeply, like she was fighting back her temper. It didn't work. Everything she said next came out in fast, rushed breaths.

"You can learn to use your magic. I'm not expecting you to fix Emeriz's problems overnight. It would be extremely convenient if you did, but we're missing a few crucial pieces of the puzzle." Ora began counting them on her fingers. "You need to practice your abilities, we need to locate the other two Descended, and we need to find a way to bring back the Haloed Sun. So let's get to Linall which—like it or not—is the only place that would have any answers to help you get home!"

Nora never spoke to me like that. It was a surreal sight to witness. Normally, she'd calmly explain the situation and disarm me slowly. This was Ora, though. Whereas Nora handled things with tender love and care, Ora appeared to be a fan of tough love.

I softened my stance and slowly approached her. "Okay."

She wrapped me in a hug like a deathtrap. "I'm sorry I lost it!" she said. "Honestly, patience isn't something Nora and I share."

"I'm sorry, too. You've been helping me, and the moment you mentioned something I didn't like, I freaked out."

"We want the same thing," she said, stepping out of our embrace. "We want to get you home. Let's start there and figure—"

Something behind me caught Ora's attention, and her eyes went wide.

"Ora?"

"Shh! Don't turn around, stay calm, and let's walk away slowly," she whispered through clenched teeth.

Curiosity got the better of me, and I turned around. A mere twenty feet from us was a crouched wild cat. It looked like a cross between a bobcat and cheetah, but with black fur and white spots. Its magnificence was overshadowed by its predatory stare.

Oh, what I would have done to have a sword on me right then... or a shotgun. I took a deep breath and forced my feet to move backward, away from the creature.

We'd only taken a few steps when my eyes met the cat's brilliant, plum-colored gaze. A connection between the animal and myself burned with intensity in my mind. A wave of calm suddenly washed over me. Warmth spread up my shoulders, neck, and flickered behind my eyes. My feet halted and my senses heightened, making me hyperaware of my surroundings.

"Come on, Tempy," Ora urged. "I refuse to be cat food."

"Hold on. Just trust me."

Not another word escaped Ora's lips, but I could feel her shaking behind me. The connection between me and the cat began to fade, and as it did, I was certain about one thing—she didn't want to harm us.

I walked toward the creature, but Ora quickly grabbed my arm. "Are you trying to get yourself killed?"

"She won't hurt us," I assured her. I shook off her hand and moved forward cautiously.

Meeting me halfway, the cat brushed her head beneath my outstretched hand. Her silky coat weaved between my fingers. I gave in to my natural instincts and proceeded to pet her like a domestic cat. The wildcat rolled around in the grass, reveling in the attention.

This was hands-down one of the coolest things I'd ever done. It was right up there with accidentally transporting myself into the world of my grandma's stories and using magic. What more did Emeriz hold for me?

"Huh, guess I shouldn't be surprised," Ora said, her voice taking on a more relaxed tone. "Your abilities do allow you to create and control most of the creatures here."

Something she said rang false.

"I don't think so. It feels more like an additional sense, not control." I scratched under the cat's chin, and she purred. "If she wanted to attack, I would only be able to sense what she was feeling. I wouldn't be able to stop her."

The sound of leaves and twigs snapped behind me as Ora made her way to us. The cat and I nearly jumped a foot in the air as she dashed over with excitement.

"Let's name her!" Ora gingerly stroked the cat's fur. The cat tensed but allowed it.

"Maybe approach a bit calmer next time, Ora. Who knows how she would have reacted to your... eagerness."

"Oops, sorry!" Ora eagerly clapped her hands together. "How about Devika? Or Thea! No, even better! Antheia!"

Every time she spouted out another name the cat became more agitated.

I patted the animal's head to soothe her. A name kept running through my mind—one I remembered from my grandma's stories. An ancient feline that had been one of the animals considered familiars to the bloodlines.

"Tundra?" I asked the creature hesitantly.

Her ears perked up, and her eyes bore into me as if saying, *"Yes, that's right."*

Looking at Ora, I shrugged. "Guess that's her name."

Ora shot me a doubtful look. "Based on what?"

"She responded to it. And I don't know... I sense it's right."

"You connected with her." Her eyes widened. "Why that name?"

"A story about familiars and the Descended of the Haloed Sun." I dropped my focus back to Tundra, not wanting to face Ora's smug smile.

"Really?" she asked in her know-it-all tone. "Can't deny your heritage now, can you?"

"I never denied that fact. It was the—" I glared back at her, deciding it was pointless to defend myself. She'd continue to believe whatever she wanted regardless. "Never mind, we should go. The sooner we find a way to get me home, the better. I'm not eager to meet Minerva or Maxwell, especially since Maxwell might already know I'm here."

Ora froze and stared at me dumbfounded.

"I'll explain on the way, but we really should get moving." Standing up, I brushed the dirt from my dress, then gestured to Tundra. "What do we do with her?"

Ora relaxed a little and shrugged. "She's your familiar, not mine."

"Here, Tundra." As we started to walk away, I clapped my hands—and much to my surprise, the cat followed.

Seriously, the coolest pet ever!

"This is bizarre," I said.

"And wonderful!" Ora gushed. "I've been waiting for an adventure like this all my life, and from my observations, I know you have too." Wearing her all-knowing smile again, she bumped my shoulder with hers.

"It's still scary."

Tundra brushed up against my leg, and I rustled the fur atop her head.

"Scary in the best way! Endless possibilities. I'm much happier here with you than I was at home." She giggled then, but there was something off about it.

"Why?" I asked.

"Oh no, I didn't mean it like that. I love my home!" She waved her hands dismissively. "It's just family obligations. My grandfather is well-known, which comes with certain responsibilities and expectations."

It was obvious she didn't want to go into the topic. Since she was a part of my best friend, I figured she'd open up when she was ready, just like Nora would.

We fell into a rhythm of conversation. I explained my run-in with the fairy and Maxwell. She asked me about life on Earth and answered my questions about Emeriz. This went on for hours until the sun had set behind the tree line, and a cool wind blew through the forest.

"We need to find a place to camp for the night and figure out a way to get a campfire going," I said, shivering to keep warm. "I'm freezing."

"Y-You're freezing? W-What a-bout me?" Ora rubbed at her shoulders to fight against the drop in temperature. "You p-put me in an outfit like this and then expect s-sympathy?"

"Hey, you said it was perfect."

"Oh, how naive I was."

"Beauty is pain," I teased through chattering teeth. "Can't I just will some jackets into existence, like I did with your clothes?"

Ora shook her head. "You're still new to all of this and your abilities strained you earlier. I'd hate for you to blindly attempt it again only to be both unsuccessful and too tired to move forward so we can find shelter."

"Thanks for your faith in me." I rubbed my arms, hoping the friction would warm me up a little.

"That's not—"

"No, it's fine. You make sense. We should save our strength until we find shelter." I shrugged. "Then maybe I can try to conjure some blankets or something."

Quick as a bullet, Tundra shot out into the darkness, leaving us alone.

Ora gestured in the direction she'd disappeared. "Great. Now our only form of protection has run off without us."

Again, I wished for my longsword. Why couldn't I have been training with it when I accidentally sent myself here?

"She's gotta eat and is actually capable of acquiring her food. Unlike us," I grumbled. My stomach groaned with hunger.

I scanned the area, looking for fallen or leaning trees, caves, or rock formations that we could settle in for the night. The last sliver of sunlight was about to disappear, leaving behind a dark starry sky. Apart from the tree line in front of us, the trees were lost in shadow. A faint turquoise glow reached out from their center just like the tree I'd connected to earlier.

Out of nowhere, something flew from the straight line of matching trees and grazed the top of my head.

"Get it off! Get it off! Get it off!" Scared it was a bat or something, I swatted my hands around and backed up. I mis-stepped and slid down into a muddy ditch.

"Temperance!" Ora cried.

I heard her shuffle down the slope, but I took a moment to lay there and allow the ridiculousness of what had just happened sink in. It was so embarrassing. Had James, Nora, and Brett been there, they probably would have been laughing at the spectacle. Just wonderful—now I was embarrassed *and* homesick.

"I'm okay!" I said, bringing myself to a sitting position. "Just covered in mud now, as if freezing wasn't bad enough."

By the time I was on my feet, Ora had made her way down to me.

"You weren't kidding." She shook the mud from my dress as best she could.

There was no way we'd get it all off. It covered the backside of my dress, my arms, and parts of my face.

"Saves me a trip to the spa when I get home," I joked, but it was lost on Ora. "Never mind."

The sound of flapping wings nearly made me jump out of my skin, bringing my attention to where a kamikaze bird perched. A fragment of moonlight peered through the branches, allowing me to see the white dove.

I stepped forward, ready to release my anger and shoo the crazy bird away. Before I could, a soothing calm washed over me, easing the muscles throughout my body.

It flew off into the night, leaving us alone. That's when I noticed what the dove had been perched on: a slanted brick and wood archway covered in vines and moss. It appeared to be some sort of ruin.

"We need to sleep somewhere," I suggested to Ora, a yawn in my voice.

"We have no idea what might be lurking in there," she whined.

"Not much different out here." I gestured to the general wilderness surrounding us. "I'm muddy, damp, and exhausted."

Ora groaned, but reluctantly agreed.

We dragged ourselves inside, but didn't venture in too far so the opening was still in view. It was so dark I couldn't tell how deep the structure was. There were no signs of animals nesting there, so it seemed like we were safe. Collapsing onto the ground, we were asleep in a matter of minutes, stomachs growling.

My heart raced as I stood face to face with the door again. This time I knew it was locked, and that I possessed the key. Worried I'd wake up any moment, I immediately reached into my pocket.

Nothing.

No! Where is it?

I frantically pawed inside the pockets of my... ball gown? Had I been wearing this each time? Before I could make any sense of this new development, the edges of the dream started to fade.

Oh, come on!

The dream grew fainter as reality came into view.

The mixed scent of campfire and cooked meat touched my nose. Opening my eyes, I found myself not in the comforts of my own bed at home, but on a damp, grassy piece of earth inside a cracked and crumbling hallway of a ruin.

In the morning light, I examined our shelter, whose walls were made of wood and stone, covered in ancient imagery and writing. Beautiful, but too faded to make anything out. I pulled my blanket closer.

Wait, blanket?

I sat up, noticing Ora had one draped over her too. Tundra had found her way back to us and lay at my feet. I observed another opening at the end of the hallway. The scent of food cooking came stronger, deeper within the structure.

We weren't alone.

"Ora."

She grunted and shifted in her sleep.

I shook her. "Ora, wake up."

Waking with a glare, she snapped, "What is it?"

I held a finger to my lips to shush her. "Someone's here."

"What?" Ora yawned, giving me a blank look.

"How do you think we got blankets?"

When she looked down and realized what I was saying, Ora threw the blanket from her, backing away like it was diseased.

"*Who?*"

"I don't know. Whoever it is, I don't think they want to hurt us." I looked hesitantly down the hall. "They gave us blankets and something smells like breakfast."

I hoped it wasn't a Hansel and Gretel type situation, and we were on the menu.

Ora gripped her stomach and smiled. "Ooh, I'm starving. Let's meet this kind provider."

Tundra had returned to my side at one point during the night. I pointed a finger at her and commanded, "Stay."

She was our secret weapon if this stranger tried to kill us.

Tundra cocked her head then settled it on her front paws, indifferent to whatever we were doing.

Keeping the blankets wrapped around us, we stood and made our way further into the ruin. The corridor led out into a massive open space. A soft turquoise glow escaped a parallel line of ancient trees. They rose above us like great sentinels guiding our path. Branches interlocked overhead in a chaotic web. It was like looking through a crochet weave in the old forts I'd made as a child with my grandmother's knitted blankets. A silence filled the air, thick but soothing. For some reason, I felt at home.

Moss and lichen grew and sprouted out of aged stone lining the path in broken patches. As we proceeded further inside, my boot kicked a stone, sending it skipping across the cracked floor. The sound drew the attention of our host, who turned from the flames.

Brilliant-white hair flowed down around her delicate face, reaching down her waist. A few shorter tendrils softly caressed her cheeks, framing a set of piercing green eyes. Her white dress was a similar style to my own, but it draped like a relaxed satin. Silver embroidery lined her sides, and a grape-colored sash sat over her right shoulder. The woman smiled, nearly glowing in the morning sun leaking through the trees behind her.

"Good morning," she said, her voice exuding peace.

"Hello," Ora and I said simultaneously.

"Where have my manners gone?" The woman stepped away from the fire and out of the path of the sunlight. The loss of the golden backdrop softened her beauty, making her look less angelic and more human. She had to be in her early forties. "My name's Rhiannon. I'm grateful I happened upon the two of you before you froze to death in your sleep."

"Thanks," I said. Then gesturing between the two of us, I made our introductions. "This is Ora, and I'm Temperance."

Rhiannon curtsied. Not wanting to come off as rude, we did the same. When she glanced at me, her eyes were cheerful, but there was something strained about them. Before I could identify why, the look disappeared, and she clasped her hands together.

"You must be hungry."

Ora and I shot each other a hesitant glance, trying to gauge what to do. If we were going to make this trip, we would need the energy to do so. We either trusted this stranger's kindness or possibly died of starvation in the wilderness. My stomach lurched and growled in answer to our unspoken question.

We followed her to the campfire. As we sat on boulders opposite each other, Rhiannon prepared our plates.

Ora eyed the food like a lioness stalking its prey. "What is it?"

"Rabbit, eggs, and biscuits." Rhiannon handed a plate to her. "There's also fruit and peppermint oil if you girls want to perfume your mouths until you reach a market to get proper cleaning supplies."

I prayed that toothbrushes existed here.

Ora didn't wait for me to receive my plate before digging in. I honestly couldn't blame her. The expression on her face was priceless and she exclaimed, "This is delicious!"

As Rhiannon handed me a plate, I smiled and expressed my thanks. The dish was not overly praised. We couldn't shovel in the mouthwatering contents fast enough, and ate in complete silence as a result. It didn't take long to finish our meals.

"Would either of you like more?" Rhiannon was still working on her own plate.

Ora patted her stomach. "Oh no, I wouldn't be able to move if I ate any more."

Rhiannon stood up to gather our plates, but Ora was quicker to do so.

"You gave us food and warmth, the least I can do is clean the dishes." Ora then promptly headed over to a stream trickling at the edge of the ruin.

Nature had really overrun the area. There was barely any evidence of whatever the original structure was.

"That's very kind of Ora." Rhiannon moved to sit next to me.

"Yeah, it's always been her nature to help others." I smiled at the thought. Nora and Ora weren't all that different.

"Have you known each other long?"

"You could say all our lives." It was half-true.

Rhiannon watched me for a moment. I'm not sure what she saw, but whatever it was she didn't comment on it. "You two must be close."

"She's my best friend." It was strange how much comfort that sentence brought me. To know that I wasn't totally alone and lost in this new world.

"Traveling with friends is always a pleasant experience." She smiled. "Where are you heading?"

"Linall," I said, hoping she wouldn't dig into the details as to why.

"Of course, for the Day of the Goddess." Her eyes went a little dreamy. "Linall puts on the best Peace Celebrations. No other city seems to capture the beauty of the day properly."

"That's what we heard." Mustering up as much enthusiasm as I could, I smiled and did my best to hide the fact that I had no idea what she was talking about.

"You're in for a treat! I'm going too. I couldn't miss it even if I wanted to." She had a gleam in her eyes, like she'd shared some inside joke. "Will your family be joining you there?"

I dropped my gaze to the grass and picked at my nails, my heart heavy. "Uh… no. They can't make it."

When I looked back at her, I found a dash of disappointment in her face. I must have looked pitiful for her to look at me like that.

"That's unfortunate," she said, her tone smooth and calming. "I hope they're all in good health."

"Yeah, they're… fine."

"I'm relieved to hear it. Family is so important." Her gaze flitted to the columns of trees surrounding us, a melancholy shadow in her eyes.

My homesickness jumped into overdrive. I wanted to be at home or at least have them with me. Grandma more than anyone else.

Why hadn't they just told me? Where were they now? Why weren't they here with me? None of it made any sense.

"Child, why are you crying?" Rhiannon placed her arm around me.

I wiped the tears, surprised to find them there. Distracted, I blurted out my true feelings. "I miss my grandma."

"I'm sure she misses you." Rhiannon patted my arm, and a part of me settled down. Something in the atmosphere pulled on my emotions to lean toward the feeling.

"No, she um..." I took a deep breath to steady my emotions. "She passed away a couple months ago."

Rhiannon stiffened a moment, before she wrapped her other arm around me in a full embrace. The fact that I was crying on the shoulder of a complete stranger should have bothered me more, but, in that moment, I found it a welcoming relief.

"Then, I was right. She misses you terribly."

"I know she would have wanted to bring me herself." I pulled away from her hug, and she looked at me in sorrow.

"Is everything okay?" Ora came running over with the clean dishes.

"We were talking about my grandma," I said.

Rhiannon stood and took a few steps away, looking at the glowing trees.

Ora froze. "What about your grandmother?"

"Just that she passed away," I said in a tone indicating that I had not spilled the beans as to who we were.

Ora relaxed but still seemed to have her guard up.

"Do you have family, Rhiannon?" I asked.

Rhiannon turned back to us with a forlorn smile. "I do. A wonderful husband, and I once had two beautiful children."

"Once had?" Ora's sympathy painted her voice.

Rhiannon sighed and crossed her arms. "I lost them both to Minerva's hands over the years."

It amazed me that she exuded no bitterness or spite at how her children died. Only sorrow and acceptance.

"I'm so sorry," I said. Wiping my tears away, I sat up a little straighter. My grandma had at least made it into her older age, but Rhiannon's children were gone before her.

Would my parents have to suffer the same if I didn't make it home?

"I'll see them again someday," Rhiannon said, looking to the treetops that provided a roof over our heads, like she was sending a prayer to the sky and heavens beyond.

Ora and I joined in her moment of silence.

"You two better be off," Rhiannon said. "You've got a long journey ahead of you." She was back in action, grabbing one of her satchels. She quickly placed the two blankets and some food inside a bag that jingled. I assumed it must have been money of some sort. "Here are some provisions to help you get to Linall, including a map. Fortunately for you, I have no need for it. I know these woods so well I could walk them blindfolded."

"Are you sure?" I asked. "It's above and beyond generous, but how can you spare this? You're making the same trip, right?"

She practically pushed the bag into my hands. "I tend to over prepare, and I'm not heading to Linall right away. Also"—her voice caught in her throat—"if it were my children out here on their own, I would hope someone would show the same kindness. Please, allow me to do this for you."

Both our worlds would be better places if more people were like her.

"Take this too," she said, holding out a sheathed dagger attached to a leather belt. "It's not much, but it could come in handy."

I took it from her and buckled it around my waist.

"Thank you!" Ora's excitement bubbled over, and she hugged Rhiannon tightly.

When Ora finally released her, I stepped forward to do the same. "Thank you so much."

Her embrace was one of a protective, caring mother, easing my homesick soul.

"You are very welcome," Rhiannon said and pulled away, looking each of us over to be sure we were ready. "Be safe and trust your instincts out there. Avoid the main roads. Bandits and rebel militia favor those. I'm certain our paths will cross again."

We said our goodbyes and headed back the way we'd come to grab Tundra. I glanced back once more. Rhiannon leaned against one of the ancient trees, grief a shadow on her face. The urge to go back to comfort her was strong, but I figured if she wanted us to witness this painful moment, she would have shared it with us. Instead of intruding on her privacy, we exited the ruin.

CHAPTER 7

FREDERICK

"Cursed horse," I spat. "If she gives me any more trouble, I will need to have a word with Brydon. Sell me a horse that wanders off? Ha!"

Calix's mount was just as valuable as mine—so if my horse had been stolen, they would have taken his as well.

I'd wanted a strong and intelligent horse with a calm temperament. Brydon, the Stable Lord in Kanthe, presented me with Neva. A magnificent creature—the purest white I'd ever seen. The man praised the horse to the high heavens, assuring me that she was the worthiest of any other steed. Up until she'd wandered off, Neva had fulfilled all the requirements.

"She'll practically read your mind and take you where you need to go. A most loyal companion," Brydon had promised, but current circumstances proved the opposite.

The earth crunched aggressively beneath my footfalls. We'd spent a sleepless night searching, which only added to my growing agitation.

What's got you all snippy snappy?

Words from the past echoed inside my mind as clearly as they had been spoken years ago. A reminder of another restless night. I shook the memory away and focused on the task at hand.

"Are you sure you do not wish to ride my steed?" Calix walked behind me, holding fast to his horse's reins.

I trudged onward. "No. I won't subject you to walking at the fault of my horse. You should ride him yourself."

"I will not ride while my king walks."

I turned to him in frustration. "You don't have to worry about propriety when it's just us. You've known me my entire life."

Although he'd only been nineteen at the time, Calix raised me after my parents passed. He was one of my few closest and highest-ranking relatives. Much to my annoyance, since my coronation two years prior, he'd been constant in his etiquette. In this instance, sacrificing riding his own horse because His *Majesty* wasn't riding one. Absurd.

"Apologies for any offense, My King. Protocols must be followed." Although Calix's words were respectful, he sounded like a guardian scolding a child.

I found satisfaction in knowing I'd cracked his facade of propriety by getting him to use that tone.

"You're an idiot," I retorted.

He took a deep breath and closed his eyes. Counting to ten and back, I assumed. Calix's way of holding his tongue.

"And another thing," I said, "stop calling me by my titles. It's just *Frederick* out here—a man free of duty." I went back to tracking Neva. "I understand you must do so around others, but you're like a brother to me."

"Apologies, *My King*."

I glared back at his smirking face. He wouldn't relent. It was obvious I wasn't going to get any further with him on the subject.

Returning my attention to the tracks, I assessed her direction. "She went this way."

A couple hours later, we'd finally tracked her down by a stream near the Eslanian Ruins. When she spotted us approaching, she immediately trotted over to us.

"If you're so eager to come back, then why did you run off in the first place?" I gave Neva a pat on the nose and placed her bridle back on. It still baffled me as to how she'd slipped out of it to begin with. "You run off again, and you'll be sent back to where you came from."

Neva bobbed her head up and down like she understood.

I placed my foot into the stirrup and pulled myself into the saddle, then looked at Calix. "Ready?"

"When you are, *My King*," Calix replied, mounting his own horse.

I rolled my eyes and nudged Neva forward, Calix in tow. Within a few minutes, we came upon a clearing surrounded by a group of Great Ancients—trees that were rumored to glow with the ancestral souls of the fallen families of Eslane.

A weight pressed on my chest, halting me in place. I held my hand up toward Calix, signaling him to pause. A long time ago, I'd learned to trust these Goddess-given instincts. Across the meadow, the early morning sun cast a prism of color through the leaves, shining violet, blue, and yellow.

Neva neighed and clomped her front hoof in the dirt.

"Steady, girl," I said gently, brushing her mane.

Two young women emerged from the trees, disturbing the illusion of color. They noticed us and stared back, talking amongst themselves. The shorter one with dark, wavy hair burst into laughter and lightly pushed the other. The second girl covered her face and looked to the ground. I observed her until she met my gaze.

The weight on my heart faded, and I lost the pull of wherever my instincts were leading me. With a light shake of my head, I broke eye contact with her. How could I let these maidens distract me?

Gently kicking the stirrups, I pulled the reins in the opposite direction of the ladies. Neva instantly became antsy and refused to move.

"Easy, Neva. Easy."

I tried to regain control, but the mare wasn't having it. Neva let out a whine and bucked forward then backward. My grip slipped from the reins, and though Calix tried to intercede, it was too late. One last buck sent me crashing into the brush, and my horse shot off into the forest alone. The hard landing knocked the wind out of me, making me see black.

"Frederick!" Calix called out, seemingly from afar.

When I opened my eyes, the brightness of the sun blinded me, making everything fuzzy. A shadow fell across its path, easing some of the sting in the back of my head, and when my blurred vision mildly refocused, I was able to identify the shadow as a woman.

Encircled by gentle rays of sun, her chestnut hair lit up with brilliant shades of red. A pair of eyes, the color of the sky at sunset, stared down at me. A heavenly crown of purple and sunlight encircled her delicate face.

The Haloed Sun?

My heart pounded at the beautiful vision before me. Somehow, I knew her.

Could it be...

"Goddess, protect me," I whispered.

"Uh, I'm flattered? But that's not quite right." She lightly touched her fingers to her lips, attempting conceal her modest smile, but her eyes sang their amusement.

The edges of the illusion shattered as my mind caught up to my sight. The sea of purple was merely the lady's dress, not the violet light of the Haloed Sun.

She was just an ordinary girl—albeit a pretty one.

I blinked away the remaining blurriness then sat up and crawled out of the bushes that cushioned my fall. I tested my limbs. I'd be bruised and achy for a few days, but there were no breaks or sprains— thank the Goddess. No longer on his horse, Calix hovered over me in concern. The girl and her companion stood off to the right.

"Are you okay?" the girl in purple asked, her hand outstretched.

Still a bit dazed and embarrassed for thinking she was the Goddess, I nodded and allowed Calix to help me up instead.

"I'm fine." With a scoff, I aggressively brushed at my clothes and adjusted my leather armor. "Thank you."

Idiot mare. Brydon would certainly hear from me now. To think I'd offered him the title of Stable Lord in Linall.

"You sure?" Her voice lingered on the tail-end of her question.

I met her eyes. "Yes, just..."

I swallowed the rest of my words, and the back of my neck went hot.

Concern wrinkled the lady's brow, while an unsure smile gently tugged at the corners of her mouth. She tilted her head, and a curly strand of hair fell delicately against her cheek, threatening to cover her right eye. I fought the strange urge to wind it behind her ear. Then, as if reading my mind, she wove the tendril back in place.

There was something about her that felt so familiar to me, but I was certain that I would not have forgotten a girl this stunning.

"Ahem." Her companion cleared her throat and giggled, snapping me back to reality.

My staring partner quickly glanced at the ground then to her friend.

I'd been gawking at her like a fool.

"Just a tad sore," I said, glancing away.

"That's a relief," the companion said. Delight twinkled in her voice, matching the shine in her brown eyes. "I mean, when we saw you fly up—"

Creating an up-and-down gesture with her hand, the companion laughed. The women's eyes met again, and they simultaneously burst into deeper laughter.

My face boiled, fuming my humiliation in the pit of my stomach. "Calix, shall we fetch my horse?"

My comment made them roar harder, and Calix snorted in an attempt to smother his own.

"W-Wait, I'm sorry," the one I'd called the Goddess said, struggling to regain her composure. However, when her friend patted her shoulder, unable to control her own giggles, the pair started up again.

Annoyed, I briskly bowed toward them. "Thank you for your concern, ladies, but we must bid you farewell." I straightened my back and stomped off in the direction Neva had disappeared, not looking back once.

Shortly after, Calix caught up to me, horse reins in hand. "That was a bit rude, My King."

"Forgive me," I said sardonically. "I did not further wish to be made a jester in their presence. The gall they had... laughing at me."

"They were deeply concerned at first," Calix offered. "The laughter came after they were certain you were unharmed." He chuckled. "It *was* rather funny."

I kept silent, battling the desire to relieve some of my humiliation by punching him square in the face.

"'Goddess, protect me,'" he imitated overdramatically.

I glared daggers at him. "I'm a *king*. They shouldn't have reacted so."

"Oh, so *now* you're king? I believe that's a fact they weren't aware of," Calix pointed out. "Had they known, I'm sure the ladies would have kept themselves more composed."

I slowed my pace. Oddly, I liked that fact. Very few interactions I'd experienced since my coronation came off as genuine anymore, but I still couldn't face those two again.

Several minutes of silence passed before Calix spoke again. "Sir, up ahead."

I followed his gaze to see Neva not thirty feet from us. Irritation settled in again, and I jogged over. When I reached her, I climbed into the saddle.

"My King?"

Turning my head, I saw Calix kneeling in the soil, observing something with a fearful expression.

"What is it?"

He looked back to where we'd left the ladies, no longer in sight. "We need to go back."

CHAPTER 8

TEMPERANCE

"Maybe we should have offered to help him track down his horse," I suggested as a strange wave of disappointment washed over me seeing him go.

"Because we know so much about horse tracking," Ora said, sarcasm dripping from her lips.

"We should've done more than laugh at him."

Ora smiled mischievously. "Someone has a—what's the word you use? Oh, crush at first sight."

"Shut up."

"You're blushing!" She poked my side. "You should have seen your face when he was staring at you!"

He *had* stared. First with a dopey grin, then with a mystified glimmer in his eyes—two sharp, cobalt pools that I sensed could penetrate my soul to where all my secrets lay. I'd been drawn into them like a moth to a flame. Perhaps it was better that he'd left. I couldn't have anyone discovering my identity. Besides...

"What does it matter?" I said more to myself than to Ora. "It's not like I'm ever going to see him again."

"Don't say that!" Ora said. "What's that phrase I've heard you utter to Nora before?" She snapped her fingers a few times before landing on what she wanted to say. "Never say never."

"Yes, but—"

"No buts from you!" Ora scolded, catching up to me. "You never thought Emeriz existed, right? So, how do you know you won't see him again? Plus…" Her teasing grin returned. "How can he not seek out his *Goddess* again?"

Ora walked ahead of me. It was strange being on the receiving end of that sort of pep talk. In my mind, I knew better, but I couldn't help one last glance to where the men had gone with the small hope that Ora was right.

"I'll admit," I said as I reached her side and latched arms, "I'm grateful for two things."

"What?"

"That we freshened up in that stream back near those ruins before running into them." I ran my fingers through my clean, air-dried curls to emphasize the lack of mud from the night before.

"Oh yes, you must look good for your new suitor," she teased.

I bumped her shoulder. "And… that Tundra went hunting when she did. I wouldn't know how to explain her to those guys."

Ora raised her eyebrows and nodded. "That would have been bad."

"I hope she comes back, though."

Ora looked around as if hoping to spot the wild cat, but then she squeezed my arm and whispered, "Temperance." Face drained of color, her eyes locked on something in the distance behind us. "We need to go now."

Following her gaze, I caught sight of a creature that could only be described as a shaved bear with a sleek build. Hideous and terrifying, something that had crawled out of a boiling tar pit in Hell. It stalked the tree line and sniffed at the air.

"What is that thing?" My words came out short and breathy.

"Kovchka." She grabbed my hand and gently pulled me away. "This beast will not bond with you."

She was right. It didn't matter how far the animal was from us. I could feel its impenetrable soul. Its intent.

He was hunting.

"We should run," I said.

"We can't," Ora replied. "Although they're mostly blind creatures, they have a heightened sense of hearing and smell. The sound of our feet stomping the ground and our scent in the wind would only draw its attention more." She tugged on my hand again, and we slowly backed away, our eyes never leaving the animal.

We were almost home free until the wind picked up behind us, blowing our hair and skirts forward. The kovchka's head immediately jolted up and turned our way, ears perked.

"Run," Ora breathed out, before darting off with me in tow.

I shot a quick glance back. The creature was catching up.

"Let go!" I shouted. "We need to put more distance between us and that thing, and this is slowing us down."

She released the death grip on my hand. Adrenaline pulsed through my veins, reinvigorating my muscles and helping me gain speed. I ducked under the low-hanging branches and jumped over fallen logs and uprooted tendrils of the surrounding trees. My breathing became erratic.

If we survived this, I needed to get my hands on a longsword! All I had was the dinky dagger Rhiannon had given me.

My calves were starting to feel like jello, and I was fading fast. I gritted my teeth and clenched my hands tightly, pushing my body harder.

When a stray tree branch caught my foot, I screamed and plummeted to the ground, rolling until I landed on my back.

"Tempy!" Ora yelled.

Before I could get to my feet, the beast was upon me, front paws planted into the soil on either side of my shoulders, blocking me from escape. Its head lashed toward my own, yellow, razor-sharp teeth angling at my throat. I threw my hands up, pushing against its neck, desperate to hold it back. It felt like touching a giant sphinx cat, but with thicker skin.

It pressed harder against my hands, and it wouldn't be long until my arms gave way. I had to think of something fast. I invoked the power I'd used to connect with Tundra, praying that Ora had been wrong. My eyes burned, and my body vibrated with energy.

The creature cocked its head for a moment, then its teeth gnashed at my face. I dodged. Nope, that wasn't going to work. Desperate, I grabbed for the knife attached to my waist. It slipped out of its sheath with ease, and the blade glowed gold in my hand as it plunged into the kovchka's neck. The hilt broke off, leaving the blade embedded beneath the folds of its leathery skin.

The kovchka reared back in pain, giving me the chance to slip out from under it. I didn't waste time and ran with everything I had.

We'd put a little distance between us and the creature when Ora cried out from somewhere on my right. Terrified, I stole a glance in the direction of her scream. One of the men from earlier had grabbed her up onto his horse and secured her safely in front of him. A small wave of relief washed over me as he rode off with her.

"Grab my hand!" a voice urgently called out from above.

I threw my hand up. He slowed down long enough to grip it and pull me onto the horse in front of him. I wasn't even fully settled when he nudged his horse back into a sprint. I wrapped my arms around his torso to keep from falling off. My position gave me a perfect view of the kovchka behind us as it barreled forward. Wanting to avoid looking at the thing that might kill me, I buried my face into my rescuer's chest. We rode for a few minutes before we came to a sudden halt. I lifted my face, my breath ragged as I scanned our surroundings.

"W-Why did we stop?" I asked, reluctant to let go of my rescuer.

"It still has your scent," he explained when my eyes met his. "I need to slay the beast, otherwise he will continue to hunt you down."

All I could do was nod in response. The kovchka was nowhere in sight, so I readjusted to climb down. Instead, he gripped my waist.

"Don't go running off," he said firmly.

"And if it kills you?"

"No need to worry about that, but I must go." He shot me a confident grin. "It's a shame really. Any kisses of gratitude will have to wait."

"Kisses?" I pulled back, appalled by his assumption and removed his hand from my waist.

"Well, if I'm going to die for you..." He quickly helped me down into a bush with small, white flowers on it, then rode back the way we came.

My head was spinning from shock. In the space of ten minutes, I'd been chased and attacked by a dangerous creature, rescued, and then dumped in a bush while said rescuer went off to kill the thing. All those events, but my thoughts zeroed in on one particular detail.

I don't want to give a random stranger my first kiss!

I didn't see Ora until her arms were wrapped around me. "Tempy!" she cried. "I'm so glad you're okay!"

"He wants a kiss as a thank you." I couldn't seem to focus on anything else.

"Really?" Ora grinned. "Lucky you."

Not wanting to let on just how upset I was, I stayed silent, as I pulled myself out of the bush. Ora still picked up on it.

"Wait, are you mad?"

"Annoyed." It came out through gritted teeth.

"But... I saw the attraction you had for him. Isn't this a good thing?"

My chest tightened in frustration, and everything came out in a rush. "What kind of trade is that? Can't he just be satisfied knowing he saved someone's life? Whatever happened to a life for a life?" My fists were closed so tight, my nails dug into my palms. "Attractive or not—my *hero* or not—I won't give away my first kiss like that."

"I didn't realize." Ora put her arm around me. "What's our plan then? Shall we punish him for his ridiculous request? Deprive him of our beauty and gratitude by abandoning them?"

"Ora!" I bumped her hip with my own.

Ora's words were teasing, but kind and reassuring—putting me at ease—but a part of me wanted to stay in place a moment longer.

What was our plan? They were risking their lives to help us and told us to stay here. On the other hand, weren't we also sitting ducks out in the open like this? What if they failed? I didn't have a weapon to defend us.

My survival instincts—mixed with my irritation toward him—outweighed my hero's command to stay put.

"Let's go," I said.

We walked in silence for a minute before Ora said, "He was incredibly handsome, though."

I laughed—typical for both her and Nora to be boy-crazy.

"Come on."

I squeezed the daggerless hilt I still had in my hand, somewhat reluctant to let it go. My thoughts wandered to the glow the dagger had exuded when I'd stabbed the kovchka. Had it been a magical dagger? Or had *I* made it glow like that?

CHAPTER 9

FREDERICK

Kicking the stirrups, I urged Neva to move faster. If we failed to kill the beast, it would hunt the girls to the farthest edges of the world. I hoped the distance we'd put between the ladies and the beast, along with the solira blossoms we'd left them in, would mask their scent long enough to slow the creature down. If it took us out, the meal we'd provide would only hold him off until he found himself hungry again. Then the hunt for the ladies would continue.

I rode up next to Calix and shouted, "When we come upon it, shoot the wire! I'll take care of the rest."

He nodded, reaching for his crossbow and latching the rope-wire in place. Up ahead, the kovchka appeared. Snarling, it plunged toward us.

"Flank him!" I ordered, and each of us took a side. "Now!"

Calix aimed the crossbow in my direction and fired. The soft thump of the bolt leaving its chamber was followed by the whoosh of the wire unraveling. Pressing my thumb against the sodalite seal on my ring, I focused on the sound between heartbeats. Instantly everything slowed around me. Time flexed like pulling back a bow string—pliable yet resistant. Bendable to my will for a short breath.

The bolt hovered in front of my face, my surroundings unmoving. I reached up to grasp the tethered shaft, gripping it with as much strength as I could. Then I channeled the moon, and focusing all that energy on the hand holding the wire, poured my Light into the cord. It was difficult during the day but still effective. The wire glowed with a bluish-white light.

Next came the jarring part—release.

As the breath departed my lips, time sped forward, sling-shotting me along with it. I yanked the bolt and the wire pulled taut. Calix matched my speed, aiming straight for the kovchka.

The wire skinned the bottom of the beast's front legs and belly, then twisted up and around its hind legs and tail. The creature yelped in anguish and tumbled into the soil as Calix and I let go of the wire. The kovchka rose from its fallen state and turned back to us. Pieces of flesh hung from its underside, severed and bloody.

We circled back. Calix drew his sword and attacked to distract the creature.

I raised my arm, calling to my Descended Relic, the Elysian Sword. A jolt, cool as snow, ran up my spine, as the weapon materialized in my hand, the blade's black steel glistening in the sun. A surge of biting energy coursed through my veins, awakening the power of my ancestors within me. The sodalite stone embedded down the flat of the blade flared with an azure glow. I knew my eyes would be burning the same hue, just as my mother's always had when using her magic at full force.

Calix made a few more cuts into the beast but couldn't successfully plunge his sword deep enough to kill. Its pelt required a more ancient weapon to slaughter the animal—one forged by Descended magic.

"Pull back!" I commanded.

Calix obeyed while the kovchka turned to the sound of my voice. I charged forward at full force, aiming for the jugular. Upon impact, my blade cut through the beast's neck with ease, severing the head from the body. The pieces of the broken creature tumbled to the forest floor, and I brought Neva to a halt, smiling at Calix.

"Well done, lad!" Calix held a fist in the air, his dark beard separated by a proud grin. "I mean—My King."

"Same to you." I bowed my head to him then glanced back at the lifeless beast. "That wire trick was different than I theorized."

"You and your crazy ideas..." He sheathed his sword and stared down at the creature.

"It's not crazy. It's genius."

Calix took a swig of one of the waterskins then tossed it to me. "Wouldn't have worked if not for your Descended abilities." He nodded in the direction where we'd left the girls. "Shall we go claim our praises?"

I grinned. After taking my own swig of water, I replaced the cap and said, "I could use some praise."

Especially after my embarrassing display earlier.

"On second thought," Calix said, "your head is big enough."

"Shut your hole." I chucked the waterskin at his head, and he caught it just before impact.

We laughed and urged our horses toward the path that would lead us to the ladies. It didn't take long to return to the rolling bundles of solira bushes which had since been abandoned.

"Where would they go?" I asked, more for my own deductive reasoning than for Calix.

"Maybe the kovchka's mate was nearby and found them." Calix dismounted, inspecting the area he'd dropped his lady. He followed her steps back to me where they combined with my lady's footprints.

"They headed East." Calix looked at me. "We should make sure they're safe."

I nodded and Calix mounted his steed once again. We kept a brisk pace until the ladies came into view. At the sound of the hooves, they stopped to await us.

Neva hadn't fully halted before I practically jumped from the saddle. Both ladies looked a tad disheveled from when we'd first met them, and the one I'd saved clutched something in her hand. A hilt separated from its blade. Had she tried to fight the beast with only a dagger?

"Are you all right?" I asked. "Why did you wander off?"

Calix dismounted his horse and followed me toward the girls.

My lady tossed the broken weapon to the side and brushed off her hands. She met my gaze, clear irritation burning behind her eyes.

"Well, who just dumps two girls in some random location like a couple of sitting ducks for slaughter with no explanation? Plus, I didn't want to—" She stopped and folded her arms, the softest blush coloring her cheeks.

How could she be upset? We saved them. Her lack of gratitude was infuriating.

"Listen, milady, we didn't just drop you off in some random place," I explained calmly, albeit strained. "We left you in an area covered in solira blossoms. Their scent temporarily blinds the kovchka's keen sense of smell. If I'd had the time to clarify that, I would have, but I felt it was more important to get you to safety while we fought the beast."

Anyone from the area would have known that.

I'd crossed the distance between us as I'd spoken. We stood a foot apart. Her blue eyes bore into mine, refusing to back down—like she was weighing the truth of my words.

Two could play that game… and I could do it better.

I grazed the stone in my ring to enact my abilities, careful not to enlighten my irises. This time, I was searching for intent and truth, not convincing her of my own. I sensed her agitation, but it didn't feel angry.

Is she embarrassed? Whatever for—oh...

My words about kissing her came back to me. I'd only meant to be playful with her to put her at ease, but she clearly misread my intention. For good reason, too. It had definitely sounded like an arrogant proposition.

Why had I said it? I wasn't Taren. Linall already had one court philanderer and was not in need of another. I did not want my subjects to view me that way. A desire to right myself in the opinion of her stony gaze pulled at my mind.

My struggle must have shown in my expression because her stance softened, and hesitation flickered in her eyes—yet she didn't look away. She stood her ground, which impressed me. My gaze flitted down to her lips, and she flinched, taking a couple steps back. Had the idea disgusted her that much?

I wanted to apologize, but to do so would be to admit what I'd done in front of Calix. I'd never hear the end of it if he knew. Later... I'd do it when he wasn't around.

"We apologize." Her companion stepped up beside her, breaking the silence. "We've been traveling to Linall on foot for a couple days. The solitude must have gone to our heads."

"Perfectly understandable," Calix said. "Why not start over?"

"Wonderful! I'm Ora, and this is..." She raised her eyebrows and nudged the blue-eyed girl's arm in encouragement.

Avoiding my gaze, she looked at Calix with a small smile as she gave her own introduction. "Temperance."

I froze. It was the same name from that night years ago. Hope bloomed inside my chest for a moment before logic righted me. It couldn't be her. This Temperance was far too young.

That woman was elderly—maybe in her sixties or seventies by now. It wasn't an incredibly uncommon name either.

After taking a deep breath, Temperance said, "I'm sorry we walked off. Thanks for saving us."

"Accepted," Calix said. "I'm Lord Baldric of Linall. You may call me Calix. And this here is—"

"Just call me Frederick," I said, worried he might reveal my title. I couldn't pin down why, but I wasn't ready for them to know. "I'm his godson."

Calix's eye twitched, probably fighting the urge to roll his eyes before turning his attention back to the ladies. "If you're heading to Linall for the festival, allow us to escort you."

While Ora expressed her excitement in traveling together, my eyes wandered to Temperance again. Scrutiny filled her stare as it flicked from Calix to me. She caught me watching and dropped her gaze. Her determination to avoid me was vexing.

Temperance began picking at her fingers nervously. "We don't want to trouble you."

Ora draped her arm around Temperance. "Don't be silly. As gentlemen, they wouldn't offer if they weren't willing."

Temperance still seemed unsure.

"Please, it would make us feel more at ease to know you reached your destination safely," I assured.

"It would get us there faster, which means we'll have more time to *make ourselves at home*," Ora added. That awakened something in Temperance.

"That would be incredibly kind of you," she said.

I wasn't prepared for the mesmerizing smile that lit up

Temperance's face as she looked from Calix to me. It was still shy and a little uneasy, but beautiful just the same.

It was my turn to drop my gaze, but I took it a step further and walked toward the horses. "We should rest and water the horses before we begin our journey," I asserted.

We needed to get out of this area as soon as possible in case we were anywhere near the High Queen's men that had the Eslanian's scrambling.

I busied myself with preparing our horses to support two riders on each mount. As I fussed with the reins, I heard footsteps behind me but kept focused on my task.

"So... just Frederick, huh?" Calix asked, utterly amused. "Are you not concerned they may put two and two together by using your actual name?"

What had I been thinking? He was absolutely right! I'd scrambled so quickly to stop him from revealing my title, that I hadn't used an alias. It might be all right. Many parents named their children after me after I was born... There was a chance they wouldn't figure it out right away, and I'd take however much time I could get. Besides, they would know for certain once we reached Linall.

"Just go along with it," I said, then pointed at his face. "And do not address me by my title while they are around."

He held up his hands in mock surrender, and I continued to prepare the horses.

"I spoke with the girls. Neither has much experience riding," he said. "Temperance seems to have a significant amount more than Ora but is still a novice. How would you like to proceed, just Frederick?"

I didn't need to look at Calix to see the amusement on his face. His teasing would go on for days.

I shot him a glare. "You're the more exceptional rider, so you should take Ora with you."

"Then that leaves you to escort Temperance." He rubbed his chin.

"It would appear so." I tried to keep my voice calm, but in my effort to do so, I missed a loop tightening the saddle.

"Look at how that happened to turn out…" Calix raised his brows and walked away to prepare his own horse.

Ora laughed, bringing my attention to a blushing Temperance. They moved over to speak with Calix while I turned back to my own preparations. It wasn't long before I heard footsteps behind me again.

"Look, enough of the—" When I turned to tell Calix to cut it with the 'just Frederick' joke, I found it wasn't him standing behind me. "Oh, Temperance, my apologies. I thought you were Calix."

"Don't worry about it." She massaged her palm and avoided my gaze.

She still can't meet my eyes.

"You'll be riding with me," I said, breaking the silence that had stretched between us.

She nodded but still didn't look up.

Had I sounded demanding?

"That is… if you have no objections to my escorting you," I tried again.

Temperance finally looked at me, making my heart pound just a little quicker. Her face was more at ease.

"I don't, but I do have one request," she said.

"Whatever you wish." I arched a brow, just happy that she wasn't avoiding me.

"Can we not…" She turned red and flustered. "You aren't expecting something more as a show of my gratitude, are you?"

My own face heated up in embarrassment.

I spared a glance in Calix's direction to be sure he wasn't in earshot. Then, swallowing my pride, I bowed my head. "I'm sorry for what I said. I didn't mean it, I swear. You seemed terrified, and I merely wanted to ease your nerves. It seems I brought you distress instead."

"Phew, good." Temperance's shoulders relaxed before she turned her attention to Neva. "She's beautiful."

I sighed, relieved she had taken my apology.

"And a whole lot of trouble," I replied. "If she keeps bolting off, I may have to trade her for one more reliable." I gave Neva a pointed grin and patted her mane.

Temperance stroked Neva's neck, and the horse responded by nuzzling into her head.

"Wow, she has taken to you rather quickly."

Temperance shrugged. "I've always had a way with animals." A dazed look crossed her face for a moment before she shook her head. "Should we go?"

"Yes." I gestured toward the stirrups. "Place your left foot here and grab the horn and back of the saddle to pull yourself up."

"Got it." With a determined expression, Temperance tried to mount Neva. Unfortunately, my mare was taller than most. She struggled to hoist herself up on her own, which resulted in her falling back into my arms.

"Whoa, you all right?"

"I'm fine." She nodded.

"Looks like we're even." My words escaped on the tail-end of a chuckle.

Her brows furrowed. "What are you talking about?"

Blood drained from my face. I hadn't meant to say that aloud.

"You laughed at me when I got bucked off my horse, so I couldn't help but chuckle at seeing you fall."

Temperance's cheeks turned rose red. "This isn't the same thing. You went flying off your horse. I just lost my footing."

Seeing her flustered, the urge was too strong to resist teasing her further. "You're right," I said. "Mine was worse by a far margin. I could have been severely injured and there you were, laughing at my pain. So, I guess you could say we're almost even."

"Hey!" Temperance slapped my upper arm playfully. "We checked to make sure you were okay first, *then* we laughed. If you had seen the air you got, you would've too."

"First of all"—I leaned in and nodded my chin toward the arm she'd slapped—"ow."

A smug grin creased the corners of her mouth.

"Second of all, it doesn't matter what I would've done, you still shouldn't have," I playfully scolded.

"Wow, talk about your double standards." Temperance feigned annoyance but met my eye again with a smile.

My heartbeat quickened, fascinated that she was actually taking my teasing and giving it right back. I was forming a retort when someone cleared their throat. Tearing my attention from Temperance's face, I saw Ora sitting securely behind Calix on his steed.

Calix eyed us suggestively. "If you two are finished getting acquainted, I suggest we get going. The horses will be transporting more weight than they're used to, so it won't be long before we'll have to let them rest again."

I realized that my hands were still around Temperance's waist after I'd caught her, and they had been during our entire conversation.

My cheeks burned, but it subsided slightly when I saw her face mirrored my own. I quickly let her go.

"Shall I assist you, milady?" I gestured to Neva.

Temperance nodded but said nothing. When her foot and hands were securely in place, I moved my hands to her sides to help hoist her into the saddle.

Once she was settled, I climbed up and positioned myself behind her. As we rode, I was hyper aware of the fact that my arms were wrapped around her. With every movement of the reins, I would bump against either side of her arms which made my blood race. In hindsight, it would have been better for her to sit behind me, but I'd been too distracted. We'd have to switch after our next break, but for the time being, I focused on the path ahead.

Chapter 10

Temperance

We rode until the sun started to set. Frederick hardly spoke throughout the ride. I couldn't blame him. It must have made him feel incredibly awkward after I fell into his arms, then hung onto him like a squirrel clutching its winter stash.

"This looks like a good place to camp for the night!" Calix said, having found an area surrounded by plush grass and low hanging trees.

They brought the horses to a halt, and the men dismounted. I had begun to climb down when Frederick said, "Here, let me help you," and held up his hand.

As gentlemanly as it was, my stubbornness got the better of me.

Instead of graciously accepting, I said, "One slip and you've already made up your mind that I'm a clumsy damsel incapable of doing anything on my own?"

"After the way you got onto the horse, I hesitate to think you'll be able to safely get yourself down." His vibrant, cobalt eyes twinkled, and he let his hand hang in the air.

I crossed my arms and stared down at him, refusing to budge.

Frederick ran his fingers through his raven hair, and I held my breath momentarily.

"No, Temperance, I believe people are capable of anything they set their minds to, you included. I'm sure your legs are stiff and sore, which can make anyone lose their footing, especially a less experienced rider. I offered my help to ensure you dismount safely."

What was my problem? Here was a guy that was being extremely gallant, even if he was a little bit of a tease about it, and I couldn't just accept it.

"Of course, if you would rather me not..." Frederick reached out once again, awaiting my response.

After a brief pause, I placed my hand in his. He held on as I swept my leg over the saddle and winced. He wasn't kidding about being sore.

"Place your hands on my shoulders."

I obeyed, and he grabbed my waist, lifting me off. When the ground was firmly below my feet, we quickly released our grip on each other. It appeared he wanted to avoid another awkward encounter as much as I did.

"You all right?" he asked.

I nodded.

"Good." He turned around and grabbed the reins to tie up Neva.

"Thanks." I walked to where Ora sat in the grass rubbing her legs, staring up at me with a huge grin.

"How was your ride with the handsome stranger?" she asked.

"Quiet and awkward." I eased my way down next to her. "How was yours?"

"Informative!" Ora said as I stretched my legs.

"Really?" I glanced up at the men as they unpacked the saddlebags.

"Yes! Oh, he's funny!" She briefly shook my arm and blushed. "He was pretty open about himself."

Frederick looked about our age, but Calix had to be in his late twenties at least.

"He's handsome," I said, "but maybe a bit older." I patted her hand then raised my arms to ease the soreness in my back.

Ora dismissed the comment with a wave of her hand. "It was just fun," she said. "Oh, but you'll never guess! How fated is this? He and Frederick both hold positions in the Linallian court and agreed to help us gain access to the royal library."

Relief washed over me like a cool shower on a hot day as I reveled in the happiness the glimmer of hope presented to us. My gaze drifted over to the men. They certainly had the air I'd expect from proper gentlemen to hold court positions, even if they were kinda goofy sometimes. But there was something more to their dynamic that had me questioning. Frederick had the presence of a man in command, and Calix treated him quite respectfully—even going as far as dismounting his own horse when Neva bucked him off. Why would he do that unless Frederick was a higher rank than him, especially when Calix was much older? Higher rank or not, who in their right mind would walk when they could ride? Unless... they held a rank one had to respect.

Frederick blatantly interrupted Calix when he tried to introduce him to us, like he was hiding something. A secret identity? Possibly, a royal one?

It wasn't completely unreasonable. Even *I* was hiding a major secret.

"Temperance? Hello?" Ora nudged me.

"Ora."

"Finally," she said, her tone smothered in exasperation. "You must be crushing pretty hard to be leering at him like that."

"That wasn't why I was staring." I folded my arms before turning my attention back to Frederick. "Who's the current king of Linall?"

It was a mere suspicion, but if I was right, this might wind up bad for us.

"Why?"

"Curiosity."

"King Fred—" After a momentary pause she breathed out the rest of the title. "King Frederick Verdelune."

Her jaw dropped, and I reached over to close it. "They both hold high enough positions in the Linallian court to give us access to the king's library, and one of them just so happens to be named Frederick."

"Emeriz herself must be watching over us," Ora declared. "We need to ask them!" I grasped her hand and pulled her back when she nearly darted away. "What? If he is the king, he can help us."

"Let's keep it to ourselves until we know for sure we can trust them," I whispered. "What if it isn't true? Plenty of people could share a name with the king. Or worse, what if they're working for Minerva and Maxwell?" We couldn't afford to get caught before we reached Linall.

"If it is really him, I doubt he would turn us over to them." Ora's face fell a little.

"But you can't be sure."

"Yes, I can. Frederick's story is well known. Minerva tortured and murdered his parents right in front of him when rumors rose that they were plotting an uprising against her."

Ora looked at the blades of grass by her feet and started to pull at them.

My gaze wandered to Frederick, my heart twisting and aching for him. I couldn't even imagine how I'd handle witnessing my parents dying in such a way.

"I overheard my grandfather say that Frederick has been playing both sides ever since," Ora said, drawing my attention back to her. "Quietly gathering a resistance, making secret allies, funding the guerrilla fighters. Even going so far as..." She glanced from Frederick to me.

"Yes?" I prompted.

Ora looked back up with a hesitant smile. "Hunting for the Descended."

Closing my eyes, I laughed bitterly. "Of course he is. Naturally. You know, because this trip couldn't get any more pointed!"

Ora kicked me. I'd said the end of that sentence a little too loud. I rubbed my face in frustration, then glared at her. She gave an awkward wave toward the guys and through a gritted smile, said, "What did you *just* say about keeping quiet?"

I also waved to the confused men setting up a fire, then turned back to Ora. "That solidifies it," I asserted. "We are not telling them. Whether it is him or not."

Her shoulders dropped. "But, Tempy—"

"If he is the king and finds out who I am, do you think he's going to let me go home?" I didn't give her a chance to answer the question. "No, he won't. He'll force me to help fight his war, regardless of what I want."

Not ready to give in, she leaned forward. "You don't know that. Maybe he'll—"

"Ora, please," I pleaded.

She opened her mouth to protest but instead sat back in defeat.

"Thank you," I said with a sigh.

"Mhm."

It was strange to see my best friend disappointed in me.

"I know it's hard, but I'm asking you to be patient." I placed my hand on her shoulder to get her to look at me again. "Besides, he made it a point not to tell us who *he* is. Obviously he wants all of this to remain private. We'll know for sure once we reach the castle. It's not like he would be able to hide it once we get there."

Ora thought for a moment, then straightened her posture. "Fine. It won't be easy, but I will channel Nora in hopes to hold back. For you."

"You're the best," I said on autopilot, and Ora suddenly embraced me. "What's wrong?"

She hugged me tighter. "You say that to Nora all the time. To have you say it to me... It means a lot. Makes me feel connected to that side of me, like we aren't so different."

Sadness shot through me. Had Nora ever felt lonely like this, or did Ora only feel this way because she was aware of her situation? There wouldn't be a way of knowing without asking Nora herself. I squeezed Ora back, letting her enjoy a moment of clarity.

CHAPTER 11

FREDERICK

After a restful night of food and sleep, we carried on with our trip. We planned to break our journey once more before reaching Linall. The delay was a necessity meant to procure confirmation that potential allies would be in attendance at the Ethereal Ball in a few weeks. We had to do everything in our power to solidify their support. Calix and I were to meet the informant in Kanthe—one of the cities within the territories of my kingdom—just a day-and-a-half's ride from Linall.

Using outside messengers was inconvenient but unavoidable. There were a select few within my own court who would sell or bury information for the right price. I lined their pockets to keep them quiet, but eventually I would need more. In the meantime, I had to play as many things close to the chest as possible.

Neva walked over some rocky terrain and stumbled, causing Temperance to grasp my waist. Her face and chest pressed firmly into my back, the rhythm of her shallow breaths beating against it. Having her body against mine sent warm tingles up my spine. Once Neva was over the rough road, I grabbed Temperance's hands, still clinging together at my abdomen, and held them fast in mine. As though I needed additional reassurance that she hadn't fallen.

I swallowed. "Are you okay?"

She lifted her head off my back. "Just briefly saw my life flash before my eyes, but I'm okay."

Relieved to hear her upbeat tone, I leaned to the side and twisted just enough to observe her from the corner of my eye.

"Falling off a horse will do that for you," I teased. "Although, she'd need to buck you off in order for you to get the whole experience."

"Aww, I feel terrible now," Temperance said with a laugh.

It brought a sense of satisfaction; the night before, she'd been quiet and distant. I sensed she'd gone to bed early to avoid interacting with us.

"Now that you understand, you're forgiven." I caressed my thumb over the top of her hand.

Why haven't you let go of her hand? I thought, in no hurry to let hers go. It didn't last.

When I glanced down, she slowly pulled free and gripped the back of the saddle. Able to move more freely, I shifted to the side and lifted my gaze to hers, but she dropped her eyes, tucking some of her hair behind her ear. A simple gesture, yet it brought me so much pleasure. Why?

I looked forward and urged Neva into a trot to catch up to the others.

"Have you made boarding arrangements in Linall?" I asked.

"Um, no. This trip was spur-of-the-moment."

It sounded like there was more to it, but she wasn't going to elaborate.

"Well, Linall is full of inns and taverns." A thought I immediately rejected—someone could try to take advantage of them. They were clearly unfamiliar with the area, which made them easy targets. "However, they could all be booked up because of the Day of Peace festivities."

"Linall gets a lot of visitors this time of year, then?" Her voice oozed concern, though I could imagine she was trying to come off aloof.

"Mostly people from the surrounding villages, but if there are any visiting royals, they tend to bring an entourage of guests."

"Great," she said, sounding defeated.

Keeping my tone as indifferent as possible, I said, "You and Ora could stay with Calix and me."

I braved a quick glance back to find her staring hard at me, suspicious and hesitant.

"What's your home like?"

"Well, every man thinks of his home as his castle." I grinned, withholding a chuckle.

Temperance snorted. "Right... Are you purposely avoiding my question?"

Yes. Why is she smirking at me?

"Kanthe is just up ahead," Calix called out, bringing my attention forward.

Kanthe's wooden gates stood tall and welcoming in the distance. Since the city had initially been settled by refugees, the walls that surrounded it were modeled in an Eslanian style. Gray stones bound together with black concrete made up the entirety of the structure. However, each watchtower was framed with towering living trees. Their leaves draped over the side like they were reaching out to those seeking refuge.

White streamers and flags lined the archway in celebration of the demi-goddess, Riona. Her crest of three doves was painted on each one with clean, bold strokes. She was the last known Descended of the Superior Goddess who attempted to bring peace when Domhnall rose to power eighty years ago.

Trotting through the gate, I observed my people. Even with the Day of Peace weeks away, festivities and merriment were in full swing. People were shopping, decorating, selling their wares, playing games, and some were even dancing. Peace swelled inside me seeing my people finding joy in these troubled times.

Then I noticed a crimson *M* painted across a blacksmith's door, and anxiety twisted in my chest like the final blow of a dagger. The windows were bashed in, and the forge stood dormant—a darkened scar in contrast to the revelry surrounding it. Minerva's raids served as a reminder of what happened when she was crossed. If her men didn't find legitimate rebels, they'd conjure one out of an innocent. An example always had to be made.

Why hadn't I been informed? He had been one of ours, the blacksmith. Calix, who had noticed too, glanced back at me. Apart from a brief flash of anger in his eyes, no one would have known he was upset. He turned around, scanning the crowds for any more signs.

At least, with Maxwell's men having already been here, we were most likely safe from discovery for the time being.

"Tempy, look!" Ora shouted and pointed to some fire performers in the square.

Temperance leaned forward, a chuckle escaping her lips. Her breath caressed my ear, and I almost dropped the reins. I gripped them a bit tighter and tilted to the right to allow her to see better.

Once we reached the town stables, I held out my arm for Temperance to hold onto while she dismounted. When she was safely on the ground, I did the same.

"It seems we're improving," I teased.

She rolled her eyes but smiled. "Thanks."

Truth. I could see clearly that she was genuinely grateful.

"Of course, milady." I bowed my head.

When our eyes met again, she backed up, gesturing toward Calix and Ora behind her. "I'm... gonna check on Ora."

I backed up toward the stable entrance, mimicking her. "I'm going to grab the stable hand."

She walked away. Keeping my eyes on her for a second longer than I should have, I collided with someone when I faced the stables.

"Pardon me. I wasn't—" The stable lord's face lit up, his laugh lines disappearing into creases around his brown eyes. "Why, Your Majesty," he said, "I'm pleased to see you."

"Brydon." The other business that brought me to Kanthe: Neva's behavioral problems. "About Neva—"

"How's my favorite mare?" He moved around me, straight to Neva.

I followed him. "Actually, she's been—"

"Ah, dear girl," Brydon addressed the horse, stroking her mane. "Pure, eternal beauty."

"It's impossible to *appreciate* that beauty when she bucks you off and abandons you on multiple occasions," I scoffed.

"I warned you that she had a mind of her own. Did I not?" he replied, still eyeing the mare.

"Yes, but—"

"Well, that's settled," Brydon said, finally looking up at me. "I'll get both your horses scrubbed down, fed, and watered. How long will you be gone?"

"An hour, maybe two," I said, the itch for argument gone.

"They'll be ready." He shook my hand, then walked to the corral to grab a stable hand to assist him with our horses.

"Were you able to discuss Neva's roaming problem?" Calix asked as he approached with the ladies.

"Yes and no," I said with a sigh, oddly calm about the whole exchange. "I'm uncertain as to why, but I couldn't argue with him."

"*You* couldn't argue?" Calix asked. "I would love to see that! I must know his secret." Calix burst into laughter, which should have irritated me, but I laughed along as the ladies wore polite smiles.

"What's all the hilarity about?" Brydon asked as he rejoined us.

I cleared my throat. "My apologies."

"Never apologize for enjoying yourself," he said, waving away my comment. "Good to see you again, Calix. Now, let's—" Brydon stared at the girls, his expression uncharacteristically solemn.

"Allow me to introduce you to our friends," I said, gesturing to each girl as I introduced them. "Ora and Temperance."

He stood in a daze, staring at Temperance.

"Brydon?" I placed my hand on his shoulder.

"Whoops, lost my head for a moment." Brydon's face lit up again, and he grabbed Neva by the reins. "I best get started."

As he led her to the stalls, he quietly whispered to her.

Ora asked, "Does he talk to all the horses like that?"

I shrugged.

"Strange man," Ora said, then looked at Temperance, whose face was scrunched up like she'd said something odd. Ora paid no mind to it. "Tempy, shall we explore while the men are occupied?"

Before Temperance could utter a response, Ora pulled her toward the marketplace.

Thinking of the potential dangers, I didn't like the idea of letting them wander alone.

"Hold on," I said. "Our business is more of a one-man job." I gestured to Calix. "Why don't you escort them around, and I'll go alone."

Calix's eyes narrowed. "I don't believe so. You will need me to oversee things."

"If Frederick needs you, Calix, we'll be okay on our own," Temperance said.

"Yeah!" Ora piped in, pulling Temperance along. "He may not enjoy what we have planned. After our journey, we could use a bathhouse, shopping, and some pampering."

We watched them go, and once they were out of earshot, I turned to Calix. "You think it's wise to leave them alone?"

"It's my duty to protect and serve you. Once we arrive safely at the castle, I'll keep them entertained." He placed a closed fist on his forehead then placed it over his heart in salute.

I watched where the girls had disappeared. "Temperance seems to have a good head on her," I said, still worried. "I'm certain she won't fall prey to anyone that means them harm."

"Right, sir." Calix nodded and moved so I could walk ahead of him.

"It doesn't mean I like it." I shot him a stern look. "Their safety is our responsibility."

"I agree. However, your safety happens to outrank theirs." Calix fell in step behind me and added, "Trust me, were you only my stubborn godchild and not my sovereign, I would have abandoned you here and paraded them through town on both arms."

We laughed, and I slammed his upper arm with my fist. "Nice knowing where your loyalties lie."

As we merged into the crowds of people, he sighed. "In the eyes of strong, beautiful women."

Even at midday, the tavern was dimly lit and filled with men and women of not-so-honorable intentions. Some drank for confidence, others drank to forget. Pints were raised to celebrate deals of the genuine and the underhanded.

The scent of smoke and alcohol blanketed the room bursting with the boisterous sounds of laughter and music. I itched to get out as soon as possible. Calix took a swig of his mead before glancing back toward the door and surveying the room.

"They're late," he grumbled.

I casually scanned the room and drank down the rest of my water. I preferred to keep a focused mind, especially as someone in my precarious position as King of Linall and a rebel leader. With such a heavy weight on my shoulders, I couldn't afford to make any mistakes. Alcohol offered nothing but risk.

I spun the blue coin—our signal to the informant. "We'll give it another hour, then leave."

I held up my goblet, and the bar maiden swiftly came to fill it. Most would fill the cup and go about serving other customers, but she stood there until I looked up at her.

"Need anything else, fellas?" she asked, leaning against Calix's chair. Messy tendrils of red and silver fell in front of her sharp eyes.

"No," I said dismissively.

Once she'd walked away, Calix said, "No need to be rude, sir. Perhaps she was only after a tip."

"She's suspicious," I griped, and tapped my temple. "I *see* her intentions are less than admirable."

"And how many people in this place aren't?"

His question was rhetorical, so I went back to spinning the blue coin on the table.

After the tenth spin, a bard approached us. "May I play you the

Last Steps of Hefeydd?" he asked. "Or the Song of the Mountain Glen?"

I stopped the coin mid-spin. The code, with both kingdoms represented. Hefeydd's last-known steps were taken in the kingdom of Kelurs, and the kingdom of Fjall was a fortress hidden away in the western mountains.

"I'm more interested in stories of the distant past," I said, offering the small disc. What he did with it would tell me everything I needed to know. I prayed to the Goddess for him to take it.

A commotion erupted on the other side of the tavern. Two drunken brutes were caught up in a fist fight over the red-and-silver-haired maiden. She stood in the corner, hand on her chest and eyes wide. What no one else could see, however, was the lie in her reaction. Whatever reason she had for starting the brawl wasn't good, that much was certain.

My eye caught the actions of another man, who moved through the bodies in the room with ease, paying no mind to the commotion. Using the distraction to his advantage, he cut the purse strings belonging to some members of the gawking audience and disarmed some of the others. I placed my hand on the hilt of the dagger at my waist, ready to strike if need be.

When he reached our table, his demeanor changed, and he stumbled into the bard. "Oh, apologies," he said.

The bard tried to laugh it off. "Quite all right."

"No, you mistake my meaning." The thief leaned close to the bard. "You have no business with these men."

The bard coughed hard, his face turning frail and white as each one that followed brought him closer to the ground.

Poison.

The thief draped his arm around the bard. "You see... *I* have business with them. You, on the other hand, have business on the other side. The real informant is waiting for you there."

The bard slumped to the floor, no longer breathing, while the killer straightened his tunic and robes. The newcomer stood no taller than five foot eight with a wiry frame—so I knew I would have the advantage on a physical level. However, his robes concealed any evidence of his strength or method as to how he'd administered the poison. He was not to be underestimated.

Not wanting to draw attention, I stayed seated but grabbed my dagger. Putting the blade to his abdomen with one hand, I pressed my thumb against my ring with the other, prepared to read his intentions.

"Who are you?" I growled.

"There's no need for that." He gestured to the blade like it was a menial problem. "I saved you from an agent of Her Highest Majesty. She's trying to snuff out any rebellious leaders like you, King Frederick."

"Why shouldn't I kill you now?" I asked, putting more pressure on the dagger.

He tsked at me. "Now, now, you don't want to make a scene, do you? Knife wounds are awfully messy. As for keeping me alive, consider it payment for saving you from the man who killed the real informant. Without my interference, he would have either killed you or run off to his High Queen to tattle."

My ability to read people was second nature, and I didn't always need to enact my abilities to do so. Every shifty move he made screamed at me to be cautious, but I was certain his words were true.

"I suppose you want something to keep quiet?"

"Yes, to join you." He shrugged, like his answer was obvious.

I nodded at Calix and slid my dagger back into its sheath.

"Of course"—he held up his hand before adding—"not for free.

My skills are valuable, in which we will discuss further at your castle. I'll meet you there in two days' time." He hoisted the bard up and pulled the dead man's arm around his neck.

Calix stood up. "Who are you?" he demanded. "What makes you so valuable?"

The shady man stared Calix down with his light cerulean eyes. "The whispers know me as Obsidian, but you may address me as Heshrin."

I fought to keep my face composed as his words sank in. He was the most sought-after assassin in almost a century. Even without my abilities, I knew he wasn't lying. No one would impersonate Obsidian, not unless they wanted a knife in the back.

"Oh, and here." Heshrin dropped a bloodstained note onto the table. "I pulled that off the informant's body out back."

He walked out, pretending the dead bard was simply a passed-out drinking companion. The bar maiden strutted over to him, and he handed off a bag of coins to her. She blew him a kiss and made her way back to the counter while he disappeared outside.

CHAPTER 12

TEMPERANCE

Walking through Kanthe felt similar to walking around the Renaissance Festival with their shops, multicolored tents, wooden carts, and booths. The streets were extremely crowded—making it difficult to maneuver—and I felt like I was inhaling loads of dirt with each step from everyone bustling about. After the third time we almost got separated, I linked my arm with Ora's.

"I feel like this trek back to the guys is making our awkward trip to the bathhouse redundant," I said.

She rolled her eyes. "It wasn't *that* bad."

"I can barely handle changing in front of the other girls in the locker room during gym class," I said with a gesture behind us. "That was... uncomfortable."

"You had your own private room, and only one woman helped you undress and took your clothes to be cleaned."

I assessed my outfit. It wasn't perfectly clean, but the dry mud and dirt had been beaten out. They'd treated it with some sort of oil to give my clothes a fragrant, floral scent. We used some of the money Rhiannon provided to buy a more appropriate travel outfit for Ora. The dress I'd enchanted for her was clean and folded inside our satchel.

We walked past a black shop, a sign with a set of crossed swords painted on it hung over the open door. I peeked inside, catching a glimpse of the gleaming weaponry on display. I took a step toward the door.

"Step away from the sharp objects," Ora said, yanking me away from the shop and back into the road. "They are way out of our budget."

"But they're authentic Emerizian longswords! Come on, just a small dagger?" I begged with a smile. "The one Rhiannon gave us broke, remember?"

"Nope." Ora bumped my arm and winked. "You can bat your eyelashes at *Frederick*. Maybe he'll get you one."

Before I could come up with a rebuttal, someone shoved us forward, right into two men. The hooded one was a little worse for wear, his limp arm draped over the second man's shoulders

"Pardon us," the second man said with a bow of his blond head and proceeded to lead his drunk friend down an alley toward a public well.

An overwhelming feeling that I was being watched pressed down on my chest and brought sweat to my brow. I turned only to find a fleeting dust devil fading away.

"Let's find Frederick and Calix," I suggested.

Ora nodded and pulled me along.

Brydon was shoveling hay into a cart when we reached the stables. He hummed while he worked, seemingly oblivious to his surroundings. The song sounded familiar and comforting. I tried to place where I'd heard it before.

As we got closer, he abruptly stopped humming and said, "Temperance. Ora. Don't you know you should never sneak up on someone?" Brydon faced us and smiled. "Especially while I'm wielding a pitchfork. Dangerous, ladies... very dangerous."

Embarrassed, we mumbled apologies.

"Just announce yourselves next time. I'd be distraught if I caused injury to either of you." The dirt caked onto his face with sweat only made the smile he gave us look even more joyful. His teeth were clean and almost perfect. It was the sort of smile that would light up a room.

It reminded me of James.

Homesickness crept in, but I pushed it down.

"That was a beautiful song you were humming," I said.

His eyebrows shot up, and he wiped his hands with a red rag from his pocket. "You liked that?"

"Yeah, I think I've heard it before." I hummed the part that sounded familiar. Brydon joined in but hummed something different. To my astonishment, the tunes melded perfectly.

Ora clapped when we finished. "That was wonderful!" she lauded.

"Every melody needs a great harmony." Brydon laughed. "Were you able to figure it out, Temperance?"

My shoulders drooped, and I fiddled with the ties on my corset. "No... Maybe it was just something similar."

"Perhaps you heard it radiating off nature or someone," he posited. "Everyone has a song within them." Brydon twisted and played with the rag in his hands. "It tells the story of that individual and helps guide them along their path in life. Some can stand alone while others may need another melody or harmony to support them. Although, amongst those that can stand alone, the addition of the harmonies takes their song somewhere... immortal."

"I love that!" Ora said. "So poetic and romantic." She grabbed my arm, gazing off dreamily. "I wish I knew what my inner song sounded like."

"I'll write you one," Brydon offered.

"You compose?" she exclaimed. Ora was so animated that I couldn't help but smile at them both.

"Yes," he said with a nod. "I'm one with many passions, and music has been my strongest love since I was a young lad. Listening to the melodies and harmonies in everyday life has the most pleasing effect on me. I draw inspiration from all kinds of places, and some"—Brydon glanced at me then nodded behind us—"from where you'd never expect it. One just has to listen."

We turned to see Frederick and Calix approaching. Both men sported furrowed brows as they partook in a tense conversation. I fought off the anxiety welling in my chest and turned back to Brydon. He was swaying with his eyes closed.

"Brydon?"

"Shh! He's *listening*." Ora folded her arms, attempting to contain her excitement.

"Very observant, Ora," Brydon said. He opened his eyes when the guys reached our group. "I shall compose something in your honor. Will you be in Linall for the festivities?"

"Yes," Frederick said. "They will be joining Calix and me."

"We are?" I glanced at him and watched his expression waver slightly.

"I, uh... thought that we had discussed it on our way into town." Frederick cleared his throat. "Would you do us the honor of joining us?"

A slightly nervous energy radiated from him, like he was worried I'd actually say no. Why would that make him nervous? And why did I find it so adorable?

I opened my mouth to answer, but Ora beat me to it. "We'd love to!" She knocked her shoulder with mine.

"S-Sorry. Yes, I'd—er—*we* would like that," I stuttered. Now I was the one exuding an anxious aura. In the last thirty seconds, it was settled that we'd stay with Frederick and Calix.

In Linall.

At the castle that we weren't supposed to know about.

With two men we hardly knew.

One of which I had a slight crush on.

It's all to get me home.

Brydon perked up like a dog offered a treat. "Wonderful!" he exclaimed. "I'll follow shortly behind. I'm stable lord of the castle now, and I will also be conducting the music at the Ethereal Ball."

Stable lord and music conductor. An interesting combination.

As fast as hummingbird wings, Ora clapped with pleasure while Frederick and Calix stared at each other.

"We'd best be on our way," Calix said. "Brydon, would you grab our mounts?"

"Of course." Brydon opened his arms to us and bowed, then headed to the stables.

Frederick softly placed his hand on my elbow and said, "I didn't mean to assume, Temperance. If you aren't comfortable with the arrangement, I apologize."

Goosebumps ran up my arm and neck at his touch. Nora would have called them *goody goosebumps* because they brought pleasure, not fear. His gentle cobalt eyes searched my face for an answer, but my mind was drowning in thoughts.

Why haven't I said anything? Say something!

I shifted my attention to Ora; it was easier to talk to her at the moment. "I'm fine with it if you are, Ora."

Everyone turned to her. She was trying so hard to suppress her smile that she sucked in her lips. Ora knew. She somehow knew exactly where my thoughts were mere moments ago. She was Nora and Nora was her, therefore she had to be able to read my face like a book.

I shot her a subtle expression of warning.

She exhaled in another attempt to conceal her enthusiasm before responding. "As I said before, we'd love to."

Calix gave a short nod. "Glad that's settled."

Frederick's smile caused my heart to skip a beat as he bowed. "It will be our pleasure to host you"—his eyes met mine for the briefest of moments—"both."

Brydon and a boy emerged from the stable with our horses in tow. Brydon led Neva, while the boy brought out Calix's horse. Neva nuzzled Brydon repetitively, clearly fond of him.

"I will be seeing you shortly, my dear." He patted her mane and gave a peck between her eyes before handing the reins to Frederick. "Continue to take care of her, and she'll always take you where you need to go. Farewell, my friends."

Frederick swung up on her back and reached out to me. I placed my hand in his and used the stirrup with my foot and followed his lead—it was much easier than before.

He looked back at me and teased, "Well, look who's finally getting the hang of this."

We were so close that his scent of lime and cedarwood filled the air around me. I swallowed to restart my breathing. "Practice makes improvement, you know."

He laughed. "True words."

"Well, not entirely true..." I said. "I've seen people excessively practice some things and are never able to get the hang of whatever it is they've practiced, myself included." I chuckled and tucked some of my hair behind my ear.

"And what is something you do not excel at?" he asked.

My lips puckered to the side, and I glanced to the right. "Hmm... Geometry."

He laughed, sending a surge through my body, energizing and encouraging.

"Not much of a scholar then?"

I felt myself get a little defensive. "I'm good at other things."

Calix and Ora were finally situated on their horse, so Frederick turned and nudged Neva onward.

"What do you excel in?" he asked.

Careful to only mention things they most likely had in Emeriz, I said, "I'm a pretty decent artist, and I'm part of a... chorus back home. I'm good at history, too, but not with exact dates." A nervous laugh escaped my lips. I couldn't understand why it felt awkward boasting about myself. Normally, I didn't mind showing off. "Longsword—"

"Really?" Frederick's voice jumped an octave as his posture straightened.

Was he impressed by that?

"I dabble," I said, trying to downplay my skill set. He was probably leagues better than me, and it made me feel shy. I hated that.

"So how does an accomplished swordswoman not have her weapon strapped to her back while traveling?"

"Why do I suddenly feel like I'm being interrogated?"

"Why are you evading the question?" he countered. "Are you exaggerating your talents?"

"You'll never know." I playfully pushed his shoulder, surprised by how much I enjoyed his teasing. As I was about to ask after his hobbies, we were interrupted by a guard at the gate.

"Sir." The guard bowed and held out a note with a blue wax seal. Once he'd secured the note into Frederick's hand, he gave a brief salute before walking back to his post. Frederick slid the note into a pouch at his side.

Calix shook his head. "We don't have much daylight left. Let's press on."

I didn't comment on the fact that the exchange was out of place, especially after Frederick's posture shifted from relaxed to rigid. Whatever that letter held already had him stressed, resulting in a quiet ride to our next, and hopefully last, campsite.

Once we made camp that night, most of the talking around the campfire was done between Frederick and Calix in hushed tones. Calix would try to engage us girls in conversation every so often, but Frederick would call him back to discuss 'a matter of importance.'

My mind flexed as it had the other day, like new muscle had webbed over my mind and I was thrown back into a memory of the campout with my grandparents and their hushed campfire conversation.

Back in my eight-year-old body, I plopped down into the sand next to the campfire's warmth and leaned against an old log. My grandparents, Henvick, and the boy stood across the embers from me, but didn't move to take a spot around the fire. Instead, they whispered amongst themselves and glanced in my direction. It made me uncomfortable.

"I know you're talking about me," I said indignantly and pulled the blanket tighter around me, trying to hide myself away.

Grandma walked over and knelt down to my level. "Tempy," she said gently, "our visitors have had a difficult evening."

"Who are they?" I whispered.

"An old friend and his nephew." She brushed some of my hair

from my face. "They're going to warm up here with us for a little bit. Try not to upset the young man any more than he already is. Don't ask him a bunch of questions."

"But, what—"

"We will discuss it later, Tempy," Grandma said, eyeing me firmly.

I crossed my arms.

Satisfied, she gestured for the boy to come sit next to me. With some encouragement from Henvick, he came and sat down. Once he was settled, Grandma excused herself to speak to Henvick and Grandpa, leaving us alone. The three of them sat together on the far side of the campfire, speaking quietly.

The boy hugged his knees to his chest, keeping his gaze on a small stick he slowly broke into tiny pieces. When it was beyond breaking any further, he traced shapes in the sand. Tears streamed down his face, each sniffle and sob making my heart tighter.

I wanted to ask what was wrong, but Grandma had told me not to.

I took a deep breath, plumping up my cheeks wide and held it. I released it slowly, like a balloon with a small leak. I chuckled at the image.

"What's so funny, Sweetheart?" The boy sniffled and wiped at his nose with his shirtsleeve.

"Sweetheart?"

He looked up at me with puffy eyes. "Isn't that what your grandma called you?"

Covering my mouth, I masked a laugh threatening to break through. I didn't want to hurt his feelings.

"It's just a pet name. Like when you think someone has a *sweet heart*, so you call them sweetheart."

"So it's a term of endearment?" His brows scrunched together.

"Sure..." Feeling awkward, but not wanting him to stop talking, I asked, "So what's your name?"

He shook his head. "I'm not supposed to tell people who I am."

"Why?"

"My parents told me not to."

"Well, I need to call you something. Let's use fake names." I grabbed my chin, thinking hard for a good alias. "You can call me... Penny. It rhymes with my real name."

"Which is?" he asked.

"It's—" Catching myself from almost spilling the beans, I lightly pushed his shoulder. "Nearly got me there! Fine, we'll just be nameless, I guess."

"Okay, Nameless I Guess." To my surprise he leaned forward with a half-smile.

Maybe he's feeling better. He's funny.

"Stupid," I joked.

The almost-smile dropped from his face. "Oh, sorry."

"No, it's funny!" I quickly assured him, not wanting the progress we'd made to disappear.

"Really?" He cocked his head toward me, the smile returning a little.

"Mm-hm!" I sat a little straighter with a nod.

Still confused by my comment, he changed his focus to the crackling fire.

"So, Nameless," I said, playing along with his joke, "why are you dressed like that? Are you in a play?"

"What? No." He arched an eyebrow at me.

"Ren faire?"

"Ren what?"

"That's a no then."

He angled his body away from me a little. "Are you teasing me?"

I crossed my arms. "No, why would I?"

"Crying shows weakness."

I rolled my eyes, punched him in the arm, and demanded, "Who are you calling weak?"

"Ow!" he cried. "*Myself.*" His face was scrunched up in pain, but he still managed to look at me like I was crazy.

"Nope, you called me weak too." I folded my arms again, daring him to argue.

He rubbed at his arm. "How's that?"

"Earlier, I was a big crybaby because of a bad dream. It's okay to cry." With a shrug, I relaxed and looked him square in the eye. "And my mom always says, *'Never judge a book by its cover.'*"

The boy scrunched his eyebrows together and stared at me. His eyes glistened strangely in the firelight.

"Are your eyes... *glowing*?" I leaned forward to get a better look.

"No, I'm not! I mean—they're not!" He shook his head and broke eye contact.

"Okay! Chill!" Pulling my blanket tight around me, I sat back to pout.

"I-I'm sorry for snapping at you," he said quietly.

I glanced over at him and saw the saddest look on his face. "It's okay," I assured. "So... what's got you all snippy-snappy?"

Tears ran down his cheeks again. "My mother and father were taken from me."

I gasped and wrapped him in a hug. "Oh no! I'm so, so sorry."

He didn't push me away and after a deep, staggering breath, he said, "I'm s-staying with my uncle until we figure it all out."

"Is that what they're talking about?" I asked, letting him go.

"Probably." He rubbed at his nose and eyes. "I'm going to be all alone."

"That's not true. You have your uncle," I said as the boy wiped his cheeks and looked where his uncle sat. "And if you want, you'll have me. I'll be your friend."

Despite the tears on his face, he smiled. "Thank you."

I returned a smile. "That's what friends are for."

"Friends." He nodded.

"Now, shh!" Holding a finger to my lips, I reached out with my other hand to hold one over his mouth. "Let's listen to them. You should get to pick what you want to do. It's stupid that they're keeping secrets. I *hate* secrets."

He raised an eyebrow and pulled my hand away. "Isn't spying on them a secret?"

"We're *knowledge-gathering*," I whispered. "It's a secret for the greater good."

"For the greater good." He straightened like a soldier and held up a fist.

Nodding, I bumped his fist with mine. He furrowed his brows and examined his knuckles.

The swell of the ocean and the incoming tide crashed over the rocks in a soft roar. It mingled with the sharp pops and cracks as the wood from our fire crumbled into ash. The background noise muffled their words into mush. We tried scooting ourselves forward on our bums to get closer, but the sound only brought their attention to us. We quickly lay down on the sand to pretend we were sleeping. A plan that did not work. Grandma scolded us and we sat back up against the log.

"They should tell us too," I muttered.

"Thanks for trying." He tossed me a half-hearted smile and yawned.

Leaning his head against the log, he closed his eyes. It wasn't long before my eyelids also started to droop, and eventually I fell asleep.

A little while later, I felt myself being jostled and picked up. With my eyes still heavy with exhaustion, I couldn't quite get them to open.

My grandma said something under her breath and brushed her hand across my forehead.

Images began to dance behind my eyelids as bits and pieces of a distant conversation reached my ears.

A symphony of howls cried out from somewhere close by.

"The choice is forced now," Grandpa said urgently. "We're all going to Earth where it's safe. They'll return when they come of age."

"Why not unite the eleven Eslanian factions? The Lords of Eslane will follow you."

Was that Henvick?

"Out of the question," Grandma said. "She and Maxwell can't know of my presence. It's enough of a risk that we're still speaking with you when her men are on your heels. If she senses I'm here, all will be over before it's begun."

Another cry from the dogs. Closer this time.

"There's no time! They're after us, so we'll lead them away from you."

"I don't like this. The boy should come with us," Grandpa objected.

"I get to decide, and I belong here," came a boy's voice.

Nameless?

"Now go!" he shouted.

The memory faded, leaving me staring at Frederick and Calix. I blinked and shook my head.

Was this another facet to my abilities? Reliving memories?

"You seem to be enjoying the attentions of a certain gentleman," Ora whispered. "You are full-on staring at him."

"Nor—I mean—Ora, shut up." A blush flamed my cheeks.

She let out a quiet squeal. "You like him. Just admit it!"

I rolled my eyes. "That's not what happened. And if I do, what does it matter?"

I really needed to tell her about the memory flashes, but the last thing I wanted was her telling me about my fate again.

Ora drooped her body so dramatically it almost looked like her bones had disintegrated.

"'What does it matter?'" she mimicked, then leaded forward and whispered, "Try a romance with a handsome king."

"*Possible* king," I corrected. "And who's to say he likes me? He's kind and considerate, but that doesn't translate into attraction." I started creating shapes in the dirt.

"You're impossible and blind." Ora crossed her arms and placed them on her knees near her chest. Her silence on the subject brought relief, however it didn't last long. "But what if he does?"

"Please, just... why?" I groaned.

"How are you not excited?" she asked, placing her hands on the ground and gripping the grass, nearly tearing it up.

My head dropped into my hands. "Because I still have no way of getting home," I lamented. "I have no family to give me direction, so I'm stumbling around trying to figure it out while also trying not to die or get discovered."

Ora pulled my hands from my face, looking me square in the eye. "I refuse to let you spoil my fun with your attitude," she said. "You will see things from my perspective at some point. Count on that. I've never been happier!"

Her comment reminded me of what she'd said before. "You said something similar the other day... about being happier. What did you mean?"

Her face softened and shoulders slumped forward. "In Merald, I'm kind of well-known."

I gave her a look that said, *Go on*.

"Outside my grandfather and the immediate royal family, no one knows that I'm Descended," she explained, gaining a little confidence. "However, my grandfather is second to the king there, his Left Advisor. Actually, he holds more power than a Left should."

She glanced over at the guys to be sure they were still occupied, then back to me. "When tyrants abused their power, my grandfather led our armies against them. First with Domhnall, then Minerva. Our king lives, but he was a second son, and thus not raised to reign—let alone lead armies into battle. So he temporarily granted my grandfather certain sovereign powers. Wars and battles are in his blood. He's our kingdom's protector. It's his duty to keep Merald safe until there is peace in Emeriz. Then, when he's learned under my grandfather, the king will fully take his place."

I blinked in shock. "Isn't the king worried your grandfather might hold onto those powers after the war?"

A small smile graced her lips. "No. Our king trusts him completely. Merald hasn't fallen to Minerva's whim because of my grandfather."

"Okay, then why the long face?" I asked.

Ora pulled a few more grass blades from the ground. "I ran away from something important to come help you." She took a deep breath. "My betrothal."

"You're only sixteen!"

"Almost *seventeen* which is an acceptable age to be betrothed here, although it didn't make me happy. It's an arranged marriage... to the prince." Ora crossed her arms like she was cold, but I knew better. Her guard was up.

"Why?"

"I'm Descended of the Tides and the granddaughter of a powerful man in Merald. Marry me off to the crown prince of Merald, and our union would make us the most powerful rulers Emeriz has ever seen. What could be better?" Ora stared into the flickering embers in a hollow daze.

"No pressure." I saw the logic, but still couldn't wrap my mind around it. Getting married right now would be an uncomfortable situation.

"It would be different if I loved the prince, but I don't. On top of that, how can I love someone with my whole heart when half of me is in a completely different world? No one could truly love *all* of me." Ora seemed to sink lower in her mood as she broke the buds of grass she'd uprooted into tinier pieces.

"Does he love you?"

Ora blushed. "Yes, which makes me feel guiltier for running. He's an honorable man—handsome too. But whenever I think of sharing my life with him, something feels... not wrong, but not *right*. Like how you feel about Brett."

I nodded, understanding perfectly.

She stared at the mess of grass now in her lap.

"What does your grandfather think?" I asked.

She tucked a strand of her chocolate locks behind her ear. "He wants me to be happy by my own definition, but he did everything he could to convince me to go through with it. He approves of the match."

"Will he be mad?" I said, suddenly nervous that this would cause some sort of banishment or shunning from her home.

"Disappointed, yes. Mad? I'm not sure. Like I said, he wants me to be happy." For the first time in the conversation she smiled genuinely, but it disappeared seconds later. "I hate letting people down, especially those I care about."

I draped my arm around her the way I did with Nora, and it felt just as natural. "That's something someone can truly love you for right now. Nora is the exact same way."

"Thanks."

"Of course," I said, then released her. "How about you come home with me? You and Nora can finally be one."

Ora shook her head and said, "I feel it'd be a safer and easier transition if she came to Emeriz. The spell that separated us was cast here, and I don't know how magic responds in your world."

"Makes sense."

That's when it hit me that I would need to tell Nora. My homesickness actually made me feel physically ill.

I was going to leave it at that, but something else gnawed on my thoughts. "Doesn't it scare you, though? Are you sure this is what *you* want?"

Will Nora?

"I'm terrified. What if in searching for myself I lose myself?" Ora watched the stars above us. "Then again... haven't I already lost half of myself?" A half-smile touched her lips. "If I don't, I'll never be a whole Descended and won't be able to help when the time comes. That's something I definitely do not want." Ora stretched her arms up and yawned. "Storytime is over. I'm going to sleep. And you"—she pointed her finger right in my face, which I playfully slapped away—"should do the same."

I chuckled and said, "Yeah, soon."

Nodding in satisfaction, Ora lay down.

My gaze flitted across the fire to Frederick, still in deep discussion with Calix. I watched as the firelight highlighted the proportioned edges of his jaw and cheekbones. Frederick must have sensed my stare, because he met my eyes. He smiled and gave a soft wave. I returned the gesture nervously and quickly snuggled down into my blanket.

CHAPTER 13

TEMPERANCE

I jolted awake, my head slightly damp with sweat and my breathing uneven. Placing my hand on my chest to calm my nerves, I glanced around to see everyone was still fast asleep, and our fire was nothing but embers.

The locked door.

The spiraling staircase.

The oppressive force coming up behind me.

This time the feeling of being chased in my dream was more forceful, and sounds of clinking metal echoed through the smoky, glassless window. To my disappointment, even with the fluctuations in the dream, the door remained unopened.

Why was it changing?

I knew that sleep would not come easily for the rest of the night, and I longed for a distraction. The dying fire popped, sending sparks into the night.

I threw on more tinder to give my nerves something to occupy them, then looked around at everyone, envious of their slumber. If I wanted to sleep at all that night, I needed to work the anxiety out of my system.

I ventured into the forest, hoping that a walk would ease my nerves, and soon reached a small opening leading out to a cliffside.

Trees parted in a semicircle around the edge of the cliff, opening the arms of the forest to the magnificent sight beyond. The entire celestial night sky domed overhead, the brightness of the moon enlightening the stillness of the river far below. The river cut through the vast thick forest valley, creating a natural border between the two sides. Leaves glistened like silver, amplifying the moonlight's reach.

Finding a nice tree to lean against, I sat back to enjoy the breathtaking view. All my anxieties over the past few days eased off my shoulders.

I watched the trees sway in the breeze and thought about my family. The history I was never told as truth.

The story of two siblings and their magical pendants was, in fact, my grandma and her sister. One born with Descended magic and one without. Grandma had shared her power by infusing her magic into an amethyst and splitting it in two. Minerva, jealous and thirsty for power, killed Grandma's sister and stole her half. My grandparents escaped with one of the Eslanian factions to Earth.

We couldn't tell Frederick and Calix. The last thing anyone needed to know was that Ora and I were Descended. Not to mention I was from a different world and Ora was from Merald. Ora had told them some story about being from one of the Eslanian nomadic factions, which wasn't a total lie on her part. Calix accepted her tale, but Frederick held something in his eyes that insinuated his skepticism. My gut told me he trusted us, but I wasn't sure he *believed* us. That was enough for me. I'd take what I could to get me home.

Then I'll never see him again.

My stomach twisted in knots.

What was my deal? We'd met two days ago.

When he'd smile at me, my cheeks instantly inflamed. His touch was always kind, warm, and nothing less than gentlemanly, and whenever he said my name, my heart would race. On occasion, I'd find my gaze shifting to his lips—curious about how it might feel to kiss him. It was my kind of luck that when I finally developed feelings for someone, they'd be unattainable to the extreme.

We were literally from different worlds. There was no future with him.

I ran my fingers through my hair. Learning about my family, my powers, and getting home needed to be my focus, not on an attractive, dark-haired, blue-eyed king. I pulled my knees to my chest and dropped my head against them, mentally building a wall around my emotions.

A twig snapped, and leaves crunched behind me.

Had Maxwell's men found me?

Acting on instinct, I slid through the brush and grabbed a fallen branch to defend myself. My heart pounded as I waited for the shadow to pass before I stealthily emerged from the brush. With the heavy branch held high above my head, I inched forward in preparation for my attack.

The shadowed figure turned abruptly and shouted, "Don't!"

The warning came too late.

My arms swung, the branch hitting the figure over the head. They frantically grabbed their head and moaned in agony. It wasn't until the shadow stumbled into the path of the moonlight and fell to the ground that I realized my mistake.

"Frederick!" I tossed the stick aside and knelt beside him, then gingerly helped him lean against a boulder.

His eyes blinked rapidly.

"I'm so, *so* sorry, Frederick!" my voice breaking in my panic. "I didn't know it was you."

I cursed myself for being skittish

The pressure building in my lungs subsided at the sound of his laughter. I examined his face and saw the pain melt into amusement.

"I just whacked you upside the head, and you're *laughing*?"

He adjusted his body to a more comfortable position and composed his laughter enough to answer. "Luckily, the blow lacked the strength to do any real damage."

I breathed a sigh of relief until I replayed his words in my mind. Lacked strength? Sure, the branch wasn't as heavy as my longsword, but the stance and motion I'd used were correct. It definitely could have caused some damage.

I pushed away my injured pride. The fact that he wasn't severely injured was a *good* thing.

"It doesn't hurt at all?" I asked.

"Not really." He raised his hand up to check for blood, wincing.

"Right, I *totally* believe you."

Frederick beamed up at me, and my breath hitched.

"Oh, it aches, believe me. Just not as bad as you think."

Something in his tone forced me to ask, "What do you mean by that?"

Smiling ear to ear he leaned closer. "I question your abilities as a self-proclaimed swordswoman, that's all."

I leaned back. "Be grateful I didn't have my longsword, or you'd be sporting a whole new look."

Frederick raised an eyebrow, but his eyes twinkled. "Only because I was aware you were the attacker. Had you been an actual threat, I would have overpowered you." Overconfidence shined through his grin.

Oh, he was *asking* for it.

A Cheshire Cat smile graced my lips. "Are you sure I'm not a threat?" I whispered, leaning closer.

Frederick stared at me with a mystified expression. He swallowed. "Yes... my lady," he said, breath staggering.

He glanced down to my lips then met my eyes again, a question burning in his own. A familiar tension hung in the air between us. Frederick thought I was going to kiss him. A jolt ran through me when I realized he wanted me to.

I slid my hand into the warmth of his, then tilted my head ever so slightly and whispered, "I see."

I gripped his hand tight and twisted it, flipping him on his stomach, effectively pinning him to the ground.

That ought to teach him not to underestimate me. A twinge of regret lurched in my stomach, but I ignored it. My brain knew it wouldn't work between us. There was no point.

"What in Emeriz—how?" Frederick breathed out, turning back over as I released my hold.

When I started high school, my parents worried about me entering the dating scene, so they encouraged self-defense classes. After all, a girl could never be too careful. I couldn't exactly explain all that to Frederick though.

"A lady never reveals her secrets." I smiled coyly. "Maybe you should stop underestimating people."

"Lesson learned, but..." A mischievous smile spread across his face.

"But what?" I groaned, annoyed that he couldn't just admit I'd pinned him fair and square.

He pulled a maneuver with his legs and my back hit the grass. He hovered over me and smirked. My shock must have been apparent, because he laughed.

"You should always anticipate a counterattack," he said.

I pulled a countermove, and the next thing I knew, we were

locked in a wrestling match, laughing the entire time. There were a few times I noticed he let me get the upper hand, but I was having too much fun to call him out on it. I thanked the universe for the legging-like pants under my knee-length dress—otherwise our match would have been seriously awkward.

After a couple matches—and Frederick teaching me a few new moves—we finally fell next to each other in a truce. I closed my eyes for a few minutes and concentrated on slowing my heart rate. When I opened them again, Frederick was propped up on his hand, watching me. His inquisitive gaze made the effort I'd made to slow my heart rate utterly useless.

"What?" I asked.

"You're not what I thought you'd be like when I first saw you," he said, a subtle amazement painting his tone.

I laughed, then asked, "Haven't you ever heard the phrase, 'Never judge a book by its cover'?"

"Yes, I have, actually." Frederick's eyes probed into mine, searching for something. When he glanced away, his brow crinkled like he was confused by what he found.

"So, is it a good thing or a bad thing... that I'm different?"

He shot me a lopsided grin. "Where would be the fun in that? You might adjust yourself based on my answer. I want to know the real you, not the mask you wear."

He had no idea.

His words were meant to be sweet, but I felt inexplicably guilty for lying to him about who I really was.

But he was lying too... Did he feel guilty about keeping his identity a secret from me?

I sat up and changed the subject. "We should wake you up every couple hours to be sure I didn't give you a concussion."

"Concussion?" He tilted his head in confusion.

"Also known as a bruised brain. If you have one, there's a chance of dying in your sleep."

"I've been hit harder in sword practice." He shrugged it off like it was no big deal. "I'll be fine."

Having been hit a number of times with the practice swords we used back home, I understood. They were weighted to feel and move like one made of steel. Even with protective gear, they left my ears ringing after a blow.

"Look at you, Sir Tough Guy." I stared him down playfully. "I'd rather be safe than sorry."

Frederick sat up and looked at me, sincere. "If it'll ease your mind, my lady," he said gently, "so it shall be."

He was so close, that I had to concentrate on my breathing just to keep it even as I said, "It will."

His eyes didn't waver from mine and squinted as if deciding something. "Temperance, are you all right?"

"Yeah, why?"

"You look…" Frederick pondered a moment, before continuing. "I find myself wondering what's keeping you awake and this far from camp."

Pulling my knees up to my chest, I wrapped my arms around my legs, laughing uneasily before I said, "Couldn't sleep."

"May I ask why?"

"Just have a lot on my mind." I studied his face to see if he'd accept that answer. I looked away shortly after, fearing that if I stared too long, my expressions would reveal everything—the homesickness for my family, the magic that breathed within my blood, or even the attraction I had for him. "What about you?" I asked.

Frederick didn't say a word, which drew my attention back to him. He observed me like he was trying to puzzle me out. My breathing became heavier each second we held each other's gaze.

Quit looking at him or you'll do something stupid.

I turned my focus to the night sky. "Are you going to answer?"

"Yes," he said, then cleared his throat. "Like you, I've got a lot on my mind." His wistful expression melted into a mischievous grin. "Also, I noticed a troublesome lady under my protection had wandered off—yet again. You make my duty difficult, you know."

"Troublesome?"

"Extremely," he said with a hint of mockery. "First my horse, now you. The wandering and willfully stubborn attract others of their kind, I guess."

I lightly punched him on the shoulder. "At least I'm not a presumptuous scoundrel."

"'Presumptuous scoundrel'?" he replied, amused. "I'll admit I can be a bit presumptuous at times, but scoundrel? I don't recall stealing anything from you."

Not yet.

Whether he realized it or not, he was setting up a heist to steal my heart, and at the rate he was going, I may as well just hand it over to him.

"Well?" he pressed when I remained silent.

"Forgotten already?" I crossed my arms and faced away from him. "I should add 'forgetful' to that title."

"Oh, I see now. Although, I didn't hold you to that suggestion." His hand came across my chin and pulled it around to face his. The graze of his fingers made me feel faint. "Shall I apologize again?"

I shook my head, unable to form words.

"Thank you. I'm glad I don't need to add 'unforgiving' to your title."

That comment earned him another glare and playful punch.

"Are you trying to start another wrestling match?"

Frederick smirked and leaned forward. "And what if I am?"

What could I say to that when he was so close? All I had to do was lift my chin and lean a little closer for my lips to touch his. My heart pounded in my ears. I couldn't. It would be too difficult to leave if something actually happened between us.

The same intensity he had before burned behind his gaze. Frederick wanted to kiss me as much as I wanted to kiss him, which made this more complicated. I opened my mouth to say something, but nothing came out. The movement brought his attention to my lips. Taking the opportunity of his broken hypnotic gaze, I pulled back.

The passion in Frederick's expression melted away. He looked hurt by my rejection, but didn't voice it.

I hated to have done that to him, especially when I wanted it just as badly.

Desperate to lighten the mood, I mustered up the best smile I could. "Then, I'm sorry to disappoint, but that's not gonna happen," I said.

"Oh," he uttered.

Just kiss the boy! I shook the thought from my mind as soon as it entered. Biting my lip, I tried to think of what to say to bury the awkwardness between us.

"At least not until later," I added.

Where had that come from? Did it sound flirty? Shouldn't I have continued to discourage it? My hormones were at war with my brain.

I gauged his reaction and watched as his knee-weakening smile returned.

"Really?" A hopeful mischief shone in his eyes, like he was keeping a secret.

I smiled. "Yeah. I'm gonna beat you next time."

He nodded in agreement and moved closer to whisper, "I look forward to *later*."

CHAPTER 14

FREDERICK

Dawn broke over the mountain ridge, flashing rays of sun into my eyes. The usual smell of damp earth and fallen leaves tickling my nose was accompanied by a new, far sweeter scent of wisterias. The origin of the fresh aroma nestled against my chest.

Temperance's hair fell around her face as she contentedly slept in my arms. I reached up to sweep the strands back with my fingertips. The way the light of the sunrise shone on her skin made it look delicate, as though one touch might break her.

She readjusted her position, pulling herself closer. I swallowed back a chuckle in hopes I wouldn't wake her. Uncertain of what provoked me to do so, I aimlessly twisted my fingers around the tips of her hair.

True to her word, she'd woken me up twice in the night so I wouldn't fall victim to the possible concussion. I was happy to see her getting rest.

My desire to know who lay beyond her skeptical gaze and teasing smile grew with every moment I spent with her.

Then there was her comment about judging others, which brought its own set of suspicions. The second coincidence tied to that night. Unfortunately, neither her name nor the comment equaled proof that she was the heir.

Maybe it was as Calix said: I'd become so obsessed with my search that I saw waves where there were only ripples.

However, the connection between us pulled me toward her like an ocean current in a summer storm—heavy and strong. We almost kissed, so I knew she felt it too.

What had stopped her?

Ora's story about them being from the Eslanian factions was a half-truth at best. Even with the lie, I knew their intentions—whatever they might have been—were honorable. The consistent, unwavering instinct from my abilities as a Descended assured me of that fact.

Besides, they were simply upholding the first law of survival throughout Emeriz: Don't reveal too much, as others will use it to exploit your weaknesses. Even I'd kept a rather grand secret about myself. Make that two. A twinge of guilt nibbled in my chest.

I needed to tell her before we reached Linall.

The sun had completely risen over the mountains when Temperance stirred in our embrace. She rubbed at her eyes then froze. Her entrancing stare bore into mine, even through her sleepiness. Changing like the seasons, her irises had transformed from their usual blue to a translucent lilac in the morning sun.

"Good morning, my lady," I said, my lips curving into a grin.

With an incoherent 'good morning,' she wriggled out of my arms and walked over to the cliff's edge. I stood but made no steps toward her. Temperance kept her gaze on the valley below and crossed her arms, refusing to look at me.

The atmosphere between us tipped, and I could sense the wall she was putting up, attempting to block the progress we'd made the night before. If I had a prayer of breaking through, I needed to act fast.

She didn't know I was king or Descended and treated me as

anyone else. I was myself when I was around her, and in a twist I wasn't expecting, she seemed to like what she saw. Telling Temperance the truth would put that at risk, but I wanted her to know me... mask or no mask. Hadn't I asked her to do the same?

If the truth pushed her away, so be it. At least I'd know I laid it all out there.

I took a step toward her, but a movement in the trees stopped me in my tracks. Sizing up its prey, a pair of glowing violet eyes watched Temperance intently from a cocoon of shadows in the brush. Cautiously, I made my way to Temperance, reaching for my dagger in the process. I positioned myself between her and the animal, then placed my arm in front of her waist to slowly ease her away from the edge and behind me.

"Frederick, don't!" Temperance knocked my weapon to the dirt and the animal retreated back into the confines of the forest.

I spun to face her. "What in Emeriz's name, Temperance?" I said, voice raised. "Had it not run off, that thing could have killed us!"

She shook her head, face full of distress, and gripped my arm. "No she wouldn't."

"It's a wild animal! What makes you think—"

"Because she's mine." She dropped her gaze. "Sort of."

Had I heard her right? I took a step back. The sound of rock sliding against rock cut through the air, and our bodies shook as the ground rumbled beneath us. On instinct, I pushed Temperance far from the edge. The earth below my feet gave way, and I fell down the cliffside. My grasping hands managed to grip the root of a tree jutting out the side of the rockface.

"Frederick!" Temperance's face popped over the side of the cliff. Relief touched her expression when she saw me dangling there and not falling to my death. "Are you all right?"

"Yes," I groaned, as my body flexed in reaction to my muscles having been yanked when I'd grabbed the root. "Go get Calix. Quickly—esh!" My hands started to slip, scratching my palms.

"Frederick!" her voice quaked.

"I'm fine! I can hold on long enough for you to grab him!"

As I readjusted my grip, the root rasped at the movement.

It'll hold. Please... let it hold.

Temperance rolled up her sleeves, lay flat on her stomach, and offered both of her hands. "Can you reach me?"

"Get Calix," I commanded through gritted teeth.

"That branch won't wait for Calix! Grab my wrists!"

Putting my faith in her, I wrapped one hand around her wrist, followed by another.

We groaned and grunted as we fought to get me up and over the side. Once we were topside, I quickly grabbed her by the waist and scooted us far from the edge. We held onto each other until the shock wore off.

"Are you all right?" she asked.

"Thanks to you." My forehead brushed against hers, bringing attention to just how close we were. I shifted the weight on my arm and felt a stinging pain burn up my palm and wrist. Sitting up with one hand still around her waist, I lifted the other to see a light trail of blood dripping from them. "You really latched on with those nails of yours."

"Sorry! Here let me help." She placed her hand over the wound and hesitated, her lips pursed.

Temperance shook her head like she'd changed her mind about something and pulled herself from my arms to grab the cloak we'd used to keep us warm the night before. She tore four long pieces from the hem to use as bandages. As she tended to my wounds, I noticed her wrists looked similar to mine, from my nails burrowing into her skin. In addition to the fingernail scratches, there were cuts from the rocky mountain side.

"Allow me to assist you first," I said, reaching for one of the fabric pieces in her lap, but she slapped my hand away.

"You can after I've finished yours." She was fueled with stubborn determination that brought a small glint to her eye.

I didn't need my Descended abilities to know there was no arguing with her.

When it came time for me to wrap her wrists, she winced a few times as I dug out any small pebbles that had been embedded into her wounds.

Temperance had saved my life without question or fear that she might fall to the same fate. If the cliff had collapsed any more, she would be lying at the bottom with me. All this for someone she barely knew.

Once I'd finished, she tried to pull her hands away, but I held them fast in mine.

"Wait."

Her brows furrowed, but she remained still.

My heart pounded as she stared at me, timid yet expectant. Lifting her wrists to my lips, I kissed them one at a time, and she made no moves to stop me. I dropped her hands and placed my own on the sides of her face then leaned in and kissed her forehead.

After taking a steadying breath, I placed my head against hers and whispered, "Thank you."

"You're welcome." Temperance pulled back a few inches to look me in the eyes. I drew my lips closer to hers, and my chest strained with anticipation when she did the same.

"Frederick! Temperance!"

Calix and Ora called out to us from somewhere in the distance—and just like that, the spell that hung between us was broken.

Temperance and I pulled away from each other. I stood and held out my hand to help her up, which she took.

"Thanks," she said.

I swallowed before saying, "Of course."

Temperance eyed our still-entwined hands then glanced up at me, a touch of pink flaming her cheeks. Clearing her throat, she gently tugged her hand from mine, and I reluctantly relinquished it back to her.

As we walked toward our friends' voices, I asked, "So that cat belongs to you?"

"Kind of," she said. "Tundra comes and goes as she pleases but hasn't hurt me. If anything, she protects me." Temperance looked over with a warning smile as she added, "So I'd prefer if you didn't kill her."

Your answer only brings more questions, my lady.

"In my defense... I wanted to protect you too."

"Which I appreciate. Feel free to slay any monsters that cross our path." Temperance tapped my shoulder with her fist. "Just not Tundra."

Calix and Ora came bounding up to us, worry etched in their expressions.

"There you are!" Ora shouted.

"What happened?" Calix asked, taking in our appearances.

Temperance brushed off dirt dusted along her skirt and ran her fingers through her hair, shaking out any debris. I noticed a small twig she missed and plucked it out. Temperance smiled gratefully.

"And what were you two doing all night?" Ora asked with an impish grin.

"Get your mind out of the gutter," Temperance said. "Nothing like what you're thinking."

Well, we almost kissed...

We hashed out the entire tale of what transpired on the cliffs to them. With a meaningful glance toward each other, Temperance and I came to an unspoken agreement that we wouldn't quite reveal everything.

They didn't need to know that I was falling for a girl I knew nothing about.

For the final leg of our journey, I decided to relax and hold off on telling Temperance my official title. All I wanted was to enjoy my last few hours of ordinary life. I temporarily let go of my responsibilities to the rebellion, the crown, and the needs of my people. Instead, I focused on what hadn't received attention since my coronation: my responsibilities and needs as a man.

I'd also chosen to hold back because of the *friendship* developing between me and Temperance. Once she knew who I was, her behavior toward me would irrevocably change. As king, mine would have to adjust as well.

Something bumped against my shoulder, and I glanced back at Temperance. My movement caused her head to quickly lift upright.

I chuckled at her sleepy smile and drooping eyes. "If you doze off, you'll fall off the horse, and I can't promise I'll be quick enough to respond."

"Sorry." Temperance lightly slapped her face, forcing her eyes to rapidly blink open a bit wider.

Guilt twinged my chest. It was my fault. If she hadn't needed to watch over me last night, she wouldn't be so exhausted.

"I promise if you hang on for just a bit longer, you shall sleep in a comfortable bed tonight," I said.

Temperance nodded and let out a yawn, which she immediately covered with her hands and mumbled, "Sorry again... That's not very attractive."

You make the teasing so easy, my lady.

"Is it important that I think you're attractive?" I asked.

"Nope," she said without skipping a beat.

Every other lady I knew would have blushed and stammered at the response or coyly leaned into it. Her blunt response left me at a loss for words, and she took advantage of it to poke me in the back.

"Someone seems awfully full of himself," she said.

I could hear the grin and knew that her eyes would be bright with mischief.

Temperance leaned close. "Sounds like someone wants an excuse to tell me I'm pretty."

Her breath warmed my skin, causing the hairs on my neck to prickle.

I did my best to ignore the sensation and jumped on the opportunity to throw her off. "I don't need any such excuse," I said. "You are lovely, my lady."

She sat back, and I immediately missed her warmth. "Thank you, good sir," she said in a mocking tone. "I am blushing oh so much from your timely and practiced response. You are quite lovely yourself."

I pulled Neva to a halt and twisted my torso as far as I could in order to look at her properly. She wasn't blushing at all. In fact, a nefarious grin had broken across her face.

"Men should never be called *lovely*," I said.

"I disagree. Some men can definitely be described as lovely."

Temperance nodded toward Calix. "Ora would certainly call *Calix* lovely."

I scoffed. "Him, lovely?" I shook my head. "What would I be defined as then? Certainly not lovely."

She tapped her chin with her index finger. "Oh, I get it. You're fishing for compliments."

"What?" I exclaimed.

"You don't have to pretend." She placed her hand on my shoulder and laughed.

"I pretend nothing. I—"

"You're getting defensive—how cute. It's okay. Everyone needs reassurance every now and then." She grinned so wide her eyes were almost slits.

How does she keep turning this back on me?

The breeze caught an errant strand of her hair. It brushed across her lips, and my fingers twitched, itching to brush it away.

"I don't concern myself with that nonsense." I turned around, suddenly ready to continue our travels. We were only a mile from the King's Way.

Temperance burst into a bout of laughter. "The lady doth protest too much, methinks. Or in your case, *the lord.*"

She said it like a common turn of phrase, but I couldn't place the reference.

"What's so funny?" Ora exclaimed. "Calix, could you please catch up to them?"

Calix was hastily at our side.

"What is it?" Ora probed, looking back and forth between Temperance and me.

"Yes," Calix said, amused. "By the rare look on his face, it seems to be at his expense."

Temperance swallowed her laughter. "*His Majesty* needed an ego boost and tried to wheedle one out of me."

His Majesty? I met Calix's eyes, brows raised. I knew he'd picked up on it too.

Calix cleared his throat. "Wow, he actually told you? You appear to be taking it so well."

Closing my eyes, I tilted my head trying to remain calm. "Calix... I did not."

"Tempy!" Ora thrust her arms out, exasperated. "And you kept telling *me* to keep quiet."

My eyes flashed open, and I turned back to Temperance. "What? Y-You—Do you know?"

"So you *hadn't* told her?" Calix asked, dumbfounded.

My gaze never left Temperance's. "No."

Her expression was one of a dog who'd just been caught in a raccoon trap, scared and uncertain.

My blood boiled a little, desperate for more information. "When?" I asked calmly.

She bit her lip. "After Calix mentioned you held positions at court. Seeing that your name was Frederick and how Calix treats you, we sort of put two and two together."

I shot a glare at Calix before returning my focus to her. "If you knew, why lie all this time?"

"It seemed like you didn't want us to know, so we acted like we didn't. Besides, you were gonna have to tell us before we reached Linall." Her attention momentarily dropped to her hands as she played with her fingers.

Looking inward, I searched for the truth of her words behind her gaze—that we'd met by chance and she'd truly kept her knowledge a secret in respect of my privacy. My blood cooled, and the pressure in my chest released, reassured that her intentions were pure. However, she still hid a great many things from me, and I would need to be wary of them.

I nodded at an apprehensive Calix, signaling that I trusted her words as truth.

He relaxed and loosed a throaty chuckle. "Don't look at me like that, boy," he said. "My nerves were more for them rather than you. Your temper can be worrisome. Remember, I helped raise you. Your tantrums were unbearable."

We all melted into light laughter, and I felt Temperance's body ease behind me. Leave it to Calix to de-stress any situation.

"Calix, you have no idea," said Ora "This one here"—She pointed at Temperance with her thumb—"could probably give him a run for his coin purse."

Temperance faked a dramatic gasp. "Lies!"

"Need I remind you of the loving nickname for your alter ego, *Tempest*?" Ora burst into giggles while Temperance went red, although she still smiled. "Fiercer than a hurricane, she is—especially if something is a threat to someone she loves. She's looked out for me all my life, even when she doesn't realize it."

Ora reached out across the space between our horses. Temperance took Ora's hand and squeezed it.

"Only time will tell who is more stubborn," Calix said. "In the meantime, we should press on."

I nodded. "Calix, would you mind taking the lead?"

"As My King commands," Calix said, flipping the switch back to political protocol. It made me dread the thought of how my interactions with Temperance were about to change.

When they were a safe distance ahead of us, just out of earshot, I decided to ask her a few more burning questions.

"Temperance, why didn't you act differently around me when you had suspicions about my identity?" I hated how pathetic I sounded.

"You mean why didn't I bow, curtsy, or praise you and beg favor?"

"That's one way to boldly put it." A slightly nervous chuckle escaped my lips.

"Besides hiding that we knew your identity... you're still just a man," she said. "A powerful one, but a man nonetheless." I glanced back at her and a sincere smile appeared on her face. "Plus, you seemed to like being treated normal."

I had. She meant well, but I couldn't help feeling a bit foolish.

We rode in silence for a few moments.

Her hand brushed against my upper arm as she said, "And I wanted to see more than the mask I'm sure you have to wear for everyone else."

My heart stuttered. "Using my own words against me, I see."

Her hand dropped from my arm. "Only the wise ones," she teased.

She'd sprung hope in me that our friendship wouldn't have to alter completely.

"Temperance, things will be different at the castle. I will be different... but I don't want us—"

"We've arrived, ladies. Welcome to Linall," Calix said.

Against the darkness of the night sky, the silhouette of Linall was carved out of moonlight. Once again, anything I wanted to express to her would have to wait.

CHAPTER 15

TEMPERANCE

Again, I stood at the bottom of that infuriating stone staircase and forced my feet forward.

Run! I yelled in my mind, but no matter how much I urged, my speed would not increase. Something was coming, I could feel it.

Don't stop at the window!

Ignored again, the dark, wispy force gripped and held me fast. The clanking metal made a repeat performance, but there was something new. With the gust of wind, the familiar and delicate scent crept into my senses.

Lilacs?

Lifting the blushing-pink-and-purple skirts of my dress, I pushed to the door. Near the top, I tried to catch a glimpse of my pursuer and tripped on the last stair. After scrambling to my feet, I turned back. No one was chasing me. There didn't even seem to be a way into the corridor.

With a sigh of relief, I faced the door. As eager as I'd been to open the door, fear imprisoned me, reflexively making me clasp the pendant around my neck, seeking strength. Not fear of what was hidden beyond, but that the dream would fade the instant I turned the knob.

Just do it!

The glowing edges of the dream flashed brightly and burned the image away, leaving only darkness.

However, instead of waking up, the blinding light diminished to reveal four people standing in front of me. They were fuzzy and shadowed, but they felt familiar—they felt close. Amidst the figures, a vibrant pair of blue eyes peered at me, the intensity of their cobalt hue unforgettable.

"How do I know you?" I asked.

"*Truth*," the eyes answered, then the four figures fell into the darkness.

I crashed to the ground, face first.

Another flash of light forced my eyes open, accompanied by a searing pain shooting through my skull. I tried to rub away the soreness.

Yep... I was definitely awake now.

"Lady Temperance!"

Someone knelt at my side and eased me into a sitting position against a dark-blue velvet chaise.

My blurry vision realigned, and my hearing cleared. I blinked a few times to push away the rest of the fuzzy outlines around everything. The return of my sight was greeted by the bearded face of Calix.

"That was quite a tumble," he said, hazel eyes filled with concern. "Are you well?"

"I'm f-fine," I mumbled, though my shoulder ached like I'd slept on it wrong. "Wait... *tumble*?"

"Yes, right off the chaise." He patted the cushion behind me. "May I ask what you're doing sleeping in the library when you have a perfectly comfortable bed in your quarters?"

Glancing around, my face burned hot. In the midst of all the books, I sat on the floor in my nightwear they'd kindly provided. I pulled the black embroidered lapels of my robe closer. Not only had I fallen asleep in the library, but I'd dropped off the side of the couch right in front of him.

An eruption of giggles sounded from the corridor, but they quickly faded. Calix glared at the door then turned back with a sympathetic expression.

Someone else had witnessed my public snooze.

I quickly reached up to do a drool check, relieved when I found none.

"Well?" he prompted.

"I couldn't sleep, so I thought reading would help."

I glanced at the thousands of books that surrounded me as memories of the night before flooded my mind. On the way to our rooms, I'd noticed this expansive library. When I'd finally settled into bed, the homesickness hit me again, keeping me wide awake. Desperate for answers, I slipped out of my room to do research.

It was the grandest library I'd ever set foot in. The smooth, white stone walls were lined with rows of dark mahogany bookshelves. Standing three stories tall, each level was supported by six matching stone and wood pillars on each side. Every one of them held firelights, which had provided the illumination I'd needed in my late-night studying.

The dim lighting hadn't prepared me for the beauty of the sunlight shining through the windows, washing over every inch of the room. At the back stood a large window that outshined the six others lining the sides. It looked almost carved out of the bookshelves surrounding it and gave view to a vast landscape of gardens and streams.

Belle ain't got nothing on this place.

Calix sifted through the piles of books I'd asked the librarians to provide.

"Ancient Artifacts and Enchanted Objects," he read. "A Brief History of Emeriz, Waking Dreams. Not exactly light reading."

"The point was to tire myself out," I said, my voice shaky. "Must have overachieved."

"That you did, milady." Calix raised his eyebrows and produced a sideways smile. "I respect your quest to find sleep and expand your knowledge, but may I ask that you refrain from doing so alone, in the middle of the night?"

I nodded.

"I will speak with the scholastedites and give you permission to take them to your chambers."

Scholastedites... not librarians? That's different.

I made a mental note to ask Ora about them later, unsure if it was a common term that I should have known.

"Thank you, Calix," I said with a smile.

"We wouldn't want to leave you unprotected and unconscious. You gave us quite the scare when your attendant came to us claiming you weren't in your chambers."

We? I couldn't help the curiosity and subtle hope of *who* else was worried about me.

"Sorry."

Calix laughed. "That's quite all right." He snapped his fingers, and one of the guards at the door promptly came over and saluted before Calix addressed him. "Please inform Lady Temperance's attendant that we have located her mistress and will meet her shortly in the lady's chambers to eat and dress."

The guard nodded, then asked, "And to His Majesty?"

My heart leapt at the mention of Frederick.

"I will report to him myself after I have returned the lady to her room." Calix stood and offered me his hand.

Once the guard disappeared, I let Calix help me to my feet, and he excused himself to speak with the nearest scholastedite. They all wore the same sleeveless, cream silk robes with gold flecks woven into the fabric. Each individual either had their hair slicked back or completely shaven. Calix returned to my side and instructed me to take any books I wished.

As nonchalantly as I could, I snagged the main books I was interested in. *Eslane Rulers: The Rise and Fall of the Great Kingdom* and *of Magic and Enchantment: Collected Stories of Rare Magical Artifacts.*

If Calix suspected anything from my selections, he didn't comment on it and escorted me all the way to my chambers.

"I'll be back in an hour to give you a tour," Calix said before he shut the door behind him, leaving me alone.

Books in hand, I walked across the room and placed them on the cherry wooden desk that sat beneath a stained-glass window. The night before I couldn't tell if the glass depicted a sunrise or sunset, but the golden circle was surrounded with interchanging pastel pinks, blues, and purples. The lightness of the colors made me suspect a sunrise ascending behind the active indigo ocean.

The room was spacious and inviting with tall ceilings and lavish, tasteful furniture. There was a desk, vanity, an armoire, a traditional floral rug, and a bed. I plopped down on the bed and lay on my back. It felt like lying on a cloud made of a soft, pale blue comforter with a damask print. Sheer, ivory fabric draped down from the center of the ornamental molding around the head of the bed—wispy and ethereal.

Where's my harp and halo?

I snuggled in deeper, but someone knocked.

"Come in," I said.

Expecting the attendant Calix had promised, I sat up to greet her. A jolt shot up my spine, and my face, neck, and hands warmed when I saw my visitor.

"F-Frederick? What are you—I mean, I expected..." I stood, brushing my hair behind my ears, then adjusted the belt of my robe.

After a brief look over my current wardrobe, he smiled and said, "That's quite the look."

I folded my arms and let out an uneven chuckle.

Yeah, this wasn't embarrassing... not at all.

"Breakfast." Frederick lifted a tray of food and stepped fully inside.

I had a guy in my room. Sure, Brett had been in my room back home, but he didn't count. This was different. Why was it different? Dad would probably flip... though he probably would have freaked more about me sleeping in Frederick's arms on the cliffs.

I silently watched him cross the room to a table on the balcony, where he set the tray down.

"I heard you had a restful sleep."

The humor in his voice caused a smile to break free.

"I heard that I worried a particular someone," I replied.

Frederick turned back to face me and crossed his arms as he leaned against the table. "Hm, did you?"

"Didn't I?" I tilted my head.

The air around us shifted, and his grin faded into an unexplainable intensity. My heart pounded as I stared into his eyes, but it nearly stopped altogether when I finally realized their color.

Cobalt. Just like my dream.

Focusing my attention elsewhere, I cleared my throat and said,

"Do you always dress up this much or is bringing me breakfast a formal affair?"

He glanced down at his outfit then back up at me. Spreading his arms out slightly, he did a quick turn to give me the full effect.

"Do you like it?"

I stepped back and placed my hand on my chin as if I were really thinking about it. He wore a black and charcoal overcoat covered in a unique fleur-de-lis print. Embroidered silver trim lined the lapels all the way down the front and around the bottom, which came to his upper thigh. Beneath the coat was a blue vest of the same print and silver trim, enclosed with buckles.

A small touch of a white undershirt subtly spilled out at the neck and wrists. Black pants and polished leather boots completed the ensemble. It was all tailored so perfectly to his broad form that the clean, stiff lines it created complemented his build. The overall effect was regal and...

Hot! Move over, Prince Charming.

Holding back a sigh, I smiled. "You look very... attractive."

Frederick cleared his throat and rubbed his ear, where I saw the subtlest shade of red bloom. Was he trying to hide it? My heart leapt in pleasure to witness him bashful.

"Thank you," he said, placing his hands behind his back and standing a little straighter. "I had to meet with my advisors early this morning. I was about to change into my training gear when your attendant came to my quarters and informed Calix and I that you were missing."

"I couldn't—"

"Sleep," he finished for me. "Seems to be a habit of yours." He chuckled and found his way over to my desk, casually grabbing one of the books to leaf through it. "We seem to have a similar taste in reading materials."

"As it goes with most people," I said, keeping my tone and demeanor as relaxed as I could, "we were bound to find something in common eventually."

If he were to discover the reason for my interest, it'd be goodbye Earth.

Unless, maybe Ora was right. There was a chance he wouldn't—

No! Too dangerous.

"I suppose that's true," he said. "Although, there are those I've known for years with whom I still have nothing in common." Frederick placed the book down. "Not many take interest in Emeriz's history or its... magic."

"Why?" I quickly regretted the question as the answer was obvious: there were those who'd kill anyone that gave a small hint at the Descended or rebellion.

His face was unreadable as he asked, "What are your thoughts on the prophecy?"

I didn't like where he was heading.

"There's too many... variables to truly have any sort of opinion."

There you go! Dance around it like a politician!

Frederick cocked his head and smiled. "I wasn't challenging you to a debate, just curious. Let's have it."

"You're a dangerous man, aren't you?" I asked, in hopes to divert the conversation.

There was a full moment of silence before Frederick asked, "Temperance, why must I pry so hard to know anything about you?"

"I, uh—" I bit my bottom lip and stared at the ground.

"Apologies, my lady," he said, drawing my attention back to him. "I value truth. I didn't mean—"

"It's a fairy tale." The words spilled out before I could think it through.

"What?" His expression softened, almost like something inside him was retreating.

"But aren't fairy tales, myths, or legends built upon some grains of truth?" I continued quickly. "So, I can't say that I don't believe it. The more I see... I'm starting to." My body and soul felt a little lighter at the admission.

Frederick had a good heart. He wouldn't throw me in a dungeon for agreeing with what he already believed, right? Opening up to him about the topic could lead me to the answer that would get me home. I wouldn't tell him everything, but I figured a few bits and pieces couldn't hurt.

The tension in Frederick's face eased, and he let out a breath. "You're a dangerous woman," he said, "and extremely brave to admit it."

Grabbing both my hands, he guided me to the table with my breakfast and pulled out a chair for me to sit. When I was settled, he crouched down next to me.

"I wish we had more time to speak in depth on the topic, but duty calls."

"We'll just have to make time later." I smiled, relieved to let go of the subject. I needed time to prepare and research more before I discussed anything with him.

"Actually, that's the reason for my visit. I wanted to warn you myself. As king, my schedule can get pretty hectic. I may not have much time to spend with *you* and Ora."

My heart sank a little, but it was better for me. More time for finding answers.

"I understand."

"Eh-hem."

Frederick and I looked toward the door, and he immediately stood. Ora was in the doorway, grinning from ear to ear.

"I better be on my way," Frederick said. As he was about to walk away, he hesitated and took my hand to place a kiss on it. "Excuse me, my lady."

After his swift exit, Ora leaned back, looked between me and the door, and shook her head.

"What?" I asked.

Ora held her hands up as if surrendering. "Not saying a word. Nora never seems to get through to you—how do I expect I will? But, my hand remains kissless, while yours..."

To hide the blush forming on my face, I turned to my breakfast and plopped a grape in my mouth.

Ora walked out onto the balcony. "Wow," she said. "The view from my window is great, but this is breathtaking." I nodded and bit into a roll with jam while Ora continued, "So how do I look?"

Her dark hair was softly curled in a low-sitting bun, a few tendrils dropping from the bottom. As she spun, pink chiffon rippled and flowed around her ankles where a print of blooming ivory flowers twisted and looped all the way up to the bodice. Gathered frills poked out from beneath the squared neckline, teasing their presence. The flounced sleeves wisped around with the slightest movement of her hands. At her waist sat a satin sash in a slightly darker shade of pink.

"Gorgeous," I said.

"I know!" she squealed and jumped. "Our attendant is amazing." She smiled like she was hiding something.

"What is it?"

She rushed to the door, motioning for someone to enter. The most angelic looking woman I'd ever met walked into the room.

"Rhiannon!" I ran over and wrapped her in a hug. "How did this happen?" I asked, pulling away with a smile.

"Fate," she said simply. "Some people are simply meant to be in each other's lives." Rhiannon's gaze glistened with that same look as before, like she'd shared some sort of inside joke. She squeezed my hands, and a warm calm washed over me.

"I've always felt that way too."

"It also helps to have connections in the right places." Rhiannon turned a bit bashful. "My husband just secured a position here and found me this one. I confess, I pressed him about it when I found out that it was you two who I'd be assisting."

"What does he do?" I asked.

Rhiannon shrugged. "This and that. I'm lucky to be married to a man with many gifts."

"She promised to introduce us to him soon!" Ora pounded on the bed in excitement. "Rhiannon, you must work your magic on her."

"Is there some place I could wash up first?" I could still feel some dirt under my nails from our travels.

"If you hadn't been missing this morning, she could've taken you with me. Instead, you decided to sleep in a dusty library." She pointed at me sternly but then fell into giggles.

"So, no bath?"

Rhiannon placed a hand on my shoulder and smiled. "You will later, but I need to at least dress you well enough for Calix to show you around. He's a very busy man, so we must go by his schedule. We'll make do with your wash bowl and soap."

"All right, beautify me." I raised my arms up to demonstrate my enthusiasm.

Rhiannon clapped her hands. "Splendid! The king provided some lovely things for you to wear."

A blush crept up my neck and cheeks at Frederick's thoughtfulness.

"Temperance, you look flushed," Rhiannon said. "Are you ill?"

My face felt warmer, and Ora said, "Oh, that's because she's *in love.*"

"I barely know Frederick," I defended.

A mischievous glint appeared in Ora's eyes. "I don't believe I mentioned *who* you were in love with."

I picked up a pillow and threw it at Ora's face.

Rhiannon guided me to the dressing table and didn't waste time getting to work while we chatted.

"You care for the king?" she asked.

I shrugged. "Doesn't matter whether I do or don't. I won't be staying in Linall after the festival."

Maybe not even that long. Why did that make me feel a little sad?

Ora groaned in disapproval while Rhiannon nodded in understanding, but neither pressed the topic further. Once she finished, I assessed her work in the mirror. My hair was styled into a curly ponytail with a braid crown on top. It was powdered and oiled to look fresh and clean. She'd selected a forest green day-gown that was light but structured. The neckline came to a V at my chest and just covered the top of my shoulders.

Not bad for a rush job.

As Rhiannon tied the ivory, green, and gold embroidered sash at my waist, Calix arrived at my door.

"You ladies look wonderful," he said, lively and all smiles. "Shall we?"

Chapter 16

Temperance

Rhiannon didn't accompany us on our guided tour, but Calix kept us plenty entertained. In the empty dining hall, he juggled apples and made silly food puns. While in the ballroom, he whisked Ora into a dance. She followed his lead fairly well but still stumbled a bit. After they finished, he turned to me with his hand extended. I kindly turned him down, assuring him that it wouldn't be a pretty sight.

"I will teach you," he said. "A lady must know the dances for the ball. For now, let's finish the tour." He promptly walked to the door and held it open for us. We took the hint that he wouldn't take no for an answer.

We exited the inner halls through two enormous wooden doors so large a giant could step through. They were swung out wide and welcoming as we were delivered into one of the few courtyards on the grounds. The space was framed off by large, squared columns made of solid wood and stone. This particular area was reserved for training in archery, weights, knife throwing, hand-to-hand, and sword fighting.

Practice swords collided in a cacophony of sound. Thuds and grunts accompanied the din as weapons smacked against padded armor or exposed flesh. I could barely hear the tap of our shoes against the concrete as we walked down the shaded hall. My fingers itched to join in on the sparring.

It'd been one of the few sport-like activities I loved and picked up somewhat well, though it took a lot of encouragement from Grandma for me to join James in learning at first.

It made sense now why they'd pushed us to learn.

A vibrating sensation squeezed my mind again, and I sunk into a memory from when I was six years old.

"Tempy, you should join the fun James and Grandpa are having," Grandma had suggested.

I twirled in my glittering dress. "But I'm a princess," I declared. "I'll get dirty or get hurt. And I've got Daddy, James, and Grandpa to protect me."

Smiling, she grabbed my hand and pulled me into her lap, which was a struggle. Not only was I growing older and heavier, but her body had weakened after battling breast cancer.

"Yes, you're a princess," she conceded. "But someday you'll become queen, and every queen must know how to defend herself."

Grandpa beckoned me to join. Still hesitant and wanting to go back to playing with my tea set and dolls, I didn't move from my grandma's arms.

She set me down and turned me to face her. "Do you know what the duty of a queen is?"

I shook my head.

"She's the protector of her people. A hero in charge of her own destiny." She leaned in and whispered, "Don't you want to show others you can protect them too?"

I nodded.

James came barreling up and yanked my hand. "Come on, Tempy!"

"The choice is yours, sweetheart." Grandma brushed some hair behind my ear and let James pull me into the open space in the yard.

The memory faded and a tear rolled down my cheek. Whatever had happened, it felt so real. She'd felt real.

It was different this time, confirming that this ability to relive memories must be part of my powers.

"Tempy?" Ora called out.

They'd gotten ahead of me, and I hurried to catch up.

As we passed by, most of the men greeted us with chaste nods or bows. Others watched us, letting their eyes linger and travel across our bodies, sending an uncomfortable shiver down my spine. Our path became blocked as one man ran across to reach a tub of water. Calix cleared his throat to get the man's attention. Ignoring Calix, the man promptly tore off his tunic, then proceeded to splash water onto his face and chest. I blinked at his rudeness, while Ora stared wide eyed and admiring.

The man stood taller than both Calix and Frederick, towering over us at the height of maybe six-three, possibly six-four. His build was broad, and muscles defined. The bronzed-honey color of his skin came off darker when set in contrast against his wet, sandy-blond hair.

All right, maybe he looks like Thor, the God of Thunder... but he's rude.

Once he finished wiping his face and hair, he turned his glistening body toward us, behaving as though he were surprised by our presence. "Hello, Captain," he said to Calix. "Or do I address you as Lord Baldric at the moment?"

"I'm always Captain to you, Taren, until I pass the position. Now, answer me, why aren't you training?" Calix crossed his arms and eyed Taren with disapproval.

"Needed a cool down, *Captain*. It's hotter than working a forge in the burning season." His snake-like peridot eyes traveled to Ora, assessing. "Although, I may need another dose before heading back."

I think I just threw up in my mouth.

"Who are you lucky enough to be escorting today?" He didn't wait for Calix to properly introduce us before grabbing Ora's hand.

"You currently grasp the hand of Lady Ora, and this"—Calix gestured to me—"is the Lady Temperance."

Taren leaned over Ora's hand, but refrained from kissing it outright, though his lips almost grazed her knuckles with a teasing air. A few droplets of water slid off the tips of his hair, splashing onto her arm.

I rolled my eyes toward the courtyard, and my gaze was immediately arrested.

Frederick stood in full training garb, sword in hand, sparring with one of his men. Swift in his movements, he disarmed the other then met my eye. He glanced down at his sword then back up at me with a smile that made my heart jump.

"Lady Temperance?"

I turned my attention to Taren who looked at me with a furrowed brow and extended hand. I attempted a graceful curtsy and ignored the hand he offered. Having him breathe on me in any way wasn't appealing.

"Lady Temperance is my ward from my estate in the country," Calix said, steering Taren back into conversation with the cover story he'd decided for us. "Lady Ora is her companion. They're here for the Day of Peace celebrations." He'd informed us not to reveal the true nature of our meeting to avoid discrimination or suspicion. Word had already been sent to his household, so they could corroborate if needed. "They're under my protection during their stay." He stared Taren down the way James and Dad did with my dates back home.

"Taren!" We all looked at Frederick, who asked, "Join me in a spar?"

It was phrased as a question, but it clearly wasn't a request. Frederick wore a smile, but his body was tenser than normal.

"Yes, My King," Taren said. Grabbing the shirt, he patted the reflecting beads off himself before addressing us again. "*Captain*, ladies... until later."

He shot Ora a wink, and the faintest pink bloomed across her cheeks. I fought another eye roll so I wouldn't offend the large man. Before Taren got too far, Calix picked up a discarded leather cuirass and called out to him.

"Soldier!"

Taren turned in time to catch it, after which Calix added, "Better don your armor. Not only is it protocol, but the king seems more... enthusiastic than usual."

Taren arched an eyebrow at the hunk of armor. "Yes, *Captain*."

Why does he keep saying "Captain" like that? It sounds a bit disrespectful.

I gritted my teeth, trying to disguise my dislike for him while I watched him jog away. As Taren dressed himself, I met Frederick's mischievous gaze. I tilted my head, to which he responded with a shrug and a small bow.

Had he sensed my discomfort in Taren's company? Or his own? Maybe... both?

All the blood rushed to my face, and I bit my lip to conceal a smile.

"Moving on," Calix said.

He led us to a corner of the courtyard enclosed by marble banisters. A man sat at the stone desk in front of a pair of doors. Papers, books, weapons, and armor were scattered across the desk.

The old man hunched over some loose documents, comparing whatever he read with a large, red, leather-bound book. Squinting through a pair of tiny, round glasses, he occasionally snorted while shaking his head.

"Cranzly?" Calix addressed him, and the man looked up with a sideways grin that scrunched up his left eye.

"Cap, my boy! How you be?" Cranzly walked around the desk and slapped his hand against Calix's in a firm handshake.

Cranzly stood just an inch or so taller than me. His white, fraying hair was pulled back in a low-sitting ponytail. Wrinkles traced the tan skin around his eyes and cheeks, then disappeared into a white, trim beard. One long, white scar lined the left side of his face from temple to chin.

Calix released Cranzly's hand and said, "Doing great, General."

"Oh, drop the *General* bull—"

"Cranzly!" Calix nodded to us.

Ora and I giggled at his attempt to shield us from Cranzly's profanity.

"Yupsie! Apologies, although I'm sure it's nothing you haven't heard before." Cranzly raised an expectant eyebrow at us.

"Yes, but that doesn't mean it's proper," Calix said.

"Phooey, depends on the lady. People should be less sheltered." Cranzly looked us over with scrutiny. "Makes for stronger folk."

Calix smiled wryly and introduced Cranzly to us properly. "This is my former superior officer, General Abe Cranzly. Currently, he serves as our Master of Arms making sure our armies are well-equipped." He patted Cranzly on the shoulder. "No matter what we try, this man has no interest in retirement."

"From the mouth of a man who never rests," Cranzly said with a chuckle. "You do everything for the boy."

"That boy is our king." He elbowed Cranzly in the shoulder.

"You treat him like you're an overprotective big brother. You're worse than a kovchka and her cub." Cranzly shoved Calix slightly.

"Better than an ornery old grandpa," Calix jested.

Cranzly narrowed his eyes but smiled. "Great uncle. Say that—it's both accurate and makes me sound younger. Also says I'm great!"

That surprised me. Apart from the skin tone, he looked nothing like Frederick.

"You're Frederick's uncle?" I said.

Both men looked at me.

Cranzly hunched forward, giving off an aura of all seriousness. "Course I am, can't you tell? Boy got all my height and good looks."

The two men burst into laughter, and we joined their mirth.

Once we settled down, Cranzly said, "Nah, he takes majorly from his father in the looks and height department, not his mother's—my niece."

I braved a glance in Frederick's direction. His attention was fiercely focused on sparring. Taren's sword crashed against his, revealing the strength he exuded into each blow. The force and skill he demonstrated was mesmerizing.

My fingers twitched, itching to wrap around a hilt.

"Ladies." Calix's address snapped me from the hold Frederick had on me. "This is where I leave you. I must lead my men in training. If you exit through that way"—he gestured to another set of giant double doors—"you will reach the main halls."

"Thanks, Calix," I said while Ora and I curtsied. "I know showing us around isn't technically one of your duties."

"My pleasure, and pardon my correction, but it *is* part of my duties to make sure our king's guests are comfortable. I might be

Captain of the Guard, but I'm also the King's Left advisor." Calix bowed his head.

"Not his Right?" I asked.

I mean, the phrase back home is 'right-hand man' after all.

He shook his head with a light chuckle and said, "No. Only one particular person may hold that position, and I lack the requirements." Picking up on my confusion, he clarified his statement. "The Queen... his partner in rule. For now, the position lies empty until such a day Frederick chooses someone worthy of the title."

"He gets to choose?" Ora shot a not-so-subtle glance my way.

Luckily, the men didn't notice, but I gripped my hands together to withhold elbowing her in the ribs.

"Yes, though he is constantly pressured to consider options with certain parameters," Calix said.

No matter what world one was in, these so-called *parameters* were most likely the same. It was 'Marrying Royalty 101.' First they must be part of a noble bloodline, if not royalty. Second, they must be wealthy, powerful, and influential.

Someone shouted for Calix, and he excused himself again, but not before confirming our dance lesson that afternoon. Then he disappeared among his men while I linked my arm with Ora's and gently pulled her toward the exit.

"Wait, Tempy!" She resisted and twisted on her heel, and I spun back with her.

"What?"

Ora clamped our linked arms closer together. "Don't you want to enjoy the view a bit longer?"

"Why? So you can admire *Taren the Terrible* some more?" I teased.

"He was nice," Ora said, trying to defend him.

"He seems hinky and arrogant." I crossed my arms. "You deserve far better than that."

"Always our brave protector." Ora lay her head against my shoulder then lifted it again with an overzealous smile. "Can I look if I promise not to touch?"

I bobbed my shoulder, urging her away. "Fine," I permitted. "We'll stay for a few minutes, but then the library. Deal?"

"Yes, ma'am." She giggled while giving me a salute. "Besides, I know there's someone *you'd* like to keep your eyes on a little longer."

"Look at the time," I said, heading toward the exit. "Best be off."

"Okay! I'll stop." She grasped my arm, yanking me back.

I eyed her challengingly, while she pretended to lock her mouth shut with an invisible key. Satisfied, I turned back to watching the soldiers. Doing everything I could to not be caught watching the king, I kept my focus on the surrounding bystanders and duels closest to me.

A boy, who couldn't be more than fourteen, was up against a far more experienced man in his early twenties. He kept knocking the boy's sword out of his hand. I watched them closely, and after the fourth time his sword hit the dirt, I knew what was wrong.

"Useless!" the older one shouted. "How am I to get a proper workout sparring a child?" Tossing his own sword to the ground, he stomped toward the other end of the courtyard. "I'm getting a drink."

You could at least correct the kid, jerkface.

The boy slowly retrieved his sword and stared at it in defeat.

"Psst."

He looked up at me, his expression strained. I waved him over, but he shook his head and glanced in the direction his partner disappeared. I hid behind a pillar and leaned over the banister, motioning him over again. Hesitantly, he obeyed.

"What's your name?" I asked.

He was thin and gangly with black curls and chestnut skin. His fierce clementine eyes framed a wide-bridged nose and sharp cheeks.

"Collin, son of Count Eros." He glanced around. "What do you want?"

"I'm Temperance, and I can help you."

"I doubt I need help from a lady," Collin said, glancing at the practice sword in his hand.

"Trying hard not to be offended here, Collin. I probably would've started you on a single-handed sword, but that doesn't mean you can't use a longsword. Here." I adjusted his grip and said, "Wrap your thumb over the crossguard and keep your other hand gripped just above the pommel." I released his hand and stepped back. "Give it a swing."

Collin's face lit up as he swept his weapon back and forth. "Whoa, much better!"

I saw his partner returning and quickly whispered, "Hang in there."

He shot me an awe-inspired smile, which I returned before moving to stand beside Ora. Collin still didn't win the practice matches and took a few hits, but he didn't drop his sword again. His partner seemed pleased about Collin's improvement.

"You know something about sword fighting?"

I turned around to find Cranzly had returned.

"I may have won a sparring match or two," I said, trying not to boast.

"Impressive." He nodded with a vague, drooping smile. "No woman around the kingdom will learn how to swing a weapon anymore, at least not in broad daylight. Not since Minerva banned women from our armies and forced those capable to fight for her. Those who refused were imprisoned or executed." He folded his arms and shook his head. "Not only that, it's seen as unfashionable now. Think they can't win a husband that way. My opinion? Everyone should learn how to protect themselves."

"I like the way you think, sir," I said.

Cranzly placed his hands in his pockets. "You know, I still have some gear for ladies if you'd like to join in on training."

"Will I get in trouble?"

If it wasn't a normal occurrence, I didn't want to bring negative attention to myself.

He waved my question away. "Let 'em be fools. You're not joining the army, so I don't see a problem sparring with you. Besides, no one would dare question ol' General Cranzly."

I looked at Ora. "Interested?"

Ora pursed her lips then shook her head. "Nope. I'm not coordinated with that kind of stuff. But you should!"

Squaring my shoulders, I looked Cranzly in the eye and said, "I'll do it!"

"I like you, girl! We'll get along just fine." His smile warmed my heart. "Come on back. Let's find you something that fits."

Chapter 17

Temperance

The lightweight female cuirass Cranzly found was a double-breasted, tailed sparring dress, made of indigo and deep-brown, distressed leather. Adjustable laces lined the sides and back to ensure a snug fit. The hem started mid-thigh at the front of the bodice, then tapered down and around to a point at the back of my knees. Beneath it I wore a pair of fitted lightweight trousers and matching leather boots. For my own comfort and modesty, I opted for an ivory undershirt with capped sleeves to wear underneath the cuirass.

"Beautiful and adventurous!" Ora squealed in delight. "The king will definitely be impressed." She tugged on my arm, guiding me to the door. "Come on! Cranzly awaits."

My lungs tensed and my stomach dropped, forcing my muscles to cease movement. They were all trained soldiers. What if I choked like I did at my last tournament and embarrassed myself in front of everyone? In front of Frederick? I attempted to swallow the anxiety riding up, but my mouth was dry.

Ora faced me, her hands on her hips. "Don't start doubting. You're going out there! I'll drag you if I have to."

"But—"

"If roles were reversed, what would you tell me?"

After a heavy sigh, I said, "Don't care about what others think. Do what you want with no regrets."

"See? How can you possibly argue with *yourself*?" she said, matter-of-factly. "Find the courage."

Her last words rang something inside me—a mantra my Grandma taught me to use in moments I was about to step out of my comfort zone came to mind.

> *"Through the anxiety and the tears,*
> *I attempt to face an inward fear.*
> *Courage is the emotion I choose,*
> *Project it outward as my muse."*

After reciting it, my heart thrummed, feeling light. All the fear I'd been holding onto evaporated like rain on the desert sand. It worked way better than it ever had before.

Almost like a magic spell...

I shook my suspicion away, ready to go out there, head held high. I was a skilled swordswoman. I had nothing to be nervous about.

"Let's go."

One eyebrow raised, Ora silently followed me back to the training courtyard. When a beaming Cranzly spotted us, he excused himself from the group he'd been conversing with. My heart picked up speed when I noticed who stood among the four people.

Frederick's eyes moved from my boots, up my figure, and stopped at my face. His mouth hung slightly open in a half-smile, and his eyes lit up with astonishment. Or was it pride?

Don't look at me like that, Frederick. I'll never calm down.

I wiped my hands on my waist like I was adjusting the fit, when in reality I was trying to dry my now-perspiring palms.

"Who's she?" Ora's voice brought me back from Frederick's magnetic pull.

"Who?"

Ora rolled her eyes. "Wow... You don't notice anyone else when Frederick's around, do you? Not even someone that looks like her."

The girl standing next to him was tall and graceful with lovely, sandy tendrils styled on top of her head. Two strands of pale-green beads draped delicately across her bronzed, sun-kissed forehead. They accented perfectly with the mint-green satin and silver brocade gown that hung on her long frame. Her heart-shaped face was genetically adorned with a dainty, upturned nose, full petal-pink lips, and sharp peridot eyes.

She looks like Renaissance Barbie... while I just—

"I know I've encouraged your crush, but you need to practice taking your focus off him and examine what's around you," Ora said.

My newfound confidence wavered. "Encourage or discourage, it doesn't matter. I'm going home, so no romance for me."

"You look ready to learn," Cranzly said when he finally reached us. He handed me a wooden longsword with strands of blue leather wrapped around the grip of the hilt.

"The whole outfit fits like a dream, if not slightly snug." I smiled and took the sword, careful to keep the blade pointed toward the ground, but also high enough not to touch it. It felt comforting and invigorating to hold one again. This was a connection to home, to myself.

"It's better for posture and movement in practice if your protection is fitted closely. Makes you feel more connected with the armor like it's part of your body. It should be the same with your sword, as one's sword is—"

"An extension of one's self," I finished.

He chuckled. "Exactly. I see you respect the practice sword as if it were a sharpened blade. That's good. Let's find out what else you know." Cranzly led us over to a shaded area off to the side of where the men were practicing.

Many of the soldiers discreetly stole glances at us as we followed behind Cranzly, even more so than when we first entered the courtyard during Calix's tour. Somehow, I could feel one pair of eyes in particular following me—ones I knew were cobalt blue. I kept my back to him, meaning what I'd said to Ora. I shook off every feeling I had about Frederick and the mystery girl, who was able to both glare at me and smile at him simultaneously.

My chest panged. It didn't matter who she was to him. I'd be gone soon.

"Let's see what you got," Cranzly said.

I wondered how different Earth's historical combat was from Emeriz. Grandpa taught me all he knew, moves which my instructors back home thought were odd but efficient. If those were actually Emerizian fighting styles, maybe I could hold my own against Cranzly.

"You wouldn't happen to have helmets we could wear, would you?" I asked.

"Are you scared for yourself or for me, lass?"

"Both—well, more for you," I said. "Safety first, right?"

I liked to use my pommel when needed. Besides, I nearly knocked Frederick senseless at the cliffs.

With a laugh, Cranzly turned to one of the soldiers near the equipment area and hollered, "You there! Get me a couple of leather helms. We got a head basher here!"

Scattered chuckles circulated from the men surrounding us, the loudest coming from His Majesty. I facepalmed with one hand while the other still held the sword.

Cranzly pulled my hand from my face. "Ah, it's nothing to be embarrassed about, but how about we keep it to light taps for headshots? Save the all-out force for the sparring dummies."

Collin ran the helms over to us and whispered, "Good luck," before he slipped away.

Cranzly and I faced each other and bowed, met our swords in the middle, and circled around each other a hundred-and-eighty degrees. I took my stance—low to the ground, left foot forward and sword on my right side near my chest with the point toward the sky.

He's older and hasn't seen battle in some time... I should go easy on him.

"Begin!" Cranzly shouted.

I stepped forward with my right foot and swung my sword at a forty-five-degree angle toward his right shoulder. He blocked it easily, so I quickly shifted my aim to his left side. Cranzly was too fast for me in his defense and blocked me again.

Taking another step forward, I aimed for a diagonal cut across his chest. He deflected the attack. I'd tried to block his blows, but the wind would be knocked out of me, or I'd feel the sting of his sword reverberate clear down to my bones.

Dang, he was spry for an old dude. I wouldn't hold back anymore. It was time for some Earth-style historical combat.

My moves took him by surprise, making him hesitate. He could still counter my blows, but I got in a few taps to his helm. A few yelps or hollers from the soldiers any time I made a hit told me we'd drawn a small audience to our sparring.

After our first match, Cranzly stepped back and eyed me as if trying to deduce something.

"You've won a match or two, eh?" he asked, repeating my humble boast from before.

I shrugged. "Could have been a tournament or two."

Cranzly laughed and slapped his knee. "You hustled me!"

I looked around while steadying my breathing and covered my mouth to release a cough. I raised my sword again.

"Ready for more?"

"How about an exchange of techniques?" Cranzly asked. "You've got some moves I've never seen, while some of the ones I'm familiar with could use some refining."

Being trained by a former Emerizian General was an offer that no swordsman or swordswoman would ever turn down. I tried to picture the jealous look on James' face when he found out that I was given the opportunity.

"Yes, please!" I smiled and relaxed my stance.

"Let's get to work," he said to me, then to the surrounding gawkers, "All of *you* get to work!"

CHAPTER 18

FREDERICK

A warrior goddess had blessed us with her presence. I'd stood motionless as Temperance had strutted onto the courtyard with a glowing smile and an air that any ruler would envy. She wielded the sword with a practiced hand and seemed more comfortable than I'd seen her since we met. Ecstatic even.

In the beginning of their exchange, Temperance displayed Eslanian moves and stances but seemed hesitant in her movements. Then, something shifted in her demeanor, and she unleashed a different style of sparring that had Cranzly on the defense.

She hadn't been lying about being Eslanian, but which faction taught this style of combat?

When Cranzly mentioned he'd decided to take on a protégé, I never dreamed it'd be her. It wasn't that I believed her to be an incapable swordswoman. It just wasn't done in Linall anymore.

For years, Cranzly had loudly and decidedly voiced that he'd bring such things back into our way of life in Linall, and I hadn't discouraged him.

After all, just because women couldn't join the army, didn't mean they couldn't learn to defend themselves. I'd always known this, but most women were still too afraid of the repercussions brought down by Minerva were she ever to find out. If Temperance could start the ripple, I hoped others might follow.

Temperance looked so focused that I wondered if she'd noticed the soldiers stealing glances or openly watching. No, not only watching... some were leering. My eye twitched ever so slightly, a twinge of jealousy gnawing at the back of my mind. The way the ensemble hugged her figure made her look unbelievably *tempting*. I made a mental note to get her some bulkier sparring clothes and armor. Or perhaps have her train somewhere private and away from their lustful stares.

Cranzly held a hand up to end the first match. Temperance adjusted her cuirass at the waist, drawing my gaze to the curve of her body. My heart stuttered.

Someone sternly grabbed my shoulder, jostling me out of the places my mind had been about to go. Calix offered me a goblet of water.

"You look thirsty, My King." Then under his breath, so only I heard, he added, "You're salivating like a dog."

"How considerate of you, Calix." I gulped down the contents of the cup and shoved it back into his hands with enough force that it pressed into his chest.

Calix's stupid smile didn't budge, knowing full well it would annoy me.

He was right to distract me, of course. My focus needed to be elsewhere, otherwise Temperance would get involuntarily pulled into the politics played at court. Keeping her safe was becoming more and more important to me. Safe from what, I didn't know—but something stirred inside me when she was near. As much as I disliked the idea, I knew I had to keep some distance between us.

"A most unladylike pastime," Persephone said from my side. "You wouldn't be pleased to see me displayed in such a manner."

I glanced at Persephone. Her bottom lip was dropped in an open pout toward Temperance. When her eyes met mine, she watched me with a deceptively coy stare as her lips parted into a deviously brilliant smile. That look had stolen hearts and won her many proposals over the years. However, since I took the throne, it had become a mask she saved for only me.

Fortunately, I'd been raised with her, and therefore able to see through her charade. Growing up, she didn't give two coppers about me, at least not until my coronation. Suddenly she was always at my side, putting on airs as the perfect, pampered princess.

I didn't need a princess. I needed—my gaze flicked to Temperance and stayed.

"No indeed, milady," I replied, my eyes on Temperance. "But then, you lack a sense of adventure."

"My *dear*... King Frederick."

My brow furrowed at her endearment.

"Why must you always tease me?" She grazed her hand down my upper arm, gently nudging me.

Why must you circle me like a territorial ferret sniveling around its next meal?

I rolled my shoulders back like I was stretching them, accomplishing my desired outcome. Persephone removed her hand. No need for her or others to get the wrong idea.

Temperance and Cranzly began their next match.

"I do so, Lady Persephone," I said, looking down at her seriously, and she beamed at the attention, "because I hope someday it'll help mold you into a beautiful woman."

Persephone's face fell instantly, and her lips quivered in anger.

This wasn't the first time I'd said something like this to her. The disappointing thing was that she never seemed to grasp the simple truth: she'd never win my affections, regardless of her beauty, because she lacked it on the inside.

Persephone never saw the point in interacting with anyone unless it raised her status, though she couldn't be entirely blamed. Her family practically raised her like cattle to be traded for more wealth and power. My empathy stopped there, however, because she relished the attention and perks she received.

Our parents had brought up the possibility of an official betrothal before mine were murdered, but with Calix's help, I'd been able to avoid a forced engagement. However, the pressure to merge our houses remained.

"If she continues on like this, rumors may spread and draw the attention of the High Queen," Persephone said. "Aren't you worried about the danger this presents to that girl? Or the kingdom? She could be taken... or worse." She appeared poised, but her tone came out like a gritted hiss. "Heads will roll, and not just hers."

My shoulders stiffened. Dame Boetius' fate came to mind. Persephone was a stark contrast to her mother, who had served as a queen's guard for my mother. Dame Boetius refused to join Minerva and perished during the purge the same night my parents died. Instead of honoring her mother, Persephone appeared to hold nothing but open hostility toward her.

"Trust in your king," I replied simply.

"Like my parents did yours—" Her face froze, and she tried to slip her mask back in place, but she'd caught her words too late.

I shot her a glare full of warning. "As your father and brother do now."

"Excuse me, My King. I came to deliver news to my brother and be on my way." With a gritted smile and the flared nostrils of an angry bull, Persephone curtsied with the utmost amount of poise and pointed aggression.

Gesturing toward Taren, I said, "I would never want to delay your departure."

Persephone gracefully floated over to Taren and elbowed him in the gut to break his attention from Temperance. They had a hushed exchange, then Persephone departed.

"Calix, remind me why I allow them to stay in my court?" I asked, my eyes glued to Temperance.

"They donate generously to your cause, and their father and grandfather are respectable men, if not a little materialistic," he said calmly. "They fight for a free Emeriz—a return to the old ways."

"Not all the old ways need to be revived. Some things can stay buried. We must move forward, expand our knowledge."

"Yes, once we find the other Descended—whoa," Calix said, awestruck by the sparring match before us.

Temperance and Cranzly's swords locked at the crossguard. She pushed upward and angled her sword in order to tap the top of Cranzly's helm with the pommel. He stumbled back and chuckled while some soldiers whooped and watched with more interest. Had he not been helmeted and she'd used her full force, that blow would have bashed his head in. She was talented.

A scholastedite approached and handed Calix a note. Breaking the seal, he read its contents. "It appears that you're done sparring for the day," he said. "The Temple of Emeriz has a new high priest and requests your presence. He states it's a matter of spiritual importance."

I grabbed the note, giving it a once over to confirm his words. "Fine."

"One more thing," Calix said, stopping me from running off.

"Treat Persephone more kindly. Her family is crucial to our cause. We shouldn't give them an excuse to take their aid elsewhere."

"She's disingenuous and unpleasant—flying about like she's better than everyone."

Calix shook his head. "You're not children anymore. You can't push someone down when you have a problem with them. Rise above it."

"Since I was crowned, that family has been trying to sink their claws into me—doing their best to convince everyone that a marriage between us is desirable." It took all my practiced self-control not to explode my frustrations on him. "No. I won't have my Queen as someone who has in one way or another sabotaged every other possible candidate. Whether they caught my attention or not, she did so. That woman spread rumors about me... about us. Not to mention, despicably throwing her brother at the problem. I can't even recall the number of times Taren has seduced a woman to get them out of the way."

Calix inhaled a deep breath and gave me a stern look. "All I'm suggesting is to show her indifference rather than hostility. For the sake of your other relationships." He nodded in Temperance's direction. "Things can get complicated for those you care for."

The fight inside me deflated at the thought of Temperance's safety. I handed the note back to Calix and headed toward the soldiers' chambers to clean up and change. As I went through the double doors, I looked back at Temperance one last time. Immersed in their sparring, she paid no mind to the gawking audience of soldiers—some rooting for her and others looking on in disapproval.

Temperance was truly remarkable.

I smiled and left the courtyard behind.

The castle chapel was a fourth of the size of the Great Cathedral in the center of Linall. It also lacked all the grandeur and splendor of its exceptional counterpart. This chapel was only meant for worship of the Superior Goddess, Emeriz. No other demi-gods or demi-goddesses of previous Descended, like Riona, were represented, while the Great Cathedral catered and gave worship to all. As Minerva had also sacrilegiously *encouraged* all kingdoms to erect a golden statue to stand alongside that of the Superior Goddess, I preferred this chapel to the cathedral.

Dimly burning candles cast soft light against the walls of brick and clay. A great, circular window encompassed the majority of the ceiling, so the light of the heavens shone through. Four small, natural waterfalls spewed spring waters inside, dispensing into a moat around the room.

I hadn't waited long when a figure dressed in emerald linen robes appeared in the archway behind the statue. The trim lining the robes was twisted and embroidered with colored threads of violet, blue, white, and amber indicating this was the new high priest.

Why have we been sent a new high priest?

"My Lord Majesty," he said, bowing deeply, and pushed back his hood.

I grabbed the dagger at the small of my back with my right hand and swung the priest into the wall with my left, holding him in place. When I raised the blade to his throat, the man chuckled.

"Your Majesty, what if someone were to see? The courtiers are bound to talk." The assassin smiled, not the least bit nervous about the blade breaking skin on his neck.

"Heshrin," I said firmly through gritted teeth, "where is our actual high priest?"

"And here I thought you might have missed me." He shot me the most pitifully fake pout I'd ever seen. "You know… after I saved your life. Thought we had something special."

"Did you murder the high priest?"

"What if I did? You gonna kill me? Lock me up?" Heshrin moved his face closer to mine. "Are you so innocent yourself? Have you not had others killed in your rebellion?"

My abilities had urged me to let him go at the tavern, but people's intentions changed all the time. If he'd killed the high priest to secure a way into the castle, I wouldn't let him get away.

I pressed my elbow into his chest, cutting off some of his airflow.

"The high priest, Heshrin?"

He smiled, deviously enthusiastic, then stuttered, "Yep, that's me."

All control gone, I slammed him against the wall again. "Where is he!"

Heshrin groaned. "Fine. You're so boring. He's not dead—just *cramped* at the moment. He'd been overwhelmed, so I offered a solution."

I processed his words for their truth. My muscles relaxed, and I stepped back. I flipped the dagger in the air and caught it before returning it to the sheath at my back.

"What solution?" I asked, irritated.

"Details, details, details. There are other things we must discuss first." He waved my comment away, like where he'd stashed our high priest was the least of his worries.

"For instance?"

"Our contract," he said. "Terms, payment, ways I can aid your little rebellion."

"What do you know of my plans?" If there was a mole, I needed to snuff them out.

"Ah-ah!" He held up a finger. "I believe those are details. Until we come to an agreement, you get nothing."

I folded my arms, staring him down, and mentally trying to will the information from him.

"*Grrr!*" Heshrin narrowed his eyes and overly mimicked my stance as though I were a menacing, idiot brute. "Do the ladies faint dead-away at that smolder?"

I bit my tongue and kept my stance firm.

Heshrin broke his imitation of me and gave in. "All right, come here."

I leaned in, straining to hear his whisper.

"I work in the shadows."

Rolling my eyes, I stepped back.

"What?" he asked. "In my line of work, any idiot can assume how I get my information. I doubt you'd be happy having me spell it out for you. Now, let's get down to business." He cleared his throat. "I will provide my services in trade for an allowance and my own private quarters in the palace."

"The priests' room's not good enough for you?"

"That hole the priests deem worthy to be called a room is fine for my guise, but not my experiments. I need space to give the creative juices air to breathe." Heshrin spread his arms out. "Somewhere more inspiring."

"How do you intend to keep up the appearance as a dedicated man of the Superior Goddess? It's more than just wearing the robes."

"Oh, you are a rule breaker, aren't you? A surprising trait for a haloed hero." He crossed his arms. "You need to agree to my terms before I reveal anything else."

"How am I supposed to agree to a deal when I don't know exactly what I'm getting out of it?" I asked.

"Not my problem. Agree to the terms, we talk. Don't, and I walk."

Accepting the terms without more information would be a gamble. He was money-driven, so if he left, he would find another wealthy benefactor. Who knew what they would use him for? I raised an eyebrow, my determination unwavering. No. There was a reason he chose me specifically.

Relaxing my stance, I gestured to the door. "Then walk."

Heshrin narrowed his eyes, studying me. My breathing slowed, and my instinct inflamed—burning away any doubt he'd let go of a deal he'd put so much effort into.

I saw his truth.

My subconscious willed him to tell me something. The silence was deafening. The longer I allowed my ability to be enacted, the more clouded my ears became. My sight sharpened, clarifying every line and color, contrasting in a way that hurt my eyes. Yet, my gaze never wavered. I didn't dare let it.

As if I'd slowed time, a smile oozed across the assassin's face like a snail over a damp floor.

"Well, well, well," Heshrin said.

My focus shattered, and my eyes involuntarily closed, shielding them from the dull ache that'd been seeping in. I blinked a few times until my eyes adjusted. Had I just tapped into the persuasion aspect of my abilities? My mother hadn't even mastered that art of our power.

"As exhilarating as our staring contest was, time is money," Heshrin said. "To move this along, I'll give you a little something." He looked from left to right, then placed his nimble fingers together in front of his chest. "You're aware I'm an assassin?"

I gave him a flat stare. "I'm aware."

"Voilà." Opening his hands palms up, he grinned and raised his eyebrows so high I thought they'd reach his hairline.

My lips pressed together, holding back a string of profanities. Frustration ripped through my chest like a kovchka tearing into its prey. My patience, almost nonexistent the entire conversation, now evaporated like steam.

"Am I supposed to be impressed? Flourish your hands again and maybe you'll convince me."

"Don't toss that aside like it's nothing, you fool! This is war, and I'm a tool—a useful one." Placing his hands behind his back, he stood a bit straighter.

At the very least, his skillset as an assassin would be beneficial in gaining and passing on information undetected. The chaos that would come were he to give his services to someone whose loyalty was pliable as a blade of grass, ready to move any direction the winds decided to blow, would be insurmountable. I didn't have to play the assassin pawn unless absolutely necessary.

"Do we have an accord?" he said with a smirk, hand outstretched.

I gripped his hand in agreement and yanked him forward. "Under the pretense that this is merely the start of negotiations."

"Of course, King Frederick. I now serve you." Heshrin tightened his hold and placed his index finger on the inside of my wrist. "*Bound in blood, the vow is made. If your word be broken, your life be paid.*"

Black veins crawled up my elbow from his finger. I tried to rip my hand from his but was unable to do so until the black faded and Heshrin released me.

"What in Emeriz's name was that?" I demanded.

"The sealing of our contract." He heaved a sigh of relief.

"What did you do? Are you a—"

"I'm no Descended. I dabble in the magical arts, but don't submerge. Only enough for what's needed in my line of work." He held up the hand I'd shook. "As for this, verbal agreements are topsy-turvy. It's easy for someone to claim they never agreed to anything, and then I've got to waste time and trouble killing them. Paper trails are out, so this is necessary."

"What. Does. It. Do?"

He smiled wryly. "If we—and by we, I mean you—don't hold up your end of the agreement we reach before our second handshake, you'll find yourself... uncomfortable."

"Uncomfortable, as in?" I asked.

The corners of his lips drooped downward while he inspected his fingernails. "Dead. Lifeless. Worm food. Finally get to meet whatever big deity in the sky, water, or cloud you believe in."

"And if you fail on your end?"

"I always hold up my end. Better for business." He smirked.

Fair was not in this man's vocabulary.

"Shall we discuss your meticulous details?" I asked.

"I require a hundred onyx along with five-hundred scepters per month, and as mentioned before, my own private chambers in the palace." He walked over to the altar and ran his finger across the statue seated there as if checking for dust. "Preferably, near the catacombs."

"Yes, because it's not unusual for a priest to be conducting experiments in his private chambers near the catacombs," I spat. Not allowing myself to imagine the kind of experiments he had up his sleeve, I reluctantly agreed. "Fine. An allowance, and I'll grant you access to one of the vacant storage rooms just outside the catacombs."

"Perfect. Now send for me when you need to."

He turned to leave, but I gripped his arm.

"Tell me where our high priest is and how you plan on playing your part."

"I've trained in many fields to make blending and disappearing effortless." Heshrin wrapped his long cold fingers around my hand and shoved it off his sleeve. "I can pose a position in any church, temple, or religion—even by way of the scholastedites. Many trades as well, although priests are best. People are more forthcoming with information to such confidants."

"So you'll use this position to weed out any moles," I said, processing the possibilities.

"If you'd like a demonstration, I'll gain more intel on your newest additions to court." I tensed, and Heshrin clapped his hands. "I could find out if one of them fancies you."

Ignoring his pointed comments, I said, "You could be just as productive without being our high priest. Just hide amongst the rest of the priesthood."

Heshrin heaved an exuberant sigh and dropped his shoulders. "By Endra's toe, you're just so—gah! New rule. Don't question my methods."

His ability to step between trite and lackadaisical was perplexing. One moment he'd be cool and composed—almost dangerous—then the next, he behaved like a juvenile child.

"You invoke the name of the first Lessor Descended of shadow and false impression. Why shouldn't I question you on that alone?" I asked.

"That's a little"—Heshrin strolled over to me, and flicked my nose with his index finger —"on the nose, don't you think?"

I fought the urge to beat him senseless. "This is my kingdom, my rebellion, my money... my contract. You will bring me the high priest, and you will also work and hide amongst the priesthood members."

Heshrin pondered over my words and ran his fingers through his platinum hair. "I must say, in some ways your persistence in these negotiations has been fun—at least original."

"We'll keep it simple. You let me utilize your skills the ways I see fit, and you get your allowance and chambers." I held out my hand. "Do we have an accord?"

"Yes, Kingly." He shook my hand.

Placing my index finger on his wrist, I repeated his words, "*Bound in blood, the vow is made. If your word be broken, your life be paid.*"

This time *his* veins glowed black like the charred branches of a lifeless tree.

Once the color faded, I leaned in. "Now we're both bound by death. Where's my high priest?"

"Fine... you win," Heshrin said, stepping over to one of the surrounding waterfalls and retrieving an object from behind it.

He approached me holding up a small circular mirror. The assassin eyed me, then brought his focus to the mirror in his palm.

"*Through shattered glass and the Goddess' grace, release the soul from this mirrored place,*" he whispered, and waved his free hand over the mirror.

Ice and fog crawled across the reflective surface. A glint of light bounced off the edge, and a figure moved beneath its glass. Heshrin dropped the mirror, shattering it across the floor. No sooner than the pieces touched the ground, they evaporated into an icy fog.

My eyes went wide, seeing the man prostrate on the floor the cloud had left behind.

"You trapped him inside a mirror?" I pinned my glaring outrage on Heshrin.

"You saw it. You really need me to clarify?" Heshrin brushed his hands together as though he were done with it.

The high priest was unharmed but confused. He didn't connect Heshrin to the incident, so we told him he'd been ill with fever-induced hallucinations. Kind soul he was, the high priest trusted that we were truthful. He even thanked Heshrin for 'taking care of him.'

Unbelievable.

CHAPTER 19

TEMPERANCE

Cranzly took off his helmet and wiped the beads of sweat on his brow.

"Tomorrow we'll meet at daybreak," he said.

"Sounds like a plan." I took off my own, the cool breeze fanning my warm face. It felt invigorating and familiar. I handed the helm to Cranzly and bowed gratefully. "Thanks for taking the time to teach me. I hope I'll be a good student."

Cranzly blushed. "It helps you have foundational skills to build off of."

He departed back to his corner of the practice yard. I glanced around and noticed that Ora, Calix, and Frederick were nowhere to be found. I'd been so engrossed in sparring that I'd become oblivious to my surroundings.

I hadn't even seen Frederick leave, but I figured that was a good thing. He'd be busy with his duties as king, and I needed to find a way home to my family. The lesson served as a distraction from the homesickness, but now that I was alone, it hit me full force. I missed so many things.

Hearing Mom rattle on to Dad about what happened in her novel or the latest neighborhood gossip. Dad belting, "Oh, what a beautiful morning," through the house the moment the sun came up. James and his many projects, never satisfied with trying just one thing at a time. Brett and his way of cheering me up any time I was feeling down, usually by putting on an impromptu comedy routine. Despite having Ora here with me, I missed Nora's steady presence.

I considered having Ora scry for me again... but that would probably make it worse.

A dust devil swirled in the dirt across from me and faded away. Kicking the ground, I resolved to stop moping and find my way home. Eager to get to the library, I rushed toward the room where I'd changed into my sparring gear. When I rounded the corner into the alcove that led to the female changing rooms, my depth perception momentarily failed me. I bumped into the corner of the wall, knocking the practice sword to the ground. But before I could pick it up, I was overshadowed and blocked.

"Excuse me." I looked up and immediately rolled my eyes. "Sir—"

"Call me Taren." He was freshly bathed, his hair slicked back in a warrior's wolf-tail.

"We just met. Shouldn't we stick to using your title?" I asked.

Even though it was the norm back home, calling him by his first name felt too personal here. This wasn't an association I wanted to encourage.

"But I sense we'll be great friends." Taren placed his hand against the wall above me and leaned in, giving me a strong whiff of all the oils he'd applied to himself. The scent overpowered my senses, and my head tensed in protest.

Wasn't he all about Ora earlier? He's fickle as they come.

"Well, I'm in a hurry, so can you back up?" I pushed against his chest, which turned out to be a mistake, because Taren grasped my hand and grazed my arm until he had a grip on my elbow, pulling me in closer.

"You'd be prettier if you relaxed a little," he asserted. "Why don't I treat you to something delicious?"

"I'm going to ignore that veiled insult and say again so your overly inflated ego can properly process it—I'm in a rush. If you hold me here any longer, I can't promise it'll end well for you." I stared him down, chin out and eyes hard.

His snake eyes twinkled like he was trying to hypnotize me. He paired it with a smile that could cut through stone.

"You're definitely not boring."

I didn't have a chance to figure out what exactly he meant by that before Taren grasped at my waist and attempted to pull me into an embrace. My instincts kicked into hyperdrive, and I bent back and shoved the base of my palm as forcibly as possible up at his nose. There was an audible crack, and he stumbled back in agony, giving me a small window to escape, but before I could take a step, he grabbed my collar, pulling me back toward him. Blood ran from his nose, dripping onto his green embroidered tunic.

"You little—"

I gripped his shoulders and pulled him down to my knee. I wasn't sure whether my knee connected to his groin or stomach, but it was enough that he fell to the floor. While he rolled on the ground in pain, I ran from the practice yards. I'd have to go back for my dress later. Lingering anywhere near there alone would be a bad idea.

Safely hidden away in my chambers, I locked the door behind me and pressed my back against it. I waited for the sound of footsteps. When none came, my emotions poured out in waves of tears and heaving sobs. I collapsed into a heap on the floor and dropped my head to my knees. At that moment, all I wanted was to go home and never see Emeriz again.

The nerve of that man, thinking he can just have his way with whomever he pleases. Once I tell Frederick, he'll...

It was then I realized that I couldn't tell him. The scandal would bring unwanted attention to me and make things far worse. I was already struggling to get the information I needed. Did I really want something else pulling me away from my search? If I didn't, though, I knew Taren would get away with it, and such a person shouldn't be allowed to think that was acceptable.

However, he was a high-ranked noble, and I was a stranger. They could choose to believe him over me by that alone. I had to hope the beat down I'd given him was enough to discourage him from acting like that toward anyone in the future.

A soft meow drew my attention to the balcony. A small, elegant cat perched perfectly on the top of a banister pillar. I wiped the tears from my eyes and stared at the creature. Black fur, white spots, and a pair of wide, plum eyes.

"Tundra?"

The cat cocked its head to the side and readied itself for pouncing. Once airborne, she transformed into her large, wildcat form. She pranced over to me and met my forehead with hers.

"Hello, girl." I giggled and allowed a few more tears to escape. "Sorry we're meeting again with me in a bad mood, but I'm happy to see you."

Tundra pulled back, then lay down, placing her head in my lap.

"I guess I should be surprised by your magic trick, but I think I've learned to expect the unexpected here."

Tundra purred as I scratched behind her ears.

"All this magic and wonder, Tundra, but I miss my family. I miss feeling safe." I rubbed my nose.

Leaning my head against the door, I stared out at the scenery beyond my balcony. A cool wind blew into my room, satisfying the heat burning my cheeks. Leaves fluttered in with the wind, and as they chased each other, they created another dust devil in the corner of my room. Tundra, suddenly uneasy, stood in front of me until the wind cut out. Oddly, the leaves fell flat and swift rather than their natural, listless drift.

"It's okay, girl," I said, patting Tundra at her side. "Just the wind."

Tundra walked in a circle as if chasing her tail, and once again transformed into a small, domestic cat to paw at the door desperately.

"Calm down, I'll let you out."

The moment I opened the door, she bolted down the hall and stopped at the top of the stairs. Her eyes bore into mine, and something inside nudged me to follow her.

Tundra walked along the dark, wooden beams near the ceiling. With her out of sight, I hoped I wouldn't look like some lunatic following a cat around. Every now and then, I snuck glances upward to be sure I hadn't lost her: a precaution to avoid crossing paths with anyone—Taren most of all. Part of me wanted to find him and let him have it verbally, but I reasoned it wouldn't be the smartest decision.

That little beatdown should've said it all anyway, right? Or angered him to the point of revenge. Would he come after me?

The library doors loomed before me. Tundra leapt from the beams and glided down the round column as though gravity didn't exist. She entered through the open doors tail high like she owned the place.

Walking in, I inhaled the blissful scent of books. Being inside the massive room put my anxieties at ease. My fingers brushed along the spines, their familiar feel evoking strands of memory.

Nora and I often exchanged books. Sometimes we'd even read together, taking turns reading the chapters aloud.

The memory made me homesick, so I focused on the rushing of the large waterfall fountain at the back of the library just below the giant window—letting the sound of the water pelting against the black rocks wash away the stress.

Tundra rubbed against my legs, waking me from my ritual. I glanced around to see if anyone witnessed my momentary lapse, but no one was there. Tundra proceeded toward the back of the library, and I followed. Once we reached the back wall, she turned right, leading us up a staircase. Déjà vu picked at me like a five-year-old picking a scab.

On the third level, Tundra sauntered over to a blank wall in a dark, dusty corner.

A dead end.

This is what I get for following an animal.

Sensing an animal's intent didn't guarantee they would lead me to the answers I needed or offer me any sort of help. It wasn't like I was Snow White.

I turned to leave, but something collided with the top of my head and yanked my hair, tugging me back around. Pure white feathers drifted through the air like a pillow burst during a slumber party. Effectively annoyed, I searched for what had attacked me. A soft coo came from the corner where a perfect, white dove sat on a small, ornate perch against the wall.

Tundra stood on her hind legs with one paw against the wall while the other waved around trying to touch the kamikaze bird.

"What do you stupid doves have against me?"

The dove cocked its head to the side, then nuzzled into its

feathers, adjusting them from the collision. I moved to leave but stopped when the bird cooed again.

I met the bird's eye in challenge. "Shoo!"

A sliver of calm dipped into my irritation, rippling throughout my chest and body. The longer I held eye contact, the more at ease I became.

"What do you animals want from me?" I asked.

The dove adjusted its stance, talons making a small scratching sound against the perch. My eyes caught on an image etched into the sconce beneath: a circle in the middle of a teardrop with tulip-like prongs. Just like my pendant.

My eyes flew to Tundra who'd somehow clawed her way up the side of the wall and positioned herself next to the dove. The animals were just getting weirder... leading me to odd places and going against nature by not killing each other.

I bit my lip and lifted the pendant to check for differences between the identical shapes. The engraved words on the back shifted again before my eyes.

"Blood of the Goddess, hear my call, paint the archway across the wall," I whispered aloud.

The instant the last syllable left my lips, an archway painted itself across the blank canvas of the wall. Heart pounding, I stepped forward to touch the fresh paint, but my hand waved at air. A painting no longer, the archway had taken on a true, physical presence.

Had I just created a secret passage? Having magic was freaking awesome!

I poked my head through to observe the dark room. The only light came from the sun filtering in through a stained-glass window, projecting a shadowed reflection of the image on the opposite wall—

a diamond with four connecting colors: violet, blue, white, and amber.

"Cool."

I braved whatever waited for me on the other side and stepped through, filled with an unbridled anticipation. When my fourth step met the stone ground, it glowed violet and the room shook violently.

I stumbled back, bracing my hand on the wall. "Okay, adventure over!"

When I turned to run out, fear crept into my soul.

The archway was gone, leaving me trapped and alone.

"Blood of the Goddess, hear my call, paint the archway across the wall!" I scratched and banged against the wall, but nothing happened.

All at once, the quaking stopped, and the purple hue disappeared. Apart from the soft light coming through the stained-glass window, the room darkened again. Nervous I might trigger something else, I remained completely still, barely breathing.

Little flecks of purple lights flitted up from the floor like dandelion seeds dancing in the wind. In one fell swoop, hundreds of them whooshed around me, whipping my hair in all directions. I covered the top of my head to protect it from the swarm of unknown magic. Altogether, they flew upward and embedded themselves into the black, rocky ceiling, creating the appearance of a night sky dappled with stars. Firelight torches lit up one by one, revealing the spiraling staircase.

Unable to inhale, my chest puffed out short breaths that transformed into laughter. Hands shaking, tears creased the corners of my eyes. Thrill and disbelief spun in my mind like a top.

It was a real place!

There'd be no alarms, no waking up, no interruptions at all. Nothing would stop me from opening the door. I smiled, dashing up and around the curving staircase. No oppressive force held me back as I rushed past the window, which in reality had glass.

I made a mental note to investigate that later.

At the top, I went straight to the door. My blood zoomed through my brain with an urgency that wouldn't be denied. Logically, I knew there was plenty of time to open the elusive door. This wasn't a dream, but uneasiness that it might all disappear nestled deep in my chest. Grasping the knob, I turned it.

Locked.

Like the window, I'd held a small hope it would be different from my dream. I knelt to inspect the lock. I grinned, confirming what I had discovered in my dream from the night before.

"This whole time..." I lifted my grandma's pendant from my neck and delicately placed its face into the lock.

The amethyst glowed, and warmth spread through my stomach and rose to my eyes as calm swept over me. The feeling wavered when I caught my reflection in the knob. My irises were a vibrant plum near the pupils and faded into a pale blue. Then, the color swirled and reverted to periwinkle blue. When the stone of the pendant lost its glow, I removed it from the lock and slipped the chain back around my neck.

This is it...

With a deep breath to quiet the anxiety throbbing in my heart, my fingers graced the doorknob. I bit my bottom lip, reining in the anticipation that after all these years, I'd finally find out what lay behind the door. Twisting it, I held my breath until I heard the click. Giddiness buzzed throughout my body.

"Yes!" I swiftly pushed the door open.

When I stepped inside, torches flared to life, allowing me to see everything that had been denied me in dreams. A few thousand books, tomes, and journals encircled the spacious round room, stacked on their sides, one on top of another. Loose sheets of paper and scrolls stuck out from between some of the books almost haphazardly. Were it not for the gaps here and there, allowing me to see glimpses of the large, gray stones making up the wall behind them, I would've assumed the room was *built* of books.

To my right stood a unique wooden desk. It was carved out of the bottom of a tree that extended twenty or thirty feet up toward the ceiling where its branches reached out, draping bundles of multicolored irises. I smiled, remembering the ones that overtook one section of Grandma's garden. They were her favorite. It was weird to see them in a tree, though. How was that even possible?

Directly across the room was a set of green, velvet drapes with gold embroidery woven and twisted into a large tree. I maneuvered around some artifacts and unusual objects to get to them. When I flung open the drapes, sunlight poured into the room. Stepping out onto the balcony, my breath was stolen away.

I could see everything from the ocean in the West to the mountains in the East. We'd arrived in the kingdom so late I hadn't truly gotten to see it. Compared to Kanthe, Linall was far more elegant. Cobblestone lined the streets of houses stacked on buildings that reached and twisted toward the sky. Colorful flowers and vines crawled up the sides, competing to reach the top. Some of the rooftops glimmered with silver tiles, creating the illusion of starlight flickering throughout the city. However, one small section of the city lay broken and charred like a fourth-degree burn.

What happened there?

I turned back to the room. A pedestal stood dead center in the middle of it all. A gemstone the size of a lemon, infused with red and purple, hovered in the air above it. The core of my soul flexed emotions both wrong and whole, projecting a calm imbalance into my heart. Entranced by the gem , it pulled me in closer until I was mere inches from it. Peace washed over me again and again, like it was trying to push out the wrongness.

Blurred crimson engulfed my vision as soon as my finger touched a chipped area of the stone. I squinted my eyes to clear my sight and tried to pull my hand from the gem, but it wouldn't budge.

My surroundings warped and twisted around me. It was like being on a merry-go-round encased in a funhouse mirror, making me nauseous. When it all came to a sudden halt, my head swam, and the red cleared to the edges of my vision.

I walked down a large, ornately arched hallway toward a blindingly white stone door. When I attempted to stop, my feet moved forward, and my hand reached out to open the door against my will.

Am I possessed? Where am I?

Panicked, I willed my body to obey me—to do anything but walk—but I continued to enter the perfectly white room. The sun's rays shone through three silver archways lining the far wall. Everything faded in and out of fuzziness.

Am I dreaming? The edges of my vision are glowing red, but it's normally purple... What's going on?

"I hope I haven't kept you waiting," said a voice that wasn't my own, its tone disembodied and silvery, reverberating deep within my mind

In the background, someone grunted and metal clinked. Unwillingly, I flipped through some pages in my hands before placing them down on a silver desk with ornate etches. My hands moved them too quickly to read their contents.

"We won't spend as much time together today, but not to worry. After today's session we'll feel closer than ever."

My insides froze. The voice sounded like it was coming from me.

A creeping horror crawled up my spine as I watched my hand caress a pristine knife. Something in the way I gripped the hilt was too comfortable.

What am I doing?

I lifted the weapon for observation, catching my reflection in the blade. Translucent skin, hair black as night, full deep-red lips with eyes to match.

It's not me. How am I not me right now?

"Frankly, I'll miss our playtime. But after this, you won't step out of line again." The knife clanged when my host dropped it on the table. "So disappointing, but effective."

She turned and terror struck me.

A man dangled from the wall, bloodied, bruised, and battered. The vision fuzzed again, preventing me from identifying who hung on the flawless, white, marble wall. I mentally pushed against my sight, trying to release myself from her body, but I was forced to continue watching.

She strolled to the man and ripped open his tunic, revealing gray, granite-like skin. He was Hulk-huge, yet his ribs protruded dangerously outward. Taking her index finger, she carved a shape into his chest. A slow burn followed her finger, cauterizing the wound as she cut through his skin. The man screeched in agony while she spoke some sort of gibberish.

Why would she carve the letter M into his chest?

The woman finished her chant and slapped her handiwork with her open palm. Veins rose and branched out from her hand, glowing bright red before bleeding into black and disappearing beneath the skin once more.

She took a step back and lifted his face. "Do you have nothing to say to your Queen?"

"I'm yours to command."

His smile disturbed me to my core. There was no hate or disgust, only admiration and obedience.

"No!" I screamed as loud as I could. *"This is wrong!"*

She turned—eyes searching—then everything dissolved.

I stumbled back to the floor of my secret room, breathing heavily, no longer surrounded by those way-too-clean walls.

"I'm finding a way home. Now!" I scrambled toward the desk and pushed myself off the floor. My legs wobbled and nausea struck. I collapsed into the chair. Elbows on the table, I rested my head in my hands. Once the dizziness cleared, I sat back, eyes still stinging.

An enclosed letter sat propped up against the pile of books in front of me. I gingerly picked it up, puffing dust particles into the air. It was written in my grandma's handwriting and addressed to Tempy.

She knew I'd get here. I'd told her all about my dreams, and she knew the entire time this world existed. Why hadn't she told me?

I broke the wax seal and opened the letter. Tears pooled when I saw her handwriting scrawled across the pages.

Dearest Tempy,

If you found this room, then our family honored my wishes by informing you of your special abilities.

Armed with the necklace and the first letter that brought you here, you are now prepared to learn more about them. You are an heir to the powers of the Superior Goddess, Emeriz.

Our powers can be a source of good and healing, but they can also be a great burden, both physically and mentally. These abilities will be a force within you, more so than myself. You're whole, while I've been divided between two stones. The other half of my gifts have remained untouched by me since I was a young girl, lost to the clutches of the wolf who wields the other side of my power.

I wasn't strong enough to stand up against her, but you aren't divided. Magic unyieldingly courses through your veins. It might be difficult to see right now, but you're substantially more powerful than her. Her survival relies on borrowed magic, while yours grows and thrives within you. With practice and patience, you could set the balance right.

If you choose to take on the wolf, this room will be a great help to you. It holds complete and accurate histories of all the Descended, spells, and journals that will assist in training and honing your abilities until you become a full power in your own right. Your ancestors dwell here to guide you both in spirit and written word. Along with my own notes, the books on the table are some I've left to help you get started.

I wish I could be there to show you all the wonder that Emeriz holds. I'm sorry that you found out about your gifts so late in life. My love for you evidently turned me into a coward. There were many times throughout your life that I almost told you but ultimately decided to give you one more day. Always just one more day of childhood—of freedom.

Love Forever,

Grammie

P.S. Throw a cover of some kind over the stone while you're present. It'll dampen the pull you feel. Just uncover it before you leave so you can get home.

I wiped my tears with the sleeve of my shirt. "What other letter?" I demanded.

I tossed the pages against the stack of Grandma's books and notes. "You should've told me! Someone should've told me!"

My body ran hot with the anger of having been lied to my entire life, followed by a drowning grief that my grandma wasn't with me.

I needed to talk to my parents.

I walked over to an empty, cylindrical vase and placed it carefully over the stone. How was the 'demon' stone supposed to help get me home?

Pressure sat in my chest like my lungs squeezed my heart.

What had that stone made me see?

Turning in a circle, I took in the magnitude of sources at my shaking fingertips.

"If I'm ever going to find the answers, I'd better get started."

My eyes fell on the documents, scrolls, and books my grandma left stacked on the desk. Picking up the letter, I smoothed it out and set it aside. The quickest way to piece everything together would be to start with what she'd provided. I just wished I had the first letter.

I grabbed a black book embossed with gold off the top of the pile and flipped through its contents. More of Grandma's handwriting graced every page. As I reached the final pages, a folded piece of paper fell out. I placed the book on the desk and opened it to the page the paper had bookmarked.

All over the page, her notes alluded to her interpretation of the prophecy and mentioned family trees she'd created over the years to trace each one of the Descended lines. After her grandfather, King Hefeydd, was assassinated, they'd all scattered into hiding. No one had been able to trace them until now. The last entry on the page caught my attention.

This paper contains the names of the Descended lines of power, heirs of the Four First Gifted, who will fulfill the prophecy.
One of my blood.
One of Neal's blood.
One of Nereida's blood.
One of Altair's blood.

"Neal's blood? As in Grandpa?" Curiosity piqued, I quickly unfolded the thick piece of paper and spread it out before me. Four separate yet thorough family trees traced all the way back to the Superior Goddess, Emeriz. The lines for *Descended of the Haloed Sun* and *Descended of the Storms* united toward the bottom, confirming my suspicions. My grandpa was also a Descended. It continued to James and me, a different coat of arms beneath each of our names. James' consisted of a lightning cloud centered around a gold lion's head. Mine was an amethyst inside similar shape to my pendant, backed by a brilliant sun with a violet center. Some sort of arrow or staff divided the image up the center.

James is Descended too... Does he know?

Under the line for *Descended of the Tides*, I found Nora's name with her own coat of arms. White and silver waves crashing into each other in an array of beautiful swirls. As I scanned down the final line for *Descended of the Moon*, my intestines knotted up like a yarn ball.

Frederick.

His coat of arms was a brilliant silver moon framed against a night sky of indigo with iridescent stars flying across it.

Was everyone I knew involved? This situation couldn't get any more ridiculous!

As if I'd tempted fate with that last thought, I noticed two more familiar names on my family tree. Listed as Grandma's parents were the names *Rhiannon (Riona)* and *Brydon*. Grandma added a little doodle next to each of them. For Brydon, a musical note and the word

Lessor. Rhiannon's had three little birds perched on a branch next to a horse.

"It's gotta be a coincidence, right?" I shook my head. "They look like they're my parents' age. They'd have to be... immortal."

It was possible. Even in Grandma's stories, she'd mentioned rare cases of immortality for the Descended and sometimes their loved ones. In the tales, Riona was considered a demi-goddess of peace that still walked among the people. She was celebrated—even worshiped.

I zoned into my memories of meeting them on our travels. When we were lost, cold, and hungry, Rhiannon provided us with food, warmth, and direction. After I told her about Grandma passing away, she seemed mournful and mentioned losing two children. One *recently.* Both Rhiannon and Brydon had stared at me like they'd seen a ghost.

I sunk deeper into the chair as the truth sunk into my heart.

A gentle coo came from the balcony, drawing my attention. Another dove sat there, watching me intently.

"You again, huh?"

The bird let out a second coo, and I sighed, dropping my head onto the wing of the chair. A sense of calm overcame me, and I let it ease the anxiety nipping at my nerves. The emotions left behind were a mixture of shock and relief that maybe I wasn't completely alone in this world. I had some family looking out for me.

Rhiannon and Brydon were my great-grandparents.

CHAPTER 20

FREDERICK

"That insufferable cretin," I mumbled, fists clenched as I strode through the halls toward the throne room. My teeth ground together just thinking about the exchange with Heshrin and what he'd done to our high priest.

I picked up my pace and did my best to push my irritations aside. It was important I arrived at the council meeting before everyone, especially since I needed to inform Calix about our new unwitting ally.

When I entered the throne room, Calix was already looking over the scrolls, maps, and documents that covered the table. Firelight-filled silver sconces lit the portraits of my ancestors and kings past. They covered the upper walls, reaching the edge of the painted ceiling with an interpretation of the sky on the night of our kingdom's creation. Indigos, sapphires, golds, and violets danced across the black expanse.

"Leave us," I instructed the guards keeping watch. They immediately stepped out, closing the doors behind them.

"My King," Calix greeted with a bow.

"*My King*? Really? It's just us here." I strolled over to him.

"You're still trying that? Really?" Raising a disapproving eyebrow, he said, "You took your time in the chapel."

"It takes time to commune at the altar of the Goddess—especially when the new high priest was Obsidian."

Calix's expression darkened. "Heshrin was posing as our high priest?"

"I've taken care of it." I took my seat at the head of the table, and he took his seat to my left, before I divulged the events that had transpired in the temple of the Goddess.

"We must figure out how to break that bond before he finds some loophole that kills you on a technicality." Calix scratched at his beard. "We'll consult the scholastedites."

Protectors of the written word, scholastedites preserved all the histories, philosophies, and advances of our world. Magical and natural. Although they studied and observed the world, they essentially lived as monks, speaking only in facts and focusing on perfecting our library.

"Just use caution," I said. "Heshrin is not someone we want on our bad side." I leaned my head against the blue velvet cushion and closed my eyes.

The double doors creaked open, and my advisors shuffled inside, their voices echoing within the domed room. The collection of them made up the highest of their ranks.

Calix served not only as my Left and Captain of the Guard but also as my Minister of War. His lands were located at our borders, with soldiers specifically trained and trusted by Calix himself. Although Calix resided at the castle, his father acted as an earl and managed on-site business.

Duke Boetius, Taren and Persephone's father, was also present. Taren stood next to him, preparing to inherit his position. Unfortunately for the duke, Taren lived wildly. Drinking, chasing women, and fighting. From the few droplets of blood on his tunic and the bruising creeping its way around his nose, he'd had a recent altercation. Duke Boetius glared at his son, wrought with embarrassment and disdain—as if Taren had just run naked through the dining hall.

Apart from his philandering, Taren clearly preferred to follow in his mother's footsteps with his eyes on becoming Captain of the Guard one day. I always sensed Persephone's intellect and strong-willed ideals would be better suited for the dukedom, however, that was something the duke would never allow. Tradition was too important to him, and as such, he insisted his eldest child inherit the title. In this rare instance, I was grateful for the duke's decision. Persephone's ideals did not align with mine, and if she were part of my council, every meeting would be a battlefield. Though, it would be better for everyone if she became the duchess rather than vying for my hand to become Queen.

General Cranzly was amongst the group as my Master of Arms, who was currently chuckling to himself with his eyes downcast toward the ground.

I stood and called my fourteen advisors to order.

"Thank you all for your attendance. Please be seated."

In unison, the men placed their right hands over their hearts and bowed their heads as they eased into their seats along the stretched oval table.

The seat to my right remained empty, reserved for my future queen. Usually, I did a decent job ignoring the gap, but the topic had pressed upon me lately, making the empty space loud and distracting. I stole a glance at the designated spot on the wall where the portrait of my parents should have been.

Imagining it there again, I saw my mother, Irene, sitting in a black velvet wingback chair, her soft black curls draped over her shoulders with a silver-and-sapphire circlet sitting across her forehead. Even with her impeccable posture and formal blue gown, she still looked relaxed. My father, Allyn, stood at her side, gently holding her left hand in his right, while his left hand rested on the back of her chair behind her head. Regal and commanding, his traditional deep blue tunic and silver satin sash draped across his chest.

A true partnership of equals that had been lucky enough to love each other. A rarity among royals and nobility. My mother actively participated in governing the kingdom and wasn't afraid to question my father when she felt there were lines they shouldn't cross. He'd listen intently to her counsel, and sometimes they'd compromise. On rare occasions, my father would pull the weight of his crown, but my mother would always support him.

That's what I wanted.

Love, friendship, and equality. A queen that would bring strength to my reign, not because she'd bring armies or money, but because she'd help me govern our people better.

Their portrait now gathered dust in a dark, lonely crypt. In Minerva's eyes, the memory of traitors was not to be preserved on the walls of history.

They were liberators... heroes. Once Emeriz was free, their portrait would return to its rightful place.

I turned back to my advisors and was met with their sullen, pity-filled expressions. They'd caught what I'd been staring at.

I squared my shoulders and said, "We've confirmed that Queen Jezzamyn of Kelurs and King Brannyn of Fjall will be present for the festivities. They will arrive in a few days. We'll cover every possible trade option that we have. By the end of the ball, we'll have secured alliances with both nations."

The group started banging the table in agreement.

"Baroness Deganit," I said, "if you could enlighten us in our agricultural trade options."

The baroness bowed her head to me then addressed the room, beginning what would be a fruitful and trying discussion of all things trade.

I breathed deeply to ease the tension that had built in my head over the course of three hours. Aggressively rubbing my face with both hands, I ran my fingers through my hair in hopes that it would restore some of my energy.

These men and women argued their viewpoints, debated, compromised, and fought to be heard. Some men had undone the first button of their tunics, while others draped their capes over the back of the chairs. A few of the women had pulled their hair back with ribbons in a disheveled manner. Scrolls, papers, maps, and books covered every inch of the table, making it nearly impossible to see the surface. We'd gone over everything from agriculture to weapons, and armor to land.

We were ready.

I stood, placing my hands on the table.

"Thank you for all the time and energy spent on addressing these matters," I said. "Please organize your documents and bring them to me for review this evening. Dismissed."

No one moved, sitting stiff as boards in their seats. They looked everywhere else but me. I narrowed my eyes at Calix, who cleared his throat and folded his fingers over each other.

"My King," Duke Boetius said, "there's one last matter of possible trade we have yet to discuss." He hesitantly stood. He swallowed and held his head higher.

Don't say it.

"Marriage." His blasé voice rang in my ear.

I dropped my head down, chin to chest, and closed my eyes. It wasn't their fault. They didn't want me to be forced into matrimony, the duke least of all. He was still pressing me to wed Persephone, but he was willing to set that aside for the good of the rebellion and the kingdom.

For the greater good.

The words from the past echoed in my mind as I raised my head and phrased my words carefully.

"I will consider any offer put to me. Dismissed."

My advisors gathered up their belongings and exited the room. I sat back in my chair rubbing my temples as the sounds of their voices and footsteps faded out the doors, leaving Calix, Cranzly, Taren, and Duke Boetius.

"You piss off another husband, Taren?" Calix teased.

Cranzly had snickered every time he'd met Taren's eye during the discussions, piquing my interest as well.

"Tell us your tale of woe!" Cranzly said, grinning like a child about to receive a sweet.

All confidence, Taren didn't skip a beat and said, "What can I say? Women love me."

"Pfft!" Cranzly, close to losing it, crossed his arms and covered his mouth with one hand.

Taren raised an eyebrow at Cranzly, while Duke Boetius grasped his son's arm. "Yes, charming," he said. "We'll be on our way."

Once the door closed, Cranzly let loose a laugh that reverberated throughout the room.

"What entertains you, General?" Calix asked.

Cranzly wiped the tears falling from his eyes. *"Women love him. Ha!* Little does he know I saw the whole thing!"

"Don't leave us in the wind! Who was the man?" Calix pushed Cranzly in the arm, urging him on.

"T'was no man! That's the best part!" Cranzly put his hands together and glanced up as though sending a prayer to the heavens. "Bless that wonderful girl. Reminds me of my dear niece, she does."

"Who was it?" I leaned forward in eager anticipation.

Cranzly looked at Calix. "That young ward of yours, Temperance."

"What?" Calix and I simultaneously uttered.

"Yep!" Not noticing the change in our expressions, Cranzly continued, all smiles. "The girl got him good! I noticed him hovering over her—you know trying to..." He clicked his tongue for emphasis. "She didn't look to be enjoying it. I was about to intervene when he put his hands on her, then out of nowhere she pops him up the nose and knees him in the groin!"

Cranzly slapped his knee with a chuckle, beaming with pride.

My good humor dissolved like a leaf in acid. I clenched my fists, slowly stood, and walked toward the doors.

In a flash, Calix was in front of me, hand on my shoulder, and I pierced him with a death stare.

"Move. That's an order."

Not her. I needed to make sure she was all right. Then I was going to beat Taren senseless.

"My King, you need to be seen as impartial right now," Calix said, holding my gaze firmly, showing no signs of backing down. "You can't attack one of your future dukes and a loyal soldier."

"We brought her here. I was supposed to keep her safe. Being accosted in a dark alcove doesn't make someone feel that way."

I pried Calix's hand off my shoulder and took a step around him.

"Frederick!" Calix's voice was gruff and unwavering, casting his brotherly authority over my heated emotions like I was ten years old again. "Calm down. You're a young ruler. You don't need rumors spreading that you're hot-headed."

"And what are they to say about me if I let that behavior happen in my own court? Especially to someone I care about!"

Compassion overtook the frustration in Calix's voice, but his eyes remained impenetrable. "I'm upset too. Those girls have a way of sinking into one's heart quickly. Even Cranzly seems half in love with them, and they met mere hours ago."

We glanced over at Cranzly, who nodded and shrugged.

"There are other ways of dealing with the situation without compromising your position and reputation." Calix placed a hand on my shoulder again. "We're in the midst of starting a war and can't afford for anyone to doubt your character now. We need allies."

As usual, Calix was right, but the anger still simmered in my chest, threatening to boil over. I opened my mouth to argue again when, rather abruptly, there was a drop of something cooler and calming right in the center of the heat. It swelled in my chest, sending a wave of serenity over my emotions. The fury I'd felt started to unwillingly fade away.

I waved the foreign sensation away with a shake of my head and looked at Calix with a new and weary calm.

"I need to see her."

"That will be difficult."

We turned toward the voice coming from the doors.

Ora stood next to Temperance's attendant, both looking concerned.

How long had they been there?

"Why?" I asked.

Ora placed her hands behind her back and said, "Because she hasn't been seen in hours."

CHAPTER 21

TEMPERANCE

I spent hours poring over all the information Grandma left me. There were a few spells she deemed helpful, tips on my abilities, more on our family history, and journal entries.

Nothing in the contents she'd provided contained an exact method of getting home. She mentioned the creepy stone a few times, along with a white scepter, and instructions for the two items. Even those were vague and incomplete. For all I knew, if I were to find that staff and execute those directions, it wouldn't be a way home. In fact, it didn't say what exactly it did, just that it would "balance the scales to an open world." Written in the margins of a few of her notes were the words, *in reference to my first letter.*

"You couldn't repeat yourself just once, Grammie?" I pressed my lips tightly and raked my fingers through my hair, effectively ruining the style Rhiannon had done so wonderfully.

I clenched my fists and tapped them against my forehead, attempting to push away the tension there. My brain kept fritzing out, making it impossible to see any connections.

Pulling the ribbon out of my hair, I walked over to a full-length mirror leaning against the books. I scratched and weaved my fingers through my scalp, causing a sensational feeling as every strand was freed from bondage. After a few deep cleansing breaths, I rested my hands on my hips.

I thought about my family. They'd planned to give me her first letter and let me decide if I wanted to pursue this path. They hadn't meant for me to come alone; that was clear from the letter I'd found. Their mistake was giving me the necklace too soon. They didn't know I'd accidentally transport myself.

Still, they should have told me before Grandma died.

I pulled all my hair to the side and secured the ribbon around it. My stomach rumbled, telling me I'd missed lunch. If I wanted to get further with my studies, I needed to do some self-care. I set off toward the door.

At least her notes mentioned something helpful. When I went back downstairs, I'd be able to call the archway back.

A whistling gust of wind blew in from the balcony, lifting and rustling the pages on the desk. I dashed over and planted my hand onto everything like a paperweight. I couldn't let them get blown away and mixed together. Looking behind me, ready to plot my route to close the drapes, I stopped.

Another dust devil oscillated around a gray figure shaped like a man. His faceless head moved back and forth as though searching for something. Logic told me to run, but fear held me firmly in place. I couldn't make up my mind before the dust devil stopped, and the figure disappeared.

"What's with this freaking room?"

I glanced around for any other supernatural activity, and when I saw none, I rushed to shut the drapes and hesitantly removed the vase from over the stone, careful not to look at it directly. Satisfied, I ran out the door and down the stairs to the wall where the archway had appeared.

Like Grandma's notes instructed, I *calmly* placed my hand on the wall and uttered the words again. *"Blood of the Goddess, hear my call, paint the archway across the wall."*

The archway painted itself across the surface, and I wasted no time exiting. Everything I'd learned so far overwhelmed me so much that I didn't notice Tundra following me until she jumped into my arms. Her plum-colored eyes bore into mine, begging for attention.

"Okay, I'll give you some love since you somehow led me there." I chuckled and scratched her head and ears while I walked. Every stroke of her smooth fur soothed the thoughts that raced through my mind.

How had Tundra known where to go? Why hadn't Rhiannon and Brydon said anything when we met? Did Frederick and James know about their powers? And who was that horrible woman I saw?

Every question brought more questions, but I hoped that some might be cleared up by my great-grandparents.

"Tempy!" Ora called out as I exited the library.

She rushed out a pair of doors up the hall with Rhiannon, Frederick, and Calix. Reaching my side, she eyed the cat inquisitively before her eyes widened in recognition.

As Rhiannon approached, she beamed at the sight of Tundra.

It was obvious that she knew exactly what the house cat really was. Her smile slowly dropped when her eyes found mine—she must have seen the emotions dancing across my face. She folded her hands over each other and cast her gaze to the ground. She knew that I knew.

"I've been in the library," I said to Ora.

"But we looked there," Ora said.

"It's a big library. You couldn't have looked everywhere." I brushed off her comment, hoping she'd take the hint to stop talking. I wasn't sure I wanted Frederick to know anything yet, including who I was.

"I scanned rather quickly…" Ora narrowed her eyes and nodded along. "I could've missed you."

Frederick approached, and I clutched Tundra's fur a little more to shade the fact that my heart had picked up pace. His brow wrinkled, and he tilted his head toward mine, inspecting my face.

Could he tell I was hiding something? Or perhaps that I liked him? My mind screamed at me to look away, to shield the emotions building inside me, but I couldn't remove my eyes from the cobalt ones I'd dreamt about.

"Temperance, are you all right? I heard what happened in the training yard"—Frederick's jaw tensed—"with Taren."

He knew? I guess you couldn't get much past a king in his own castle. Hopefully I hadn't caused him any trouble.

"I'm sorry. I didn't mean to hurt him. Well, I did, but—" I felt my cheeks burn and glanced down to Tundra. "I'm fine."

He placed one hand on top of Tundra's back while the other grazed my wrist beneath.

My breath caught. To any bystanders, it would appear like he was only petting Tundra. Nobody would see the sly move of his hand on mine. Heart pounding like a wild drum, I glanced around. The others had moved a few paces back, conversing away from us and giving us some level of privacy.

"You have nothing to apologize for, my lady. In fact, your defensive abilities are impressive."

With one glance at that lopsided grin, my knees nearly turned gelatinous. It took all my concentration not to fall to the ground.

"Between our match at the cliffs and watching you spar," he continued, "I'm not surprised."

I bit my lip, trying to conceal my glee at his concern and compliment.

"Thanks, Frederick—or is it *Your Majesty*?"

His hand brushed over Tundra's back and stopped when his fingers touched mine.

I swallowed and was unable to bite back my smile. His touch made me way too happy.

"Right now, *Frederick* is just fine." His face relaxed and serenity oozed off his aura, pouring into mine.

My heart fluttered, and an inexplicable feeling of comfort and balance washed over me again—a feeling of coming home after being away for a while. How did that emotion keep overwhelming me when we'd only just met?

Tundra stirred a little in our hands, and we broke eye contact.

"That cat looks an awful lot like..." He shook his head, bewildered. "Uncanny."

Of course he'd noticed. He was way too observant. I would have to keep my guard up around him—a task that was getting more and more difficult to do.

"I don't know what you're talking about." I shrugged. "Maybe you should get your eyes checked."

He rolled his eyes, though his smile stayed. "Fine, keep your secrets. No one can hide the truth from me forever."

That was for sure... given what his powers were. Grandma had listed the abilities his line of Descended possessed. While there were some confirmed, and a few she merely suspected, she was certain that Frederick had the gift to *see* truth and the intention of others.

He was probably already aware of the feelings I had for him. How was that fair? And could that mean he knew who I was? I needed to figure out how his abilities worked exactly.

"I'm sure you're right," I said.

Frederick arched an eyebrow, and concern touched his eyes. "You sure you're all right?"

Not knowing what urged me to do so, I laced my fingers through his and squeezed his knuckles as reassurance. "Trust me, I'm good."

He returned the pressure and nodded. "Taren's ego is damaged a little, but you don't need to worry about him. Calix and I will handle it. But, please, tell me if he or anyone else bothers you."

"I promise."

As soon as he let go and stepped away, the others were beside us again. Tundra jumped from my arms and climbed up to the beams in the ceiling.

"You don't look ready for our dance lesson, Lady Temperance," Calix said, assessing my current state of dress. He gently smiled. "Perhaps, we'll practice after dinner?"

Desperate for a proper bath, I quickly agreed. "I'd be grateful."

"We'll meet you ladies in the dining hall for court supper." Calix bowed to us, then addressed Frederick. "Shall we, My King?"

"Yes," Frederick said with a bow of his head.

We curtsied then turned to leave. Before I took a step, Frederick grabbed my hand and spun me back around, placing a kiss on it. A blush crept up my neck and cheeks. He walked away, glancing back once more before disappearing around a corner.

He's not making the whole no romance thing easy.

Rhiannon and Ora cleared their throats, and my smile faded when I saw their expressions.

"Shut up," I said and walked between them toward our destination.

"We didn't say a word. Did we, Ora?" Rhiannon shot me a knowing grin as they matched my pace.

"I don't believe we did," Ora caroled and hugged me tightly.

I softly shoved her off.

When we arrived at the doors to the bathing rooms, a group of ladies blocked our path. The blonde leading the pack was the same one who'd been with Frederick at the training grounds. She whispered something to her friends, and they fluttered over like a flock of magpies. Paying no mind to Rhiannon and Ora, she kept her attention on me.

"Who do you think you are?" she hissed.

"Excuse me?" I said, stepping back.

"Who. Do. You. Think. You. Are?" She placed a hand on her hip emphasizing her displeasure.

"I'm Temperance, but I don't think that's what you're asking, so how about you save us some time. You tell me who you are and get straight to the point," I said a little more curtly than I probably should have.

Her jaw dropped, eyes growing lethal. After a glance back to her ladies, she continued. "Speaking to me like that shows your ignorance of the knowledge and propriety of this court. I'm Lady Persephone Boetius. You met my brother, Taren."

Of course they're related.

"Yes, what about your *handsy* brother who deserved what he got?"

Persephone scoffed and raised her head high. "Not only did you reject the courting of a high lord and friend to the king, but you assaulted him."

"I'm sorry that his education failed to teach him what the phrases 'no' and 'leave me alone' mean, but I won't apologize for teaching him myself." I crossed my arms and lifted my head to match hers. "Maybe now he won't underestimate the women he courts."

"Most women would be thrilled to have caught Taren's

attention—highborn, heir to a duchy estate, and a highly ranked soldier." Persephone looked me up and down. "A significant step up for a dirty swamp-crawler like you."

My stance wavered. I knew I didn't look great right now, but Frederick didn't seem to mind.

"I guess this simple swamp crawler is looking for more than wealth and an advance to my lowly station," I retorted. "It seems I want horrible qualities like class and respect for the general well-being of others." Shrugging, I smirked. "But that's just me."

She pursed her lips before a grin broke across her face.

"You simply have your eyes set on a much larger prize, don't you? If it's Frederick you're after, he's a king, and you're a minor distraction before matrimony."

The all-too-familiar way she said his name sat heavily in my chest. They probably grew up together in this court. Perhaps he'd even courted her. She knew a side to Frederick that I never would and fit all the requirements to court him, while I...

I opened my mouth, but nothing came out.

"A thousand pardons, swamp crawler. Was that rude?" Persephone pressed her fingers to her lips. "I apologize."

It took every semblance of control to conceal how her words had cut me, but I held firm.

"Ladies, we must go," Persephone said, clapping her hands.

The group surrounded her like a pack of hyenas around a fresh carcass. They then let out a collective animal-like giggle as they walked away.

Rhiannon wrapped her arms around me, and Ora held my hand.

"Don't you dare listen to her, Temperance," Rhiannon said. "Trust me, if she'd known who she was truly speaking to, she would never have addressed you so."

"What do you mean by that?" Ora said, eyeing her nervously.

I took a deep breath, letting the effects of Persephone's insults roll off. "Ora, she knows, but it's more than that."

I looked at Rhiannon with a half-hearted smile. With the knowledge of our relation, I could now see my grandma in her features, and James too.

"I have a lot of questions to answer, don't I?" Rhiannon beamed.

"Oh, definitely," I said.

"Eek! My dress!" Persephone screeched, the echo amplifying the sound to a painstakingly high frequency.

Persephone's maidens started bopping around her like scattered hens. A few blotted away at three separate parts of her gown, attempting remove something.

"Pesky little rodents!" Persephone frantically looked up to the ceiling, her expression twisted in anger.

One of her ladies spoke hectically, "Milady! Three doves! A sign of—"

"I know the symbolism, Hartley! I doubt it was Riona's will that I be pelted with her dove's excrement!" Persephone sneered.

Ora and I laughed loudly, unabashed. Persephone and her group shot withering glares at us before scurrying away and out of sight.

Rhiannon chuckled to herself, eyes narrowed, and chin lifted. "It appears when you spew filth out of your mouth, filth is pelted down upon you."

"Now that's what I call karma," I said. The three birds flew out a nearby window, and I turned to Rhiannon. "*Riona's* will, huh?"

Her expression in response reminded me of the *Mona Lisa*. What other secrets did she hold?

Rhiannon refused to discuss anything until I'd bathed and she was styling my nearly dry hair in my room—much to Ora's dismay.

"It's been long enough!" Ora whined. "Questions must be answered." Her finger fell on me first. "How does she know? And why are you okay with it? You nearly bit my head off when I wanted to tell Frederick and Calix."

"Because... she's my great-grandmother," I said.

Rhiannon and I looked at each other, her smile a mirror image of my dad's.

"I've been bursting to tell you," Rhiannon said, "but my daughter was clear that she wanted your path here to be your choice. She worried that family might sway you toward something you wouldn't truly want. Instead, we kept watch from a distance."

I laughed. "You and Brydon should've told me anyway. We wouldn't have stumbled around so much."

"Whoa..." Ora held up her hands. "Brydon?"

"Rhiannon's husband and my great-grandfather," I explained.

Ora plopped down on my bed, stunned silent.

Rhiannon stopped combing through my hair and hugged me from behind. "I was with you the entire time, dew drop. Trust me."

"The doves?"

Rhiannon pulled away from me, pride shining in her face. "Clever girl. Yes, one of a few ways."

"I suspect you're also responsible for Persephone's misfortune earlier?" I asked.

She curtsied, accepting the accusation.

"It was risky to approach us the way you did," I said. "I was raised not to talk to strangers." I spun one of the bottles on the vanity.

"You trusted Ora, and she's not from your home." Rhiannon cocked her head.

Ora and I glanced at each other before she said, "That's not technically true. My other half was raised on Earth and is Temperance's best friend. I'm also Descended. My abilities allow me to scry, not just here, but into Earth. It's clearest if done through Nora's eyes directly."

Rhiannon froze. "What?"

Ora explained her parents' story and how Grandma helped them by splitting her soul.

Rhiannon began styling my hair again. "I wonder how she knew to perform such a spell... That sort of magic is dangerous and unpredictable. You never know what traits will manifest without being raised with the others, let alone if the person would even survive."

"With what I know about them both," I said, looking at Ora, "they're wonderful."

Rhiannon laughed. "Knowing Ora, I'd have to agree."

I turned to look at Rhiannon. "You didn't teach Grandma that spell? Aren't you Descended too?"

Rhiannon twisted my head forward again so she could keep working. "That's a bit more complica—"

Ora gasped. "You're Riona! King Hefeydd's daughter who fought for peace against Domhnall in the First War of Power. Everyone thought you'd died and became the Pure Demi-Goddess, the epitome of peace." She turned to me. "Not only do we celebrate the Superior Goddess during the festivals, but we also honor Riona for her sacrifice."

"You couldn't have told me this sooner, Ora? If you had, I might have figured it out before I found that room."

"Room?" Rhiannon and Ora asked simultaneously.

I told them everything. From my altercation with Taren to

following Tundra to the library, finding the staircase, and all that I'd experienced in the room. I left out the part about the stone, as I wasn't quite ready to relive that moment.

"James and Frederick are Descended too?"

For the first time in my life I couldn't read Ora's expression. I merely nodded.

"Whoa." The comforter on my bed puffed up around her as Ora fell back on it. "We've all found each other. The prophesied."

I glanced at Rhiannon for clarification of Ora's statement.

"According to my daughter's interpretation, yes." Rhiannon sighed and walked to the small vase that'd been on my breakfast tray that morning.

Ora leaned up on her elbows with furrowed brows. "What's that supposed to mean?"

Rhiannon returned to me with a few tiny, white buds of solira blossoms and weaved them into my hair. "It means that, although my daughter was more sensitive to the meaning of the prophecy—due to her abilities—her interpretation is simply that. *Her* interpretation."

"So you don't believe the prophecy is about us?" I absently played with my necklace.

"I believe that the four of you are key to restoring balance to the magical and political energy in the world. However, I don't believe it's the will of the Superior Goddess that you do. She's shown no concern in the past."

"So you believe in the Goddess?" I asked.

Rhiannon heaved a sigh. "I believe all things here came from somewhere, and history tells us it was from her. Until proven otherwise, that's the truth in my heart. Whether or not she is a cosmic being is another matter."

"You don't think she's a real goddess?" Ora said. "Aren't you one?

I mean, clearly you don't age." Ora twisted onto her stomach and plopped her chin in her hands.

"There are those who believe the female heirs to Eslane were gifted with powers resembling that of the Goddess'. Others believe our line was born of her womb. Descendants by blood to Emeriz herself."

"Which do you believe?" I asked.

"It used to be the first, but after my experience with the powers I inherited, I question the truth of the second."

"What do you mean?"

"My gifts... they were not safe with me." Rhiannon's voice wavered.

"That can't be true. You're so serene. I'm always less anxious around you." I hoped my comment would comfort her.

"That's because they no longer reside in me. The temptation is not there to use them."

It seemed mysterious speaking patterns were a family trait.

"Please, Rhiannon, tell us everything. No more secrets or lies." I picked at my fingers. "I'd hoped you'd know how to get me home, but it sounds like you don't."

Rhiannon sat down in the chair across from me.

"My powers were born amidst destruction and emotional turmoil. When I was seven years old, the Eslanian Palace—my home—was invaded. My brothers and uncles were assassinated alongside my father and his council members. Hardest of all... my older sister and the true Descended of the Haloed Sun."

"What?" I whispered in disbelief.

"As the second daughter, I was never meant to have magic. When she died, her abilities transferred to me even though I hadn't reached the age of empowerment."

"Age of empowerment?" My eyebrows scrunched together.

"You aren't able to physically learn to use your powers until you turn eight and the Haloed Sun dawns," Rhiannon said. "Though a sun of that kind hasn't appeared since Minerva rose to power."

"Yeah, I've never seen one," Ora said. "But clearly the Descended lines have continued."

Rhiannon nodded and continued. "For the safety of those lines... I was happy to never see that purple hue again. People assumed Minerva destroyed the Descended, so they stopped hunting them. The Haloed Sun's absence also weakened her power and the power of anyone else gifted in any sort of magic.

"I escaped with my mother and her lady-in-waiting. They were careful to mask the news from me as to who'd been killed. While we were sneaking up a hallway, a group of enemy soldiers boasted of the murders of my father, brothers, and sister.

"I only have flashes of what happened next. My powers awakened, my eyes burned violet, and my blood flowed slowly as I walked out of the shadows. All I remember is somehow those men were slaughtered, and I remained standing. My hair had turned from blonde to the blackness of a crow's feather. My body vibrated with the metamorphosis of new power, and my sister's birthright was thrust into me unwillingly. No other Descended power had ever been transferred in such a way before. It didn't belong to me.

"We escaped, but I didn't have my grandmother or sister to teach me. I practiced the little I knew from watching my sister train. Healing, creation, binding, and general magic. I stayed clear of the darker sides of our abilities and focused on the gifts that would bring good. With time, my hair returned to its natural blonde, and life was peaceful.

"At eighteen, I fell in love with Brydon. Not long after we

married, the Eslanian camp we were hiding in was discovered. Domhnall's soldiers attacked, wreaking havoc and bloodshed throughout. My mother gave her life to save those she could. However, the rumors of my gifts had reached the ears of a local commander and Brydon was taken for questioning and tortured for information.

"Anguish pierced my soul, and something I couldn't control overcame me. My heart turned cold, my eyes burned, my blood boiled, and my hair blackened again. I attacked the prison. I'd lost my entire family... I wasn't about to let them take my husband too. I slaughtered everyone that got in my way.

"After I rescued him, we fought for years against Domhnall's forces. I became destructive so that one day my people might know peace again. At the Battle of Roz Mountain, we only barely reached our victory. I overlooked the death on both sides. All emotions faded at the view of desolation I'd let loose upon my people... and the darkness I'd led them into.

"In that moment, I considered the life growing within me and vowed to never use my Descended gifts for destruction. They weren't born into me therefore my emotions were easily manipulated by them. My children would know peace. Besides, once my daughter turned eight, my powers would begin to wane as hers grew. That's how balance is kept."

"Will I lose control?" I asked, a sliver of trepidation in my heart.

Rhiannon shook her head. "You're different, like my daughter. All the power born in you flows through your veins naturally. I have no doubt you can be trusted with them."

A balloon of anxiety expanded in my chest. "What if I can't? I don't know if I can carry the weight of this entire world on my shoulders."

Rhiannon placed her hands on my cheeks. The balloon deflated and calmness washed over me. No wonder I hadn't had a full mental breakdown... She'd been keeping my sanity intact.

"Grandma gave half her power to her sister, Ivy," I said, my voice shaking. "Can't I do something like that?"

Did I truly want to give up my gifts? Go home and leave this world's problems to sort out for themselves? If I could just give them away to someone else who could use them for good, would that ease the guilt of leaving it all behind?

Tears shone in Rhiannon's eyes. "If you could find a stone strong enough to store your gifts, what would happen if it fell into the wrong hands? We can't risk Minerva or anyone else gaining that much power." She shook her head. "It must live and die with you. You could go home and never return. Long enough away from here, and your powers could become dormant."

Ora sat up on my bed. "How are you immortal if your Descended abilities faded?"

"Faded is the keyword. Every Descended can still use minor powers later in life," Rhiannon explained. "And if a Descended reaches full power in their lifetime, they can achieve immortality. After we left the fight and faked our deaths, we slowed our aging process and raised our girls. We assisted those in need where we could, but we didn't stay around long enough for anyone to catch on.

"Word spread, morphing into rumors. Soon, full-fledged stories were created, and a legend was born, giving way to a new perception We kept it alive by helping others from time to time. I keep to small feats, especially since I'm no longer at full power. The people need some form of hope and peace to keep in their hearts during trying times. I let them believe I'm a demi-goddess that actually participates within their world."

Ora and I stared at Rhiannon, overwhelmed. I knew we were both bursting with questions, but neither of us could bring ourselves to ask them.

"We're running late, so let's finish this later." Rhiannon faced Ora. "Why don't you head down to the dining hall, and we'll join you shortly."

Ora groaned as she rolled off the bed and headed for the door. "Fine," she said, "just don't take long."

After she left, Rhiannon went to work on my face. Once she finished, she slipped me into a lovely blue gown with sparkling sapphires and silver embroidery along the trim of the scooped neckline. The sleeves reached the elbow, and the same glittering trim lined the ends. My hair was softly curled and pulled into a braided half-updo. The braids were weaved with the white flowers Frederick had left on my tray that morning.

"I dare say our dear king won't be able to look away from you," Rhiannon said. I was about to deny it, but she cut me off. "Ah-ah! Don't argue with your elder, and please don't close yourself off to the experiences you're given. You can't make an informed decision if you don't truly delve into our world."

"But what if I choose not to come back? Two people will be hurt and separated. I don't want to experience that, and I definitely don't want to do that to him." I ran my fingers over the smooth satin sash at my waist not daring to look up.

She lifted my chin. "You need to talk to him, dew drop. If not about love... at least what you learned. Descended should trust each other."

"If I tell him, he'll force me to stay." As soon as the words left my mouth, I knew they were false. He'd been nothing but considerate of my feelings since we'd met.

"You won't know if you don't speak up." She gave me a wink and a smile. "Now, off to dinner with you."

CHAPTER 22

FREDERICK

Multiple conversations filled the spacious community dining hall. A few were about the festival or personal matters, but most were circled around Temperance and Ora—the mysterious relations of the King's Left. One slept in libraries and practiced swordplay while the other flirted salaciously with all the eligible men of the court. Some admired their beauty and bravery, while others held no appreciation for what they considered rebellious nature. False and ridiculous tales of their breeding or the lovers they had blanketed the air.

After our interaction in the hall, Calix lectured me again about showing too much attention toward Temperance in front of others— a task I found difficult due to the discussion being held a mere table away. The desire to shut them all up festered in my chest.

"Why must it take so long to wash up for a meal?" said one of Persephone's followers with a giggle.

"You saw how repulsive she looked when Frederick and Calix delivered those girls here," another lady said. "Positively filthy."

"At least the *cloud hopper* had the intelligence to bathe at a reasonable hour," Hartley snickered.

"Unfortunately, it didn't improve that one much." Persephone's tongue cut like a viper. "As for that Temperance girl, she's far worse.

Between the soot from her travels, the dust from the books, and her practice with the soldiers, the results were appalling."

Her ladies snickered, stoking the anger inside me, but I bit my tongue. The last thing Temperance needed was me verifying the truth of the rumors with a tantrum. Instead, I sat there fuming while Persephone continued spitting venom.

"It wouldn't astonish me to hear that it took her rubbing herself against a wash plate to get herself clean." A roar of laughter erupted from all the ladies at her end of the table. "I only hope she'll at least have the courtesy to replace it since there'd be no cleaning our clothes with it when she's done."

I clenched my fists, telling myself not to explode at her. I wouldn't give her the attention she was clearly angling for.

"Not only that, she's a danger to the court, playing soldier like that. If the High Queen were to find out—"

I slammed the table with my fist. She and her maidens could spread lies about Temperance's looks. Anyone with eyes could see how beautiful Temperance was, so Persephone would end up looking stupid for saying otherwise. But outright painting a target on Temperance's back by calling her a danger? I would never stand for that.

I stared Persephone down until her eyes met mine. All humor drained from her expression, while mine remained as stone—my eyes unyielding. Persephone quieted her disgusting opinions and steered the conversation toward their gowns.

Somewhat satisfied, I turned my attention to Ora and Calix who looked at me with concern. Ora sent me a grateful smile then glared at Persephone and her friends, while Calix pointedly scanned the rest of the room. Taking his cue, I did the same and found many eyes were on our table watching in confusion. Assuming they were wondering why

I'd hit the table, I grasped my goblet, held it up and shouted, "Here's to a good meal!"

There were a couple of 'hear, hears' in agreement throughout the dining hall, and then everyone returned to their meals. Calix went back to telling Ora one of his funnier stories from his boyhood days and she laughed.

I was grateful for that. There was no need for any negative thoughts or feelings to go through Ora's mind, and by extension, Temperance's.

Absentmindedly picking at a slice of crusty bread, my mind ran through today's meeting. I traced the sodalite ring, etched with my Descended crest, to sharpen my thoughts, but halfway through my bread, the room quieted. All eyes collectively wandered toward the grand staircase on the opposite side of the banquet hall.

There, Temperance stood in the entryway on the edge of the stairs.

By the Goddess, she was *lovely*.

Clean, oiled curls framed her face with rows of solira blossoms on each side. I smiled.

Were they the same ones? No... Rhiannon could have picked the flowers from the gardens. But if Temperance asked her to... was it a sign that I could have hope?

Her blue dress set her ever-changing eyes on fire—a fierce sapphire that penetrated every barrier I'd set on my emotions. Seeming shy and uncertain, her gaze drifted around aimlessly while she slowly reached for the pendant around her neck. Unnaturally slow.

The silence was more deafening than before. Every breath I took and every beat of my heart pulsated in my ears above any other sounds. Glancing around, everyone else also moved slower than normal.

My eyes shot to my ring where my finger still rested directly on the stone. Hastily, I let go of the stone and cursed under my breath at my unconscious stupidity. My brain swirled at the time adjustment. The usual sounds of conversation filled the tables, and my heartbeat left my ears.

"Tempy!" Ora was at her side in an instant. "We're over here."

Calix cleared his throat discreetly, drawing my attention to him.

A rather large grin drew across his face. "I thought so," he said, having seen my eyes fade.

"Not a word," I commanded.

Calix snorted out a laugh, earning a glare from me.

Ora and Temperance approached us, and I'd never been more grateful for our casual dinner seating. Each table in the hall sat eighteen people, twenty if anyone sat at the heads, which no one did. Only at formal affairs or official kingdom functions did I, as King, sit at the head of a main table. My father believed in mingling with everyone at court. It kept his hand close to the pulse of his subjects' true views and opinions.

Luckily, the only remaining spot at the table was the one directly across from me. I couldn't stop the smile that escaped through my defenses.

The men at our table stood, as tradition required it when a lady entered. Calix pulled out the chair for Ora while Collin did so for Temperance.

Ora thanked Calix, to which he humbly bowed his head toward her and walked back around the table to his seat next to me.

"Thanks, Collin," Temperance said. "It's nice to see you're both a gentleman and a promising swordsman." She shot him a genuine sideways smile.

Collin's face lit up as he awkwardly bowed his head.

"After your kindness, it's only right to treat you so, milady."

Once the ladies were settled, we seated ourselves, and Collin returned to his seat on the opposite side of Ora.

"Hello, Your Majesty." Temperance's small smile seemed to take on a new meaning. "I'm seeing you more than I expected."

My heart raced, and I swallowed my nerves, flashing her a grin. "I hope you aren't displeased with my company, my lady."

"Not at all." She blushed a subtle shade of pink.

"What kept you?" I asked.

Her eyes darted toward Persephone's table then moved back to me. "Started off the day late, which made everything else run behind."

"Is that so?" I glanced over to Persephone, wishing I could scold her for whatever she'd said or done to Temperance.

She'd already inadvertently spread those rumors about Taren getting smacked around by Temperance, and purposely instigated the conflicting one that the two were lovers. Taren was irate about the first, which thrilled me. Although I knew the truth of the latter, a sliver of jealousy gnawed at me.

"Plus"—Ora bumped Temperance in the arm—"a lady must dress to impress, Your Majesty."

Temperance's smile stiffened, and Ora yelped in pain.

"Oh no... Something bite you, Ora?" Temperance assessed her with concern.

Glaring back at her, Ora said, "Yes!"

Temperance returned a satisfied smile and took a bite of her bread while Ora rolled her eyes.

"So you're dressing to impress me?" I asked, unable to resist teasing her.

Temperance coughed down her bread, nearly choking. Instinctively, I reached across the table and held her hand, rubbing the top of it with my thumb, until it passed. Ora giggled, and Calix attempted to withhold a chuckle, though he eyed me with subtle disapproval. *For her safety, be careful with your attention,* his eyes said.

Temperance pulled her hand from mine to take a sip of water. I wanted to reclaim her hand but thought better of it.

"That's not what she meant," Temperance said.

"That's what I heard her say." I shot her another smile.

Red faced, she stumbled over her words. "N-No, she meant that one should dress appropriately for any o-occasion, and that it takes time. Then she addressed you. Ora didn't mean *I* dressed nicely for *you*."

Why did it bring me so much satisfaction to see her tongue-tied? Was it because it gave me a glimpse behind the mask she started to wear around the others at court? Or was it the way her cheeks heated, turning her face a gentle pink, softening her features? Who else did she show this side to? No matter the reason, I found it adorable.

I raised an eyebrow which put her immediately on the defensive again.

"N-Not that I—er—someone wouldn't want to, and you're—" Temperance leaned back against the chair and shook her head. "You're messing with me, aren't you?"

I held my thumb and pointer finger close together. "A little."

She crossed her arms. "Bully."

"Oh no, is a bug gonna bite me now?" I teased.

Without missing a beat, she leaned forward to say, "Fortunately for you, I don't think it could reach you."

"Maybe I find that unfortunate," I quipped.

"You wanna get bit?" She chuckled and spun her fork before skewering a carrot.

"Maybe just a nibble."

Temperance, who'd been about to take a bite of her food, now stared at me blankly with her fork hanging unmoving in the air. Ora watched the scene, fish-faced, eyes darting between the two of us. The silence hardened, and I questioned if I'd slowed time again.

Why in the world had I said something so forward... so suggestive? In this crowd of people, anyone could have heard us.

Calix cleared his throat, bringing me out of my self-scolding and back to reality. Temperance finally placed the fork into her mouth and effectively avoided eye contact by staring at her plate.

If I didn't say anything, I worried she'd think me a pervert, so I opened my mouth to change the subject, but Temperance started laughing. I looked at Calix, who returned my questioning gaze. After she finally calmed down, I apologized for my impropriety which she immediately accepted.

"Sorry, but that line was kinda cheesy," Temperance said, flashing me a breathtaking smile. "And... annoyingly charming."

Relief flooded through me, and I leaned forward, smiling. "Such high praise."

"I thought you valued honesty," she said.

The atmosphere swelled with the magnetism that always seemed to draw us together and into our own little world.

"Touché, my lady." A yawn escaped me. "I apologize. While some people were studying late in the library, others wandered the halls most of the night due to their inability to sleep."

Mimicking me, she lay her elbows on the table. "What would ever deny His Majesty rest?" Her hands rose to her chin and a mischievous half-smile graced her lips.

I froze, making sure no one in the hall was paying attention before answering truthfully.

"I can assure you, *my lady*... there has been only one thing on my mind preventing me from sleeping." I held her gaze earnestly in mine. "I think you know that."

The mood shifted, and she broke free of the spell that entranced us. Temperance pulled back, her face paling.

"Excuse me." She stood and proceeded to the door leading to the gardens.

Ora moved to follow Temperance, but I stopped her.

"Ora, please, will you allow me to speak with her?"

She nodded, and I exited the now-half-empty dining hall to go after her. I pushed through the door and into the lush, colorful landscapes that filled the castle gardens. The sun had begun its descent, covering the deserted grounds with its dimming light. It'd be dark soon, and the celestial beauty of the gardens would fade to shadow. Enough of the light remained, leaving a soft golden hue over the vibrant flowers.

I walked through the stone paths, searching every which way for her. The sound of rushing water from the creeks and fountains met my ears, and I moved toward it on a hunch. At the back end of the gardens there was a quiet, secluded area near the creeks. There she sat on a stone bench with her legs to her chest, crying into her arms.

"Temperance?"

She abruptly stood and wiped her tears away.

"Did I say something to offend you?" I asked.

"No." Shaking her head, she crossed her arms. "You've been amazing."

"And this is bad?" I smiled and stepped closer.

"Yes—no. I mean… not bad, just complicated." She looked down. "I need to tell you something."

"I'm listening." I walked to her and gently grasped her hands, which she instantly pulled away from.

"I'm not who I said I was," she said, her voice barely above a whisper.

"I suspected that. I still—"

"Please, Frederick. Let me finish."

I pressed my lips together to show her I'd remain quiet. Temperance fiddled with her fingers as if she were cold, but after observing her and reading her intent over the course of our time together, I'd come to know better. She was nervous. Why?

She took a deep breath, then said, "I'm who you've been searching for."

"That's a bold statement." I chuckled and reached my hand out to her face, but she took a step back. My hand dropped to my side.

"No, you don't understand." Temperance rubbed at her wrist and scanned the area. "It'll probably be easier to show you." She grabbed my hand and guided me to a fountain. Water from the creek flowed into it in a steady stream. "Take off your jacket."

I raised a brow. "Brazen enough to command a king, are you?"

She shot me an awkward smile and added, "Please?"

Warily, I slid it off and draped it around her shaking shoulders.

"What are you doing?" she asked.

I placed my hand on hers to stop her from removing it.

"You're shivering."

"Thanks."

Temperance rolled up the left sleeve of my shirt to reveal some of the now-scabbed-over scratches from her rescue at the cliffs. We sat on the stone barrier of the fountain and leaned over the edge for her to submerge my wrist into the cool water.

"Temperance?"

"Shh!" Her eyebrows drew together as she focused.

I watched as her gentle hands caressed my wrist below the rushing liquid. It felt relaxing, rapidly putting me at ease until she gripped the scars tightly in both hands. My skin warmed in the cold water, and I brought my gaze up to Temperance's.

Her eyes sent a shock through me as if I'd fully submerged my body into the cold water of the fountain. Temperance's once-blue irises were now ablaze with a vibrant violet fire. Her gaze remained on her task in the water, but mine stayed fixated on her. As the heat around my wrist faded, so did the light from her eyes. I lifted my arm from the fountain, completely healed.

"You couldn't do this—not unless..." Our eyes met, and the truth bled crystal clear in hers. "You're Descended of the Haloed Sun."

Temperance nodded and grasped at the pendant she always wore. "And the four of us are supposedly the prophesied."

"*Four* of us?" I twisted the crest on my finger, my mind on high alert.

"You, me, Ora, and apparently my brother, James, are descendants of the Four First Gifted," she explained.

"Ora? A-And your brother? How do you know all this?" My thoughts moved faster than I could speak.

All that time I'd spent chasing rumors and hitting wall after wall, and in a single moment, the other Descended had fallen into my lap.

"My grandma compiled our ancestries and traced it to all of us." Temperance rubbed at the back of her neck. "As for my brother, he's Descended of the Storms, like my grandpa."

At the mention of her grandparents, I came to a realization, seeing her in a whole new light.

"It's you," I breathed, dumbfounded.

She looked at me like I had two heads. "Yeah, I just said—"

"No." Elated, I gripped both her hands in mine. "We've met before."

Her expression softened. "That's not possible. I'm not from here. I live on—"

"Earth," I finished, and she tensed.

I enacted my abilities so she could feel the sincerity of my next words. "You once shared your blanket with a young boy going through the worst night of his life. Brought him warmth, laughter, and friendship. Gave him the courage to decide his own fate."

"Nameless?" she whispered.

I nodded and gently squeezed her hands.

"I know your grandparents helped one of the smaller Eslanian factions escape to another world," I said. "Not well-known, but Henvick explained the secrets of it before he died." My voice cracked at the memory of him being slaughtered next to my parents. "Cranzly's filled in the other blanks since then."

Temperance wrapped her arms around me but didn't speak a word. Her warmth radiated into my soul, easing the pain of the memory and lifting the weight of that night.

Moments passed before Temperance spoke again.

"There's more. But please hear me out before you respond. Okay?"

Regrettably, I pulled away from her embrace and nodded. I pressed my thumb against the stone of my ring, in tune with my gift in seeing truth.

Temperance gasped lightly when she saw my eyes glowing.

"You showed me your true self," I said. "I must do the same." I laughed softly. "I'm able to discern—"

"Truth," she finished with a delicate smile. After a deep breath she stood to pace in front of me. "Neither my parents nor my grandparents told me about who I am. I thought Emeriz was a fairy tale. They made sure of that, it seems. Maybe they were trying to protect me and my childhood. But, seriously, not a single word my whole life? Then Grandma"—she choked on the words before she could get them out—"passed away."

I held out a handkerchief to her, which she took gratefully, grazing my fingers as she did so. Dabbing tears from her eyes, she explained how she was transported here and trapped without knowing how to get home. Then she told me about a secret room and revealed her grandmother's interpretation of the prophecy.

"I've never been trained in my powers!" she lamented. "I really need to talk to my family about all this, but I'm stuck here." At the end of her story she stood still, staring at me expectantly. "What are you thinking?"

A mixture of emotions bounced around in my gut, and I was unsure of which one to run with. Pure joy at being reunited with her, astonishment that the prophecy seemed to be true, hope that Emeriz could be saved, exhilarated that her destiny was intertwined with mine, and lastly, fear that she appeared unhappy with all of this.

"It's a lot to take in." Not looking away from her, I sighed. Nothing in her story indicated she was lying.

Her shoulders relaxed. "Trust me, I know."

"Maybe this is all fate," I said. She tensed again, and I stood and approached her. "All of us have found each other... You were brought back to help us."

"I have absolutely no idea what I'm doing. Not with my powers or this world. I need to get home. My family is probably freaking out." Temperance dropped her gaze to the ground. "That's why I came to Linall. I needed access to the information in your library. Ora mentioned you were knowledgeable about the Descended. We didn't realize how much, though."

I did my best to mask my disappointment but must have failed, because she once again apologized.

"You shouldn't be sorry." I took her right hand in mine. "I've been fighting for so long, and you were thrown into all of this. I believe you have the potential to live up to your abilities and the heart to see it through. But I shouldn't have pushed."

I couldn't let her endure what I had to... even if it hurt the rebellion—hurt me—to let her go.

"We'll find a way to reunite you with your family so you can decide for yourself."

Tears of relief slipped down her cheeks. "There are a few things I'm reluctant to leave behind. One in particular has become a complication."

I wiped away one of her tears. "What's that?"

Temperance stared unwaveringly into my eyes. "It's more of a who..."

The balance in the atmosphere tipped, drawing us into that same space we were always brought to.

Realization hit me harder than a wooden sword in practice. "I'm your complication?"

Temperance broke her gaze, and instead of answering my question, she ran her fingers over the scratches that remained on my right wrist. "I should heal—"

I leaned my forehead against hers, and the air filled with an intensity neither one of us could deny anymore.

"Temperance, I feel the same."

She sighed and lifted her chin up ever so slightly, filling me with hope.

Determined not to lose another opportunity, I pressed my lips to hers. The want I had for her ached in my chest, awakening more feeling in me than any other lady before. I slid my hand against the side of her neck, braiding my fingers into her hair as I deepened the kiss. Her arms wrapped around me, pulling us closer and pressing her curves against me. Then, in a moment that felt too soon, she parted her lips from mine.

I examined her flushed face. "Something the matter?"

She shook her head. Her smile nearly caused me to buckle to the ground, and I fought the urge to kiss her again.

"Are you sure?" I asked.

"Positive." Her tone was sincere, but something in her eyes told me there was more going on in her mind.

It'd been years since I'd felt so happy. Looking into her sweet face, I decided that I'd officially ask to court her. There'd be obstacles, a few of which she'd already named, but I could help her through them. I'd keep her safe.

"Temperance, there's something I've been wanting to discuss with you since you hit me over the head with that stick."

"What? I need to work on my technique?" She laughed.

Relinquishing my hold around her waist, I took both her hands in mine and moved us to sit on the bench. Mentally preparing myself as I'd never done this before, I gripped her right hand in mine and looked her in the eyes.

"I've been—"

Ora and Rhiannon came running up the path, shouting for Temperance.

"It's time for our dance lesson!" Ora grabbed Temperance's hand and pulled her toward the door to the corridors of the castle.

Temperance offered me back my jacket.

"We'll talk soon, okay?"

"Yes. You wouldn't want to feel the wrath of Calix."

I accepted the jacket from her and did my best to smile as they carried away the girl I didn't want to part from.

CHAPTER 23

FREDERICK

The next few days were busy with preparations for the Ethereal Ball and arrival of the foreign rulers. My schedule was filled with meetings, reports, and hearings of every nature that concerned the kingdom. Up at dawn, and not sleeping until the moon sat at its highest, my only reprieves were meals and training with the soldiers.

Unfortunately, I found my time with Temperance limited, which she accepted with pure understanding. A feat most ladies of court didn't have the patience for. We'd have breakfast in the mornings within her chambers and brief polite conversation at dinner, but Calix made sure we never sat across from or beside each other—an action that frustrated me on two counts. First, it kept me from her, and second, Calix felt forced to do it. Rumors had worsened over Calix's agenda of bringing his relations to court. They believed he was attempting to gain more power by marrying me to one of them, which was absurd

However, it prevented me from officially asking Temperance to court her. Doing so could make things worse. Instead, I focused our private conversations on other topics: Emeriz history, the Descended, magic, and our families. My least favorite discussions were the ones about her going home. Every time the subject came up, a pebble of irrational homesickness would twinge in my chest. She wasn't even gone yet, but the thought left me feeling lonely.

She'd gotten closer to an answer. Something to do with her Descended Relic, the Genesis Scepter, which remained unaccounted for. We'd snuck into the library one night, trying to find answers together, but some sort of magic prevented Ora and I from breaching the entrance to the secret room. Temperance tried bringing some of the books and scrolls out with her, but as soon as she had exited the archway, they would disappear from her hands and reappear in their proper place in the room.

We resolved to have Temperance report her findings to me, and I'd make recommendations as to what she should search for. When she delivered a sketch she'd made of what the staff looked like, recognition plagued me.

I was lost in thought trying to place the memory when the back of my head was smacked, knocking my crown off center.

"Ow!" I glared at Calix, his presence looming over me like I was a misbehaving child.

"Stand up and focus!" he snapped. "They're about to enter."

Adjusting my tilted crown, I walked to stand beside him in the center of the room, ready to meet the monarchs from Fjall and Kelurs. Only Calix and I would be attending the conferences with them.

Queen Jezzamyn and her elder brother, Lord Petit, were first to enter the room. They followed the same hierarchy that Eslane had, where the firstborn woman inherited the crown before men, in representation of the Superior Goddess. The queen wore a golden crown with emeralds that dipped down to a point just above her nose, drawing attention to her fierce green eyes. Her brother shared the feature, and like her, his eyes were made brighter in contrast to their dark skin.

The two leaders flaunted their most profitable trade of dyes and textiles through their lavish and exuberant attire. Kelurs controlled the majority of the garment trade with the most valuable goods supplying the Kingdom of the Haloed Sun at Minerva's demand. Only the people of Kelurs could wear or use the same goods sent to her imperial kingdom.

I bowed and shook hands with the queen. Then, keeping our hands grasped, we leaned our heads together: the traditional greeting of their kingdom. It represented the third eye, an ancient ability their people lost not long after the fall of Hefeydd.

After greeting Lord Petit in the same manner, I turned to address the new arrivals from Fjall. With sharp features, they appeared statuesque and ferocious. They wore less flamboyant shades than Jezzamyn and Lord Petit, but no less intricate in design. King Brannyn approached, accompanied by his Left, Freya, and his nephew, Drystan, the crown prince. Punching a fist into the palm of our opposite hand we bowed to each other. Known as some of the toughest warriors in all the kingdoms, their main sources of trade were weapons, armor, and coal.

Fjall was a solitude for fairies—which created unrest in their kingdom because it drew Minerva's interest. There were those that worried the High Queen would soon go mad again and invade, regardless of their strong armies and rough terrain. She'd tried before, only to be held back not only by their nearly impenetrable fortress and large numbers but also by the mudslides and constant rain.

Her goal was to obliterate the fairy race, except those younger than ten. These younger fairies, called Squirts, had the gift of seeing magic auras, and Minerva used them to hunt down those with power.

"Welcome to Linall, Your Majesties," I said and gestured to the table. Once everyone was settled, I took my seat. "I've gathered you here to negotiate a three-way alliance between our great nations. Together we will revolt against the tyranny of the pretender, High Queen Minerva. We've all felt the weight of her reign, and I say no more! We will restore the peace known to our world before the fall of High King Hefeydd."

The silence was deafening. Everyone glanced at one another, contemplating.

Queen Jezzamyn broke the silence first. "You speak great words of rebellion, but what have we to gain by engaging all-out war with the pretender? Our nation's all benefit from her rule."

"Yes, she hardly interferes with the affairs of our realms," said Lord Petit from beside her. "At least when compared to those she's burned down or infested with multitudes of soldiers, making them impoverished and dangerous."

"While I don't like being roped up like a dog by her," King Brannyn said, "it's better than the alternative." He stroked his beard. "Because she fears us, she leaves us be. Besides, I'm attempting to smother a civil war threatening to break out within my kingdom."

"She pins us down, My King!" Freya contradicted. "Our fortress has become our cage. I am tired of being a bird without wings. If he offers a possible solution, hear him out. We didn't travel all this way to tell him 'no' outright."

Wings, huh? Interesting phrasing. Could the rumor that Freya was a fae be true?

"Putting Minerva out of power could prevent your civil war by uniting them in a common cause," I added.

"Or make it worse," Prince Drystan scoffed, his gruff voice skeptical.

"The scales sway closer to the opposite, Your Highness," Freya lightly scolded Drystan, earning her an eye roll from him.

"We aren't asking you to join without gaining something in return," Calix said. "We're prepared to trade."

"Bribe," Drystan muttered.

Brannyn slammed his fist on the table in front of the young man, staring him down. Drystan merely rolled his eyes again.

"Let's hear it then," King Brannyn said, urging me to continue.

Calix and I dove into our plans we'd prepared: tax cuts on traded goods, soldiers to protect their caravans as they transported them, along with grain and gold. After our proposals they seemed more at ease, but not fully convinced.

"We've discussed payment but not why we should help you," Queen Jezzamyn said, brow furrowed. "You're a young king trying to follow your parents' example. Who's to say that you won't walk us straight into that grave next to them. Why risk it?"

I met her fierce gaze head on.

"When Minerva's naval forces took the islands surrounding your kingdom—raping and pillaging those lands, my father negotiated with Merald to pirate and attack those ships from below. They beat them back from reaching your mainland, isolating them to those islands. You now have open trade and protection with Merald and safety from further attacks from Minerva's forces."

I turned to King Brannyn.

"When your kingdom lay under siege all those years, it was Linall who arranged food and supplies to be snuck into Fjall, thus preventing your people from starvation."

"I owed your father that debt, not you," he said sternly.

"Then consider this putting myself in your debt," I replied, looking to Queen Jezzamyn. "In addition to what we've already discussed, I'll provide men and ships to help take back your islands. In return, you'll provide uniforms to my soldiers and discounted cloth to all our nations.

"And in return for you providing soldiers, weapons, and armor to our cause, King Brannyn, we'll lend you a grouping of some of our best archers to aid in pushing Minerva's remaining troops from your mountains. Additionally, we'll take any Fae as a citizen in our cities and assist in freeing those imprisoned."

Addressing everyone at the table, I concluded, "Once we rebel against her, we'll be able to openly trade goods anywhere, with no limitations on who they're being sold to. After we succeed, no person, magic or not, will live in fear of her killing touch."

Freya and King Brannyn looked at each other, and with a nod from her king, she spoke. "If we decide to do this, our custom requires a marriage to solidify the alliance. Prince Drystan must marry a lady from your court."

Elated that they were open to an alliance, a breeze of relief eased the anxiety from my chest.

Thank Emeriz they don't require me to marry!

"Of course," I said to Freya, then turned to Queen Jezzamyn. "Do you require a seal of marriage?"

"No," she replied. "We don't consider people as property to be traded as others do. We marry for respect and love."

"Then how else do you secure your kingdom?" King Brannyn said. "Our traditions help us bolster our lines and bring out the best in our leaders."

"It is the heart of a man or woman that brings strength to those who lead, not their blood," Queen Jezzamyn replied.

Drystan had the look of someone about to spit. "What a load of drivel. Ultimately, our hearts fail us."

Sighing, I sent Calix a sidelong glance and noted his equally exasperated face. We jumped into the exchange to get the conversation back on task. Thus began the negotiations with Fjall and Kelurs.

After hours of back and forth, I finally called for a break, stating that we'd resume the following day, and Calix and I offered to show our visitors around the palace and its grounds. Freya's attendant, Ariella, joined us with her daughter, Taylee. Their fiery red hair was a stark contrast to Freya's dark locks, but they shared the same olive skin. Ariella and young Taylee wore flowing red gowns, differing from the black, tailored style of their mistress. The only commonality was the feather adornments worked into their ensembles.

"Through here, we enter the training grounds," I said. "Our men are currently training our newer recruits." Gesturing out toward the courtyards, I hoped that seeing our men in action might help convince them further to our alliance.

"Not all are men," said Queen Jezzamyn, who stopped walking and stared up ahead.

Seeing Temperance train with Cranzly brought a smile to my face. Since she'd demonstrated so much proficiency with the longsword, the general decided to improve her skills with the one-handed shortsword. Temperance picked it up quickly, as she had some experience training in shortsword—though she still favored longsword.

Calix's polite smile melted into one of pride. "Lady Temperance is my ward."

"Wardship?" King Brannyn said, raising a brow. "She's an orphan?"

"I'm afraid the statutes of her wardship don't permit me to reveal such information. You understand?" Calix clasped his hands behind his back with no visible signs of deception in his expression—unless one had my abilities.

"Yes..." King Brannyn stroked his beard and watched Temperance carefully.

It was risky to be secretive of who she was, but if we lied and someone checked facts, that'd be far more dangerous. This way brought speculation and nothing else. Being a ward suggested she was highborn, so no one would wonder why she was allowed at court, let alone staying within the palace.

"You don't worry about Minerva coming down on you for breaking her law and allowing women into your armies?" Drystan asked, his eyes on the sparring match between Temperance and Cranzly.

Calix waved his hand in dismissal. "She's not joining the army, but you can't say a woman shouldn't know how to defend herself. Besides, she's of the adventurous sort. When she wants to try something, she does it."

Cranzly knocked the wooden sword from Temperance's hand, sending it sliding across the dirt a short distance ahead of us. Temperance dodged the blow he was about to inflict and ran toward her weapon, leaving a stunned Cranzly to chase her. As he closed in, she slid through the dirt on her right leg and grabbed her weapon. The general was almost upon her when she twisted up on one knee with her sword pointed at his belly, and his weapon held back by her left hand.

"Vanquished!" Temperance breathed heavily but didn't waver from her position, a smile lighting up her entire face.

Whoa.

Surrounding soldiers hooted and hollered.

Cranzly joined in and, dropping his sword, offered her his hand. "Where'd you learn that maneuver?"

"City softball when I was twelve." Temperance laughed as she took his hand to stand and dusted herself off.

Cranzly cocked his head and furrowed his brow.

"Never mind." Temperance shook her head. "Game from home."

"We'll tell 'em I taught you that," the old general said with a chuckle.

"Deal," she said.

Taylee sprung from Ariella's grasp and propelled herself forward, feathers and ribbons whipping in the wind from the tulle of her skirts. Temperance was momentarily startled by the girl's sudden appearance at her side, but her expression melted into one of adoration as she placed her hand on her chest.

"You're just about the cutest thing!" she exclaimed. "Where'd you come from?"

Temperance glanced up at our group, realizing she had an audience of more than just soldiers. An awkward chuckle escaped her lips, her gaze met mine, restoring her comfortable smile. Taylee swung her hand frantically at Temperance.

"What's your name, cutie?" Temperance beamed at her, bending closer to her level.

"Taylee," Ariella said from her place next to Freya, before turning to her mistress and whispering into her ear.

Freya raised a brow. "Really?"

Neither made any moves to interrupt the exchange between Temperance and the girl. Ariella's eyes sparkled, while Freya's chin tensed, her face unreadable.

"Your dress is very pretty, Taylee," Temperance said.

"Thank you!" Taylee spun, her dress lifting her skirts in full circle.

"Careful!" Wide-eyed and laughing, Temperance quickly held down the flying bundles. "Ladies should keep their skirts down."

"Come here!" Taylee's mood changed in a blink, and she gestured for Temperance to kneel.

Holding her hands up in mock surrender, Temperance knelt down. Taylee squared her shoulders and gave as proper a bow as she could muster. When Taylee's head popped up from her curtsy, she gingerly removed the multicolored flower crown atop her head and held it out to Temperance.

"Bow your head," Taylee demanded and laughed in pleasure when Temperance obliged. Once the girl secured the crown upon Temperance's head, she squealed in delight. "Now arise as Queen!"

My chest tightened. With a locked jaw to hide my worry, I watched Temperance thank the five-year-old.

If Taylee was a Squirt, they would know who Temperance was now.

By the Goddess, no.

Prince Drystan entered my line of sight approaching the two. Taylee rushed to hug him. He softly smiled at the child before tousling her hair and sending her skipping back to Ariella. Drystan bowed to Temperance in the Fjall greeting. After a moment of hesitation she mimicked his gesture.

When Temperance raised her head, Drystan took her hand in his. "Lady Temperance, I'm Prince Drystan of Fjall. That was a skillful victory."

A blush formed on her cheeks, pulling a shy smile with it. "Thank you."

Don't let him see you look like that!

Drystan bent to pick up her wooden sword. "It's unfortunate you lost your grip in the first place. May I demonstrate?"

Temperance glanced my way before nodding. Drystan adjusted her grip on the handle, then proceeded to stand behind Temperance, leading her arm through a few movements.

"Feel better?" he asked.

Temperance nodded, and he stepped away, grabbing her free hand in his.

"May I request to walk with you after your exercises?"

No. Not her. Don't choose her! I screamed in protest inside my head, remembering the agreement Fjall and I had just come to.

"Doesn't she have her dance lesson after this, Calix?" I asked as indifferently as I could. "You two will open the dancing at the ball, after all. Practice is necessary."

"Prince Drystan, your Linallian dances could use some work," Freya said. "Why not join them?" She smiled encouragingly toward the prince, though her eyes held a threat.

Drystan turned the question to Temperance. "Would you allow me to join you?"

Temperance glanced at Calix who, much to my irritation, nodded.

I fought back the urge to punch him in the shoulder, which was more difficult when my eyes met hers. My eyes wandered toward the ground, afraid she'd notice the jealousy spilling over.

Why did it always feel like she could see my truth?

"As long as it's all right with my guardian, Calix and *My King* then it's okay with me." Her tone was hesitant but kind.

Drystan bowed over her hand and placed a kiss on it.

He's the prince of an allied kingdom. DO. NOT. PUNCH. HIM.

"Well, we have much to see and discuss," I said. "Shall we continue?"

Wanting to separate the pair as soon as possible, I led the group of royals out of the practice yards.

CHAPTER 24

TEMPERANCE

Drystan placed his hands on my waist, guiding me into the next lift. It was a maneuver that was supposed to look effortless and fluid, but it came off more like a sack of potatoes being plopped into a wheelbarrow. My partner rolled his eyes as I stumbled back slightly.

You asked for this, buddy. No one forced you. I glanced at our ogling royal onlookers. *Not me, anyway.*

Had there been a slab of glass between us and them, King Brannyn and his entourage would have had their noses pressed right up against it. I chuckled, imagining it.

Drystan arched an eyebrow at me but said nothing. He hadn't said a word since he'd asked to join my lesson. At least he wasn't some creepy older dude. He looked around James' age—maybe a year or two older. He had long black hair, that was sleek and pulled into a braid down his back. Unlike his uncle's long braided beard, Drystan was clean shaven.

I stole a glance at Frederick and wished I was dancing with him instead. On the other hand, I also hoped he'd leave. Not only was I dancing with someone else, but Drystan was no better at the activity than me.

Frederick briefly smiled before his face tensed, and he looked away. He seemed... concerned? Upset? I couldn't completely tell, but he certainly wasn't thrilled with the situation.

"Ahem." Drystan stared down at me, his left hand hanging in the air. He waved his fingers, encouraging me to take it.

Lifting my left hand to his, we turned. The skirts of my dress billowed up around my ankles as we spun. The motion reminded me of my dream. The image of the skirts of my ball gown fluttering against the steps of the staircase came to the forefront of my mind.

I dropped my left hand and raised my right.

It'd been three days since I found the staircase and the room. Why was I still having the dream?

Lost in thought, I nearly forgot to switch hands. No matter how much I tried to focus on the steps, my dream kept bubbling to the surface.

The locked door.

The spiraling staircase.

The oppressive force coming up behind me.

The smoke-filled window that entrapped me before was no longer a foggy mess, but clear as crystal. When I entered the room, Frederick and Ora were among the three figures standing across from me, but the last was the gray wind-blown figure I'd encountered the first time I'd entered the room in reality.

They'd disappear, leaving me alone with the Genesis Scepter in hand. Approaching the stone, I'd extend the staff toward it, only to be met with the face of the torturess. Red eyes, black hair, and a sharp, blood-red smile that sliced across her face. Then there was nothing. I'd woken up with more questions.

Was the woman Minerva? Where was the staff? Who was the shadowed figure?

While guiding me into a lift, Drystan and I stumbled again.

Drystan's reflexes were quick, and he grabbed my waist before I hit the ground.

"Are you well?" Drystan's sharp eyes widened, assessing my condition as he helped me regain my balance.

"I'm fine," I assured, my cheeks warmed with embarrassment as I righted myself and glanced around the room.

Ora attempted to conceal her laughter. When she failed to do so, I covered my face and joined her.

"Ladies?" Calix said sternly. "Can we continue?"

Biting back our chuckles, we nodded.

Calix addressed Drystan and me. "Now... gently, Prince Drystan. Gently. Linallian dances are more symphonious than what you're used to. Temperance, focus more on your partner and less on the clouds you should aim to dance like."

Calix turned back to his own partner, Ora, and I curtsied to Drystan.

"I promise to do better."

Drystan bowed to me while Frederick headed toward the door. Before he exited the ballroom, he met my gaze with kind eyes and a laugh in his smile.

Drystan pulled me back into the dance, picking up where we left off.

"Was it interesting?" he asked after we'd found our rhythm.

"What?"

"The conversation you were having with yourself." Drystan kept his head up but aimed his gaze at me.

"I wasn't talking to myself."

"Not out loud," he said.

Was he a mind reader or something? How would he know? We

spun around each other. Then, as if he'd heard them, he answered my thoughts.

"Your face is rather expressive." This time, he turned his whole face to me. "It changed quite frequently."

A blush crept up my cheeks. He didn't sound like he was making fun of me, but that didn't make it any less embarrassing. I'd have to watch what I said around him.

"What's distracting you?" he asked.

"A riddle inside a dream," I said, hoping he'd take my vague response and that would be the end of it.

He spun me into the next lift of the dance. "Ah... I like riddles. Perhaps I could assist."

"I wouldn't want to bore you." I laughed, trying again to kill the subject. I didn't need anyone else to find out about me.

"Feel free to speak your mind," he said, his eyes holding a sincerity that warmed my heart. Much like how I felt around Brett back home, but Drystan was just a little more stoic.

Maybe, if I was extremely careful with my wording, he could help.

"It's a recurring dream, but lately it's been changing," I said.

His lips pursed, and he glanced at the ceiling in thought.

"Has your life path changed recently?"

"Yes," I said hesitantly.

"Sounds more like divination." Drystan grasped my right hand in his as we stepped toward each other for a step, then backed away. We repeated the movement with our left.

Crap... Time to backpedal.

This probably wasn't the best idea after all. How had he possibly jumped to that conclusion?

I shook my head. "It's not like everything in my dream has happened."

"But some of it has?" Drystan raised an eyebrow and reached his hand around his back.

It would look more suspicious if I avoided the topic altogether.

"Hypothetically... sort of." I mimicked his movement and grasped his waiting hands behind my back. "It's probably just memories manifesting in a strange way."

He led us into a turn. Keeping hold of one of my hands and releasing the other, he twirled me in a circle until we were facing each other in a proper dance frame.

"If you say so," Drystan said, glancing at the flower crown that still sat on my head. "But it sounds like more to me."

"Mind expanding on that?" I asked.

He rolled his eyes and sighed before leading me by the waist.

"If you roll your eyes at me again—prince or not—I will pop them out."

Drystan laughed. His straight, high cheekbones that made him look like a gargoyle plumped up, filling in his narrow face. The transition made a remarkably attractive difference. I smiled, proud of myself for cracking him a little.

His laughter quieted, returning his stony expression. A hint of a smile remained, making him seem more relaxed.

"My kingdom is a safeguard of sorts for fairies. As a result, I'm well-versed in many forms of magic. In my education, I've found that there are multiple methods of divination, some rarer than others."

Drystan eyed me as if gauging my reaction. My face flushed, but I attempted a casual smile to mask my fear of discovery.

"Dream divination is the rarest," he said. "Only one family is known to possess the trait. Throughout history there were those who used spells to mimic it, albeit not accurately."

"Fascinating." Trying my best to appear indifferent, I smiled again.

"Indeed." Drystan's eyes narrowed as if aiming to solve the riddle of me.

It's time to change the subject.

"Why are they watching us?" I nodded toward his uncle and Freya.

His shoulders tensed, and I sensed another eye roll coming on.

"And don't even think about rolling your eyes at me again," I warned.

"Ah, fine. No more." He briefly released one of his hands from our grip and moved it diagonally across his chest. "Promise."

I assumed the gesture was the equivalent to a pinky swear.

"We have an agreement with your king that's to be sealed with marriage," he continued and spun me out, then back. "I'm to choose a bride from this court."

I nearly lost my footing again. No. Was that why Frederick left? Why would he let them even consider me? I'd thought that he and I—

"King Frederick agreed to this?" I asked, during one of the turns. I glanced at our onlookers, then turned back to Drystan. "Does the girl have any say in it?"

"Of course she does... But why would someone turn down a throne?" Drystan spat out his last words bitterly.

My thoughts shifted to Ora and Frederick. She ran away from a crown and an arranged marriage because she didn't love him. Frederick seemed to want nothing less than a marriage of love either. But he might not have a choice in the future. Even so, why would he force it on me? It didn't make sense... especially after our kiss.

"If she doesn't accept, we select another," Drystan said stiffly.

"What if no one accepts?"

He smiled reassuringly. "If everyone says no—which is unlikely—better for me. No offense."

"None taken." I laughed in relief, happy we understood each other. Neither of us wanted this.

After one last spin, we faced each other and bowed. Everyone clapped for us.

"Did we just make it through with no mistakes?" I asked, almost giddy.

Drystan grinned back at me. "Indeed."

"I guess Calix was right. Having my head in the clouds earlier wasn't helpful."

"I wasn't in the best of spirits before, which also didn't help." He smacked his fist into the opposite hand and bowed, which I reciprocated. "Would you mind if I continued to join you in your practicing until the ball? I'm not eager to bond with someone again in order to work on my dancing skills."

I knew where he was coming from. Our practice had been awkward enough.

I curtsied as gracefully as I could and said, "Yes."

Ora and I had barely exited the ballroom when I received a surprise attack hug from behind.

"Temperance!" cried Ariella. "I'm so happy to see you again!" Her grip was so tight my elbows dug into my sides. "Freya told me to wait, but I was too excited."

"Again?" I asked.

Ora blinked at the woman like she was insane.

"Sorry." Ariella released me. "It was brief, and I was in my true form."

Her true form?

It took a moment for my memory to catch up.

Waist-length fiery red hair—worthy of a shampoo commercial—framed a pair of ruby-colored eyes. The skirts of her gown ruffled in a hodgepodge of red, orange, and yellow chiffons that moved with the delicateness of a flickering flame. The bodice was decked out with a uniform array of feathers to match the bottom. Red chiffon draped from a pair of red arm cuffs, creating the illusion of a sleeve.

I swallowed the awkward chuckle that threatened to escape my lips.

"I didn't recognize you without your... wings."

"You're the fairy that saved her?" Ora asked, her eyes widening before she gave me a disbelieving look.

"Thank you for your help," I said. "I'm glad to see you're safe."

Ariella smiled and squeezed my hands. "It's one of our sacred duties to protect you. Though, I didn't know for sure it was you until—"

"Ariella." Freya stood among us, looking fierce. Her silver eyes shone in contrast to her sleek, black hair that faded into silver at the tips. Each strand was folded over her head to one side, revealing a small section above her ear cut so close to the scalp it looked buzzed. It too was painted silver.

Black illusion lace crawled up the front of her dress and wrapped around her neck in a mandarin-style collar. Raven feathers jutted out from the neckline covering her shoulders. Throughout the body of the gown, a mishmash of silver-and-white threads twisted and overlapped diagonally across the surface of the black satin, creating a winged pattern.

"I instructed you to wait," Freya said, eyes narrowed, waiting for an explanation.

"I waited through her sparring and dance lessons," Ariella said. "If you expected any longer then you've forgotten who I am." She stifled a chuckle and performed a minor curtsy before adding, "Mistress Freya."

"It baffles me how the majority of our race hasn't been exposed with you amongst our ranks." Though Freya's words were savage, her tone was jesting.

They were *both* fairies?

"Um, excuse me." All three sets of eyes fell on me. "Yeah, hi. Isn't it a bit risky for you to reveal who you are?"

"Need we hide ourselves from a child of the creator?" The humor in Freya's voice vanished in an instant. "You are the Descended of the Haloed Sun, heir to the Superior Goddess. Uncrowned Queen of Eslane—at least what's left of it."

How did they know? Even if Ariella and Drystan suspected, there was no way for them to know for sure, right?

I attempted to seem amused by her statement.

"What gave you that impression?"

"You mean, apart from the violet shade in those eyes of yours?" Freya asked.

Had my eyes been glowing? No, I wasn't using my powers.

"My eyes are blue," I asserted with a shrug.

With a near dead-on Drystan impression, Freya rolled her eyes.

"Ariella and I are fairies." She let the statement hang in the air, like it had meaning.

I tilted my head. "Okay... and?"

Ora leaned over to explain, "Fairies have advanced sight. They see colors and edges clearer and sharper than any other creature. Your eyes must look more violet to them. Not to mention, their race was created by one of your ancestors, so they have some talent in divination and creation magic. Limited, but still there."

"Oh," I said.

"How is a Descended naive to all this?" Freya said, head cocked to the side as though trying to work out my thoughts from another angle.

"As I told you, Mistress Freya," Ariella said, "she was startled by me on that beach... like she'd never seen a fairy before."

"Why's that?" Freya asked.

"You said *apart* from my eyes," I said, averting her question. "What else brought your suspicion?"

Freya chuckled, clearly exasperated. "Taylee indicated as much by placing that floral wreath on your head. Until we reach adolescence, we have the gift to see auras of magic, Descended included. Taylee's been trained to only crown one with the soul of the Haloed Sun."

I gaped over at Ora. "Anyone with a child fairy can find me this easily, and you said nothing?"

"Fairies are scarce!" Ora defended. "The young ones almost unheard of. Domhnall massacred most of them, and then Minerva kidnapped or murdered any she could get her hands on. Initially, she wanted to create more, but then she failed—creating the kovchka instead. Then she turned on them."

"That's all kinds of wrong!" I said, my voice shooting up an octave.

"In a way, they're proof that she's not Descended." Ora folded her arms and softened her voice. "Without their support, she'd be outed as a fraud. So she kills or forces them to her will with Catatonia Mist."

"Catatonia Mist?" I asked.

"A strange substance Minerva concocted that takes away someone's free will," Ora explained.

"That's barbaric," I whispered. My heart weighed down inside my chest like a medicine ball.

"You're sympathetic?" asked Freya, a flash of hope gleaming in her eyes.

"Only a heartless idiot wouldn't be," I replied, my fingers dug into my palms.

"An alliance between us would be beneficial." Freya bowed to me in the Fjall fashion.

Everything was crystal clear now. They had known who I was from the get-go and made some sort of agreement with Frederick. There was only one thing they could want from me.

"You want me to marry Prince Drystan." The words came out more bitterly than I'd intended.

"I wouldn't be so down on the prospect," Freya lightly scolded. "Our kingdom is filled with Eslanian refugees, particularly the monks of the Superior Goddess. They can train you in your gifts. With a marriage to a viable kingdom, you can unite the Eslanians and rebuild."

She made a fine argument, but my plans were set. I was going home before making any decisions about my role in Emeriz.

"And if I'm not interested?" I asked.

"That would be foolish." She laughed.

"Then I guess I'm a fool." Not breaking eye contact with her, I shrugged. "One who's free to choose my life on my terms."

We eyed each other, neither one of us backing down.

I sensed our staring contest was some sort of test, so I stood a little straighter and raised my chin. In return, she relaxed her stance and smiled.

"Calix mentioned when you wanted to do something, you did it without hesitation," Freya said and took a step closer, assessing me. "I can appreciate that you are not so easily swayed."

"Thanks," I said.

"At least spend time with our prince. He's every bit as worthy of your hand as *others*."

Freya smiled at me as if to insinuate something. It seemed the discussion was closed as she and Ariella turned to leave.

Ora and I had headed in the opposite direction when a strong gust of wind blew through the halls, and a storm cloud appeared above our heads. A foggy, gray figure appeared within the vortex. Moments later, it disappeared, and the hall became quiet and still.

Whatever that thing was, it was getting bigger.

Frantically turning around, Ora and I scanned the area to be sure it had, in fact, left our presence. I listened closely for anything unusual, but all I heard was a pair of footsteps rapidly fading in the distance.

CHAPTER 25

TEMPERANCE

My boots clacked loudly against the steps of the spiral staircase as I descended with my sixth pile of thick books and scrolls. It reminded me of the sound of hooves meeting the cobblestones, making me feel more like a workhorse than I already did. Sweat dripped down my temple and neck, my fingers aching from the weight. I plopped them down on the floor next to the painted archway with no regard for delicacy.

"That was wrought with meaning," Ora said with a wide-eyed blink.

I slumped down next to the pile of books, letting out a long breath.

"If I have to go up and down that stupid staircase one more time I'm going to hurl." I leaned my back against the stone of the interior wall, absorbing its cool touch.

Surrounded by her own piles of books collected from the scholastedites, Ora sat cross-legged, going over the handwritten notes I'd passed her through the archway. Eyebrows raised, she turned back to her research on the staff, clearly not wanting to encourage any more complaining from me.

"I may have found something." Without looking up, she held one of Grandma's journals up to the archway. "It looks like poems, but it might be more."

We'd found that only my grandmother's journals could pass through the barrier as long as I passed them through.

"With all the dead ends we keep reaching it might be faster to resolve this archway problem. Then you can just come inside." Sighing wearily, I reached through the magical barrier and snatched it from her hand. "At this rate, I'll never get home."

A sad smile crossed Ora's face.

"Ora, you've known from the beginning the plan was to go home."

She turned the page and the sound ripped through the air, echoing in the silence of the hall.

"It's the only way to make you whole," I tried again.

"Unless you decide not to come back," Ora said softly, still staring at the book in her hands.

I understood her fears, but I'd already decided that Nora deserved the option to be reunited with her other half. If Nora agreed, I'd come back at least once.

"No." I shook my head. "I'd help you first. Once you're whole, we'll decide together."

"And if Nora doesn't want to?"

I reached through the barrier and placed my hand on her shoulder until she looked up.

"She will. I'm incredibly persuasive."

We laughed.

"Nora probably feels the same as you do. Incomplete, wishing she was braver and more outgoing. Just like you want to be cool and collected in your emotions."

"Promise?"

I held up my pinky finger as I always did with Nora.

"Promise."

Smiling, she linked her pinky with mine.

"You have another reason to come back anyway." She released my finger.

"Which is?"

Ora glanced briefly toward General Cranzly standing guard at the end of the hall. I'd allowed Frederick to entrust him with our secret, so he could protect us in case anyone came snooping.

When she was certain he wasn't paying attention, she turned back to me. "Oh, I don't know... Maybe the king who kissed you a few days ago?"

"You mean the coward who kissed me then pushed me into the arms of another man to strengthen his alliance?" I asked flatly.

"You don't know that." Ora raised an eyebrow.

"Don't I?" Counting them off on my fingers, I addressed the events. "I bore my soul to him, revealing who I am. We kiss. I'm introduced to Prince Drystan. Frederick watches our first dance practice then disappears for three whole days. No explanation, note, or personal visit. Just Calix dropping off breakfast, and the personal research Frederick's done to help me get home. Then I have to find out from—"

Not wanting to state the real reason for my bad mood, I rubbed my temples to ease the tension.

"Something has been bothering you today. What is it?" Ora's eyes narrowed, ready to fight whatever upset me.

"On my way to sparring this morning, I overheard Persephone talking to her hoard of worshipers." I stared up at the meteor-like black ceiling, watching the colorful sparkles dance across it. "She said, 'Frederick has barely left my side during my visits with Prince

Drystan. Jealousy must consume him at the possibility that the prince might choose me.'"

Ora scoffed. "Persephone is a snotty little brat. Frederick would never choose her. Trust me. I've seen how he looks at you versus how he looks at her, and it's vastly different."

"Why is he pushing me on Drystan then?" I said, looking at her with a sigh. "I don't see him staking any sort of claim."

"Ugh!" She wadded up a scrap of paper and chucked it at my head, but it bounced against the barrier. "You're sometimes just—bah! If you two don't see it and communicate, then maybe you shouldn't be together."

"Excuse me, ladies," Cranzly interrupted. "I need to see to an important matter. Mind finishing up soon so I might tend to it?"

"Everything okay?" I asked.

"A cadet of mine has scrambled eggs for brains—been screwing things up a bit." He chuckled. "Need to remind him of what's important."

"We're almost done," Ora said.

"Thank you." Cranzly smiled and walked back to his chair, grunting as he reclined back into it.

I turned back to the journal Ora handed me earlier and said, "What'd you find?"

"I'm not sure these are mere poems," Ora explained. "I suspect maybe spells or a code of some sort."

Observing the book, it was clearly well-used. Like it had been carried and hauled around for years. The spine was tattered and wearing away.

"Turn to the last page, final sentence," Ora directed.

I did as she asked and read it aloud. "'The sword holds the staff in its heart under the eye of the moon.' Sounds like..."

"The forces of the staff through the mouth of the flowing river that shall be linked with the moon as it draws its sword over the realm," Ora whispered.

"Two physical representations of the Descended. Which means she stashed the Genesis Scepter with the sword. If we find the sword, then we find the staff!" My heart pounded in anticipation. This was the breakthrough we'd needed!

Scrawled next to the words was a date. It was around the same time I'd met Frederick as a kid.

"The sword and moon in the prophecy refer to Descended of the Moon," Ora said. "Which means..."

"Frederick has to have it," I breathed.

"Looks like you have a pretty good reason to speak with him now."

Ora crossed her arms like she'd won something.

Finding Frederick should have been the first thing I did after leaving the library. Cranzly offered to escort me, but I turned him down. Ora wrinkled her brow when I used the excuse that I was meeting Brydon at the stables for a riding lesson.

After he left us, Ora turned to me, one hand on her hip and the other pointing at me.

"Liar."

I shrugged. "I did promise Brydon I'd visit."

"What happened to, 'I need to find a way home fast?'"

"Still true. I just..."

I had no rational justification for avoiding Frederick. What could I say? I liked him but hated that he hadn't done anything to stop the King of Fjall and the fairies from pushing me and Drystan together?

Or that I wondered if Persephone was right about me being a... temporary distraction for Frederick? Or if my feelings continued to grow, it would make it that much harder when I left?

"You *just*?" Ora crossed her arms and cocked her head, daring me to deny the real reasons I wanted to avoid Frederick.

"Whatever! Can't I spend time with my long-lost great-grandfather without getting the third degree?"

"Hey! I don't know what that last part means." She pointed at me again, then held her hands in the air. "But fine. Be impossible. I'm gonna go practice scrying and check on my grandfather."

My stomach churned with homesickness. "While you're at it, can you check on my family?" I asked. "Maybe Nora has seen or talked to them." Ora gave me a long-suffering look, and I stuck out my lower lip. "Please?"

She sighed, then smiled. "Sure. If you go talk to Frederick."

Laughing in disbelief, I crossed my arms. "I haven't seen or spoken to my family in weeks, and you won't check on them unless I flirt with a boy?"

Ora mirrored my stance. "Look where your mind is. I never mentioned flirting with him, but that's a better idea."

"Ora, that's not—"

"Ah-ah! That's the deal. Bye!" She spun on her heel and walked away, tossing a wave over her shoulder.

Brilliant move on her part. Usually I could wear Nora down and help her see things my way if she let me talk long enough. That, or she'd get fed up with my stubbornness and let me do whatever.

I let my arms drop to my sides as I watched her go. I turned and made a left at the next intersecting hall, knowing it would lead me to a courtyard I could use as a shortcut to the stables.

Though set up similarly to the practice yard, this courtyard was more formal with marbled platforms and cobblestone floors. Lush, colorful flower beds filled the space instead of soldiers. A few people draped sheer white fabric down and around the eight surrounding pillars, readying it for the Ethereal Ball the next night.

A crash of thunder rumbled in the sky, and it started to rain. I'd get soaked if I went to the stables, no matter which path I took.

I leaned my head against the nearest pillar and sighed, watching it fall. Breathing in the cool mist the wind carried in from the courtyard, I closed my eyes to enjoy the peace that fell over me. The damp floral aroma seeped into my soul, lifting the weight in my chest and cleansing away my anxieties.

I stepped away from the pillar and accidentally bumped into someone. They dropped a tray of supplies. Spools of thread, ribbons, needles, buttons, and trims clattered to the ground scattering in multiple directions. Faint snickering traveled from up the corridor.

"Ay! Watch wha—" The middle-aged woman who I'd bumped into eyed me, and the blood drained from her face. She immediately dropped to the floor. "Forgive me, milady."

I felt so guilty as she frantically picked things up and tossed them back onto the tray erratically.

"You stole the words from my mouth," I said and knelt down to help her.

She held her hands up. "No, milady," she protested. "Your dress will get dirty."

"Don't worry about it." I shook my head, continuing the task of cleaning up. "Really, this is my fault."

When we finished and stood, she curtsied a bit awkwardly.

"Thank you, Lady Temperance."

Word got around fast in this castle if she already knew my name. I guess I did sort of stand out like a sore thumb compared to the other ladies at court.

"It wouldn't have spilled if I wasn't daydreaming. I'm sorry, Lady…?"

She blushed. "Oh, I'm not a lady. You may call me Miss Angelanya. Your dress though—let me wipe—"

Miss Angelanya stepped back and bowed her head low to someone behind me.

My face flushed the instant I laid eyes on them. A mocking smile ripped across Persephone's face as she stood between Frederick and Drystan, setting my lungs ballooning again, which didn't mix well with the rapid beating of my heart at seeing Frederick.

That smile on him…

Turning to Miss Angelanya, I placed my hand on her shoulder.

"Sorry again," I said, "but I'm supposed to be at the stables."

I'd rather be drenched than deal with the three of them. I stepped toward the rainy courtyard.

"It's raining, Lady Temperance," Persephone said, her tone sickly sweet in contrast to her daggers for eyes. "Your skirt is already filthy from squatting down on the floor. We wouldn't want you to look completely unpresentable."

Almost in synchronized fashion, both guys rolled their eyes. I chuckled—a sound I'm sure they hadn't been expecting.

"Oh, it's raining?" Straightening my posture and placing a hand on my chest, I glanced from the rain then back to her. "Thank you for your astute observation."

Drystan bit his lips trying to contain a smile while Frederick covered his with one hand.

Unappreciative of my sarcasm, Persephone's plastered grin faltered.

"A little water never hurt anyone," I said and stepped back with arms spread wide into the drizzling weather, showering in its glory. I spun until I stood in the center of the flowers and turned back to my audience, bringing their attention to where the dirt had been on my gown. "Would you look at that? You don't even notice it now."

Through the rain, I could make out three smiles and a pout. I spun one last time, tossed a wave over my shoulder, and exited the courtyard toward the stables, not looking back.

Brydon was humming that same familiar tune when I came rushing into the stables dripping wet.

"Whoa there, girly!"

He quickly grabbed a blanket that'd been draped over a nearby stall and wrapped it snuggly around me. It smelled like hay and itched against my skin, but it was warm. Brydon ushered me to sit next to a small furnace.

"'Whoa there, girly'? I'm not a horse." My laugh came out closer to a shiver than an actual sound of amusement.

"You could catch something going out in the rain like that," he said, rumbling about across the room. "And you're not capable of curing disease."

"Why?" I asked.

He placed a hot cup of tea in my hands. "Don't know. Not one of your ancestors could. It seems you're resistant but still susceptible. You can ease the pain but not heal it."

"Like cold meds. I can cover up the symptoms, but I'm not a cure."

Brydon eyed me, confused. "Not completely sure what you're saying, but sounds like the gist of it, yes."

I sipped on my tea as Brydon pulled up a stool across from me, drinking his own. He didn't say anything, letting me warm up by the crackling furnace as he hummed. I took a long breath, inhaling steam from the minty tea. It reminded me of late nights with my dad, sipping a concoction of spearmint and chamomile to help when my dreams made me especially restless. My shoulders relaxed, and I shifted deeper into the blanket.

"Clearly you're stressed. Don't deny it, I can tell." When I finished my cup, he placed it on a table behind him. "Not only did you run out here in the rain, but you've got that crinkle in the middle of your forehead, and you aren't talking. Your grandmother used to do the same."

I stared down at my fingers and picked at them, remaining silent.

"How about a distraction?" he offered. "You can sort your thoughts, and I can get some help. Sound good?"

"Yes."

He clasped his hands together and led me to the first stall.

"Neva!" I said, beaming when I saw her.

"She needs a good brushing," Brydon said. "Use long strokes along the hair growth, not against it." He handed me the brush and headed out the stall. "Oh, and sing to her."

"Sing?"

"Or hum, if you'd rather." He shrugged. "It soothes her."

"The songs I know aren't exactly from around here," I whispered.

"Good thing it's storming out and it's just us here," he replied softly, then went about his other duties, leaving me alone.

"Okay, what kind of music are you into, Neva? Pop? Rock and roll?"

Neva nuzzled me with her nose. Laughing, I brushed her back. Between the rough sound of the bristles sliding against her hair and the pattering of raindrops against the roof, I felt content. My breathing matched Neva's, surrounding me with an odd calm. A song popped into my head I knew would make me feel at home.

"Neva, how about hearing one of my mom's favorite songs?" I tousled her mane, and she tapped her hoof twice. "I'll take that as a yes."

The lyrics of Tracy Byrd's "The Keeper of the Stars" flowed through me. My voice strained at some parts, not quite able to get a few of the notes right, but the feeling was there. As I sang, I found myself inside a memory.

While doing the dishes, Mom listened to her iPod and sang along to this song, completely unaware of her surroundings. Dad and James came in after yard work, and I looked up from my book. Dad held one finger to his lips, signaling James and me to keep quiet. When Mom reached the chorus, he wrapped her in his arms, pulling her into a dance while he sang along.

I told them to 'get a room' before James added an 'actually, ew don't.'

A few tears slid down my cheeks, and I smiled at their fading images. I'd done all I could to conceal how much I truly missed my family. The research, dance lessons, and sword fighting had all been minor distractions.

At the close of the song, I leaned my head against Neva and let myself cry. Two hands gently gripped my upper arms and twisted me into a comforting embrace. I buried my face into his chest.

In muffled sobs, I said, "I miss them so much. I want to go home, where I belong. But then this all fits too. I don't know what to do."

He cupped my damp curls and pressed his lips to the top of my head. That's when I caught a scent. Lime and cedarwood?

I lifted my head and immediately took a small step back, face burning.

"Frederick?"

His hand shifted from the back of my head to rest on my cheek.

"Disappointed?" Frederick said, peering down at me with a small empathetic smile, making my heart beat harder.

"No. I thought you were Brydon." Way too aware of how close he was, I fiddled with my fingers, but didn't dare move. I liked him near me a little too much. "How long have you been here?"

He brushed a few hairs out of my eyes. "Right before you started singing. Nice song. Not a bad voice either, though you were pitchy in some parts."

I laughed and tapped him lightly in the gut. "Who says you're an expert, hmm?"

"My ears." He caught my hand before it made contact with his stomach again.

I didn't take my gaze off our entwined hands.

"How do you do it?"

"Do what, my lady?"

My thumb traced the outside of his and I replied, "Take my mind off things."

"*Things* meaning your family?" he asked.

I nodded, but didn't look up.

"Maybe because I can see the truth of your emotions, and not just because of my powers." He gently squeezed my hand. "I know what it's like to be separated from your parents. It's an unimaginable pain— one you never quite get over."

Inhaling a deep breath, I met his eyes.

He blinked and swallowed before speaking more softly. "I care about you. I don't like seeing you in pain."

I put some distance between us.

"I'm confused. Persephone..."

"Pay no mind to Persephone. She likes to get what she wants, but I assure you, I'm one thing she'll never have." Frederick's expression turned sheepish, and he rubbed at the back of his head. "Cranzly gave me a good talking-to about confusing you."

So, Cranzly had heard everything.

"You're the one with 'scrambled eggs for brains'?" I teased.

"Correct." He looked down then back up at me with that smile of his.

Dude, you're killing me here. You can't be this hot.

"I'm encouraging Persephone to be their choice," he continued. "The last thing I want is for them to choose you, so I'm sitting in on their visits together." He reached out to pet Neva, which conveniently brought him closer to me. "I need to be sure she doesn't try to pull something."

"But there's still a chance they might pick me, right?" I whispered.

"Yes. Unfortunately, we can't just lie to them and tell them you are already betrothed or something, because if they discover the truth... it could shatter the alliance, and they would still pursue you anyway. But if they extend an offer, you could refuse."

I groaned and dropped my head into my hands.

"But that's just it! I don't even want to be in the running. I want to be taken off the board completely."

"I'll take care of it," Frederick said and pulled my hands away from my face to look me straight in the eyes. "I promise."

"Lots of promises today." I sighed. "I trust you."

"Good. Now, Cranzly mentioned you had something to tell me."

"Yes!" The excitement from when we found the information bubbled to the surface as I explained what we'd found in my grandmother's last journal. "So they have to be together! Do you remember anything about that night? Did my grandma mention them at all?"

"I'll look into it," he said, and my heart sank.

It felt like we'd take one step forward only to take two steps back.

"As much as I'd like to stay here in our private haven away from court, it stopped raining." He held out his arm to me. "May I escort you back?"

I hadn't noticed until that moment, but his hair and clothes were damp with rainwater. He'd run through the rain just to talk to me.

The thought warmed me to my toes.

I curtsied and placed my arm in his.

"You may, My King."

CHAPTER 26

FREDERICK

While I was locked in a fierce stare down with the Elysian Sword, the majestic item shone brightly. The tempered metal winked from its sacred place upon the mantle of the Superior Goddess. Moonlight bestowed her grace through the clear, domed ceiling of the chapel. Her watchful eye touched every space of the circular room—lightening every reflective surface masterfully like placing a candle inside a vase of etched glass. Every light seemed to reach for the sword. Taunting me.

I clenched my hand over my chest. Why hadn't I told her?

Although the time I'd spent with Temperance earlier had been short, I felt grateful for those few hours. She'd talked more about her home, family, and closest friends. I enjoyed watching how animated she became while she spoke of them, but the moment she finished telling a story, sadness would glaze over her eyes. She'd cover it by smiling or asking me questions about myself.

When I heard her singing in the stables, I'd hoped she would come around to the idea of staying in Emeriz. That, maybe, I was helping her come to that decision, but that thread of thinking was cut the moment her tears fell.

Of course she wanted to be with her family. That need of hers shouldn't have stung me so much. I would have given away every power in my being to have mine back. Even understanding that, what had I done? I evaded the truth selfishly. The moment she mentioned the sword, I remembered. The head of the Genesis Sceptre resided at the hilt of the Elysian Sword, put there years ago by Temperance's grandmother.

I hadn't known the *whole* time where the staff lay. The night I originally met Temperance, I'd awoken to a prick of my finger and a flash of light. Then I glimpsed Henvick sheathing my mother's sword. We had to depart to draw Minerva's men away from Temperance and her grandparents so they could get away. I never had the chance to ask Henvick about it before he'd been executed.

Yet, after I'd spouted all about my appreciation for truth, I'd turned around and hid this from her. Looking once more between the hilt of the sword and Temperance's sketch of the staff, I crumpled the piece of parchment in my hand and tossed it across the room.

"Leaving trash on the floors of the chapel is a rather blasphemous act," Heshrin said as he eased himself out from behind the altar with the stealth of a snake exiting its hole, eyeing the sword as he did so. "From how hard you've been staring at this thing, I'd guess it offended you in some way. Want me to make it disappear?"

"I pay you to spy on others, not myself," I scolded.

"I didn't intend to. You just happened to be tonight's guest." He chuckled wryly. "You'd be surprised by the number of people that come in the dead of night to confess their darkest to the Goddess, thinking no one would overhear. It's taken all my energy not to respond as the Goddess. Make them shudder at their hypocrisy."

"Anything noteworthy?" I said, picking myself up off the floor and brushing the dust from my trousers.

"Not to you. For my pockets, however, plenty." He shrugged and tossed a piece of meat into a darkened corner.

"What did you just say about trash in the chapel?" I crossed my arms and nodded toward the discarded meat.

"It's for a friend."

In the next instant, the meat disappeared into the shadows. I didn't get a good look at the creature, only a flash of two plum orbs reflecting in the light. Had that been Tundra?

"Right!" Clapping his hands together, Heshrin effectively brought my attention away from whatever lay in the darkness. "I actually do have some information you'll find interesting, kingly."

"Listening."

"Fjall's come to a decision as to who they've chosen for their future queenie."

My chest tightened, already knowing the answer before he spoke.

"Your Lady Temperance. No surprise given who she truly is." He laughed when I stared at him blankly, unsurprised that he knew.

If we weren't careful, everyone would inevitably discover who she was. It would become more difficult to protect her if we didn't control the situation better.

"You'll do *nothing* with this information other than making a few extra gold from me to keep your slimy mouth shut." I gripped his shirt, my gaze unflinching. "What you *will* do is protect Temperance at all costs."

"I'm to stalk her for you? Make sure she's not whisked away by another suitor, is that it?" Heshrin grinned. "Jealousy doesn't suit you."

"I doubt you want such a powerful ally as her in the hands of Minerva."

I could *see* deep within his soul that he wanted Minerva out of power. For what reasons I didn't know, but it was good enough for me.

"Now go," I commanded.

Laughing maniacally, Heshrin left me alone in the chapel with my thoughts.

It was becoming more and more dangerous for her to stay in Linall. No, in all of Emeriz. If word got back to Minerva or Maxwell, they would burn the world to get to her. Everyone would be safer if she went back to Earth. *She* would be safer.

I knew this, but something inside urged me not to let her go. Not yet.

I approached the altar and whispered a promise to the scepter.

"Just one more day. After the ball, I'll give you over to her."

CHAPTER 27

TEMPERANCE

The Day of Peace had arrived, and the Ethereal Ball would be held that night in honor of the Goddess. My skirts swished delicately against the floor of my chambers, causing momentary déjà vu. The dream haunted me yet again, clear and sharp.

The locked door.

The spiraling staircase.

The oppressive force coming up behind me.

In the dream I'd race up the staircase, stop at the window, open the door, and finally see the pedestal with the mysterious stone. Frederick stood on my right, Ora to my left, and the ghostly gray figure directly across from me on the other side. Then, they disappeared, leaving me alone with the Genesis Scepter.

Ever-changing, the dream manifested new details that put me on edge:

First, the heart-crushing fear I felt within the dream nearly paralyzed me when I reached the window. Second, I'd seen what to do with the staff once I entered the room with it. The final difference didn't hit me until Rhiannon revealed the dress I'd be wearing to the ball.

Stunning skirts layered in blush and lavender tulles came billowing out from a blush bodice detailed with dimensional appliquéd lace. The petals of the flowers matched the colors of the skirts with an added accent of green, creating a leafy, vining effect. Twisted tulles gently kissed my shoulders, creating cap sleeves.

Mixed emotions overwhelmed me as I stood in the literal dress of my dreams, praying it wouldn't become the dress of my nightmares. It was lovely, but I had the fierce urge to tear it off my body.

This couldn't have been a coincidence.

Ora, Rhiannon, and Miss Angelanya didn't understand my hesitation in wearing it. I wasn't about to mention the dream and ruin their enthusiasm for the night.

My eyes drifted to my vanity. I'd awoken to breakfast, a bouquet of white solira blossoms, and a small gift wrapped in blue velvet. Inside the package lay an exquisite hairpiece. Gems and pearls twisted around each other in shades of ivory, green, and mauve, all held together with gold wire.

Rhiannon finished styling my hair in a curled half-updo and secured the beautiful hairpiece at its base. While she did so, I read the handwritten note once again.

Temperance,
I intended to present this to you in person, but you were sleeping soundly with Tundra curled up next to you when I arrived. I never imagined myself being jealous of a cat. I leave this note to prove that I, King of Linall, did attempt to see you before tonight.
Yours,
Frederick

A calm sense of security quieted my nerves. It was silly to think that the hairpiece would bring me luck or protection, but I wore it like a shield.

Frederick would keep me safe.

Ora and I were jostled around the lavishly decorated halls by people overcrowding the area, drunk with merriment.

Desperate to get out of the suffocating atmosphere, we maneuvered through the sea of formal tunics, capes, extravagant ball gowns, and masked performers. We finally reached the hall guarded by two soldiers at the entrance with four more guarding the inner atrium.

"Lady Temperance," the soldiers greeted me before turning to Ora with glittering eyes. "Lady Ora."

As naturally as breathing, Ora coyly twisted her finger around one of her loose tendrils and curtsied.

One of the guards gestured for us to enter, his eyes never leaving Ora.

We started to enter when someone rammed into the back of me.

"Apologies," said the guy wearing an elaborate face mask—he took hold of my hand to keep me from toppling over.

"No harm, no foul." I curtsied and turned to leave but was held in place by the man's grip on my hand.

A shiver ran down my spine. The stranger was uncomfortably familiar, regardless that the only feature I could make out were his eyes. The irises were nearly the same color as his pupils, with a slight carnelian hue.

"Excuse us." Yanking my hand away more forcefully, Ora and I passed through the archway, leaving the staring man behind.

"You're drawing some attention," Ora said, her eyebrows raised suggestively.

"Pff... please." I shuddered thinking of his overly smooth hand touching mine ever again. "Speak for yourself. Those guards were drooling all over you."

"Much like your swordplay, flirting is an art." She nudged my shoulder. "It must be fed with practice."

"Are you a mermaid or siren?" I teased.

"Two sides of the same coin." She grinned from ear to ear. "You haven't seen your last surprise from either part of me."

We found Calix waiting with some of the other lords and advisors, ready to escort Ora and me into the ballroom. Not liking the idea of having all eyes on me, I begged him to open the first dance with Ora. He explained that the court knew me as his ward. As the legal equivalent of a daughter, and Calix being unmarried, we had to open the dance. When I'd shyly asked why Frederick didn't open the floor as king, Calix said Frederick never danced at the balls.

"Shall we?" Calix bowed and offered an arm to each of us.

"Lady Temperance?"

Two voices called out in unison. Collin and Drystan approached me, eyeing each other warily.

"Yes?" I asked.

"May I escort you in?" Collin asked, not caring for the higher station of the prince.

"Looks like the lad beat me to it." Drystan sighed, smiling at me. "Unless you'd prefer me."

Collin glared at him, and I blushed.

"Calix will be my escort," I said. "Maybe Ora could be persuaded."

"Lady Ora?" Collin held arm toward her.

Smiling, she nodded and wound her arm in his.

"I shall press on alone." Drystan bowed, a little disheartened, and returned to his uncle.

Calix and I took our place in front of the procession. Nausea threatened as the opening horn sounded, and the herald announced the arrival of the council.

CHAPTER 28

FREDERICK

"You're late," Cranzly chastised, matching my quick pace. He eyed my hands as I attached the caplet to my formal tunic with a brooch of the royal seal.

"You're late eight times out of ten, Uncle," I jested. "Did Calix put you up to this?"

"He's about to lead the procession into the ballroom, therefore, too occupied to scold you." He flicked me just beneath my crown. "Also heed my words, not my example, boy."

"You and Calix do like to smack me around. Ever think it's your fault I have 'scrambled eggs for brains'?"

"Told you about that, did she?" Cranzly said, beaming with pride. I couldn't tell if it was for himself or Temperance. Maybe both.

"Yes, thanks for that," I said sarcastically.

"Smart girl."

I raised an eyebrow at him and said, "It's treasonous to speak ill of the king."

"Get over it. Calix and I won't be around forever." He shrugged. "You need someone who can take you down a peg or two when needed. She'll do the job splendidly."

"She's leaving, Cranzly." The words tasted bitter on my tongue.

"Not yet."

Tonight she will.

I intended to show her the Elysian Sword by the night's end. The longer I waited, the more it felt like a betrayal to her.

We reached the end of the King's Atrium—my personal maze of secret passageways—and I traced a circle on the door with a crystal while reciting the words, *"Goddess, offer your protection and light the path with your direction."* The door glowed white, and the torches burned out behind us, leaving us in darkness. The door silently slid open, but I halted in the shadow of the doorway before stepping through. We had to be certain no one would see us appear from thin air who didn't already know about the passageways.

My heart leapt at the sight of Temperance as she and Calix stepped through the grand double doors and into the ballroom filled with lights and chattering lords and ladies.

"Being escorted by my brother is pathetic," Persephone whined to Taren.

I held my hand up, signaling Cranzly not to go further. Taren was aware of the King's Atrium, being a member of my personal guard, but I did not want Persephone to see me.

"You were the one who couldn't procure the arm of Frederick or Drystan," Taren ranted, glaring at his sister. "If Father hadn't insisted on this, I might have had another lady at my side, but I'm stuck with you."

"Why are they fawning all over that girl anyway?" Persephone scoffed.

"Lady Temperance," Taren corrected.

Persephone paid no mind to it as she spat out more complaints: "She speaks to those beneath her, helps them, is friends with them. Then there's her brutish need for battle play with no concern of the risk that poses to Linall. When she's not doing those things, she's enclosed in the library. She couldn't dance properly when she arrived either. Where's Calix been keeping her? Under a rock with the guerilla fighters?"

"Stop with your incessant gossiping," Taren said. "I would prefer her next to me than you. She'd be more pleasant to banter with, even with the risk of physical injury. It's also thanks to your lie about her liking me that I pursued her and caused that misunderstanding. It's your fault I was demoted a rank in the army."

A mix of gratitude and irritation swelled within me at Taren's defense of Temperance. However, he still had a long way to go to make up for what he'd done.

"You won't have to worry about her much longer," Taren continued. "Prince Drystan chose her. She'll be gone soon enough."

"True, perhaps sooner than you think." Persephone shook her head. "Her behavior exhibits nothing of being a lady. Filthy little dirt grubber."

"Too far," said Cranzly, stepping forward to intervene, but I held him back, emerging from the corridor myself.

"My King," the two addressed me with a bow.

Hands behind my back, my eyes never left Persephone.

"You're right, Persephone. How could I be so blind?" I asked.

Lifting her head, Persephone's minxy smile appeared. The herald announced another member of the council, leaving the room nearly empty.

"Temperance shows kindness to everyone," I continued. "She learns to fight, not only to protect herself but others as well. She studies diligently so she might understand more about the world. Honest and sincere, she puts those she cares for before herself. You're absolutely right—those aren't the actions of a lady." I took a step forward, hovering over her. "They are actions of a queen."

Persephone sucked in a sharp breath, all smugness gone.

The herald called their names.

"Thank you for pointing that out to me." I stepped back and nodded toward the entryway. "I believe they're calling for you."

A wavering, stony smile crossed her face as she placed her arm in Taren's and walked out.

Chapter 29

Temperance

I'd spent countless hours in the beautiful ballroom during dance lessons, but it hadn't been alight with life until that moment. Soft white, silver, and sapphire linens draped down the pillars, accenting the depictions of the night sky painted across the ceiling—a view made even more celestial from the candlelit reflections of grand chandeliers. Their light bounced off iridescent paints illustrating the stars. Four three-story windows poured in the natural splendor of the skyline the inside was desperately trying to imitate.

Bustling with the cheerful attitudes of the guests, the room was awash with an array of color. Excitement bubbled inside me as I took in the glittering skirts—a feeling that was short-lived once Calix and I reached the edge of the staircase.

All eyes were on us, so I slapped on my best "Miss America" smile to hide the nerves threatening to overtake my body. My thoughts were on rhythm with my footsteps as I descended to the ballroom floor.

Don't. Trip. Don't. Trip.

Once we reached the floor, it took all my control not to sigh in relief, but I did soften my grip on Calix's arm.

Smiling, he placed his hand over mine and whispered, "The worst part is over."

"One of the worst." I laughed quietly as the next couple

descended. "Girls back home dream of having a storybook entrance like that, myself included. The reality is terrifying, though."

"If you're worried about the dance, don't be. You're ready," he reassured.

The other council members and their escorts took their turns down the steps. Each set formed a semicircle around the bottom of the stairs, ready to receive the king when he arrived.

Descending with Collin, Ora was the epitome of a mermaid princess. Rhiannon must have been inspired by the dress I'd created for Ora when we first met. The top was nearly identical, but the skirts of this gown belled out at the waist in the form of flounces. Various shades of blue rippled out in waves throughout the ruffles.

The leaders of Fjall dressed in their signature black, gray, and red. Feathers or wings accented their attire in different shapes and forms. Queen Jezzamyn and her brother were awash with colors vibrant and striking. Both were accessorized with bold, bejeweled gold collars, similar to ones worn by pharaohs in ancient Egypt.

"Long live His Majesty, King Frederick!" the herald's voice boomed over the crowd.

Everyone held a bow or curtsy waiting for their king to address them. My legs and arms followed their lead, but my head remained up and admiring. I'd rarely seen him wear his crown of sapphires and silver, and even those few times, he'd still given off a relaxed vibe. Tonight, Frederick's regality projected across the ballroom.

His navy overcoat was embroidered in a diamond pattern with silver thread, lined at the lapel and cuffs with matching silver trim. When he caught me staring, he grinned.

Frederick descended the stairs as he addressed the crowd.

"Welcome. Today is the Day of Peace, and we are honored to have visitors from Fjall and Kelurs join us in our celebrations of the

Superior Goddess. I'd like to thank them for their efforts in opening more paths in trade and friendship." Frederick reached the bottom step. "Let us begin with the opening dance."

I reached for Calix's outstretched hand when another presented itself. Frederick stood before me with his right hand extended invitingly.

Whispers broke out around us, and—unable to deny his king—Calix stepped back.

As I reached up to place my left hand in his, Frederick shook his head slightly and eyed my right hand. Confused, I switched to my right hand. The small action caused more whispers among the spectators, and anxiety twinged inside me.

He squeezed my hand, the warmth gentle and reassuring. In a graceful, practiced movement, Frederick positioned me to stand to his left, and wound his arm around my waist, pulling me in closer. Side-by-side and with our right hands still clasped together, he led me onto the dance floor.

We were so close, my heart thudded, and my stomach filled with butterflies. His lime and cedarwood scent tempted me to lean in and get lost in his embrace. I couldn't do that, though. What in the world was he thinking? We were supposed to take attention off of me. He was the king—one who didn't dance at this ball. What kind of message was he trying to send?

Yet, there was the large part of me that didn't care because he was holding me.

When we reached the center of the ballroom, Frederick nodded toward Brydon and the orchestra.

I looked around and found everyone's eyes on me. Panic moved in. It felt like my lungs expanded and plummeted into the pit of my stomach, effectively scaring the romantic butterflies away. Closing my eyes, I waited for the music to begin.

"Breathe," Frederick said, his deep voice resonating in my ear, the heat of his breath shooting through me and reminding me I wasn't alone on that dance floor. He was there. My worries waned, and I blocked out any thoughts but him. "Keep your eyes on me. I won't let you fall."

You're emotionally too late.

With my free hand, I crushed the skirts of my gown to ease some of my nervous energy. The rhythm of his breathing brought comfort, and soon mine synced up with his.

"Brydon told me to let the music lead us," Frederick whispered into my ear, sending goosebumps down my spine. "This is his gift. I guess we're improvising."

How was I supposed to do this without practice? Calix had said that I could dance anything as long as the lead had a steady hand, and the couple trusted one another. I just had to trust Frederick. Something I found easy to do.

The moment the music touched my ears, all my fretting disappeared, and Frederick led us into our first steps. Its familiar melody engulfed me like a long-lost favorite song. After I discovered who he was, Brydon explained his special family gift. He wasn't Descended, but what they called a Lessor. He could hear the song of someone's soul and manipulate sound. I smiled when I realized the melody was the same as the one Brydon had hummed whenever I was around him. Was this my song?

A harmony entered, intertwining with the melody, blending into a seamless balance. Lovely and intriguing, it pushed and pulled on my emotions as Frederick led me around the dance floor.

Brydon had also said soul songs could complement each other.

Could this harmony be—

"If you blush like that, everyone will know," Frederick whispered during one of our turns.

Scared he'd read my mind, I asked, "That I'm nervous to be dancing in front of them? Speaking of which, shouldn't everyone join in now?"

He smiled gently. "Thanks to Brydon's song, no one knows the dance."

"Aren't we making this up as we go?" I glanced at the still bodies circled around us.

Frederick pulled me into a framed position. "They don't know that. And I wasn't referring to the dancing."

"What will they know?"

"About your affection for me," he said with a confident grin.

My mouth nearly dropped open in awe, but I played it off with a bashful laugh.

"Someone is feeling pretty sure of himself."

His eyes shone. "Actually, keep that up. It only helps me more."

"With what?" I raised my eyebrows.

Frederick released my waist, and naturally, I raised my right hand to his and began the next turn.

"Keeping my promise to you," he said as we switched hands. "If I'm officially courting you, no one would dare ask for your hand." Frederick raised our clasped hands above our heads and brought me in at the waist into the next turn.

I bit my bottom lip to contain the smile breaking across my face. "So, basically, you mark your territory, and the other pups find another tree."

"That's a unique way to put it, but yes." He laughed and spun me out gently.

"Now you're banning all possible suitors from me?" I teased.

His face fell, and we returned to the framed position, moving in a waltz-like fashion.

"I thought that's what you wanted."

"I didn't want to be forced into marriage. I never said anything about not being courted by anyone else."

"Who am I preventing you from?" Frederick's eyes narrowed.

"Guess I'll never know…" I feigned a sigh.

"You're impossible."

"You're jealous."

"Yes."

His direct response momentarily froze me. Never had a three-letter word made such an impact on my heart.

The music swelled to its climax, and its pace quickened. He led me into a small span of turns and lifts until the notes softened, and we were brought back to the frame position. Every impulse to tease him dissipated, and all I wanted was to assure him of my feelings.

"There is someone," I whispered.

Frederick stiffened and looked away.

"He saved my life and arrogantly thought it was okay to ask a stranger for a thank-you kiss…" He met my eyes again, his smile returning. "Then I saved him." My heart pounded as I finished with, "I like him a lot."

The song slowed toward its end, so Frederick spun me out one last time until we stood across from each other. Bowing to one another as the music ceased, Frederick's gaze never broke from mine, unraveling a plethora of emotions within me. I didn't want our dance to end.

I didn't want any of it to end.

CHAPTER 30

FREDERICK

Applause broke the trance-like hold Temperance's gaze had on me. I held out my right arm to her, and she took it. Once we reached the others, I kissed her hand before relinquishing it to Calix. A satisfying blush bloomed across her cheeks while she gazed at me, soft and ardent.

That expression will be the death of me.

Prince Drystan cut between us.

"Lady Temperance," he said, "may I have the honor?"

He hadn't wasted any time. I resisted the urge to steal her away, knowing a dance from him wouldn't sway the feelings she had for me.

"Sure," Temperance said. She curtsied and sent a regretful look my way as she took his arm.

Whispering a curse to the Superior Goddess, I made my way to Queen Jezzamyn and King Brannyn. If the dance hadn't been enough, it was crucial that I made everything perfectly clear to my allies. Temperance wouldn't be taken from the Linallian court unless it was her decision.

"Never in my life have I been put in my place so wordlessly," King Brannyn said as I approached.

"Untrue," Freya said. "I do that constantly, but you never pay attention." She eyed Brannyn wearily before shifting her gaze inquisitively on me. "Though, I don't display it so theatrically."

"Any other lady of my court may consider your offer, but—"

"This is not the time nor place to discuss such matters," Queen Jezzamyn interjected. "Let's enjoy the evening. Besides, her guardian, Calix, mentioned she chooses her own path." She turned to Fjall. "If she wants your prince, she'll accept him."

"Indeed. We'll not have war over it. After all, who would dare question the choice of the Eslanian heir," King Brannyn said. "Her presence at your side solidifies our decision to join you. The Descended of the Haloed Sun has our protection, and *you*, King Fredrick, have our fealty."

My eyes darted to Queen Jezzamyn who showed no reaction to the news of Temperance's identity. Somehow she and her brother knew. Had that been why she'd defended Temperance's decision?

"Kelurs is with you too," Queen Jezzamyn promised. "We will not betray the descendant of our Superior Goddess. It would bring dishonor and negative karma to our realm."

I hated how many people knew her real identity. If too many others discovered the truth, I worried it would reach Minerva. However, that knowledge had saved the situation.

We needed to be more cautious moving forward.

If she leaves tonight, though, does it really matter?

"Thank you," I said, returning their bows and looking upon the merriment below us. Hopefully the alliance wasn't fully dependent on her presence.

My gaze followed Temperance all over the ballroom. Dancing nearly every dance, she smiled and laughed, unaware of the eyes that watched with hope and expectation.

CHAPTER 31
TEMPERANCE

Dancing with so many couples on the floor breathed new life into the atmosphere, sending me on an internal high. I danced with Calix, Drystan, and Collin multiple times, but Frederick hadn't danced again. A few times I caught his eye, and he'd smile in such a way I thought I'd crumple to the ground with giddiness.

During a turn on my last dance with Drystan, I noticed Tundra walking along one of the beams, eyeing the meat on the refreshment table. I prayed she wouldn't cause a scene.

A frosty-blond man moseyed over to Tundra's area. He leaned on the wall beneath her and casually picked around the food on his plate. He tossed a piece above him right into her mouth. Without looking up, the lean man smiled.

Looks like you've made more friends than just me, Tundra.

Laughing, I turned my attention back to Drystan.

"What?" Drystan arched an eyebrow at me.

"Oh, the things people do when they think no one's looking." I chuckled, and he remained silent. "Never mind."

Drystan and I grasped hands and circled around each other, stepping inward and back out.

"Would you consider taking my hand?"

"Aren't I already holding it?" I joked.

Rolling his eyes, a rare Drystan smile graced his lips. "Are you promised to King Frederick?" he asked, pulling me back into the framed position.

"I'm not promised to anyone, but we…"

No words followed. Not even I understood what we were. If I found my way home, what would we be? If I didn't, would we…

"Understood," he stated.

"I didn't finish what I was saying."

"Sometimes the clearest answers are in the lingering silence." Drystan bowed to kiss my hand. "I hope our friendship can continue."

"Definitely."

It dawned on me then that I'd just received my first-ever marriage proposal. Only in Emeriz.

I shook my head and yawned as I watched him walk away. I looked out the windows trying to gauge the time. I figured it had to be close to dawn. Then someone yanked me to the dance floor.

"Hey!" I protested.

"We must dance. I don't like it either," he said.

He was the one who fed Tundra. I didn't want to cause a scene, and one dance wouldn't kill me. But if he tried anything, I wouldn't hesitate to pop him on the nose.

Glaring at him, we took our places. While we danced, his movements were agile and light, but robotic on some level. The man hardly looked at me.

He wore black, tailored robes embellished with a silver trim, lavish enough to be a noble, but his behavior did not support the image. Ebony gloves with a silver tree threaded in the palm covered his hands. A familiar, eerie feeling tickled the back of my mind. At the end of the song, he yanked me off the floor, away from the others.

"Here." He nodded to our clasped hands, crumpling something into mine.

"Do I know you?" I said, jerking my hand back.

"Name's Heshrin, and that's all you get." He pointed to my hand. "Just open the note."

Unfolding the now-scrunched message, I recognized Frederick's handwriting: *Follow him.*

Looking around, I noticed Frederick was no longer with Fjall and Kelurs.

"Didn't you understand the note?" he quipped and stared hard at me. "He's not here."

The expression made me shiver as he loomed over me. This guy gave me the heebie-jeebies.

"Now come along," he said over his shoulder, walking away.

I placed my faith in Frederick and followed the strange man.

CHAPTER 32

FREDERICK

Hidden in shadow, I leaned against the wooden lattice on a deserted balcony overlooking the gardens. The moon had begun its descent behind the vast Eslanian mountain range. Just like the bulbous moon, my time with Temperance was also disappearing.

"Hello?" Temperance's voice carried out into the crisp night air.

She walked to the railing hesitantly. Still unaware of my presence, she clutched it and smiled, inhaling the cool breeze—transcendent in the glow of the soft moonlight. I seeped her image into my memory.

"Breathtaking," I breathed.

Temperance turned toward me, her smile widening.

"This view is gorgeous," she said.

Walking toward her, I glanced at the moon then brought my gaze back to her.

"Right, that is too."

Temperance bit her lip and shyly cast her eyes downward.

By Emeriz, why send me someone I have to say goodbye to?

"I'm surprised you followed Heshrin," I said. "Knowing you, I worried you'd tell him to bug off."

She rubbed her hand up and down her arm. "If I hadn't recognized your handwriting in the note, I would have."

"I wanted a few minutes alone with you." I joined her, gripping the railing next to her hand. "Have you been enjoying yourself?"

"Yes! I've never been to prom, but tonight has to be ten times better than it would ever be."

"Prom?"

"It's like a ball hosted by my school," she explained.

"You've never attended?'

She shook her head. "Never been asked."

"Imbeciles," I scoffed.

"What?"

"You'd be my first choice." I covered her hand with my own. "My only choice."

She gazed at me in wonder. "You'd be mine."

Holding hands, we watched the moon in peace for a few silent minutes.

"Frederick, why don't you normally dance at balls?" she asked. "Beyond the fact that you don't want to give the ladies at court the wrong impression."

"The night we met—and I don't mean when Neva knocked me off like a dimwit." Temperance chuckled, and I continued. "When we were children... that was the night I lost my parents and Henvick in that ballroom."

Temperance squeezed my hand, her eyes never wavering from my own.

"The Ethereal Ball marks the anniversary of their deaths, and I know it must sound foolish, but celebrating this day feels..."

"Like you're somehow dancing on their graves?" she asked.

"Yes."

Temperance stared out into the gardens. "So why dance with me? I hate that I might have caused you to feel that way."

I cupped her cheek in the palm of my hand and turned her face back to me. "Temperance, I care about you. Your presence eases that pain, that loss. When I'm with you, no matter what we're doing, I don't feel alone. Dancing with you was about us, nothing else."

I kissed her forehead, sealing my words.

She blinked up at me, searching for something. When the breeze picked up, she shivered and rubbed her arms. I removed the cape from my shoulders and draped it across her own. Using it to my advantage, I tugged against it to bring her closer and ran my hands up and down her arms to give warmth to them.

"What are you thinking?" I asked.

"All night I've felt like everything is ending. I know I need to go home, but being here... I feel balanced." The warmth of her hand touched my cheek. "Then there's the people tying me here."

Her hand dropped back to the railing, leaving my cheek exposed and craving the heat of her touch.

"I guess it doesn't matter right now. It's not like I'm going home yet."

By the Goddess, I hate this.

"About that..." Lost for words, I called upon the Elysian Sword. It materialized in my hands, and I presented it to her.

She drew in a sharp breath, reaching long, elegant fingers toward the blade. "Is this what I think it is?"

"Yes," I said. "Notice the pommel?"

"It's the top of the staff," she exclaimed, excitement lighting up her face. The expression sent my heart racing but also brought a twinge in my chest.

"I'm sorry." I bowed my head and readied myself for her anger.

She leaned forward, trying to peer into my face. "For what?" she asked.

I took a deep breath. "I've had it this whole time. As a relic of my Descended line, only I can wield its power. It's blood-linked to me."

I explained all I could remember from the night her grandmother must have merged the items together.

"Why didn't you tell me?"

I was taken aback by the sadness that came through her tone. She should have been furious, and justifiably so.

"I wrestled with myself all night about telling you," I said, looking into her eyes. "Call me selfish, but I wanted one more day with you."

Shame filled me as I dropped my gaze to the object that would sever our ties—possibly forever.

Temperance's hands found their way to the sides of my face.

"I forgive you."

"Just like that?" I desperately searched her eyes for answers, her intentions. She'd forgiven me so easily for something that didn't deserve it. Where was her frustration?

"Just like that," she repeated.

Overwhelmed with awe at her ability to constantly surprise me, I found myself speechless. I lifted her right hand from my cheek and kissed the palm of it.

She blushed and pulled her hands away, clasping them behind her back.

"You could have gone home," I whispered.

"Maybe, but it's weird—I'm sort of happy you waited. If you waited any longer than tonight, though, I would've kicked your butt," she teased.

"Don't forget who won most of our matches at the cliffs," I threw back playfully.

"Hey! I held my own, and with my training lately, I can take you. Name any day. Any time."

Our laughter faded as soon as the last words left her lips. There was no other day. Once she figured out how to use the scepter, she'd leave.

"We still need to find out how to use it, right?" I grinned, failing to mask my enthusiasm about her being stuck longer while she worked out how to use the scepter.

"About that..." she said, avoiding my gaze.

My heart sank, pulling my smile with it.

"I know what to do thanks to my dream divination." She nervously twisted her grandmother's necklace back and forth. "But I don't know how to get it out of the sword. That could take time."

"About that," I groaned.

Exasperated, she dropped her head into her hands.

When she raised her head, I said, "Merging them together like this took great magic. These relics are blood-linked to our individual powers. Your grandmother used that to combine them, so it'll take both of us to separate them.

"So what do we do?"

"You need to make a blood bond."

She cocked her head and said, "Like... I cut my hand, you cut yours, and then mix our blood together?"

"No!" I leaned back a little. "What in Emeriz's name?"

"It's an old, weird custom on Earth." She clasped her hands together. "Just tell me what to do."

Gripping the hilt with my right hand, I positioned my thumb on the sodalite that sat on the guard while I held my left hand hovering at the point of the sword.

"Hold the amethyst in your necklace, and get ready to prick your finger on the point of your staff."

Temperance obeyed, and I continued. "Good. On the count of three, prick your finger and hold it. One. Two. Three."

We simultaneously pricked each point, allowing our relics to draw blood. The decorative etchings of the blade filled with deep crimson then glowed white. My heart slowed, muscles tensed, face flushed, and my hand tingled with cold.

Temperance's irises illuminated with a violet iridescence, and by her expression, mine glowed blue. We watched each other until a restorative surge raced through me. Focusing back on the sword, we released the points, and I held it out to her hilt side up.

"Try it now."

Inhaling and exhaling deeply, she reached out to retrieve the staff.

"Hey, kingly," Heshrin's voice called out, "you're needed in the ballroom."

"I'll be there in a moment. Leave," I snapped.

"Sure. I'll just inform the Grand High Priest Maxwell, that you're too busy smooching your intended to receive him."

The blood drained from my face. Heart pounding wild with worry, my eyes didn't leave Temperance's as I dismissed the sword from our presence.

I couldn't let him find her. From what she'd told me, he'd already seen her when she first arrived in Emeriz and called her by her name. He had too much knowledge already for my comfort. If he figured out who she truly was and saw the sword in my possession, Maxwell would have two Descended within his grasp.

"Temperance, this has to wait."

She removed the cape from her shoulders and attached it in place around mine. Not wasting any more time, I grabbed her hand, and we exited the balcony.

"Take her to the library," I commanded Heshrin as we stepped inside the doors. "Protect her with your life, because trust me, your life depends on it."

I turned to Temperance, gripping her shoulders. "Lock yourself away until I come for you."

"Must she depart?" Maxwell's honeyed voice said. "Such a shame."

My body tensed, and nausea swirled inside my stomach from hearing his voice again. There were only a handful of times over the years that I'd been forced to meet him. Why now? Why again? Why this night?

Temperance looked Maxwell over, fear in her eyes.

"We only shared a brief encounter earlier this evening," he continued. "I was hoping to spend a little more time together."

"When was this?" Temperance asked, bemused.

"Ah, of course you didn't recognize me." Maxwell bowed. "I was dressed in my performance mask and attire."

Had he been here all night? He would have stood out if he'd been dressed like this: lavish, black velvet robes, embroidered with colored thread representative of the Descended, framed a white satin tunic. A blasphemous traitor to the faith shouldn't be worthy to wear the garment. Stitched between his shoulders on the back of the sacred robe was a large scarlet *M*, in support of the pretender he'd placed on the High Throne.

I stepped toward Maxwell, cautiously placing myself in front of Temperance.

"Your Excellency," I bowed to him, his face never leaving my eyeline. "I didn't expect you to be here tonight."

"Clearly," Maxwell said, his gaze shifting to Temperance. "Would you allow me the honor of dancing with the lady?"

"Thank you, Your Excellency." Temperance curtsied as she spoke. "But I'm turning in for the night."

Ignoring her polite decline, he held out his hand.

"I insist."

If he'd been here unbeknownst to anyone... how many others had he hidden amongst the hundreds of attendees?

Temperance looked to me for help but must have sensed the delicacy of the situation in my eyes, because she took his hand.

"Excellent." He gleamed like a viper finding its prey.

It took all my self-control not to stop this from happening, but one wrong move and everyone would be in danger. It would be the night I lost my parents all over again.

Maxwell led her to the dance floor, fanning the flames inside me. Temperance squirmed slightly and glanced over her shoulder at me with a fearful expression. Chills shot down my spine. I'd let the innocent mouse be in the proximity of a snake.

If you hurt her, Maxwell... I'll kill you.

CHAPTER 33

TEMPERANCE

My heart pounded with fear. Undeniable, irrevocable fear.

Maxwell oozed a pointed lethality, living up to the image Frederick and the others had described. Anyone who could abuse their influence to convince masses of people that Minerva was the true heir to the Superior Goddess had to be dangerous.

I scanned the ballroom. The crowds had lessened significantly due to the late hour with only about a hundred remaining. They stood stiff and silent as we took our first position.

"Begin!" Maxwell barked at Brydon.

Brydon looked at me, and I nodded. A shadow crossed his face, but he turned to the ensemble to begin.

"Seems you're already in command, my dear," Maxwell said and spun me out forcefully. "Such progress in a short amount of time. Have I arrived too late?"

"I don't know what you mean," I said.

He yanked me back into the framed position. "Why are you here, Temperance?"

"To visit my guardian, Calix." I kept my face muscles stony to mask my anxiety.

"Quit pretending with me. I know who you really are," he breathed into my ear, sending creepy crawlies down my spine.

"It's the truth." My eyes flitted over to Frederick, the sight of him giving me courage.

"Don't lie. Given our past, you should know better." His grip on my hand tightened, crushing my knuckles together.

"Ah—I've never met you before." I attempted to pull my hand from his, but he squeezed harder.

"Stop playing this game!" he hissed. Skipping the next moves in the sequence, he held me firmly in the framed stance. "Last I saw you, you didn't look this young." Eyes narrowed, Maxwell assessed me—cold and curious. "You're capable of slowing your age progression, but it seems you've reversed it."

He knew I was a Descended! But how was that possible when I'd never met him?

I wanted to push him away, but the faces surrounding me—and most importantly, the tightness in Frederick's gaze—warned me off.

Instead, I stared him dead in the eye.

"You're mistaken."

"Stop lying!" He spun me out so hard he gave me whiplash.

I caught a glimpse of Fredrick, who looked like a bull about to charge.

Maxwell pulled me back into his arms. "At first, I thought seeing you on that beach had been a trick by that wily fairy to distract me. But when we received the letter about someone using magic to influence the king, I knew it'd be you."

He ran the back of his fingers down the side of my cheek. I jerked my face away.

"I see you missed me."

Frederick, it's time you cut in! I screamed inside my mind. *Anyone, cut in!*

"There's no need for you to stir up an uprising." He pulled me in a little too close for comfort. "Come with me. Minerva will honor the original offer she extended to you."

"Offer?" Something about that stopped me. In order to convince him I wasn't whoever he thought I was, I'd need more information on just who that was.

"Playing the fool doesn't suit you. Let's depart, and we shall sort out the details with the High Queen." Hand pressed against my lower back, he started to lead me away.

This guy was a lunatic! I dug my feet in and pushed against his chest.

"No, let me go!"

A shrill, eardrum-shattering screech rang out from one of the flutes in the ensemble. Maxwell tossed me to the floor to block out the sound with his hands. Even with covered ears, the sound echoed and vibrated in my mind, making everything unfocused. It took all the strength in me not to let the pressure pull me into unconsciousness.

The sound finally faded out, and Maxwell shouted, "After that conductor! He's a Lessor!"

Three soldiers in black uniforms, each embroidered with a red *M* across the back, raced off in separate directions. My head spun when Maxwell yanked me to my feet.

"Unhand her!" Frederick stood six feet away, sword drawn and blood dripping from his ear. When had he gotten closer?

At least fifty more of Maxwell's men emerged from the crowd. How had he concealed all these soldiers?

A nefarious grin graced Maxwell's face. "She is suspected of treason against the High Queen," he said. "I'm within my right to take her for interrogation."

My mind flashed to that white room and the interrogation I'd witnessed. If the woman in my vision was Minerva, would that be my fate? Forced to join her ranks? My will ripped away? Or perhaps she'd just murder me and steal my power like she had with my grandma and great aunt.

"What evidence do you have?" Frederick demanded.

Linallian soldiers and various lords remained at the ready with hands on the grips of their sheathed weapons. Fjall and Kelurs even appeared ready for battle. To my relief, Ora and Rhiannon were nowhere in sight. Hopefully they were somewhere safe.

"You can never be too careful with who you can trust these days," Maxwell said. His grip tightened, cutting off the circulation to the rest of my arm. "Not even within your own circle, which has expanded recently." He nodded to Fjall and Kelurs, then whispered to me, "Your idea, I presume?"

I shook my head.

"You will not take anyone from this kingdom under mere rumor and suspicion," Frederick said and extended the Elysian Sword forward, murder in his eyes.

Both Maxwell's men and the Linallian soldiers officially drew their own.

"I outrank you, Your Majesty," Maxwell asserted. "Attempt to save her if you wish, but it will be viewed as an act of rebellion." He twisted me into his embrace, facing outward, and placed a gold dagger to my throat. "Is her life worth a war?"

CHAPTER 34

FREDERICK

Not again!

I gritted my teeth and battled the desire to release the wrath of my powers on him. With so many innocents in the room, I couldn't risk the danger of using my light. Burning or blinding my own men wouldn't help the situation.

When the sound rang out, I'd used all my strength to get to Temperance, but the power had been too overwhelming. Every sound that reached my right ear came through muffled and faint.

"This situation feels familiar." Maxwell leaned his head against Temperance. "Yes... like the night of your parents' deaths."

Temperance trembled in his arms. I strangled the grip of my sword, wishing it was his neck. Tonight would end differently. I would save her.

I pushed down the memory attempting to resurface and consoled her instead.

"Temperance," I said, "focus on me."

Her tear-filled gaze pierced through me, homing in on my own. Reflecting fear, faith, and determination, they reminded me of another set of eyes. Ones that'd believed in me too.

"You made a choice back then." Maxwell hovered the tip of the blade up around Temperance's cheek and back down her neck. "You chose your throne, your people, your own life over your dear parents."

"Shut up!"

"You've seen firsthand what happens when you defy the High Queen. Need I remind you?" He inched the knife closer to her skin.

"Let her go, and we can preserve this Day of Peace," I pleaded.

"Dawn is drawing near. The Day of Peace has ended." Maxwell laughed. "But you're wrong. Interrogating her is in the name of peace. It's the only way to ensure whether or not she's innocent."

Temperance found her voice again and said, "Please... I'm not who you think I am."

He teased her collarbone with the tip of the knife until it hooked itself to the chain around her neck, pulling the pendant up.

"You still lie when the evidence hangs from your neck?"

"I'm not—"

"You are! I'm helping King Frederick, as his heart's been stolen by a manipulative wretch," he hissed at her, before addressing me. "This woman uses men for her own ambitious desires, using you to fan the flames of a needless rebellion." The blade nipped at her flesh, drawing blood as he spoke to her. "You set me aside for Neal, then set Neal aside for this boy?"

"Grandpa Neal?" Temperance whispered.

Maxwell thought Temperance was her grandmother? It suddenly made sense. Temperance had mentioned that she was what her world called a 'doppelganger' of her grandmother. Previous Descended of the Haloed Sun were rumored to look very similar to one another as well.

"Grandpa?" Maxwell stiffened, his face twisting into a sneer. "You're their granddaughter. This changes things."

Maxwell sniffed her hair then looked at me. His aggressive

demeanor completely faded into a conciliatory one. "You let me take her to sort this whole mess out, and I promise not a hair on her head will be harmed. All will be forgiven."

"Not on your life." I took a step forward.

"Ah-ah." Maxwell waved a finger, then said to Temperance, "My dear, you don't want anyone to be hurt, do you?"

"If you think—"

"I'll go," Temperance said with a calm, faraway expression.

"How delightfully predictable." Maxwell chuckled and lowered the knife ever so slightly. "Come along."

"No!" I shouted.

"You don't have the nerve to do what must be done," Maxwell chided. "You're too weak."

"Not weak—merciful. But if you take her, I will show you no mercy."

"Frederick, please," Temperance pleaded. "Protect your people. I'm just one person."

Her words felt like a punch to the gut. She'd uttered the exact words my mother had the night she died, shattering the barrier that kept the memory hidden. Mother begged me not to use my powers to save them, and to protect the legacy of the Descended and ensure the prophecy. I was to watch and wait. Then they dragged her from my arms and made me watch as they tortured and murdered her.

Temperance was the key to everything. Fate brought us together twice now. Emeriz was only safe if she lived.

"Trust me, this is for their protection." I bore my gaze into hers, begging her to listen. To have faith in me once more. To fight.

Temperance raised her head slightly, her expression resolute.

"What a touching display, but she agreed. Farewell." Maxwell lowered the blade from her throat.

A mistake on his part.

Temperance elbowed Maxwell in the stomach, and he dropped the knife. As it slid away, she stomped on his foot and turned, punching him in the nose, followed up by a knee to the groin. He grasped at his injuries while she raced to my side. Pride and relief spread through me like the warmth of the sun after a rainy day.

"As I said, she won't be going anywhere." I smirked.

Maxwell held up his hand to prevent his soldiers from attacking. He must have thought he could end the standoff without bloodshed, but I knew better. Temperance needed to get out of here.

"The scepter," I whispered over my shoulder to her, keeping my gaze zoned in on Maxwell. "Go."

Temperance gripped the pommel and removed it. As she did, the stem of the scepter appeared, revealing its true form: A glittering staff of white steel, intricately etched with gold details. What once served as the pommel of my sword was now its head, a sharp-edged four-pointed star with the symbol of the Superior Goddess within. The staff adjusted to her height and the head of the scepter grew to the size of her fist.

"Isn't that interesting? The Elysian Sword possessed by the King of Linall, and the Genesis Scepter hidden within it," Maxwell said with a laugh as he straightened up. "Naois!"

A large man, closer to a giant, charged toward us from the side. Before I had a chance to react, Calix shielded us. Naois' flanged mace smashed into Calix's stomach and blood splattered across the pristine tiles as he crumpled to the floor.

Chaos broke loose.

"Protect the king!" Taren shouted, and Linallian soldiers beat Naois back from us.

No!

The Elysian Sword slipped from my grasp, clattering to the ground as I frantically gripped Calix in my arms. Temperance picked up the blade, holding it out in a defense position while she clutched the staff in her other hand. Taren and the rest of my guard protectively surrounded us. Touching the stone on my ring, I focused on slowing down our surroundings. Everything went still and quiet, apart from Calix's ragged breathing. Sorrow raged through me as I examined his mangled abdomen.

Must this day always be my curse?

Tears stung my eyes. I grabbed Temperance's wrist, pulling her into our frozen moment in time. Without me saying a single word, she knelt down, dropping the weapons into her lap. She pressed her hands against his wounds, ready to heal him.

Wincing, Calix squeezed her arm and shook his head violently.

"No time. G-get her home," Calix uttered before slipping into unconsciousness.

I hated it, but he was right. My brain already felt like it was on fire. If I held us there any longer, it'd drive me to insanity. I needed to let go.

I released my thumb from the stone and laid him on the floor.

"What are you doing?" Temperance cried. "I can help!" Her cheeks were red and wet with panic.

I stood and pulled Temperance up, securing the scepter in her hands and the Elysian Sword in mine. Time snapped back into a normal sequence, so fast it made my head spin.

"You there, get the King's Left to the infirmary!" Taren shouted before he and the rest of my guards rushed us up the stairs.

The Linallian soldiers that stayed behind engaged in full combat with the enemy below us. Fjall and Kelurs were escorted with us to the King's Atrium.

"Follow Temperance," I commanded Taren when we were secured inside. "Get her to the library safely!"

Temperance looked at me in shock. "Are you crazy? Give me a sword—let me help. I'm not running off while everyone is in danger."

"Maxwell wants to get his hands on you, and I will not allow that to happen," I said. "You're too important to Emeriz... and to me."

"But, Calix—"

"Your family, Temperance," I said. "That's where Calix wants you to go."

The fight in her demeanor changed, softening a little.

"You don't play fair."

"Sometimes a ruler can't... no matter how much he wishes differently," I said, then addressed the other rulers. "Go to your kingdoms. Raise your armies. Your kingdoms are now targets of rebellion by association."

"We're with you, King Frederick," Queen Jezzamyn said. "We won't abandon our word at the first sign of trouble."

"We'll fight with you!" King Brannyn drew his sword while Freya and Ariella performed a sequence of hand gestures that morphed their outfits into Fae battle armor. "Drystan, go with Lady Temperance. Keep the heir of Eslane safe."

Taren's expression froze in a state of shock, and he moved to stand behind Temperance alongside Drystan.

My attention moved to Temperance, and I lifted her hand to kiss it.

"It's time for you to go, my lady."

Tears streamed down her cheeks, but she squeezed the scepter firmly and nodded. Her hand slipped from my fingers as Drystan and Taren rushed her through the atrium.

"You're a Descended too, Frederick," Freya said. "You should go with them."

"My duty is here," I said. "Freya, Ariella, make sure all civilians are pulled out of harm's way. We weren't able to secure everyone while Maxwell danced with Temperance."

They nodded, and I turned to the others. "Maxwell wouldn't arrive unprepared. He'll have Catatonia Mist. We must find him before he uses it to bend everyone to his will. I'll do what I can to counteract the effects with my light."

Maxwell already figured out my secret when he saw the Elysian Sword in my possession. For the first time in my life, I could release the full extent of my abilities in battle.

For my parents. Henvick. Calix. Temperance.

I was ready for blood.

CHAPTER 35

TEMPERANCE

We raced through the King's Atrium with Taren at my front and Drystan protecting my back.

"Why are we taking you to the library?" Taren asked. "We should be getting you out of Linall."

"Keep moving!" I pushed against his back to urge him to go faster.

"Your king commanded you to take her where she says, not question her choices," Drystan said.

"As Her *Majesty* commands." Taren rushed around the next turn in the maze until we came to the end of a passage. "This is it."

"Open it and let's go!" I demanded.

"There's no telling where Maxwell's men could be lurking. Stick close and quiet." Taren eyed me skeptically, like he didn't believe I'd follow his order.

"Okay. Go." I pushed him lightly on the shoulder, encouraging him onward.

Taren used some sort of crystal to trace a circle on the door then recited, *"Goddess, offer your protection and light the path with your direction."*

The frame glowed white, and every torch behind us burned out, leaving us in darkness when the magic faded. The door slid open, and we stepped through. Moments later, it closed and left no trace that it'd ever been there at all.

Directly across from us stood the open double doors of the library. I moved to step forward, but Taren held up a hand to stop me. The sound of metal clinking against metal could be heard in the distance, but not close enough to be anywhere near us.

Surveying the hall, Taren drew his sword and moved toward the library doors, then gestured for us to follow. I was two steps out when the sound of rushing footfalls came from our left. Taren crouched behind one of the doors while Drystan pulled me into the corner of the shadowed alcove. With his back as our defense, Drystan hovered over me, hand on my head.

"There's no one here," one of Maxwell's men said.

"Keep searching for her," a second soldier responded. "His Excellency demands it."

"Let's check here."

No, not the library!

Getting to that room was my only shot to get home. If they managed to keep guard over it and block our path, I was screwed.

"Wait for Taren," Drystan whispered. He then jumped from our hiding place and cut down two soldiers in three calculated slashes, then turned to the remaining four.

"Death to the pretender queen!" Drystan shouted, then ran up the hall toward the ballroom.

The soldiers chased after him, leaving Taren and me alone in the abandoned hall. Drystan was going to get himself killed because of me. Me and my stupid destiny, predetermined by the blood that ran through my veins. All so I stood a chance of getting home. Was that even fair to anyone? How many would die protecting me?

My body trembled, and I squeezed the stem of the staff to stop my hands from shaking. I desperately wished I had a sword, but doubted I could use it in actual combat—not when I was shaking so badly.

Taren reached my side and said, "Let's go."

I couldn't will my limbs to move.

"Be brave." Taren gripped my shoulder and looked into my face. "Where's the girl who bloodied my nose? Where's that fire that helped you take down the grand high priest back there?"

I looked back at him but said nothing.

Taren brushed away the tears from my eyes. "You're kind of pretty when you cry."

Hand still on my cheek, he closed the distance between us, alighting a flame of agitation within me.

I slapped him, halting his advances.

Taren rubbed his cheek, but grinned. "Thought that might snap you out of it."

He stood and extended his hand, but in defiance I ignored it, getting up on my own.

I couldn't let my fear distract me. If I didn't try, then all they would have done to help me would be in vain. Instead, I used my fear to fuel my survival instincts.

Taren and I rushed into the library. It was deserted with only the main chandeliers to light the room. My sight homed in on the stairs, and I rushed forward with Taren hot on my heels.

We'd only reached the water fountain when Naois' raucous voice called out from the doors, "His Excellency will be pleased."

The humongous man barreled toward us, winding up his mace like a baseball bat. Taren moved to shield me but was overcome by three enemy soldiers before he could do so. Naois swung the mace at me, but I ducked and whipped the scepter toward him. The point slashed through the bottom of his upper arm.

He screamed in pain and dropped the mace. His wound burned at the edges of the opening, searing the outside of the cut.

"Temperance, run!" Taren shouted, still occupied by the other three soldiers.

I sprinted for the stairs but wasn't fast enough for the long strides of Naois. Enraged, the large man lifted and hurled me like a pebble from a slingshot. Flesh ripped open as my body skidded across the rocky terrain along the fountain base, exposing fresh blood. I groaned and attempted to lift myself up, but my hand slipped. Catching myself before I was impaled on the staff, its point slashed across my cheek.

Naois' heavy steps shot water into the air nearly above his head. It was clear nothing would stop him from following Maxwell's orders.

Get up! I screamed inside my mind, urging myself to move.

I needed to heal myself. Closing my eyes, I focused on the feel of the cool water running over my body, imagining it wiping the injuries away. Heat resonated off my wounds, but I was too late.

Two large hands gripped my neck, lifting me into the air. My limbs jostled like a rag doll as he punched my body into the wall behind the waterfall. Pain shot through every nerve, knocking me breathless. In my weakened state, the staff slipped from my grasp, plopping into the water.

"His Excellency wanted you alive," Naois said, tightening his grip, "but he told me that if you fought, or if I deemed you a threat to the High Queen, to do what's necessary. And you've managed to piss me off!"

Desperate for oxygen, my fingers scraped and pulled at his hands. My toes hovered near the surface of the water, waving around for any surface to alleviate the strain. I put my feet against the wall and tried to push him off, but he pressed all his weight on me—holding me still. Any time I tried to call out for help, water poured into my mouth.

I'm never going home... This is how I die.

My life was fading, like the shredded tulle pieces of my gown as the stream washed them away.

CHAPTER 36

FREDERICK

The sounds of battle reverberated in my ears, pounding in my mind like a heartbeat. I slashed in practiced movements.

Shing. Clang. Slash.

Another man down—I turned to the next.

Shing. Shing. Clang. Slash.

The soldier's abdomen met the venomous fang of the Elysian Sword. Its point sliced through cloth and flesh, leaving a trail of ice and frostbite behind. Only in my hands did the sword possess this element. Fog rose like steam from the blackened wound as he collapsed before me.

"Frederick! Behind you!" The enemy was cut down by Drystan wielding two swords.

We stood back-to-back to defend our position.

"Temperance?" I shouted.

"Library with Taren," Drystan said. "We ran into some trouble, so I led them away."

We turned our attention back to the battle fighting side by side. Maxwell was my target. With his men nearly overtaken by my army, I hoped we'd capture him soon.

We'd beaten back Maxwell's men outside and into the main courtyard. King Brannyn, Queen Jezzamyn, and Lord Petit fought alongside each other. The trio delivered fierce blows to those who entered their circle. Freya and Ariella stayed within the castle, caring for the wounded and protecting them from harm—Calix among them.

Shing. Shing. Slash.

Another enemy soldier fell at my hand. Slick blood coated my blade, dripping off the tip.

"Mists!" shouted one of my captains.

Thick gray fog crept across the cobblestones and swirled into the air around our faces. Cranzly and his unit furiously passed out containment masks to our men. There weren't enough, and my men dropped faster than they could secure them. Some were already under the spell of the smoky substance.

"Find the source!" Jezzamyn shouted.

Mist filled my airway like smoke, burning through my nose, throat, and lungs. Muscles became strained and heavy, pulling me to the ground. As a Descended, all the mist could do was slow me down. My will remained my own. Faster and faster the substance crawled up the wall, creeping inside the castle. The more it consumed, the more my forces turned on their own.

Comrade battled comrade.

"Wound! Don't kill!" Cranzly shouted.

"King's Guard, surround!" I commanded.

Eight of my masked men encircled me, swords drawn, to defend against anyone who approached. This would take more of my light than I could produce naturally. Kneeling down, I placed the Elysian Sword's point into the ground. I removed my ring, sliding it into place in the center of the pommel.

"Celestial guardian of the night, protect us with your sacred light."

A beam of light circled me and grew outward, safeguarding those within. Mist inside the sphere evaporated in an instant, and those under its control were released.

Knowing what I'd done, Cranzly led our troops.

"Stay within the circle!" he commanded. "Let them come to you!"

Each of our soldiers who crossed into my sphere of protection rejoined our side, while Maxwell's were taken prisoner or killed. Goosebumps rose on my skin, and my blood ran cold from the pressure of overextending my abilities. A sharp pain dug into the center of my forehead. I wasn't sure how much longer I'd be able to hold on.

Goddess... protect us!

The sun peeked halfway over the mountain ridge when the ground beneath us trembled. A violet light blew through our surroundings, and an exhilarating new energy ran rampant through my veins—foreign yet familiar. The invisible cords that bound me for so long were finally severed, releasing an unburdened power within me.

A blazing violet ring hugged the sunrise.

Greeting the Haloed Sun, I smiled. I concentrated on the energy humming within me and pushed on my abilities further than I ever had in the past. The sphere expanded out toward the borders of my kingdom, clearing away the mist and freeing those under its influence.

The most gratifying word rang out from our foes: "Retreat!"

Chapter 37

Temperance

A wild snarl erupted inside the wide expanse of the library, echoing the throaty call of a wildcat. Naois' hold around my neck instantly disappeared, plummeting me into the water. Pain shot from my knee to my thigh as it crashed into the bottom of the fountain.

I inhaled so fast I coughed incessantly. Naois' screams intermingled with the growls for a few seconds then faded into silence. Tundra devoured the brute as I dragged myself out of the fountain.

My esophagus burned as the contents of that evening's dinner spilled across the floor. Whether it was the sight of her ripping off his face and intestines with her fangs, or a side effect of being strangled, I heaved again. Both... definitely both.

After rinsing my mouth out, I moved to stand, only to crumple back down in agony. The injuries I'd sustained were too extensive. Luckily I was drenched in water, so I didn't need to submerge myself back into the fountain to heal. Keeping my mind on my breathing, I meditated on my injuries closing and the pain subsiding. Some of the cuts across my skin transformed to faint, pink scratches.

I reached for my pendant in hopes of using the amethyst to

amplify my healing, only to grasp at air. I sat up, desperately searching. My heart plummeted when I saw it.

Next to the hand of the man that nearly killed me, lay the broken gold pendant.

"No!" I crawled over to it, examining the shattered pieces.

It was over.

Without the necklace in one piece, I could never open the door again.

I could never perform the ritual.

And I would never be able to return home.

It'd only be a matter of time before Minerva and Maxwell got their hands on me. People were dying because of me. Everyone fought so hard to ensure I was safe, and now it would all be for naught.

Tears slid rapidly down my cheeks. A hollowness filled my soul, and my heart ached with defeat.

"Temperance!" Taren called. "What are you doing? Run!" He continued to fight off the three men on his own. One of them managed to slash one of his arms. He stumbled but ignored the injury, crossing swords with gritted teeth.

With the weight of everything I'd lost bearing down on me, my body refused to move.

I would never see my family or friends again. Nora and Ora would never be whole. All they would ever know is that I went missing and would assume I was dead. There was a chance that very soon I would be.

Taren cried out. He breathed heavily, clearly running out of steam. An enemy managed to bludgeon him in the stomach, knocking him to the ground.

My breath caught. The scene was all too similar to how Calix went down trying to protect me and Frederick. The same thing was about to happen to Taren. A fire lit within me.

I didn't get to help Calix, but I could help Taren.

My sorrow shifted into anger, and I forced myself to my feet. Adrenaline pumped through my veins, and I used it to ignore the pain throbbing through my body. I clutched the Genesis Scepter in my hand, determined that no one else would be hurt because of me.

I just wish it was a sword.

A violet light flashed, and the scepter shifted into a white, steel longsword. I smiled, knowing that this new development in my abilities was something I could get used to.

Tundra came up beside me, ready to pounce.

"Tundra, attack!" On my command, we both rushed forward, Tundra taking one of the men and I the other.

Taren staggered back, eyes heavy with relief and awe.

I was able to get a slash into the leg of one enemy soldier, burning through his flesh and bringing him to his knees. I knocked the sword out of his hand. As angry as I was, I still didn't have it in me to actually kill someone. I swung up, knocking him out with the pommel. He fell to the floor, unconscious.

After Taren and Tundra took out the other two, the exhaustion and pain I'd ignored caught up with me, and I collapsed.

Taren was at my side immediately. "Lady Temperance, let's go before that beast attacks us."

"Tundra's mine," I snapped, pushing his hand off my shoulder. It still ached, and I didn't need his weight pressing down on it.

"It's still a wild ani—wait, what?" He looked at me like I was insane. "You named it?"

"I don't have time to explain right now. Just help me up!"

When he helped me to my feet, it felt like I'd collapse again under the weight of my dress. The skirts were soaked, making the gown even heavier than before.

"Knife," I whispered to my weapon, and it obeyed, shifting into a small, white dagger. I proceeded to cut out the puffy crinoline from the inside of my dress and stepped out of the slip. At my command, the staff returned to its normal state.

"Where to?" Taren asked.

"Nowhere," I said, and pointed at the broken necklace on the floor. "I needed that in order to get there."

My family and friends back home would forever be out of my reach. I ran a shaky hand through my hair and bit my lip, grieving the loss of my parents, my brother, and my grandpa.

I'd lost them all.

Taren retrieved the pieces and held them out to me. "Maybe you could fix it."

"Do I look like a jeweler and a locksmith?"

"I don't understand why you'd need a locksmith, but don't you have creation magic? I mean, you just used it."

I blinked at him in disbelief and almost kicked myself for not thinking of that before. Grabbing the pieces from him, I held them in my hands and thought back to when I'd made clothes for Nora. The only parts that needed fixing were the pendant mount and chain, the amethyst remained a full piece. I closed my eyes, focused on the magic inside me, and envisioned what I wanted to create.

Heat crept up my hands, arms, neck, and then flickered behind my eyes while an incredible pressure of energy thrummed through me. When the pressure subsided and the heat left me, I opened my eyes.

Resting in my hands was my grandma's necklace, whole again.

Tears of relief welled in my eyes, but I fought them back. I had no time to waste.

"Let's go, pretty boy." I moved to run, but without having healed myself, my body was at its limit.

Taren's arm wrapped around my waist to support me like a crutch. Grateful of the relief of pressure, I didn't push him off like I normally would have. We'd gotten up three steps when he lifted me off my feet and ran up the stairs.

"Hey!" I objected.

"Get over it, Your Majesty!" he said. "This is faster."

"Stop calling me that!" I concentrated on healing myself more. Once we reached the third level, I directed him where to go.

"We're here. Put me down."

Taren obeyed. "And where's here?"

I called for the door. *Blood of the Goddess, hear my call, paint the archway across the wall.*

As always, the archway painted itself across the wall, and Taren's eyes widened.

"Never thought I'd say this, but thank you, Taren," I said sincerely.

He nodded away his momentary shock and saluted. "It's my duty. I'll wait here for you."

There was no need for him to stay. If everything went according to plan, I'd be gone. My heart constricted. Was leaving what I really wanted? Everyone was fighting for their lives, and I was running away like a coward.

When Frederick told me to go, I did it without a second thought—trusting that he knew best. I'd never been in a real battle before, and this wasn't sparring practice or a tournament with rules and regulations protecting me from harm. I'd barely made it through that fight.

They had all made it seem like it would be better for me to disappear to safety. Would I only bring them more trouble if I stayed?

"No," I said. "Rejoin the fight. Protect Frederick, please."

"I can't leave the heir of Eslane undefended."

"Where I'm going, I'll be fine."

"Where's that?" he asked.

"Home."

I walked through the archway, letting it disappear behind me. Scepter in hand, I took my first step, living out the reality of my dream. My skirt slopped against the steps, and I slipped halfway up the staircase. I used the windowsill to catch myself from falling, and the staff ran through the glass, shattering the stained art into pieces.

A blackened mist entered through the glassless window, infiltrating my senses. My body became heavy, making it difficult to move.

I fought against the effects of the smoke, its weight pushing me to the stone floor like an impenetrable gravity. I ignored the pain and dragged my body up the rest of the stairs. Crawling on all fours, I made my way to the door. When I tried to grip the handle, my fingers danced across the tip, unable to grasp it.

Miraculously, a bright white wave of light burst through the window, burning away the mist. No longer pinned down by the substance, I wrestled with the pendant and placed it into the keyhole. I felt the warmth of my eyes glowing and heard the click of the lock, then rushed into the room and shut the door.

Taking a moment to breathe, I leaned against the wood, squeezing my necklace in one hand and the staff in the other. I'd made it. I'd actually made it.

I stared at the stone in the center of the room, tears pricking the corners of my eyes. Remembering the ritual my dream revealed to me,

I approached the pedestal. Like a sword into its sheath, I slid the scepter into its rightful place beneath the faintly glowing stone hovering above the staff.

> *"Goddess, bathe the land in violet light,*
> *And bring the worlds into your sight.*
> *As Heir of the Haloed Sun,*
> *I swear to take on all that I can bear*
> *To purge the darkness with the dawn*
> *And ensure the Descended will live on."*

The stone emitted a violet light that expanded through the room. Adrenaline surged through my veins, my body awakening to something ancient and powerful.

I was whole.

Balanced.

I gripped my grandma's necklace and closed my eyes, letting it wash over me. My fingers traced the pendant face, shifting the tulip-like prongs up. My breath caught. I looked down at the necklace and watched as the amethyst oscillated back and forth.

It worked. I was going home!

Almost giddy, I kissed the cool metal, savoring the moment.

"Retreat!"

Limping as fast as I could to the balcony, I pushed open the velvet drapes to identify the frantic cry and immediately shielded my eyes. A ring framed the sun, casting purple shadows across the land.

The Haloed Sun.

I overlooked the carnage. Some of Maxwell's men laid down their weapons, but others tried to flee. Freya and Ariella ordered Linallian soldiers to move the wounded inside.

They were hurt because of me.

Ora came rushing down a set of stairs and gripped Frederick's arm. He barked orders at Cranzly and Drystan, then followed Ora.

What about Calix? This was all my fault. How could I leave now?

Tears spilled down my cheeks. All I'd wanted for three weeks was to go home. Back to my family. My friends. My life.

But at what cost?

I'd found family in Rhiannon and Brydon, friends in Ora, Cranzly, and Calix. And with Frederick, something more. They'd all helped me. Protected me. I couldn't abandon them.

I stared at my hands, contemplating the gifts I was given. These hands could heal—could save. Frederick was wrong; it wasn't time to go just yet. I still had some work to do.

I moved the prongs back into place and raced out the door.

CHAPTER 38

FREDERICK

Ora and I burst into my private infirmary where Calix lay unconscious. With the battle concluded, my men focused on sealing off the kingdom and hunting Maxwell.

Tears rimmed Ora's eyes. "He's not responding to any medicinal potions," she said. "We were just talking to keep him awake while they stitched him up. But... he—"

"You did what you could, Ora," I said, sitting next to his pale form.

"I'll take her to rest," Rhiannon said, moving to usher Ora out.

"Rhiannon?" I pleaded.

Knowing what I desired, she answered solemnly. "I no longer carry that power. There's only one, apart from the Superior Goddess herself, who possesses it."

She shut the door behind them, leaving us alone.

"Calix." Grasping his hand in mine, I felt his weak pulse. "You can't go. Not yet. We're supposed to free Emeriz together."

My head dropped to the bed in tears. Every emotion I'd repressed up until that moment came rushing to the surface. While I prepared myself to say another goodbye, a commotion echoed outside the door before it swung open.

"Miss, you're not permitted—"

"Let her in, that's an order," Taren scolded the soldier who'd been guarding the door. "The king would wish to see her."

Like a golden ray of sunlight, Temperance emerged. Slightly unbalanced, she hurried toward the bed. We were alone again.

Temperance should have been able to go home now that the Haloed Sun had returned. Why had she stayed?

"Here, let me," she said, resting a comforting hand on my shoulder, and I shifted so she could take my place. Leaning over Calix, she pulled back the sheet covering his torso.

"You're hurt," I said.

"He's dying." She pointed to the bowl of water behind me. "Get a wet cloth and don't ring it out."

I obeyed and deposited one into her hands, which she spread over his abdomen. Immediately, blood seeped through, mingling with the water-soaked cloth. Gingerly, she placed her hands on top, growing still and silent.

Threads of hope tightened around my heart.

After a few moments, her hands dropped away, and she stepped aside.

Calix groaned, stirring from his unconscious state. I removed the cloth and found the wound completely healed. Not even a scar marred his flesh.

"You did it," my voice cracked. "Temperance! He's—"

I heard a thud behind me and panic flooded through me once again. When I turned, Temperance was sprawled on the floor, unconscious.

"No!" I knelt down, pulling her sickly body into an embrace and tapped my fingers against her cheek. "Temperance?"

No response.

"Open your eyes!" I demanded, but her pulse was barely discernible.

Nothing.

"What's happened to her?" Calix asked, finally conscious and sounding panicked.

"She healed you then collapsed. Temperance, wake up! Please!"

Her eyelids blinked open, rapid and uneven.

"There you are! You need to heal yourself. Here." I grabbed a cup of water from the table above us. My hand shook, letting some of the water escape as I lifted the goblet to her lips. "Drink this... use it."

Temperance swallowed the entirety of the cup's contents before I tossed it aside. Her eyes closed, crinkled and twitching while her muscles tensed then relaxed.

"It's not working..." Her voice was broken and soft.

"I know you're tired but try again. We can't give up."

A faint smile touched her lips, and she reached up to guide my face to hers, uniting our lips.

Once parted, her words were barely audible, but almost serene. "I figure... 'If I'm going to die for you anyway.'"

I spat out a bitter laugh and pressed my forehead to hers. "Don't repeat the words of an arrogant fool."

Temperance caressed my face, then nuzzled her head into my chest. "I'm tired."

Her hand dropped from my cheek, and she went limp.

"No," I pleaded, hugging her tighter. "I can't lose one of you at the cost of the other. I need you, please!"

Not her. I couldn't bear it if it were her. Must everyone I cared about come to such violent ends?

I glanced at Calix, who was sitting up at the edge of the bed, looking at the scene with horror. When I turned back to Temperance, she wasn't breathing.

"Guard!" I shouted.

Taren, who looked a little worse for wear, and two guards crashed into the room, swords drawn.

"Lady Temperance?" Taren said, sincere concern painting his voice.

"Find Rhiannon and Ora!" They were halfway out the door when another thought occurred to me. "Heshrin too!"

When they were gone, I kissed Temperance's forehead. "She could have gone home, Calix. She would have been safe!"

Not a minute passed when the trio entered the room.

"They hadn't gotten far, and Heshrin seems to have been outside the entire time." Taren eyed the assassin suspiciously before stepping back out.

"Temperance," Ora and Rhiannon exclaimed.

"She's not breathing," I said. "Can you do anything?"

"As I said before, I don't have the power anymore, and even if I did, she's not..." Rhiannon didn't need to finish her sentence for us to know what she was about to say.

I turned to Heshrin. All this time, I'd suspected what he'd been up to in the catacombs. I prayed to the Goddess that I was right.

"Then, you! Bring her back."

Completely unaffected by the atmosphere in the room, Heshrin shrugged and said, "Necromancy is a fickle and delicate art. She would only be returned to you for a few minutes."

"That's all she'll need! Then she can heal herself, right?" My gaze met Rhiannon's.

"That's unnatural." Rhiannon stared at Temperance's lifeless body in my arms. "We can't guarantee the results. She might not have her powers if Heshrin reanimates her."

Ora knelt in front of us, eyes glowing an iridescent shade of silver and a hand clasping the medallion around her neck.

"What are you doing?" I asked.

"Trying something! With the Haloed Sun returned I feel stronger, and—you know what, we don't have time for me to explain."

Hope sprang forth once more. I'd felt the same pull when using my Light to clear the Catatonia Mist from the kingdom. I didn't know what she could possibly do as Temperance was the one with healing abilities, not Ora, but I wouldn't turn down any attempts to save her life.

After a deep breath, Ora uttered a spell.

> *"Mirrored in our own images and reflected in our eyes,*
> *I attempt to break their sacred ties.*
> *We connect in the only way our hearts will allow,*
> *Even when it severs the immortal vow.*
> *And then someday the time may come,*
> *That we come together as one."*

Ora's eyes closed, and when she opened them again she met my gaze with one of confusion. Then her gaze dropped to Tempy lying limp in my arms, and horror darkened her features.

"Tempy! What happened? Who are all of you?" She desperately glanced at her surroundings like she'd never seen this place or any of us before.

Temperance mentioned Ora had a connection to her other self... Could this be her?

"She's not breathing," I said.

"Did you try CPR, nimrod?" Ora moved Temperance from my grasp, laying her flat on her back. She then proceeded to pump her hands up and down on her chest. "When I say, blow air into her mouth like this." She demonstrated, then looked at me again. "Got it?"

I nodded.

Satisfied I understood, she continued pressing down on her chest. Every time Ora commanded it, I gave my breath to Temperance.

Whatever this is... please work.

Minutes passed, and the only thing that seemed to change were the amount of tears streaming from Ora's face.

"Come on, Tempy... please," she whispered in desperation.

Rhiannon squeezed Ora's shoulder, tears welling in her own eyes. "Dear girl, it has been a valiant effort, but I think it's time."

Ora's body went slack and she sat back, the glow from her eyes fading to their natural brown. She looked utterly shattered at her friend. "I thought Nora could save her. She—*I* wanted to save her.

Rhiannon wrapped her in a comforting embrace where Ora proceeded to sob into her shoulder.

No! No! No! This will not happen! I grasped Temperance's hand in mine and kissed it. *Forgive me, Temperance. This may not be what you wish, but I must try. I can't lose you.*

I looked at Heshrin, who glanced between the sobbing Ora and Temperance's still form like he was puzzling out an equation. "Heshrin, I command you to bring her back."

"Frederick, I don't think that is wise," Rhiannon protested, voice cracking. But she had not specifically forbidden it.

"Do it." I kept my gaze locked on the assassin.

He sighed. "Oh, kingly, if you wish her back as a mindless, undead puppet to stare at you for the rest of eternity, that I can arrange. But resurrection... as I said, she would not live long. Revival only lasts moments, and in rare cases, minutes if the Goddess allows it to be so."

"I don't care. Do it! If it fails, you can do it again."

Heshrin clicked his tongue. "Sadly, you only get one shot at this. Once a body is revived, failed attempt or not, there is no reviving it *ever* again; even if we are successful and she manages to heal herself."

"If she dies here, it's not like she can die again. If you bring her back, it'll give her time to heal herself, or at the very least…" I looked down at her still form, a part of my soul shredding to pieces. "I could say goodbye."

"Rhiannon said this could affect her abilities if it works. What if she can't heal herself?" Calix asked.

"We won't know until we try." Ora sniffled and rubbed her nose. "We are wasting time that Tempy doesn't have. Do it!"

I shot her an appreciative nod, relieved someone was on my side.

I turned my attention back to Heshrin. "Are you claiming that the great Obsidian, master of death, isn't powerful enough to conquer life? You know you want to. Curiosity will plague you if you don't. And if you succeed… imagine the possibilities."

Heshrin's eyes narrowed and he smirked. "Ever the rule-breaker you are. I suppose anything is possible now that the Haloed Sun has dawned. If I draw from its fresh power, perhaps a miracle could occur."

Heshrin knelt by Temperance's other side and held his hand over her heart. His eyebrows raised. "Her soul is still connected to the body."

"Truly? Are you certain?"

"You question a necromancer if they are certain?" Heshrin shot me a glare but didn't give me a chance to answer. "This may be possible. These are once in a lifetime circumstances. I need you to permit me to do this without questioning my methods, and even then, I do not guarantee results. Do you wish to proceed?"

"Yes." It didn't require a second thought. I'd pay whatever cost to save her.

"Very well." Heshrin reached into a pouch on his belt and produced a jagged iridescent crystal that glowed with a faint golden light.

"A soul shard?" I asked, horrified. "Where did you get that?"

"Does that matter? You want a chance at saving her, don't you?"

I did, but would she forgive the use of another's soul to save her own if it wasn't willingly given? If Heshrin had stolen that soul from one of his victims?

"Soul shards are illegal! That thing should be destroyed, and you should be arrested for making one," Calix said, voice strained. He stood at the edge of the bed eyeing the assassin with open displeasure. If not for the experiment to save Temperance that Heshrin was about to perform, I'm certain Calix would already have him in shackles.

Heshrin looked from Calix to me, frowning. "Kingly... for someone who promised no questions, I'm hearing quite a lot of chatter."

When I didn't respond, my hard stare piercing into Heshrin's, he sighed in frustration. "Fine, a high priest gave it willingly on his deathbed and donated it to the Order of the Haloed Sun. I merely *procured* it for my own use."

Only one thing could confirm whether his words were true or if he were merely lying to sate our consciences so we would allow his experiment, but I couldn't bring myself to do it. Regardless of his answer... I couldn't risk losing her. I met Calix's watchful gaze, awaiting my confirmation of Heshrin's truth.

I nodded, and Calix's shoulders dropped slightly. He trusted my word. I ignored the guilt of the lie.

I turned my attention back to Heshrin and Temperance. "Do it."

"The shard fulfills the requirement for a spirit of the dead, but it also calls for a spirit of the living," he said.

"Would it kill them?"

The assassin shrugged. "This is new territory. Anything is possible. A person with magic could soften those odds, theoretically."

"I'll do it," I said without a second thought.

A unanimous "No" came from those around me.

"The world can't wait for another Descended of the Haloed Sun to be born. The prophecy surrounds her... This could be my part in it," I said.

"And if you die, you think she'll ever forgive herself?" Calix countered.

"No more than I could possibly forgive myself if I don't try."

"Silence," Rhiannon commanded, and the room went still.

Rhiannon delicately pulled away from Ora's embrace, then stood and walked the few steps to Temperance. She knelt down and lifted her great-granddaughter's head into her lap, softly stroking her hair. "I will do it. I've slowed my age progression for long enough. I can give the lifeforce that she needs."

I opened my mouth to protest, but Heshrin spoke first. "Can we just choose someone already? Her soul is intact but getting fainter with every moment and the Haloed Sun is rising further."

Rhiannon squeezed my shoulder. "I have outlived my children. I'm ready to be reunited with them if that is the cost to save my great-granddaughter. It's time to pass the gauntlet to the future generations."

I could lose Temperance's affection for allowing this, but at least she'll live. And I hoped Rhiannon could make it through too. I moved away from Temperance, and Ora did the same.

"Turn her toward the window," Rhiannon said and opened the drapes, allowing a trail of sunlight into the room.

They repositioned Temperance in the center of the haloed sunlight, and Rhiannon knelt by her.

Heshrin leaned over Temperance holding the shard between his hands and began an incantation.

> *"Goddess, accept this toll, restore to this mortal a living soul.*
> *Heal the body from their fatal wound*
> *And deny Death his right to consume.*
> *A spirit of the living. A spirit of the dead.*
> *Partake of their combined lifeforce instead.*
> *Tis not a soul Your Grace should reap.*
> *Awaken them from eternal sleep."*

"I've never felt this much power." Heshrin opened his hands, and the shard hung suspended in the air, glints of gold and violet light escaping the crystal. He then placed a hand over Temperance's heart and the other over Rhiannon's. She cried out as a golden mist emanated from her chest and drifted down to Temperance's.

I could hear the whispered pleas of the others in the room, praying for the Goddess to intercede. To save her.

Hear us, Emeriz. She is your kin. Your descendant. Your hero. Save her.

A webbing of wrinkles bloomed over Rhiannon's smooth, unblemished skin, while her shining hair thinned and dulled to a soft gray. Her body tilted back and forth as though she could collapse at any moment.

"The old woman is fading," Heshrin called out and winced.

No.

"Frederick."

A warmth blanketed my entire body as I searched for the one who called my name. Ora and Calix watched the scene with hopeful horror, but the voice hadn't belonged to either of them.

The voice spoke again inside my mind, *"The moon has yet to descend, and your abilities are still at their peak. You can lend her your strength."*

My heart stalled when I realized who the voice could be and confirmed it in my heart to be true.

Goddess, I'm no healer or necromancer. What can I do?

"The Descended share a bond unlike any other. A balance. Hold both your ring and her pendant between your hand and hers now, or she will be lost. This is all I can do. There are rules even I must follow."

I ignored the bitterness brewing in my soul that she would not do more, but I sprung into action. I slipped off my ring and knelt beside Temperance, unclasping her necklace. I held the jewelry between our hands and laced our fingers together. I focused on the heat of the sun and thought of what I wanted to accomplish, then sent a prayer up to the Goddess.

A weight pressed on my chest, and my eyes warmed with the heat of my powers being enacted. Never breaking my gaze from Temperance, I concentrated. My body weakened and I became dizzy, but I didn't care. Her color slowly returned to her face, but she still seemed pale.

All at once, the golden light surrounding us faded and the shard imploded into a cloud of shimmering dust. My body felt utterly drained and my head was aching, and Rhiannon and Heshrin looked a little worse for wear, but we were all alive.

Temperance's head shot up, her eyes wide while she gasped for air. Her irises flashed violet, then returned to normal.

She stared up at me and relaxed. "Hiya."

Laughing from relief, I gathered her in my arms, which caused her to hiss in pain.

"Apologies." I loosened my grip a little, the smile never leaving my face. "Heshrin just brought you back, but you have to heal yourself now."

Temperance's eyes glowed, but after a moment she crumpled further into my arms.

"It hurts... I can't." Her voice weak and quivering, she gave into the pain.

Was Rhiannon right? Had her death ripped away her powers? If that were so, would I lose her still? But her eyes had flashed violet, perhaps they were only weakened?

Rhiannon shifted closer to us, her aged face both familiar and not. "You healed Calix without being properly healed yourself. Normally, it wouldn't have affected you so much, but he was on the brink of death which is why your body couldn't handle it."

"Rhiannon?" Temperance's eyes widened. "What happened to you?"

"Shh... I'll explain later," Rhiannon said.

Heshrin, still catching his breath, held his hand above Temperance's chest, a self satisfied expression crossing his face. "Her soul is strong, but her body is weak."

"If she can't heal herself, will she—"

"Calm yourself, kingly. She'll live, thanks to me." Heshrin stood and ran his fingers through his hair. "I will be expecting a high compensation."

Temperance looked up at him. "Thank you, Heshrin."

The assassin stiffened a moment, and I wondered what could be going through his mind. Perhaps he would say something sincere for onc—

"Yes, I'm practically a living saint." With that, he abruptly turned on his heel and sauntered off, whistling a jaunty tune.

Blessed by the Goddess, yes. A saint? No. But I was not about to argue with the man who had helped save the life of someone precious to me.

Ora came to Temperance's side, her bloodshot eyes still glistening with fresh tears. "This whole dying thing... Can you not do it again? It wasn't fun."

"I didn't die," Temperance said, but when no one said anything, she looked at me in question. "Did I?"

"We will spare you the details for now. You're alive, and that is what matters," Rhiannon said, softly.

"I tried to help you too, by summoning Nora," Ora said, then rubbed her head. "Though, if this is the migraine that Nora feels anytime I scry into her head... then I feel bad for myself."

"Nora?" Temperance asked.

Ora nodded. "I thought Nora could help, and with the Haloed Sun back, my magic felt stronger, so I took a shot. She tried something called CPR, but it didn't work."

"Thanks, for trying," Temperance breathed.

"Frederick helped her with part of it." Ora wiggled her eyebrows at Temperance, grinning.

Temperance blushed, and my face burned.

"Are you healed now? Can you move?" Ora asked, her teasing demeanor melting back to one of concern.

A smile tugged at the sides of Temperance's mouth as she moved to sit up but winced. "Ow. Definitely cracked some ribs, and my body aches everywhere. Why can't I heal myself?"

Rhiannon brushed some strands of Temperance's hair back. "You have been pushed to your absolute limits. There's no telling what effect the night's events may have had on your abilities. For now, Ora and I will go fetch the physician. You need some form of medical attention and some medicinal potions and poultices."

Ora looked like the last thing she wanted to do was leave, but she followed Rhiannon out the door.

Calix stepped forward. "My King, I suggest we move her to the bed."

With his help we were able to move her with fairly minimal discomfort. At least she said it was minimal. Her pained face implied otherwise.

When Temperance was settled in the bed and I was sitting beside her, Calix placed a kiss on her head. "Thank you for saving my life, Lady Temperance."

"You're welcome." Temperance reached up to squeeze Calix's hand. "You can drop the title, you know."

"I'll keep using it for now." Calix raised an eyebrow at me, amused. "I sense I'll need the practice."

"Practice?" Temperance asked.

"Farewell." Calix departed, leaving her question hanging in the air.

Fully understanding his implication, I smiled.

Temperance sighed then leaned her head on my shoulder. "Can I sleep now?"

"Just until the physician arrives."

"Can you hold me until then?"

"I'd love nothing more. And I'd like to see anyone try to take you from my arms."

"Will you stay by my side all night?" She yawned and sunk deeper into our embrace.

I laid my head against hers and breathed, "Yes."

CHAPTER 39

TEMPERANCE

The rhythm of Frederick's breathing in harmony with his heartbeat soothed me. I inhaled his familiar scent of lime and cedarwood, but found it tainted by blood and sweat. The smell brought flashing memories of the violence from the night before.

Or was it only hours ago? My sense of time was completely wrecked.

Frederick lay beside me, his body warming and comforting my own. My arm was draped across his chest, while my calf interlocked with his, keeping us secure on the bed meant for one. With my lingering aches and pains, it wasn't the most comfortable position, but I didn't care. The thought of being any further from him made me feel uneasy.

The medicinal potions certainly helped, but will I ever be able to heal myself again?

"My lady?" Frederick's husky voice tingled in my ears, sending goosebumps down to my toes.

I opened my eyes, but my gaze stayed on the open window, studying the lilac-hued landscape of the Haloed Sun. A sign of the Descended's return.

My return.

"How'd you know I was awake?" I asked.

Frederick twisted one of my curls around his finger. "For one, you weren't snoring anymore."

I slapped his chest playfully, then buried my face into it to hide my embarrassment.

"I was only teasing." He chuckled and pulled me closer.

The movement pressed on my ribcage confirming that I probably still had some cracks, and I sucked in a breath.

He froze and softened his hold on me. "I apologize. Did that hurt?"

"I'm okay."

He was quiet a moment, and I wondered if he'd sensed the lie in my words.

I didn't want him to worry. When the physician left, Frederick told me what they had all done to save me—Rhiannon especially. After all that sacrifice, the least I could do was put their minds at ease.

I braved a look at him and attempted to lighten the mood. "But it's the worst. Not only did I snore, but I'm far from loveliness right now. Look at my dress—I can only imagine what my face and hair look like."

"If you remember, our appearances during our travels were rough too." Frederick turned his attention to the tattered skirts of my dress, rubbing his fingers across the snags. "Your dress may be ruined..."

I groaned and dropped my head back to his chest.

He chuckled softly and lifted my chin, forcing me to look into his sincere cobalt eyes.

"But you're still radiant to me."

My heart leapt.

"I wish I could freeze this moment," I said.

His cheeks turned rosy.

"What?"

He held up the hand that was securely around my waist, to reveal his thumb pressed against his ring. "I already have. Or at least slowed it down."

It was then that I caught the hint of a luminescent glow rimming his eyes. Grabbing his hand, I maneuvered it up around my shoulder and pressed my lips to it.

Frederick grinned and repositioned us on our sides so we were facing each other.

"Where is everyone?" I asked.

"Giving us some time alone since..."

He didn't have to say it. I'd found my way home, and we both knew I couldn't stay. No matter how much the guilt of their sacrifice pressed down on me or how much love I had come to feel for them, it was time to leave.

I'm such a coward. I get to go home to safety while they all deal with the aftermath my presence caused.

"I'm leaving such a mess behind, huh? I don't know how you can look at me like that."

"Very easily," he said.

"Why?"

"You're a hero, Temperance. You restored the Haloed Sun, allowing me to use my powers to their full extent. Maxwell's men had to retreat, saving countless people." He kissed my hand. "You healed Calix in spite of your own condition."

"My presence caused the battle. Calix got hurt because of that, and Rhiannon gave up her everlasting youth to save me. You should've let Maxwell take me."

"Never."

"But—"

"Never." Frederick's eyes locked hard on me, immovable in his conviction. "That battle was coming eventually, with or without you. We all chose to save you. Even if you leave… with the Haloed Sun, magic is at full strength. Others will rise up."

"Doesn't that mean Minerva is too? What if they fear her more? What if they don't want to fight?"

Frederick cut me off with a kiss.

"So, negative thoughts get me kissed?" I asked, confused. "Good to know."

He ran the back of his fingers down my arm. "You get kissed because, as a ruler, you need to look at every angle so you're prepared for anything."

"But I'm not a ruler, so why kiss me?"

"I have many reasons as to why I want to kiss you."

He kissed me again.

Running my fingers through his dark hair, I deepened the kiss. My heart beat wildly, and Frederick's grip around my waist tightened. He was such a good kisser that I felt I could bear the pain of his embrace very easily.

He broke off the kiss, and whispered, "Temperance?"

"Uh-huh?" My head was too foggy to form actual words.

"Let's take a walk," he suggested.

When we stood, all the aches and pains ignited again, and I found it difficult to catch my breath. Frederick wrapped his arm around my waist, propping me up.

"Thanks."

"What?" He leaned his left ear toward me.

"Thanks," I repeated.

"Of course." He beamed down at me.

Cocking my head, I examined his right side. A drip of dried blood left a trail down his ear. He must have blown an eardrum.

I haven't been able to heal myself, but what about other people?

Curiosity got the better of me, and I cupped his ear in my hand. I focused on healing it and felt my magic enact behind my eyes. When it ebbed, I dropped my hand away and a twinge of a headache pressed against the back of my skull.

"Whoa! That's back." He rubbed his ear with a look of awe, but it quickly faded to worry. "You shouldn't have done that until you fully recovered."

It appeared I didn't need water to heal anymore. I wondered if it was because of the Haloed Sun or the strength he'd lent me. Frederick and Ora had mentioned their powers felt stronger, and I wasn't an exception. An unbridled magic raced through my veins, and I could clearly heal others, so why couldn't I heal myself?

I caressed his cheek. "With the Haloed Sun, I'm stronger now. Fixing your ear is nothing."

"Can you heal yourself?"

I shook my head. "I tried healing myself every time I drank water last night, but nothing. I might need more time. Rhiannon said I pushed myself too far. It'll be okay, and between the potions and poultices last night I am feeling much better. I'll go to the doctor when I get home. I promise."

"If my lady says so." He gripped my healing hand and squeezed it.

We made our way to the deserted gardens. Everyone was off elsewhere, clearing away the evidence of the ball and its horrors. Guilt wrapped around me like a boa constrictor. I may not have been at fault, but I'd been the cause.

"Stop it," Frederick scolded, gently. "Maxwell did this. Not you."

"How—"

"You have sighed every fifteen seconds since we came out here," he said.

How did he already have me so nailed down?

"We can't be responsible for other people's actions. Last night happened because of the decisions that both Maxwell and I made. We are at fault, not you." Frederick peered into my face, begging me to understand. "What's important now is that you're safe, which means—"

"I need to go home," I said, not looking away.

He nodded. "Maxwell escaped, and who knows what he has planned next."

A burst of high-speed winds gusted around us as a dark whirling storm cloud brewed across our path. Lightning danced through the puffs of moisture, leaving echoes of thunder. A figure stood in the center of the mini storm.

Right now? Seriously!

Frederick gripped my hand and moved in front of me, ready to block whatever was coming. Ora came running to stand next to us.

"Where did you come from?" I shouted over the wind.

"I was coming to find you when I saw this," Ora said, staring at the meteorological impossibility.

The microburst faded, revealing the mysterious figure in full detail. Tears instantly flowed down my face when I recognized who'd been haunting me since I got to Emeriz.

"James!" I dropped Frederick's hand and propelled myself at my brother. All thoughts of my injuries were forgotten in that moment, because he was a piece of home that I had been missing.

A smile lit up his face. "Tempy!"

I nearly tackled him to the ground with my death grip around his neck. He staggered back a couple steps to catch himself from falling, but he hugged me back just as tight. My body tensed from the pain, but I pushed past it. I'd missed my family so much I was not about to break off this reunion.

"Are you okay?" James released me only to grab my shoulders and assess my condition.

"Some bumps and bruises, but I'm fine! You've never looked more wonderful to me than you do right now."

He arched an eyebrow and spoke through the side of his mouth.

"Wish I could say the same, sis. *Yeesh*, you look like crap."

"Shut up!" I laughed and hugged him again. "You try fighting off enemy soldiers, nearly dying in the process of saving someone, and see if you look any better."

James pulled back and stared at me. "Come again?" he said.

"Yep! You missed all the action."

"No fair! I'm geared up and everything." He held up a massive mace and gestured to his Emeriz-appropriate attire.

"Trust me, you didn't want to be here. How's Mom and Dad?"

"Worried sick," he said, lowering the mace. "Mom's pissed at Dad and Grandpa. They were gonna tell you everything when we got to California, but then I saw you disappear. I've been trying to get here ever since." He straightened his posture like a proud cockatoo. "Looks like my power could no longer be denied."

I laughed. "Sorry to burst your bubble, but... I think it had to do with something I did here."

"Are you trying to steal my *thunder*, sis?"

Ora cleared her throat, approaching us with a hesitant wave. "Hi, James."

"Nora?" James pointed at her, looking between the two of us confused.

"I guess Grandpa didn't tell you everything." I sighed and made the introduction. "James, meet Ora, Nora's other half. Literally. Her soul was split at birth and divided between worlds. Long story."

Not looking away from Ora, he smiled. "Awesome."

Ora looked petrified and stiff, so much so that one light breeze might have knocked her over.

James had arrived in a glorified storm cloud. That would be intimidating to anyone. Still...

James nodded at Frederick behind us, still standing where I'd left him. "Who's that?"

A pebble of guilt weighed on me. I'd run away without a second thought.

"King Frederick, ruler of this kingdom and Descended of the Moon," I answered.

"Sweet!" James waved at Frederick, which Frederick reciprocated with a minor nod.

"Be right back," I said, returning to Frederick's side.

"Hi," I said softly, a little embarrassed that I'd just abandoned him.

"So, that's your brother?"

"Yep."

Frederick softened his tone. "I hope you return someday."

My heart sank, but I smiled. "I have some pretty good reasons to."

"Never thought I'd be so grateful for complications." He rubbed the back of his neck. "I wish I could kiss you."

"Why can't you?" I asked, tilting my head as I bit my lip.

The gesture brought his attention right where I wanted it to, but he cleared his throat.

"It wouldn't be appropriate with your brother present."

"He's got eyelids." I pulled against the lapel on his tunic and pressed my lips to his.

Frederick made no effort to break us apart and pulled me closer instead.

"Oh man! I do not need to see that," James protested.

We broke off the kiss, and Frederick touched his forehead to mine. "Was that supposed to help me let you go?" he whispered.

An irrational fear twisted my stomach. "Don't forget me."

"Impossible, my lady."

"Tempy!" James shouted, making me jump apart from Frederick.

Chuckling softly, Frederick was a little more poised at pulling away from me.

"Mom and Dad don't have to know how long it took me to find you."

No, they'd waited long enough.

"You should go," Frederick said. "As tempting as it is to have you stay, you've been missing your life back home since we met. I'll feel better knowing you're safe until things stabilize here."

Stop saying all the right things! You're trying to make this easier, but it's only making it more difficult.

I wanted to say goodbye to everyone, Rhiannon especially. I needed to thank her for everything. Without her, I would've never survived this entire journey. I scanned the surrounding area hoping to get a glimpse of her, but she was nowhere in sight. But I worried if I didn't leave now, I might not go.

"Will you tell the others goodbye for me? And take care of Rhiannon and Brydon, please. I owe them so much."

"I swear it." He placed a kiss on my hand, then held it over his heart. "Goodbye, Temperance."

When I turned to leave, his hand didn't let go, twisting me back around.

"Sorry," he said. "My mind has accepted your departure, but it seems my hand hasn't."

My heart fluttered. "I'll miss you too."

Frederick let go, his face becoming serious and somber.

I walked straight to Ora, and we wrapped our arms around each other, holding on tight.

"Thanks for everything, Ora."

"I'm going to miss you so much!" Crying, she squeezed me tighter.

"I'll tell Nora soon."

We pulled away from each other, smiling despite our tears.

"*See* you around," I joked.

"I believe it is I who will be *seeing* you." She dangled her medallion in the air between us before walking to stand next to Frederick.

I wiped tears from my face. "Let's go before anything else happens."

"You sure?" James said, hesitant.

"Yes... for now."

Watching Ora and Frederick, my heart panged with the urge to return to them. Instead, I turned to James. "I'll take us home. Where are we going?"

"Earth, dummy," James teased.

I pinched his arm.

"Ouch! Fine, Grandpa's."

Pendant in hand, I pressed the prongs up and spun the amethyst, my heart picking up pace. I grabbed James' hand.

I closed my eyes and imagined my family's faces. The smell of the hydrangeas in Grandma's garden, covered in flowers and greenery. The soft touch of their cat, Syd's, fur. The window seat I'd spent hours reading on during vacations...

I felt the winds of Emeriz fade and the pull of Earth grow.

When the pendant stopped spinning, the prongs clicked back into place. Opening my eyes, the view of my Grandma's lush garden from the dining room window welcomed me home. My reflection in the glass of the window showed that I still wore my tattered ball gown.

It must only change when one goes to Emeriz.

"Tempy?" my mom's voice called out, a catch in her throat.

Mom, Dad, and Grandpa stood from their seats in the living room. Next thing I knew, we were in the center of the room in a group hug, tears mixed with smiles and lots of kisses.

Mom shooed back everyone to hold my face in her hands. "Sweetheart, what happened? And what are you wearing?"

Before I could answer, she swallowed me up in a suffocating hug, a blubbering mess.

"Mom, I've hugged giants that didn't squeeze this much," I said, voice somewhat strangled.

She finally let me go and led me to a chair. "Tell us everything," she demanded.

"Honey," Dad said. "Let her shower, change, and get some rest before we interrogate her."

"Yes, please," I begged.

"All right. Come on, I'll help you out of this... corset?" My baffled mother led me to the bathroom for some much needed R&R.

"Wait," I said. "What have you been telling everyone?"

"You were already supposed to be gone the first two weeks so that was covered," Grandpa said, "but for the past week you've been hospitalized with a virus. I've got some... Emerizian connections at the hospital. There's still a lot to tell you."

James laughed and pulled my phone from his backpack.

"I've been handling all your text correspondence! None of your friends are the wiser."

My jaw dropped. "Who said you could speak on my behalf? What did you say and to whom?"

"Oh, you'll have a lot to talk about with some people. The guys in particular." James waved my cell back and forth.

Home for only two minutes, and I already wanted to kill him.

I struggled to break free from my mom's grasp to beat the crap out of him.

"Hey," Mom soothed, "I monitored what he said, don't worry. James, give the phone to your dad."

James tossed the phone to Dad while Mom and I headed to the bathroom. I laid my head on her shoulder, inhaling the familiar scent of her Vaseline lotion. It was calming and warm, and I relaxed like I did when she'd carried me to bed as a kid.

I was finally home.

CHAPTER 40

FREDERICK

Temperance disappeared from my view faster than evaporated steam. I focused on the spot she'd faded away, willing my eyes to leave the vision of her standing there.

"She'll come back," Ora said, breaking through my forced illusions. "She promised to make me whole again."

"If she did, then I don't doubt it." I shot her a half-smile.

Ora bounded off enthusiastically toward the castle, unaware of my white lie. There was a tiny sliver of doubt that nibbled at my mind.

When she'd reunited with James, she appeared natural. So free.

She was with her family now. Safe. If it were me... would I give all that up?

Heshrin slithered up next to me. "Wake up, kingly," he said. "Shouldn't you be polishing your crown and licking your wounds from last night's disaster?"

"I'm grateful that you saved her life last night and you will be compensated accordingly, but I don't have time for your nonsense." I gritted my teeth and walked away.

"Kingly, kingly, kingly." Heshrin draped his arm over my shoulder, a wry smile tugging on his lips. "No nonsense, only intel."

"Listening."

"As I've said before, the things one says when they think no one is listening are fascinating."

"Your point?" I asked.

Heshrin folded his arms. "You will never guess who just came to confess to the Superior Goddess with a guilty conscience."

Freshly bathed and dressed, complete with my polished crown, I sat on my throne, my expression grim. Calix stood at my left, with Duke Boetius standing below in front of the dais. Taren escorted Persephone into the throne room. My blood boiled, but I gripped the edge of the velvet-lined arms to keep my composure.

"Your Majesty," she said, her honeyed voice lost in the air.

Calix stepped forward with the charges.

"Lady Persephone Boetius, you are charged with high treason against His Majesty, King Frederick, and the Kingdom of Linall."

Persephone's gaze jumped back and forth between everyone's faces.

"What evidence do you have to back this accusation?" she asked.

Calix laid them all out for her.

"We have a witness to your confession in the chapel. You sent a letter to Grand High Priest Maxwell relaying privileged information regarding Lady Temperance. We questioned your ladies, and they confirmed everything. They were more than willing to oust the traitor that caused their fathers, brothers, or lovers to be severely injured."

Persephone crossed her arms. "Had His Majesty been wiser with where he put his affections, none of this would have happened. For the sake of the rebellion—of the people—you should have just let Maxwell take her."

"Don't speak of what you don't know, sister," Taren warned.

Persephone shot him a dirty look. "I tried to warn you all that she was a risk to Linall—to the cause. I saw her using magic and spending a little too much time with Fjall and Kelurs. Who knows what secrets she revealed. Better to turn her in on our terms rather than invoke the wrath of the High Queen were she to find out some other way. That grubby title-seeker caused all of this."

Unable to listen to her idiocrasy any longer, I stood and announced, "Temperance is a Descended."

Persephone's pinched up face melted into shock.

"And not just any Descended." I took a step forward, and she immediately took one back. "Heir to the Superior Goddess and the throne of Eslane. Descended of the Haloed Sun and queen in her own right."

She searched for the truth of my words on the expressions of Calix, her father, and Taren. Her shock turned to fear.

"Not only did you move against your king, but you performed treasonous acts against a foreign sovereign. An ally. The penalty of which requires no less than death." My voice boomed against the walls.

I had blamed myself, but no—this all happened because of her! I would not stand for it.

"King Frederick," Calix said, but I held up my hand, silencing him.

If I had it my way, I'd let her rot in a cell the rest of her life with only the rats to keep her company.

"But... given our history, and the continued devotion of your father to our cause, I've settled on banishment. One step within the borders of Linall, and you will be brought to court to determine the method of your death."

"My King—"

"I'm not *your* king!" Just the sound of her voice inflamed the anger inside me. "You put my people in danger and exposed us! Temperance was forced into hiding. She may never come to our aid in the future now. My powers were revealed to the world, outing me as a Descended! And why did all this happen?" I pointed at her and took one step down. "Your ego, jealousy, and ignorant betrayal!"

"Please... Linall is my home!" Persephone screeched through tears.

"Maybe that thought should have crossed your mind before you nearly handed your home over to Maxwell," I snapped.

"My King, might I offer another solution?" Duke Boetius asked, not the least bit bothered by his daughter's situation.

It was only fair to let him speak on his daughter's behalf. He'd only do so if it benefited himself or the kingdom. I was still fuming, but I clenched my fists and returned to my throne.

"I'll allow it."

"Persephone acted in hopes of securing her future and protecting the kingdom—albeit a little misguided. Perhaps she could make it up to Your Majesty?" the duke suggested.

"You think I would marry this traitor?" I said, my tone dripping with disgust.

"That wasn't my implication," he replied and waved the thought away, eyeing me. "I recommend she assist the rebellion as another option."

When I realized where he was going, I looked at Persephone. "I guess there's one alternative..."

She doesn't deserve it.

"Anything!" Persephone dropped to her knees, pleading.

"Our deal with Fjall requires a seal of marriage. If you marry

Prince Drystan, therefore solidifying our alliance, I will forgo your banishment."

"An arranged marriage?" she said, gaping at us.

"A royal one," I retorted.

"Father, Taren, please!" Persephone looked at her kin, receiving no comfort from either man.

They have some honor, unlike you.

"Banishment or marriage. Either option is better than death, wouldn't you say?" Staring her down, I sat back against the cushion.

The room stayed quiet for a minute before she gathered herself up off the ground.

Her eyes downcast, she curtsied and said, "I accept."

"Dismissed." Not giving her any more attention, I addressed Taren. "Confine her to her quarters. Apart from meals and meetings with Fjall, she's not permitted to leave. Any correspondence to or from her will be checked beforehand. Prince Drystan will reside in Linall until the end of the season, finalizing the details of our treaty and her dowry. Then he'll take her to Fjall."

Once we were alone, Calix squeezed my shoulder.

"It's the right call," he assured. "It gets her out of Linall, keeps the duke loyal, and secures Fjall."

Even with the truth in Calix's words, I was still left wanting. Persephone deserved far worse.

The weight of recent events bared down on me. Too much of my life had been turned upside down, and I was desperate to clear my head. I'd found the Heir of the Haloed Sun. Fallen for her. Nearly lost her. Then had to say goodbye to her. But what had my head spinning the most... The Superior Goddess had spoken to *me*.

I shrugged off his hand and headed for the hidden entrance to the King's Atrium.

"I'm going for a ride." The blank space amongst the portraits of former leaders of Linall caught my eye, stopping me just short of the door. The glaring injustice that had haunted me for so long could finally be remedied.

I stared at the barren spot. "And hang my parents' portrait back in its rightful place."

CHAPTER 41

TEMPERANCE

For the first time in years, I had a blissfully dreamless sleep. When I finally awoke, I stretched and winced in pain before checking the clock on the nightstand to find that it was three in the morning. I'd slept for twelve hours.

Later, my parents would be taking me to see the Emerizian connections that grandpa had at the hospital. They wanted to be certain there were no longstanding injuries and that I would heal normally. Now that I was on Earth, my powers felt significantly dampened. Even if my ability to heal myself had returned, I doubted it would be strong enough to do anything.

I slid myself out of my grandma's patchwork quilt and headed to the kitchen for water. I rubbed my eyes as I walked down the hallway, trying to shake the foreign feeling pulsing inside me. After growing accustomed to Emeriz, I figured it'd take a day or two to assimilate to Earth.

When I entered the dining room, I found my grandpa sitting at the table.

"Grandpa?" I said, my voice raspy. "Why are you up?"

"Morning," Grandpa replied, looking up from his book and removing his glasses. "With what you must've been through, I didn't want you to wake up alone."

He poured a glass of water from the pitcher on the table and handed it to me. I drank it in one go.

"Thanks."

With concern knitting his brow, he watched me. "Want to talk about it?"

"Let's wait until everyone's awake. I don't want to go through everything twice."

"I'll help you break it down for them. Why don't you practice on me first?"

I told him everything, leaving out a few subtle details, like a certain budding romance. He listened intently, occasionally asking questions here and there. By the time I finished, it was five in the morning.

"Sounds like much has changed back home." He took a swig of water. "I will never be able to repay Rhiannon for what she did. I take comfort in knowing that she and Brydon are still around. Good on her for protecting Frederick during his travels, and by extension, you."

"What? She wasn't anywhere near us while we were traveling together."

He laughed. "Tell me, what are Rhiannon's symbols?"

"Three white doves."

"And the lesser known..." He leaned forward with a twinkle in his eye. "A pure white horse."

The click of the puzzle pieces was almost audible in my mind.

Brydon had shown exuberant amounts of attention to Neva and would defend her tendency to disappear. And Rhiannon and Neva were never in the same place at the same time.

"Neva is Rhiannon," I breathed, staring wide-eyed at Grandpa.

She'd seen and heard so many things between me and Frederick—

how embarrassing! What else had I done around her without knowing?

"Maybe I shouldn't have told you." He patted my hands.

His words stung like a wasp. My family's secrets had led to everything in the first place. I'd *died*—actually died—and was only brought back magically while others paid the cost.

"No." Clenching my fists, I couldn't control my cutting tone. "Why didn't you guys ever tell me anything?"

"We always meant to," he said, stumbling over his words. "But as we watched you grow and enjoy your childhood, it became more difficult. Before we knew it, you were a young woman, and she was sick. So your grandma compiled her journals, prepped your parents, and wrote the letters."

"That's essentially what the letter in the room said. Didn't have much other useful information, like how to get home, though," I said.

"Right." He retrieved a thick envelope and a clear glass sphere from the writing desk in the corner. "From what you've told me, you know most of what she shared in this first letter. But it could fill in some missing pieces." He placed the letter in front of me and held up the sphere. "This will give you access to the room, but like the entrance in Linall, you will only be able to exit the way you entered."

He put his hand on my shoulder.

"What you do from here is and always will be up to you. Your parents knew the risks when you were born."

"Mom too?" I asked, unable to wrap my mind around how anyone from Earth could possibly be okay knowing their little girl would be destined to save another world.

"Yes," he said with a nod. "She's the daughter of one of forty families we helped escape Emeriz. We share a community of sorts." Grabbing his work gloves, he headed for the back door, stopping just before stepping out. "That reminds me. Before she died, your grandma reached out to someone who can help you develop your skills. His name is Ethan Barley, grandson of an Eslanian high priest of the old order. He's been raised and taught in their ways. If you choose to go back, just say the word and I'll contact him."

Ethan? As in Sophia's brother?

"Haloed Violet Community Center..." I said, realizing the exclusivity of the club now made sense. They were all Eslanians.

My phone buzzed with a text alert. Nora's name appeared on the screen.

"I still have to tell Nora."

"I'd speak to her father first, but..." Grandpa nodded. "She deserves the choice, just like you."

"One more thing—can we not tell them that I almost died? If I decide to go back, I doubt my parents would agree if they knew."

"I won't lie. Not anymore. You were right in your anger that we never told you. Your parents know where your destiny may lay and the dangers that come with it." With one last glance, he headed out to the garden, leaving me alone.

I watched the condensation drip down my water glass, contemplating all the questions I still had but was too mentally exhausted to ask. Especially since the interrogation of my parents would be just as tiresome.

What did *I* want?

The next month passed relatively normally. I kept myself busy with school, family, friends, and training. My injuries had mostly healed. Though it took some time before I could swing a longsword again, and I still wouldn't be competing any time soon. Grandpa moved in with us temporarily, thinking it would be wise to be nearby in case I decided to go back. He spent his free time training James and me in Eslanian swordplay and our powers. The latter proved more difficult to do here but was still possible due to some sort of magic barrier he'd enchanted the space we practiced in with.

Most of my magic training was personal study of my grandma's fifty journals and her portable sphere that allowed me access to the secret room. Every time I entered, it awakened my memories, and the pull of Emeriz would get that much stronger—making my choice all the more difficult.

I hated being blind to what was happening over there. Could I make a double life work? Or would I have to give up one for the other? When was I supposed to tell Nora?

Nora stood near the choir room door with Mark, her useless Morp date two weeks prior. Mid-dance he left her to get back together with his ex-girlfriend. Luckily, her night was salvaged thanks to James and Brett taking turns dancing with her.

Mark and his girlfriend were already on the fritz again, and he was leaning in hard with his flirt game. Nora didn't look thrilled about it. Placing my lunch on the ground, I got ready to interfere, but James beat me to it.

"I think you've done enough damage, Mark," James said, dropping his hand on Mark's shoulder and escorting him away. "Why don't you scurry back to your hole like the little groundhog you are?"

Mark stomped off like a two-year-old.

"You okay?" James asked Nora, squeezing her shoulder.

"Yeah, thanks." She tapped her hand against his elbow.

"Be more blunt next time." He bent down so their heads were level. "Most guys don't pick up on subtleties."

She nodded.

"James!" Sophia shouted through the fence from the parking lot. James headed over to her and started chatting. She'd been his Morp date, and by the looks of it, they'd hit it off.

James and my friends appeared so at ease, it made me jealous. Sure, I'd still laugh and joke around, but it was different. The mask of the girl I used to be was slipping, and it was a daily struggle to hide my true thoughts at times. It felt like something was missing.

Seeing Sophia brought thoughts of Ethan. I still hadn't reached out to him. Honestly, I wasn't sure I ever would unless I decided Emeriz would be part of my future.

"Hey." Nora sat next to me, grabbed the ear bud I wasn't using and placed it in her ear. She then stared at me like she was waiting for something.

"What's wrong?" I asked.

"You are."

Of course I couldn't slip anything past her. To Nora, my emotions were always crystal-clear. I fiddled with my grandma's necklace in silence.

"Is it that boy you told Brett about? You know, the reason why you turned him down for the dance? The one you never mentioned to me? Which, by the way, I'm still mad about!" Nora held her finger to my nose in challenge.

"Well, isn't Brett just a Chatty Cathy lately..."

Nora relaxed her posture. "He was just venting. What *I* want to know is why you told him and not me about this mystery guy."

Frederick... I'd been desperately trying not to think about him. Every time it was like my grief compounded tenfold.

"Sorry. I figured I might never see him again, so what's the point in telling anyone? I only told Brett because I had to." It was half the truth at least. I mainly kept quiet because, in order to tell her about Frederick, I'd have to tell her about Emeriz. About Ora.

"Did you kiss him?"

My cheeks burned and I closed my eyes in pre-wince mode, waiting for the punch in the arm that was coming. And she delivered.

"You totally did! Details now!"

Unable to help myself, I asked, "Which time?"

That got me another slap on the arm and a squeal, irritating the study group across from us.

"You want to study in silence, go to the library," Nora scolded them.

Careful Nora, your Ora is showing.

"What's he like?" She practically sang the question. "Did he help nurse you back to health when you got sick at the end of the trip?"

My heart fluttered thinking about how Frederick had in fact saved me by lending me his strength.

"He's a gentleman, but a total dork. Only around me, though. He banters but is incredibly sincere." Talking about Frederick lifted my heart, and I couldn't help baring my soul to Nora. "Not seeing him actually aches and strangely makes me feel... homesick."

"I'm happy for you friend. Not that you miss him, but that he had that influence on you."

"Ever the romantic, aren't you?"

"Hopelessly." She laughed, then turned serious. "And I know I've said it before, but I'm glad you're okay. I was really worried when I heard you got sick to the point you were hospitalized. I even had a nightmare where you died, and I tried to give you CPR. It didn't work and I woke up crying. It felt so real."

Because it was.

I looked away, the guilt once again pressing on me. I'd hoped that

Nora would have written it off as a bad dream, but hearing her say it didn't sit right with me. I was lying to her.

I met her gaze and leaned back in shock. Her irises were a glittering silver.

"Nora, how long have you had your migraine today?"

Taken a little aback she said, "A few minutes. Why?"

Ora must have been watching.

Nora groaned, then something sparked in her expression, and she shook me.

"It worked! Temperance!" Nora wasn't in the driver's seat.

"Ora?" I looked around to be sure no one was listening to us. "Put her back! Is she in Emeriz?"

"No. When I let go, she'll probably think she daydreamed for a bit." She wrapped me in a hug. "I've missed you so much! We all have. Some more than others."

Frederick missed me?

My heart pounded with glee.

"Same. What's happening? Is Rhiannon okay?" I asked.

"She is well. Brydon advanced his age progression too. When people ask what happened, they just claim Maxwell cursed them."

I owed them so much for what Rhiannon gave up for me, but I didn't know how long Ora would be able to talk to me to I moved on to my next concern. "Have there been any attacks?"

"No, it's quiet on that front," she whispered. "It gives us more time to prepare, but why we aren't in a full-scale war yet is—oddly—off-putting."

"Has anyone said anything about who I am?"

Ora shook her head. "Frederick took care of that. No one knows."

"How's that possible?"

"Besides those few amongst our allies, Maxwell was the only one who knew, and so far, he hasn't revealed it to anyone. According to Heshrin's intelligence, not even to Minerva," she explained. "Since Frederick used his powers in front of everyone, he steered all Descended rumors to himself."

He did that to protect me? If Maxwell made it back to Minerva, why wouldn't he say anything?

I squeezed my pendant. "Have they found out who tipped Maxwell off in the first place?"

"As far as I know, they haven't." Ora rubbed at her temples but kept her focus on me. "I'll have to go soon. Holding on is starting to hurt. First, I want to ask, are you coming back?"

When I opened my mouth, nothing came out. I still didn't have an answer.

A moment later, her silver irises faded to their natural golden brown, and I missed my opportunity. Nora woke up from her daydream.

Could I live the rest of my life wondering, 'What if'? What would happen to Emeriz if I stayed on Earth? Would I regret not stepping in to help fix the mess I left behind?

"Sorry, I must've zoned out," Nora said, but I barely registered her words.

"I've got some family stuff this weekend, so I won't be able to hang out." I packed up my backpack.

"That's fine. Are you okay?"

"I'm not feeling so great, so I think I'm gonna have James take me home." When the bell rang, I stood and shouted, "James!"

He looked at me, and I dangled the pendant in the air, indicating for him to follow me.

"Seriously? Yes!" He pumped a celebratory fist, then excused himself from Sophia.

My nerves wouldn't stop vibrating as I waited for Frederick to return from his ride. I couldn't just walk up to him in the castle. We'd need to figure out the best way to introduce my presence in Linall again.

"They'll be back soon," Brydon said, shoveling hay out of the stall we stood in. "Now that you're here, Rhiannon will sense you and cut his ride short."

Brydon still looked strong for his age, though his wrinkles were more pronounced and his shoulders hunched a little more. His smile was the same as ever, kind and comforting.

He glanced in the direction of the stable entrance. "I can't imagine it'll be much—"

Horse hooves pounded against the cobblestone inside the stables, followed by a bellowed neigh. Brydon stepped outside the stall while I remained frozen in place.

"Hello, beautiful," Brydon greeted Rhiannon—or in that moment, Neva—and led her into the stall. "Where'd you leave our king stranded? Someone was hoping to see him."

Neva nuzzled me with her nose.

"I've missed you too, Rhiannon," I whispered. "Quite a secret to keep from me. I'm happy your age hasn't affected your horse form it seems."

Another set of hooves echoed through the stables, and a familiar voice set my heart racing.

"Take this horse back to Calix. I abandoned him an hour's ride up the King's Path."

"Yes, Your Majesty," a stable hand replied.

Brydon bowed. "King Frederick, your horse is just inside this stall."

Frederick walked up to Brydon, not even bothering to look inside. "I don't care where that blasted horse is! She abandoned me, again."

"Ah, but she always takes you where you need to be." Brydon pushed an irritated Frederick into our stall.

When Frederick's eyes snapped onto mine, all the strain left his body.

Brydon pulled on Neva's bridle and led her out of the stables. I shot Brydon a grateful smile as they exited. No need to have my great-grandparents chaperoning us.

My gaze met Frederick's again. The intensity of his stare panged against my heart, sending my nerves into overdrive.

"Hi," I said and waved with a trembling laugh.

One month of separation, and all I could say was, 'Hi'?

Silence.

With a deep breath I said, "James and I... are going to split time between Emeriz and Earth."

He stared at me, emotionless.

I cleared my throat. "We can't stand by and allow others to suffer when we can help."

More silence.

I so desperately wanted to know what was going on behind those cobalt eyes.

"It took some major arm twisting to convince them but my parents did agree. Albeit with some set ground rules." I counted the list off on my fingers. "I have to keep up with my schooling on Earth. Stay connected to friends and life experiences there. I'm not allowed to fight in direct combat until I'm eighteen and graduated. We have to wait until school's out to combine Nora and Ora. Also, other than the few who already know, no one else can find out who we are."

Frederick's gaze flicked down and back up, his expression unreadable. I picked at my fingers, anxious that he still hadn't said a word.

Was he mad? Did he blame me for what happened?

"Emeriz has stayed with me all this time. I've missed everything about this world."

His eyes searched mine, but his face remained impassive.

"I missed... you," I finished.

He tilted his head slightly.

I guess he's over me. That was fast.

My heart shattered at the thought, but I refused to look away. "Of course, when we visit, I don't have to stay here. I'm sure Rhiannon and Brydon would—"

Quick as lightning, he closed the distance between us and stopped my words with a fervent kiss. His fingers weaved through the hairs at the nape of my neck. Heat raged through me from our entangled lips and down to my toes. As he deepened the kiss, a small gasp escaped my throat.

"Tempy? Where are you?" Ora's calls came from outside the stables. "James told me you're back!"

They couldn't catch us like this!

Frederick's grip remained firm, his lips continuing to ardently trace mine. He stayed focused on his task, like he was carefully memorizing the shape of my lips with his own.

"Brydon! Rhiannon! Have you seen Tempy?" Their voices faded away, and I was grateful they hadn't explored the stalls farther.

I relaxed, allowing myself to enjoy Frederick's affections. My muscles loosened, and I gripped his shirt to keep from completely collapsing. All too soon, he pulled back enough to lean his forehead against mine.

"Welcome home, Temperance."

ACKNOWLEDGMENTS

Temperance and Frederick's story has lived in my heart since high school, capturing my imagination and holding onto it until I could finally bring it to life on the page. Along the way, countless people have supported me in my journey, and I am deeply grateful for their encouragement and help.

First, I would like to express my heartfelt gratitude to Jimmy, Terri, and Mike at MoonQuill for believing in the potential of my story and expertly guiding it to its fullest expression. Terri, your expertise, patience, and dedication have made all the difference, and I am incredibly grateful for your partnership. A special thank you to my editor S.R. Crane for her exceptional work on my manuscript.

Thank you to my brilliant cover designer, Emilie, whose artistic magic and creativity brought my vision to life in the most fantastical way, and I couldn't be more grateful for the enchanting cover you've crafted!

I am forever grateful to my husband, Paul, for his boundless love and support as I chase my dreams, no matter how big, small, or downright ridiculous they may seem. Your belief in me never wavered, and you have gone above and beyond to make sure I reach each one— often while keeping a smile on your face and offering endless encouragement (even when I'm buried in my latest writing obsession and you have to remind me to eat or sleep). I love you with all my heart, and you are woven into every love story I write, making each one a little more magical because of you.

A huge thank you to my family, who endured my constant storytelling and fact-dropping at the dinner table. No matter how wild my antics or far-fetched my stories, you always stood by me, making me feel like I could conquer anything with you cheering me on. Your love, patience, and acceptance gave me the confidence to grow and chase my dreams, and for that, I'm incredibly grateful. Extra brownie points for my little sister, Becca, who fished this manuscript out of the trash can in high school when I was convinced it was time to give up, then proceeded to scold me for doing so. Your faith in me—and your tough love—was the spark I needed to keep going!

There's a group of women I will never be able to thank enough—Sara K. Anderson, Chantel Fleming, Ashley Bustamante, and Elise George. Without you, I would never have crossed the finish line in completing this book. You four talked me off every ledge, helped me push through every bout of writer's block, held my hand through every rejection, and celebrated every win, big or small, in the writing world. I will never forget (and will forever be grateful for) the countless rereads and revisions—no matter how many times you say you loved reading it again. Your sharp eyes, thoughtful feedback, and dedication brought this story to life in ways I never could have imagined. Your humor and unshakable encouragement lifted me when my writerly spirit was fading, always pushing me forward. You all are my rock, my sounding board, and my absolute favorite people to get lost in a book with.

An extra thank you to Ashley, for designing the beautiful printed edges.

A big thank you to Amber and Candace, the original inspirations behind Nora and Rhiannon, for planting the seeds of love and confidence in my story that helped it flourish.

To all the members of the Writers of the Round Table, I'm so fortunate to be a part of this community of super cool writers. Purple Shirt Mafia for life!

A huge shoutout to some of my amazing mentors and favorite authors who fueled my journey with their bucket of publishing wisdom and endless encouragement. Lisa Mangum, for being totes awesome and knowing all the things that help shape myself and all writers out there. Dennis Gaunt, for being one of the first people in the industry to read this entire manuscript and enjoy it! Julie Wright, for lighting the way and showing me what's possible!

A special mention goes to the American Night Writers Association for hosting such an incredible conference year after year. This event not only provided invaluable opportunities for growth but also allowed me to forge lifelong friendships that have profoundly shaped both my story and my voice as a writer.

Thank you so much to my incredible readers! I'm overjoyed to have you on this journey with me, and I'm so grateful you've made space in your hearts for these characters. Your support brings the magic to life!

Above all, I give my deepest thanks to my Heavenly Father for blessing me with the gifts of creativity, storytelling, and the bonds of friendship. It is through His grace that this story has come to life, and I am forever grateful for the guidance and inspiration He has provided along this journey.

About the Author

H.C. Lane has loved weaving tales and capturing the world through words from a young age. Ever since catching the storytelling bug, writing has been a constant companion in her life.

When she's not writing, Hannah enjoys spending time with her husband, two cats, and corgi, all of whom provide endless inspiration and support. A lover of creativity in many forms, she also spends time sewing costumes and cosplaying for writers' conferences and renaissance festivals, often drawing design inspiration from her own stories.

Hannah's debut novel marks the culmination of years spent honing her craft, and she is thrilled to share her first story with readers everywhere.

She's happy to connect with readers at hclane.com.

Thank you for reading a Cozy Unicorn original novel. We sincerely value the support from our readers and would greatly appreciate it if you could take a moment to leave a review. Your opinion helps the author and supports their ability to continue writing fantastic books for everyone to enjoy!

Additionally, we're looking for dedicated beta readers to join our street team. Email cozyup@moonquill.com for more info.

Still want more? Scan the QR code below to subscribe to our mailing list for notifications about new releases. You'll receive 4 complimentary e-books!